REVENGE

OF THE

FORGOTTEN

Revenge of the Forgotten
The Cursed Gods Series
Book 1

Dany Crooks

Revenge of the Forgotten

ISBN: 978-1-965434-00-0

Developmental & Copy Editing: Katie Wolf

Cover: Maria Spada

Map: Ophelia Illustration

Chapter Header & Scene Break Illustration: Marta Riva

To those who never felt like they belonged.
I created a home for all of us.

Author Note & Trigger Warnings

Revenge of the Forgotten is a book about loss, love, and a lesson in how to pick yourself back up when you've been knocked down a few too many times. Themes in this book might be hard for some to read.

If you wish to see a list of Trigger Warnings, flip to page 459. If you **do not** wish to read the Trigger Warnings, flip to the next page.

SPOTIFY PLAYLIST
(Scan me with your Spotify App)

I Would've - Jessie Murph

Snow Angel - Reneé Rapp

when the party's over - Billie Eilish

Watch The World Burn - Falling In Reverse

Over My Head (Cable Car) - The Fray

Last Hope - Paramore

It Will Come Back - Hozier

Always Been You - Jessie Murph

What Do You Make Of Me - Beth Crowley

Me and the Devil - Soap&Skin

Beautiful Things - Benson Boone

run for the hills - Tate McRae

Lose Control - Teddy Swims

Can't Catch Me Now - Olivia Rodrigo

die first - Nessa Barrett

Legends Never Die - League of Legends &

Against The Current

Triumph - Bishop Briggs

WILDFLOWER - Billie Eilish

Two Ghosts - Harry Styles

Misguided Ghosts - Paramore

TOLEVARRE
CALDOR OCEAN
LITTERA
IMBER
ORO
SOLUM
VATES
STELLA
AERIS
THE MINES
SEA OF ROS
PAX
FORTIS
ATROX
DEMUTO
ARDOR
AMORA
FRAUS
VINCERE

Prologue

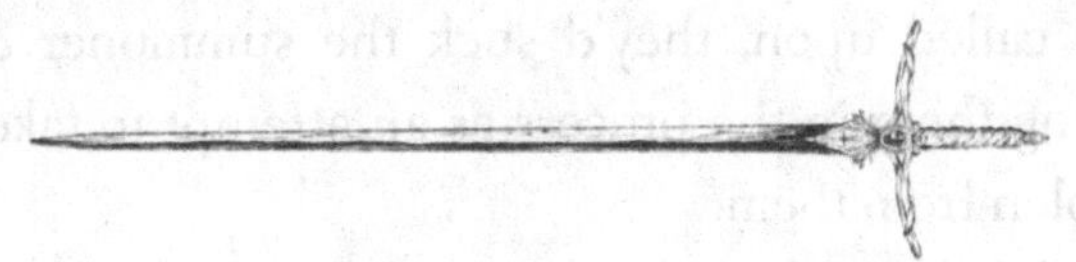

BLOOD POOLED IN THE PALM OF HIS HAND AS HE PRESSED HIS
dagger with enough pressure to cut through the first couple layers of
skin. Bridger looked up to see the other three doing the same. He
met a piercing gaze, eyes bluer than the sea beyond the cliff.

"Are we sure this is what we want to do?" Khort asked, eyeing
the group. The small fire they'd started roared to life as the cold
winter air licked their skin.

"I'm not letting her win." Vega's voice was hoarse, her makeup
staining her rosy cheeks from the tears she'd wept. "I will do this
with or without all of you," she replied with finality.

Vega had lost so much in such a short amount of time. Her sister
blindsided everyone around her with not so much as a whisper of
what she was plotting or who she'd been scheming with. Marlena
took the lives of innocent people, her parents included. But Vega
was here, still willing to fight harder than anyone.

The small, sad smile she shot Bridger warmed his insides, rattled
his bones, and solidified his decision. There was no going back—he
would fight until death beside them, beside her. "I'm not going
anywhere."

Vega took her ocean eyes off Bridger the moment Arlet spoke. "Me either. I have nothing left to lose but you three. The consequence of dying together is better than living without you."

"If we fail, we die. Everyone understands what happens here, right?" There were tales that the dead gods could be summoned, but no one had ever heard of it being done. Rumor had it that if one was successfully called upon, they'd suck the summoner dry of their powers, killing them in the process as an attempt to take back what had been stolen from them.

Bridger slid the dagger across his other palm and placed it back into the sheath on his thigh. He reached out his hand, offering it to Khort, who looked at his bloodied palm, his green eyes flicking around the small circle.

Khort had the most to lose here. His parents were still alive somewhere in Tolevarre, undoubtedly waiting for their son to find them. Khort nodded. "We get to my parents as soon as we can. Promise?" They all nodded in return. He reached for his blade, sliced both of his palms without a wince, and linked his hand to Bridger's.

Arlet followed suit, taking the dagger Vega handed her to slit her palms, and reached out to connect her hands with Khort and Vega.

Vega's eyes found Bridger's again as she reached for his hand and gave it a little squeeze before she spoke—their circle was complete. "I love you." Her voice quivered with anticipation.

Bridger took in the sight of her, frazzled and yet somehow still so fucking gorgeous, so strong, so capable. This woman was going to change their world. "You're the air I breathe—my life. I'd follow you to the underworld if you asked," Bridger responded.

Vega's eyes wandered over the three of them: her closest confidants, her best friends, and the love of her life. Her breath hitched in her throat, but a cold fire burned behind those icy eyes. "You two, thank you for everything. I wouldn't want to do this life without either of you."

Tears rolled down Arlet's cheeks. "This isn't goodbye, Vega. I believe in you. If anyone can do this, it's you."

There was no more time to waste. With the power of the god of gods running through her veins, Vega flipped her gaze to the stars above and took one last deep breath.

The trees around the meadow's opening began to rattle with fresh wind. Vega was summoning something dark, something they'd never want to mess with unless they were absolutely desperate.

They were desperate.

"I call upon you today for protection. For guidance. For our people. I call upon you to bond these bloods, to help us make what's been wronged right. To avenge the innocent lives that have been lost. To kill my sister."

Bridger put his head down and shut his eyes despite the urge to scoop Vega into his arms and shield her from the hurt she was feeling. He tightened his hand around hers, letting her know that he was with her every step of the way—forever.

He felt something watching them, his body vibrating with the darkness closing around them. Vega stiffened, alerting Bridger that she felt it too, but they all knew the consequences if she broke the connection now.

She continued to speak. "We come seeking your help to defeat the evil you saw growing within the original gods. To protect the people of our realm from the wicked inside it."

The urge to defend was too much to ignore. Bridger's eyes shot open, his powers roaring to the surface as the fire shot thirty feet into the air. The commitment to protect was so deeply rooted inside of him, but he wouldn't move his hands until the last second, keeping their connection to whatever or whoever had joined them.

Khort opened his eyes, sweeping the horizon like he might shift and take off into the night sky at any second.

"Bind us. Let us fight. We are stronger than her together. We can get the revenge you never got the chance to see." Vega's voice grew louder.

The wind picked up. Khort flinched, but Bridger shook his head and mouthed, *No*. Vega would alert them if she felt this going south. Bridger didn't want to die before he had the chance to fight back.

"Do not let us die like you did thousands of years ago!" Vega's voice rang through the air above them.

That seemed to do it.

A shock went through them, starting with Vega. It blazed through them one by one, a cry of agony flying out of Arlet's mouth as the power shuddered through her. None of them could run to her aid if they tried—they were stuck in place by the power consuming them.

A voice inside Bridger's head said, *"I saved her. Do not waste this opportunity."*

1

"Oh, and Chase?" Vega didn't hide the venom icing her tone. He looked up from the floor, tears streaming down his face, skin blotchy from crying. "Go fuck yourself."

Vega slammed the door in her husband's face. The worn building rattled with the force. Vega ignored Old Man Morris's irritated banging on the wall from the commotion and Chase's shouting as she stormed into the rain-soaked night.

The image of another woman's bare ass on her *clean* kitchen table would be burned into her memory for as long as she lived.

It was a wet walk to the bar a few blocks away, and the entire time, Vega squeezed her hands so tight, little crescent moons formed in her palms. The world spun around her, nausea causing her stomach to churn like Lake Michigan on a cold winter's day.

She'd gotten off work earlier than anticipated tonight, the rain affecting the traffic at the scummy diner where she worked. Vega had stopped by her and Chase's favorite Thai place to surprise him with dinner.

But she was the one who got the surprise instead...

When the door chimed, announcing her entrance into the

raggedy dive bar, Vega's leggings were soaked with cold rainwater. No one looked up from their drinks or the pool tables, and the staff didn't welcome her. She wiggled out of her coat, hung it on the rack by the door to dry, and then found a seat at the bar.

"What can I get ya?" The woman behind the fading counter looked like she hadn't slept for weeks, and her voice was rough with the sound of someone who smoked a pack of cigarettes a day.

"A shot of your cheapest whiskey, please." Vega passed a damp twenty-dollar bill across the counter and snatched her phone from her pocket while she waited.

Ten missed calls and twenty-eight texts.

Before he could show up here and persuade her to listen, Vega turned her location off and imagined what Chase's face would look like when he got the notification that she'd revoked his right to know where she was at all times.

She hoped his sorry ass sobbed a little harder.

The bartender returned with her change and the small glass of amber liquid. Vega tipped the shot back, ignored the burn in her throat, and slid the rest of the money back. "Another," she blurted.

The bartender cocked her head. Question marks seemed to float above her head while her eyebrows scrunched in the middle. Maybe she wasn't used to girls Vega's age coming in and slamming shots of cheap whiskey, or she saw Vega needed to get something off her chest. Whatever it was, Vega took the bait. "I just walked in on my husband cheating on me."

Right after fucking me before I left for work. She didn't say that last part out loud to protect what little dignity she had left. She'd worried about this the day he asked her to marry him because nothing in her life ever stayed good for long. Vega vividly remembered when he got down on one knee just months into their relationship, the smell of the salty water wafting off the Pacific Ocean, the way the sun made his sandy-colored hair glisten, and the way his round face lit up with excitement when the single word, "yes," slipped through her lips. But behind her excitement hid the doubt she would always have when it came to any bit of happiness life allowed her to have.

"This one's on me," the bartender said. Vega's eyes welled with tears, but she forced them away, blinking rapidly. "I hope you clocked him right in the nose." The woman's response made Vega chuckle, but it didn't heal her hurt.

"I should've, huh?" Vega asked. The bartender only nodded in response before walking away to tend to her other patrons. Her thoughts wandered back to Chase and *Jessica*. What did she look like? Did she hear Chase snort when he laughed so hard he couldn't breathe? Vega hadn't heard it in so long. Did she come from a good family? Had Chase met them? Did he love her?

She bit the inside of her cheek hard enough to taste blood.

Vega wasn't destined for greatness. She'd known that from a young age. She was destined to be the girl everyone always compared themselves to when they were having a bad day. They would think things could always be worse because look at poor Vega, she couldn't ever catch a break! *"At least we aren't Vega,"* they would say.

In six short months, Vega would turn thirty.

By fifteen, she'd lost her mother to cancer after watching her suffer for nearly a year.

By seventeen, she'd been kicked out of the home she'd been adopted into when they found weed in her backpack.

By twenty-one, her scholarship money ran dry.

By twenty-seven, she'd been fired from her big girl job at Chicago's most prominent marketing firm after it sold to a Fortune 500 company.

And now, before she turned thirty, her life was being flipped upside down by an unfaithful husband.

Her life had always felt like a long string of bad luck, as if someone above got off on watching her struggle. There weren't many moments in her life Vega could look back on and smile, none that made her feel warm and fuzzy.

That was until she met Chase.

Chase came from a good family who went to Colorado every winter for ski trips. A family with lots of siblings and Sunday FaceTime calls. A family with enough money to invest in their children's futures—they were the all-American dream.

And Vega had holes in her memory no one had answers to. She couldn't remember going to elementary or middle school, couldn't remember what her childhood home looked like before her mom moved them to Seattle to start treatment. All she knew was nothing ever worked out.

A therapist once told her it was her brain trauma-blocking.

The bartender never cut her off. Vega didn't care how she was supposed to get home or if she even went home... *Here we are again.* Her thoughts started to run together. *Gonna be just me, myself, and I. Again.*

Her inner demons flooded her mind, stirring up another wave of nausea. Vega felt like she was seeing herself outside of her body, floating above in a haze as she reached across the bar to the new shot. Her stomach twirled at the sensation, and as much as she tried to push away the feeling, it sunk its talons in, taking hold.

Ringlet curls bounced in her vision before she blacked out entirely.

Lightning struck, and wind whipped around her. Her stomach lurched, the feeling of falling seizing her body while visions clouded her perception.

The out-of-body experience didn't let up. It only intensified when Vega realized what she was seeing. She and three others were circling a fire, their palms crusted with blood from matching cuts. Her voice rang over the crackle of the large flame.

"We fight for our realm, for our lands. We fight for our people and for those who can no longer fight for themselves. We fight together."

The girl with the pretty curls reached out and squeezed her hand. "Together."

The two men in the group looked at one another, the tallest nodding his head with a surety Vega had never seen before. "And we fight until our dying breaths."

For one split second, her eyes locked with his, and Vega felt like the world stopped. *Those eyes.* She knew those onyx eyes. The spinning feeling in her stomach shrank, and with a gasp, Vega was back in the Chicago bar.

Somehow, she was still sitting upright on the barstool. Vega turned to look around the bar, her black-painted fingernails digging into the bar top for support. Her knuckles were white from the grip she held as she hoped not to fall off of the stool and embarrass herself.

No one in the bar seemed fazed. At the billiard table, a man with peppered hair reracked the balls on the table, smoke spiraling above his head from the lit cigarette between his lips. The bar was as it was before she slipped into her mind.

What the fuck was that?

The bartender came over, noticing the shift in Vega's mood. "You okay?" Her dark eyebrow raised, almost touching her hairline.

"Fine. Where's your bathroom?" Vega spoke, her voice quivering. The woman pointed to the other end of the cramped room. The scrape of her stool against the floor caused looks from the other patrons, finally taking notice of the new face in their midst. Vega speed-walked to the bathroom and flung the door open with a bang.

A full-length mirror sat in the corner. Vega's long, dark brown hair was down, billowing around her shoulders in loose curls. The eyes staring back at her in the mirror were ice-colored. Her skin was as white as a piece of paper, and sweat glistened along her brow.

She braced herself against the wall, hands on either side of the mirror. "Jesus Christ." She'd stopped believing in God a long time ago. "Get yourself together."

Vega once had dreams like this that would keep her up at night—of herself in a life she couldn't remember, with people and places that weren't like anything she'd ever seen. It had taken years of therapy after opening up to Chase about them to realize it was just her mind playing tricks with her, trying to fill in the gaps she'd forced herself to forget from a childhood of trauma.

A woman in a biker jacket walked into the bathroom, and Vega shoved herself off the wall as swiftly as she could—no one needed to see her talking to herself. The woman stared at her before she slipped into a stall. Vega turned the sink water on cold and splashed her face.

Do not break down now.

The phrase had become a motto for Vega over the years. Anytime something happened where she felt like she might spiral out of control, she reminded herself that no one was going to pick her up if she crumbled.

If she closed her eyes and focused, she could hear the words floating through the air, as if they'd come from someone else and not her.

Vega turned the water off, dried her face with a scratchy paper towel, and toddled back to her seat at the bar. She smiled at the bartender when the woman looked her way, realizing that it seemed more like a grimace as she caught her reflection in the bottles across the bar.

Can't you be normal for one fucking minute?

Vega hung her head in her hands as the door chimed with a new arrival. Someone sat down on the empty stool next to her—as if there weren't plenty of empty seats elsewhere.

The voice next to her was melodic and smooth. "Can I get two of whatever she's been drinking?"

Vega never understood the saying "a voice smooth as butter" until now.

She locked gazes with the woman sitting beside her. Vega's stomach did that free fall thing again, and she steadied herself against the bar's edge for the second time tonight to keep from falling off the stool.

Vega knew that face, had seen those spiral curls too many times to count.

The muted smile on the girl's face was relaxed, and her shoulders dipped in relief as she took a large breath.

"It took me a lot longer to find you this time."

2

Vega couldn't strip the look of shock from her face. Her mouth hung slightly ajar, all thoughts gone from her brain, and she had to remind herself to breathe.

The girl laughed lightly, radiating warmth into Vega from the sweet sound. Her curls had the volume she'd only ever dreamed of having, and her amber skin glowed despite the dim bar lighting. Vega got an ethereal feeling when looking at her.

God, she's beautiful.

The bartender slid the shots at them. "Fifteen-fifty." Without hesitation, the woman slid some cash across the bar top, only taking her eyes off Vega long enough to thank the bartender.

Vega finally realized she was gaping and clamped her mouth shut. The girl's eyes ticked down Vega's body, raking her eyes over her rumpled clothes. Vega threw her arms across her chest, suddenly self-conscious about her appearance.

"You look like shit," the other girl said, throwing her head back to take the shot.

"Excuse me?" Vega asked, the feeling of astonishment dissipating quickly. "Who are you?"

"I'm Arlet. You grew up calling me Arlie. Once, you just called me Lee, which I hated. I didn't like you much then, either. You were very mean in that life." She eyed the shot beside Vega. "You gonna take that, or can I? It's been a long week."

That life?

Vega reached down and pinched herself to make sure she wasn't dreaming, ignoring her question. Arlet must have taken her silence as an answer because she grabbed the shot and tipped it straight down the hatch.

"I've seen you before," Vega finally admitted, unsure of what else she could say.

"What?" Arlet asked, stunned.

"I've seen you in my dreams. I-I saw you today, just a little bit ago. In my head." Vega started to feel nauseous again—or maybe the nausea had never really left.

Arlet leaned back, her fingers tapping on her chin while her eyes clouded over in thought. "That's new." She raised her hand to signal another round of shots.

Vega didn't object.

"What do you mean, *that's new*?" Vega watched Arlet's every move.

"In your other lives, that's never happened. You've never had dreams of me." Arlet's brows creased in the middle, and she bit her lip, still pondering as she reached for the new shots. She extended one in Vega's direction. She hesitated to grab it. "I'm not going to bite you, Vega."

Her name on the stranger's lips sent Vega flying out of her chair. The stool would have clattered to the floor if it weren't for Arlet's catlike reflexes.

"How do you know my name?" Vega's voice was shaky, warbling with shock.

Arlet shrugged, her eye contact unwavering. "Because I'm your best friend."

Vega was paralyzed in shock, fear, disbelief, or a combination of all three. "You're crazy. Absolutely mad." She scoffed.

Arlet sighed, took both shots, and patted the cushion on the stool Vega had vacated. "According to your favorite book, we're all mad here." Arlet spread her grin as big as possible, mimicking the Cheshire Cat.

"How—?" Vega cut herself off, stepping back from the stool. Her boot scuffed against the sticky floor, gaining the attention of the other patrons again.

"Everything okay over here?" the bartender asked, her eyes narrowing in suspicion.

Arlet smiled sweetly. "Oh, she's fine! We haven't seen each other in a long time, and I surprised her." Arlet wiggled in excitement, momentarily turning her attention to the woman. "We've been best friends all our lives and haven't seen each other in *fifteen years*." Her words oozed with elation. The bartender settled quickly as if under some kind of spell.

"How sweet." She smiled big despite missing a bottom tooth. "You two let me know if you need anything, okay?" The bartender padded away after Arlet nodded enthusiastically.

"Who are you?" Vega felt like a broken record. Had her little episode earlier fried her brain?

"I told you. I'm Arlet... and I'm your best friend. Maybe you *are* drunker than I thought. Should I walk you home?" Arlet stood up.

Vega kept some distance between herself and what she was beginning to believe was a stalker. "I am *not* letting you know where I live," she huffed.

"I already know where you live."

Vega yanked her coat off the rack by the door. Her throat constricted, fear making her skin tingle. "Stay away from me." She walked backward out of the bar, keeping her eyes on Arlet, who only rolled hers in reply.

Once back outside in the wet Chicago night, Vega turned on her heels and picked up her pace. Her feet were heavy against the sidewalk, water splashing up her legs.

She kept checking over her shoulder, scared she was being followed. The last thing she wanted to do was go home to her apartment, where Chase might be, but at the very least, it would feel like a safe space after whatever this mess was!

The building loomed in the distance. Vega beelined for it, stumbling her way up to the entrance. Her fear did nothing to sober her up.

Vega's breathing was ragged after climbing the stairs to her floor. Drunk or not, she would always avoid the death trap this place considered an elevator. She'd lost track of how many times the fire department had come to pry someone out.

Vega fumbled with the keys in her chilled hands, the metal jingling against each other. They slipped through her damp fingers and hit the floor with a rattle. "You've gotta be fucking kidding me." Vega stood in place, looking down at her keys—defeated by the day, by her life. *Don't tempt the universe,* she noted. It was in the mood to show her how lousy things could feel in a single day.

Without attracting any more unwanted inconveniences, Vega stepped inside her apartment and put her back against the door. Her heart rate still sputtered in her chest. *What the fuck was that girl talking about tonight?* If she hadn't pinched herself at the bar, Vega could have chalked this up to a silly dream she'd laugh about in the morning.

The apartment was dark, the only light coming from the glow of the streetlights outside the kitchen window. It was quiet—too quiet. She was alone.

Vega finally let herself break down. When the first tear fell, so did Vega. She slid down the door and let out a sob she was sure her neighbors heard. Her shoulders heaved while the tears continued to fall. She cried for all she had already lost and what was unavoidably going to happen next.

Who was she supposed to be now? Chase was her everything—but she wasn't his. There was no coming back from what he'd done.

Vega's hand slid across her face, wiping away tears and snot. She laid her head back against the door with a thud as her mind began to see all the red flags she'd been blind to over the last several months.

Chase staying late at work, leaving on business trips that came out of nowhere—his excuse being the new position he'd taken leaving no room for proper planning sometimes.

Her heartache turned to rage in the blink of an eye.

Vega let out a guttural screech, the echo vibrating off her eardrums. How could she have been so stupid, so gullible?

There were plates laid out on the table, presumably for the dinner Chase was making for his *fucking mistress*. Vega stomped over to the table and swept the ceramic to the floor. They hit the tile, shattering into a million tiny pieces around the kitchen.

Once the first piece shattered, there was no stopping the destructive path Vega went on. Pictures were ripped off of the walls, their glass frames mixing with the smashed plates on the floor. Anything around the apartment that was Chase's wasn't safe—his clothes were ripped to shreds, in ribbons around the apartment.

Vega continued to scream, letting the hurt and confusion from tonight's events pour out of her. She didn't care if she woke her neighbors, if the cops were called, or if someone broke down the door to make sure she wasn't being murdered.

She didn't stop until the rust stained porcelain bathtub was full of water and Chase's laptop sat at the bottom with little bubbles floating to the surface.

Vega's eyes fluttered open, and the light from her open blinds made her squint. She groaned, throwing the blanket over her head. If it weren't for the smell wafting into the bedroom, she might have fallen back asleep.

Bacon.

She sat upright, her hair wild from a fitful sleep. Clothes from last night, a towel, and the pajamas she'd meant to wear littered her bedroom floor. *How drunk was I?* Vega rubbed her temples, racking through her fuzzy memories from the night before.

Vega dressed in clothes strewn on the carpet, avoiding Chase's shredded clothing like they'd grown eyes and were staring directly at her.

The smell of breakfast hinted that Chase had come home to talk. Vega didn't bother brushing her teeth—there would be no kisses. She crossed her arms across her chest defiantly, ready to ask him if he thought making food would solve their problems.

Except the person in the kitchen wasn't Chase.

"Do you still like your eggs scrambled with cheese and hot sauce?" The angelic voice brought Vega's blurry memories back. When Vega didn't answer, Arlet peeked over her shoulder.

Vega fought to find her words. "How. The fuck. Did you get into my house?"

Arlet looked back at the food in the frying pan. "This is an apartment," she deadpanned.

"I'm calling the cops." Vega spun towards her bedroom, hoping she remembered to plug her phone in to charge. *Fuck, what did I do with my phone?* She didn't make it three steps before Arlet was blocking her path.

"You can't do that," she warned.

"I most certainly can, and I am! This is fucking ridiculous! You followed me home from the bar and broke into my *apartment*!" Vega sneered, but her voice raised in fear.

"You left the door unlocked. I didn't break in," Arlet admitted with an air of innocence.

"That doesn't make this okay!" Vega's palms were sweating. "I need an explanation... and not the 'I'm your best friend' one you gave me last night because I'm not sure anyone would believe that shit." Her memories of last night started to trickle back in.

"Gods, okay, okay. Are you going to be mean in this life too?" Arlet stalked back to the small kitchen, grumbling about ruining her breakfast surprise while she turned the stove off.

"What do you mean by that?" Vega needed answers. *Now*.

Arlet sat on the arm of the couch and took a deep breath. "Your name is Vega Caelum. You're from a realm called Tolevarre. Fifty-five years ago, your sister betrayed our realm and some of our ruling families, overthrowing your parents and the others who held seats in the Curia at the time." Before Vega had time to ask, Arlet explained, "The Curia was our form of government. There were twelve seats, all held by the twelve original bloodlines."

Vega stood as still as stone, plotting how to inch closer to her front door without this beautifully deranged woman noticing. She took one step to the left.

"The ones who didn't side with her were killed. Slaughtered, technically." Arlet told stories with her whole body. Her hands moved as she spoke, making grand gestures as she explained big points. "You, me, and some of our best pals tried to defeat her, but there's one thing about your sister that I need you to understand." She paused, meeting Vega's gaze intently. "Your sister is always one step ahead. She's not stupid. She's one of the most brilliant people I've ever met. I swear once we're on the way home, I'll explain this in more detail, but for now, you'll just have to trust me."

Vega opened her mouth to say something, but Arlet held her finger up. Vega scoffed.

"Long story short, your sister cursed you to forget everything and banished you to this realm, to Earth. If and when you get killed, your life starts over again—always as someone new, somewhere new, but always on Earth. You're always alone, with nothing."

"I'm not alone," Vega lied.

Arlet looked around, her eyebrow raising in a look that said, *really?* She moved on without saying anything. "You've died twenty times, and I've been the one to find you every life."

The room seemed to grow smaller as the minutes ticked on. *How can this girl do this with a straight face?* Vega felt like she was on *Punk'd*, her mind working in overdrive to understand what Arlet was talking about.

"This is the longest you've been gone, and it took me way too long to track you down this time. I couldn't even feel you for ten years. We thought maybe..." Arlet's sentence trailed off.

"That I died?" Vega asked, reading her expression easily.

"Maybe, but you can't die."

"We all die one day." Vega took another step to the left.

"If you die, your sister wins. Marlena can't win." Arlet's voice strained with fear.

The name hit her like a ton of bricks, and an itch in her brain stirred. She had to say the name out loud. "Marlena." The familiarity of it felt weird on her lips.

Arlet shot up. Her eyes were void of the fear that had once been there—it was replaced by something close to hope. "Yes. Marlena. Blonde hair, ice-blue eyes, devastatingly beautiful. We hate her. You haven't also forgotten the cardinal rule of hating the same person your best friend hates, right? You brought that back from here." Arlet motioned around the room but meant the world outside of it. "About thirty years ago, and it's always stuck."

Vega nervously gripped her right wrist. A scar went all the way around her delicate skin and connected at the other end. It was slightly raised and faded enough to be mostly unnoticeable. Vega had no idea where it'd come from but couldn't remember a time when she didn't have it. Sometimes it would tingle, making her rub the skin to distract herself from the sensation.

When Arlet's eyes landed on the brand, Vega hid her hands behind her back. It felt like Arlet was seeing her, *really* seeing her and who she was on the inside.

"Where did you get that?" Arlet asked.

Vega kept her hands hidden, still attempting to scoot herself closer to the door without being too obvious.

"Vega, stop moving towards the door. I'm not going to kill you."

Vega halted. "I don't know what you're talking about."

Arlet sighed, rubbing at her temples. "Where did you get the brand?" she asked again.

"I don't think that's any of your business," Vega finally responded.

Arlet moved towards her. Her tight black pants, long-sleeved black shirt, and black boots made it easy for her to blend into shadows. It was the same outfit she'd worn last night.

Arlet pulled her shirt sleeve up. A matching scar spread around the length of her wrist. "You're not answering me because you don't know where it came from, but I do. I remember it like it was yesterday and not fifty-five years ago."

Vega's breath caught in her throat. What were the chances two strangers had the same scar in the same place?

"What the fuck!" Vega's eyes shot up from Arlet's wrist. "Who are you?" Vega wanted answers now. Real answers, not this wild tale that she was from a different realm with magic and an evil sister.

"I already told you that. A couple times now." Arlet raised her eyebrow. "Are you still drunk or do you have memory issues in this life? Oh no." She gasped, her eyes growing wide.

Vega took another step away from her. The fear she felt last night after leaving the bar began to fill her chest, tightening the muscles around her heart. The panic set in at the same time she felt an electric shock zing through her body, and everything went black.

Rain pelted Vega's face, the sound of the ocean churning behind her. Her reflection caught her eye in the puddle below her feet—she was so young, an age she'd never seen herself as.

Vega's hands shook, curling into fists as she inhaled sharply. "I can't stop it!" Her young voice sounded defeated, a hint of frustration lingering while little blue traces of electricity bounced in the center of her palms.

"Yes, you can! Don't focus on the lightning. Let that go. It's distracting you!" a blonde, only years older, yelled, keeping her distance. "I watched you do it before! I know you can do it again, Vega!"

Little Vega stomped her foot, threw her hands to her side, and tossed her head back to let out a scream so mighty, so unnerving, that thunder rolled in the distance.

The rain let up, the clouds moving faster overhead. "Oh my gods, you're doing it! Ha-ha! Vega, you're doing it! You can really control the weather!"

The giddy blonde tackled her, and when Vega's breath was stolen from her lungs, she gasped back to life. She lay on the floor of her Chicago apartment, staring up into Arlet's hazel eyes.

"Vega, gods, are you okay?" Arlet gently dabbed a moist cloth on Vega's clammy skin.

"What is happening to me?" Was this the beginning of a mental breakdown?

"I'm not sure. Can you tell me what you saw?"

Vega sat up, fighting the spots in her vision. "It was me. A young me. I-I've never seen. I can't rememb—" She couldn't find the words she was looking for. She stared at the wall on the other side of the room. "I can't remember anything before fourteen. I've never seen myself as a kid." Vega paused, grabbing the cloth from Arlet and using it to wipe her brow. "There was a blonde girl there. Our eyes—they were the same color." A headache began to bloom around her temples. "I had lightning coming out of my hands." She rotated her hands over to stare into her palms. "And I stopped a storm."

Arlet was still crouched down next to her, her eyes glazing over like they had in the bar last night. Her curls bounced when she shook her head, and her eyes refocused. "I don't understand how you're remembering." Her voice was a whisper. "That was Marlena. You saw your sister. The curse is doing something. It's—gods." Arlet stared at the floor, thinking out loud. "The power is exerting itself because it's coming to an end..."

Vega pushed herself off the floor when she felt stable enough to stand, Arlet following suit. "This is batshit. I don't know who you are or what kind of game you're playing, but I need you to leave." Vega's voice was firm.

"What?" Arlet asked, her eyes wide.

"I didn't stutter. I need you to leave." Vega nodded towards the door.

"Vega," Arlet said in protest.

"No. Please, get out of my home." Vega walked to the front door. "My whole life was turned upside down last night when I found out that my husband has been cheating on me. I went to the bar to wallow, and for some reason, you decided to take advantage of a woman down on her luck." Vega bit her lip, forcing the sadness away. *Do not show this woman any weakness.*

"That's not what this is," Arlet pleaded, yet to move from the middle of the room. "Do you really think someone could make all of this up?"

The question rang in Vega's ears. "Ya know, I don't know what to believe right now."

Arlet took a breath and nodded. "Fine."

The tension in the room rose the closer Arlet got to the door. Vega stood tall in her beat-up pajamas, shoulders square when Arlet stopped in front of her and met her stare. Her stomach was tied in knots, queasy with fear, but she refused to show it.

"I know this is a lot to take in."

"Unbelievable, actually," Vega scoffed.

"Time is running out. Tolevarre is falling to a darkness far worse than anything any of us have ever seen. I can get you your memories back. Your life isn't this dark cloud you think it is. There's been a lot of heartbreak, but there's been so much good too."

Vega opened the door. "Get. Out."

Arlet stepped over the threshold. "I've never given up on you, Vega. I'm not going to start today. You'll be able to find me if you want."

Vega slammed the door shut, not giving her another moment to speak. She flipped both locks and pinched herself for the second time in twenty-four hours—the pain was subtle.

She still wasn't dreaming.

3

Vega's body felt weighted down as she slumped into the living room and collapsed on the couch. She blew air through her lips in an exasperated sigh. "What the fuck is my life?"

She rolled to her side, noticing her phone on the coffee table. Had it really been there the whole time?

Reaching out, Vega paused before the phone was in her hand, distracted by the ring sitting on her phone screen. She sat up slowly, tucking her legs underneath her as she inspected the ring.

The imperfect rectangular stone in the middle sparkled like the night sky, accented with diamonds fanning out like the petals of a flower. The closer she brought the jewel to her eye, the more depth it seemed to reveal. The stone in the center was unlike anything she'd ever seen before, so otherworldly. The black color was deep, reminding her of coal under a Christmas tree. When she turned the gold band, the jewel twinkled in the daylight filtering through the open curtains.

It somehow felt familiar in her hands.

Vega spun the ring between her fingers before sliding it onto the fourth finger of her left hand. Where she usually wore the wedding band she'd flushed down the toilet last night.

It fit like it was made for her.

There was no way to chalk this up to a wild dream anymore. A dream wouldn't explain how Arlet knew so much about her.

Starting with her last name. Caelum wasn't a name she'd had in thirteen years. When her mother died, she got what some would call "lucky," and the home she'd been placed into as a foster wanted to adopt her immediately. Her last name changed to Brooker, but Papa Brooker, as he'd requested to be called, was a fucking creep, and getting kicked out at seventeen might have been a blessing in disguise. Her last name changed to Hughes when she married Chase at twenty-four.

Caelum was a dead name. The name didn't even feel like hers anymore. It hadn't been on anything she used in her adult life. Not an apartment lease, not a job application—hell, not even her college applications showed any implication of the person she'd been before being adopted.

Arlet also knew about the odd scar on her wrist. Vega's hand slid to it, her fingers sweeping gently over the raised line. Arlet had the same scar in the exact location. What was the likelihood that two people donned a carbon copy scar on their bodies?

Her eyes wandered back to her hand, her attention focused on the ring. Arlet had left it as a little breadcrumb—a reminder that this wasn't a delusion her brain was making up.

When she eventually picked her phone up from the table, there were eighteen missed calls and thirty-five unread texts from Chase. Vega could try and make the relationship work like he'd been begging in the texts, but the trust was gone, irreparable. Vega didn't know what was supposed to come next, what she was supposed to do now.

Vega lay there for hours, turning over the last twenty-four hours in her mind. She was running late for work—as usual—because of it. If Bobby didn't fire her tonight, it would be a miracle.

Doing her best to sneak in the back door of the sixties-themed diner, Vega scurried to the computer in the office to clock in.

"Did you think I wouldn't notice you were over thirty minutes late?" Bobby's gruff voice stopped her in her tracks, her hand hovering over the computer screen.

Vega sighed, turning slowly while her hand fell to her side. She'd wished thousands of times he would hire a manager for this place and disappear forever. "I'm sorry, Bobby, really. I had a bad night that turned into an even worse morning." She wasn't sure she'd ever get rid of this brain fog.

Bobby was a bulbous man who always smelled like stale cigarettes. His dark hair, or what was left of it, was slicked back on the sides in what Vega imagined was grease from the flat-top grill. He was in his fifties, with faded, cheap tattoos up his arms, and was currently on his fifth marriage. *I should ask him who his attorney is.* Vega pursed her lips together, holding back a bitter laugh at the thought.

"It's always a bad day for you. What other excuse do you have?" The large man tapped his foot impatiently.

Vega knew she owed him an explanation. "I walked in on Chase cheating on me last night." She lowered her voice in embarrassment, eyes darting to the floor to avoid the lack of empathy on Bobby's face.

"I'm not surprised," he spat.

Bobby's words shouldn't hurt her, but they did. Vega inhaled deeply and met his dark eyes. "Should I clock in, or would you like to add to my terrible, horrible, no good, very bad day by firing me?" Vega cocked her head, waiting for his response.

He didn't get the reference, slanting his eyes at her. "You get one more chance, Vega." He held up a nubby finger as emphasis. "One. If you mess it up, you're gone. Do you understand?" Bobby scolded her like she was a kindergartener.

She nodded, turning to the computer screen to clock in, and tied her apron around her blue diner dress uniform. "I hear you loud and clear." Vega's jaw was set in a hard line, teeth grinding against each other.

"Good, now get out there and help Susan. She's gonna be so pissed at me that I didn't fire you." Bobby glared at her until she was through the swinging doors.

The shift went by almost as slowly as Susan moved between her tables. That would be Vega—sixty-two years old, still serving tables at a sullied diner because she couldn't afford to retire.

The woman sneered at Vega, bumping against her at the coffee station. "You're in the way," she said, her tone sharp.

"What crawled up your ass and died this time?" Vega snapped.

"You. Always coming in late like it doesn't affect others around you. You millennials have no respect for anyone." Everyone hated Susan here, Bobby included. But who else was he going to get to work for him at his atrocious diner besides a crabby, washed-up old lady and a down-on-her-luck almost thirty-year-old?

Every booth had rips in them, and the bar seating wrapped around the inside of the restaurant was missing stools. The sign reading Bobby's Diner was a hazard to walk anywhere near, hanging on by a wish and a prayer. Vega would be surprised if it lasted one more winter, the salt from the roads eating away at the metal base.

God, I hate this fucking place. Vega finished pouring the three cups of coffee she needed and stepped away from the server station. "Stop worrying about me so much and try not to forget table ten's side salad this time!" Vega didn't lower her voice, giving the kitchen staff behind the window a good laugh.

"You need to learn to respect your elders, Vega!" Susan was as red as the tomato on the burger under the heat lamp.

"Respect is earned," Vega said with a wink while bringing her tray down from its resting spot on her shoulder to distribute drinks to her table.

The rest of the shift went by without a hitch, and Susan avoided her at all costs. She walked out with $100 in her pocket—a good night for crummy old Bobby's Diner.

On her way home, Vega stopped at the corner store for the cheapest wine she could find.

The owner sat behind the counter, his permanent scowl on display in the stark lighting. "You look awful. Smell like wet dog," Gregor said with his thick Romanian accent.

As if Vega didn't have enough to worry about, she had to deal with this asshole. "Yeah, in case you haven't noticed, it's spring in Chicago. Rain happens this time of the year." She usually stopped here at night after a long shift and bought a bottle of wine to sip while she and Chase watched whatever trashy reality TV show was on. Tonight, she bought two bottles for herself—praying to anyone who would listen that Chase wasn't home.

Gregor grabbed the bottles and scanned them as he continued to talk. "Your husband was in here with a pretty blonde last night. At first I thought it might be a sister, but they were too cozy for that." He slid the bottles into separate brown bags. "Trouble in paradise?" he asked, eyes wide with excitement. Gregor was a leech, living off the misfortune of others.

"Do you ever mind your own business?" Vega snapped. This wasn't a conversation she wanted to have with Gregor.

The chuckle that left his lips was thick, filling up the room like a bleating sheep. "Bad day?"

Vega's response was the loud *whack* against the counter her hand made when she slammed a twenty-dollar bill down. "Just give me my change." Her voice sounded defeated and tired, which might have been why the man did as he was told for the first time since Vega had known him. She packed the bottles into the bag slung over her shoulder and gave the man behind the counter a sarcastic salute as she slipped back out into the unrelenting rain.

The walk back to the apartment took half the time it usually would. Vega was sick of being rained on—physically and metaphorically.

Old Man Morris stood outside the mailboxes in the main lobby of their apartment building, keys rattling against the metal door. "Ah, Vega. I got a package of your husband's outside of my door today. Would you like to stop by and get it for him?"

Vega didn't slow her pace, dashing to the elevator. Morris was *a fucking weirdo.* Always staring at the younger women who lived in their building, offering to help them put their groceries up when he caught them in the hall. He liked to sit in a lawn chair on the stoop during the summer and comment on dress lengths as women walked by. Their landlord never said anything to him because Morris had been living here since the dawn of time.

How he'd ever been married was a mystery to Vega. "He can get it himself." She hit the Up button, adjusting the bag on her shoulder.

Riding in the death trap that was this elevator was more appealing than joining Morris in the stairwell. He always took the stairs so he could brag to his friends at Monday night Bingo that he was still getting around just fine!

The elevator dinged upon its arrival at the ground floor. Vega stepped in, hit her floor number, and began to press the Door Close button a hundred times like that would speed the door closing.

"... should keep the noise down!" was all she heard before the door snapped shut.

Vega leaned against the wall of the elevator when the machine roared to life, creaking as the cable jarred the box. Vega's stomach dropped, her heart speeding up as she ascended in the elevator that was built before Prohibition.

She forced herself to focus on something other than the sounds the elevator made on its climb, her eyes fixed on the lights around the buttons lighting up at each new floor. They flickered between floors three and four, and the elevator lurched to a stop, sending Vega tumbling to the ground.

"What the..." Vega screeched, landing on her knees with a thump. Her bag flew off her shoulder, slamming to the floor—pink wine puddled around her. "No!" she cried, ripping the bag open to save whatever she could inside. One bottle was shattered, but the brown bag kept the glass contained.

"Fuck!" Vega was losing her mind. Slowly but surely, she knew she would break.

All the blood left her body when the realization sank in that the elevator was no longer moving and the doors hadn't opened to her floor. Vega hopped up, scrambling to the buttons. "No, no, no," she muttered to herself as she continuously pressed the Open Door and Fourth Floor buttons. "This can't be happening." She slammed her hand onto the door with an open palm hard enough to feel the sting of the impact.

An unwelcome wave of nausea rolled in the pit of her stomach. "All I wanted to do was get black-out drunk and forget who I am tonight. Is that too much to ask for?" Vega screamed to the ceiling, knowing no one would answer back.

Frantically, Vega began to press the Emergency Call button, but nothing happened. Her breathing hitched, chest tightening—a panic attack was creeping in.

The corners of her vision went fuzzy, and she tripped over herself. *No, not a panic attack.* She was about to black out again. Vega reached for the handle on the wall, attempting to steady herself before she was thrust into her mind.

A calloused hand reached out to grab hers, and Vega's eyes fluttered up to meet the gaze of the most handsome man she'd ever seen. His delicate grasp contradicted the way his eyes locked on hers with feverous intent. He dipped his head, never breaking their eye contact as he placed a light kiss on the back of her hand.

"No wonder they've kept you away from us for so long. A striking young man like yourself wouldn't last a night around a bunch of hormonal teens." Vega heard her voice swirl above her head, so melodic and carefree.

"I'm sure I could hold my own." Her voice was met with one so unlike hers: deep and mysterious.

"Is that a challenge, Dimico?" Vega asked with a playfulness to her tone.

"Please, call me Bridger. And it could be, if you'd like."

Her laugh echoed off the walls of the grand home, winter decor hanging from chandeliers and taking up space on the mantles. She sounded so *happy*.

Vega couldn't take her eyes off him. His hair was the darkest color of obsidian she'd ever seen, nearly matching the color of his eyes. He ran a hand through it when he noticed Vega's eyes dragging down his body, a smile fit for a god lighting up his naturally sun-kissed skin. He towered over her by a good six inches in her heels, his shoulders were broad, and his all-black suit with small gold accents hugged his toned physique—his suit tailored to fit perfectly.

"I'm not so easily won over," she admitted with a wink.

"You're not the only one who loves a good challenge, Kitten."

The nickname made her cheeks burn hot. "Kitten?" she asked.

"Black nails, black dress, a spitfire attitude. I'd say this kitty has claws, regardless of how badly you're trying to keep them hidden." He licked his lips as his eyes trailed down the length of her body.

A shiver traveled up her spine when his eyes made it back to hers, jarring her out of the vision she never wanted to end. Vega's eyes shot open as she came to on her hands and knees in a puddle of wine.

Frightened, she popped up, only to end up on her ass from the rush in her head from standing too fast.

Her breathing was ragged, chest heaving from the rush of adrenaline. "What is happening to me?" She'd seen his face in dreams before—the dreams that haunted her years ago. *But now he finally has a name, just like Arlet and Marlena.* Once the vertigo subsided, Vega pushed herself up. She thumbed the Emergency Call button once more and let out a defeated sigh when nothing happened again.

"Hello? Can anyone hear me?" Vega wiped at her face, tears free falling down her pink cheeks. She knocked on the door again. "Help! I'm stuck in the elevator!" It wasn't that late. Someone was bound to hear her pleas for help. Morris would make it up the stairs at some point, right?

"My phone. Shit, where's my phone?" Vega lunged for her bag and rummaged through its wet contents until her hand felt the slim device at the bottom. Everything inside was soaked, including her phone, but the screen lit up. Her fingers tapped against the sticky glass.

"9-1-1, what's your emergency?" the voice on the other end asked as Vega pressed the phone to her ear.

"Hi, I'm stuck in my building's elevator." Vega sniffled, backing up against the cold metal wall and sliding to the floor.

"Ma'am, you need to press the Emergency button. It'll alert the elevator service company." The woman's tone sagged in annoyance.

"Yeah, um, I've already tried that. It's not working. Can you please send someone out before I have another panic attack?" *And see shit that isn't real.* Her patience was wearing thin—not just with the woman on the phone, but with life in general.

"Is there a fire? Are you hurt?"

"No, there's no fire, and I'm not hurt," Vega responded. *Yet.*

This was the third time she'd blacked out, visions materializing in her head. Vega was starting to believe this was the start of a nervous breakdown, maybe an undiagnosed mental health issue.

"What's the address of your building?" Fingers tapping on a keyboard echoed through the phone.

Vega gave the monotone woman her address, pulling her legs into her chest to make herself as small as she could. She was still in her work uniform, smelling of fried foods and grease. The little blue dress with the white apron built in did nothing to keep her warm, and neither did the wet raincoat wrapped around her.

"I've contacted your local fire department. They will get to you as soon as they can."

She took her bottom lip between her teeth. "How long do you think it'll take?" She rested her chin on her knees.

"I'm not sure, ma'am. If you smell smoke or this turns into a dire situation, please call us back, and we'll try to get someone out faster." Which translated to, *If this turns into a real emergency…*

"Okay, thanks." Vega didn't wait for her to say anything else before ending the call. Tears poured down her cheeks, and Vega threw the phone across the small box, unconcerned if it shattered into a million pieces.

Maybe I am cursed. No one's luck is this bad.

Since she was stuck in here for the foreseeable future, Vega crawled across the small space on her knees and ripped the intact bottle of wine out of her soggy bag. She twisted the cap off the cheap bottle and chugged until she felt like she needed to come up for air.

The wine warmed her belly as she rested her head against the wall, eyes closed tightly, and fingertips tracing the branded ring around her wrist.

Arlet claimed to know where she—they—got them. But did she understand why it itched, burned, why it tingled so severely she couldn't sleep sometimes?

As if it could hear her thoughts, the scar started to itch.

Vega brought the bottle back to her lips.

4

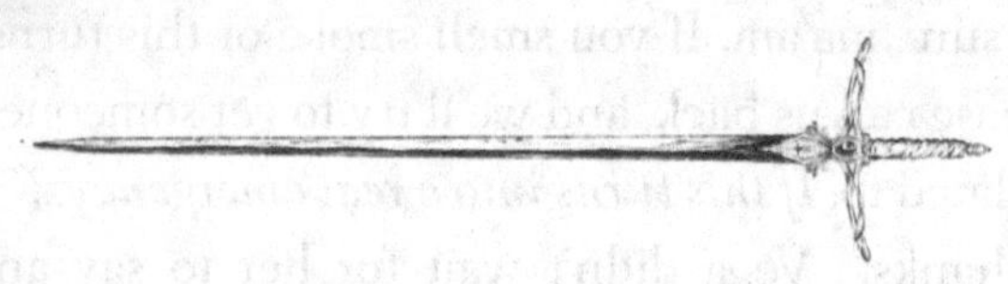

Bridger's leg connected with the punching bag swinging from the iron bars crossing overhead, a pop booming through the open-air training arena followed by the quick snaps of his left jabs and right hooks.

The people of Vincere were either asleep, tucked into their beds, or at their posts where they'd spend the night until the sun rose and they were relieved of their duties.

Bridger, on the other hand, was rattled out of his sleep by a dream that had once been real. The images were trying to sink their claws into a part of his brain that had been cleared of those memories ages ago.

He'd worked so long, fought so hard to forget her—to forget the feelings he'd once had for her. To rid himself of the emotions that took hold whenever he remembered what he'd done—who he'd chosen.

The memory felt so real—so much so that when he'd woken, he forgot where he was and found himself reaching out in his large, empty bed to feel for her.

Like she hadn't been missing from that side of his bed for almost fifty-five years.

After pulling a dagger from the sheath on his leg, Bridger threw the blade. It soared through the air end over end until it stuck into the center of its intended target. The red bullseye stared back at him, a crack splintering down the center of the thick wood.

Bridger's fists were red from the force of his punches, sweat trickling down his bare chest until droplets formed under his feet. He'd been out here for hours, fighting the nostalgia that made his body buzz from the all-too-real dream.

Is it a dream if it's something that actually happened? He groaned at the thought, plopping himself onto a stool in the corner. Bridger hid his face in his hands, pushing the damp pieces of hair that fell over his brow back into place.

Vincere was meant to be a place that felt new, void of the demons haunting the rest of Tolevarre. The training facility and underground barracks were built over thirty years ago as a way for Bridger to run from the place he'd once called home—as a new and improved location where the best warriors Tolevarre had to offer could come to train.

Designed to weed out the good from the great, the great from the extraordinary. Vincere's location had been hand-picked by Bridger himself—southwest of Aeris, sitting below Demuto at the southernmost point of Ardor's territory. He chose the vast openness offered here, far away from the city where he could breathe, far away from Fortis and the family who still called those phantom streets home.

But lately, with the rise in rebel camps popping up all over the realm, Bridger wasn't sure there was any place he could hide that didn't remind him of what he'd done.

Each territory took after the land around it and the god that blessed its people, pulling from the natural textiles found there.

They all had their individual charms, and each felt vastly different from the others.

Ardor was desert lands. Their buildings were orange, made out of brick with clay molded over top to keep homes cool in the brutal months of summer.

It sometimes felt like a world away with its stark difference in landscape. It was the only territory in Tolevarre with deserts, sand dunes, and heat indexes that reached 120 for eight months out of the year.

He was alone under the moonlight, grateful for the cool night air giving him a break from the usual sweltering temperatures Ardor was known for.

Bridger had lost count of how many times one of his soldiers collapsed and was rushed to the infirmary during the summer months. Being a warrior in Bridger's army wasn't easy—but it was better than it had been under his father's control.

Before his thoughts could wander back where they didn't belong, Bridger felt the wind pick up, stirring unnaturally through his fingers.

The packed dirt of the training pit crunched behind him, his elevated hearing making it impossible for him to be snuck up on. "Marlena." That was Bridger's way of hello to the ruler of their realm.

"It's awfully late for a training session, don't you think, Commander?" Her voice had always been so different from her sister's. Vega's voice was smooth like velvet, but Marlena's was pitched, sharper than the tip of a fresh blade.

Bridger turned to face Marlena, her long, ice-blonde hair braided into a coronet around the top of her head. The leather pants, sheer top, and pointed boots didn't match the palm trees swaying in the breeze behind her. Marlena looked every bit of the evil ruler she was as she sauntered over to him.

"It's awfully late for an unexpected visit, don't you think, Your Majesty?" Bridger repeated her words back to her in a cold response.

"I told you to stop calling me that." Marlena sneered.

Bridger smiled. It didn't touch his eyes like it should. "Then why wear the crown?" His eyes darted to the single ring woven into Marlena's braid. A black iron crown glimmered in the moonlight, marking Marlena as a woman destined to rule, but it could easily be mistaken for a dark angel's halo.

And Marlena loved nothing more than subjecting the people underneath her to live her personal version of perfect—everyone else's hell.

Her face was unreadable as she blatantly ignored his question for one of her own. "What's on your mind?"

"Couldn't sleep," he answered while standing from the stool.

Marlena's eyes dipped to his shirtless chest, then ticked back to meet his gaze sharply. "Anything you'd like to talk about?"

He and Marlena were friends once. A lifetime ago. But he'd been a different person then.

Bridger could lie, but what was the point? He didn't fear Marlena like the rest of them did. "I had a dream about them." He paused. "About Vega."

Marlena couldn't hide the distaste distorting her face at the mention of her sister.

It was about time Vega reappeared—it'd been too long this time around. Bridger knew Marlena was waiting for the day she never did, when the curse finally ran dry, taking her sister with it.

"We're coming up on year fifty-five." Her voice rang with a sense of longing. "Aren't you ready to let go of her forever?"

Bridger rubbed his right wrist. "I have."

Marlena's eyes, the same color as Vega's, locked on to the wrist he was absentmindedly running his fingers over. "Does that old thing still bother you?"

It always bothered him when Arlet made contact with Vega. Bridger was sure that's what triggered his dream. Sometimes, if he concentrated, he could still feel Arlet and Khort—not like he'd once been able to, but they were still there regardless of how much power he used to keep them blocked out. Four souls connected by one person, and her curse had been active too long.

Curses didn't last forever—they either needed to be broken or released. If neither happened, the power of the curse eventually died, taking the cursed with it.

"Don't ask questions you know the answers to." He'd been trying to convince her to attempt to break the bond since he'd taken over her army. Bridger would do anything to never worry about feeling the connection he shared with them again, as small as it might be nowadays.

"But then how would I know my sister is stirring?" Marlena took a step closer, looking up to meet Bridger's stone-cold gaze. She reached out and touched his jawline with her fingertip.

Bridger grabbed her hand and placed it back by her side. "Marlena, do you think I'm dumb enough to believe you need me to know when Vega is on her way back to our realm? That's not the reason you need me," he said matter-of-factly.

Marlena's eyes twinkled under the moonlight, a faint smile pulling at the corners of her mouth as she pretended to look around at the training arena with interest. "Yeah, but then I wouldn't be able to see the look on my sister's face when I rip the bond out of you three before I kill her for the last time." Marlena's face shifted to the look of a serpent ready to strike. "And I've told you before, my dear commander, that I want nothing more than to see the look on Vega's face when she finally realizes, once and for all, that not only have I won every single time she's tried to stop me, but I also got the only thing she ever wanted." Marlena breathed a contented sigh. "You."

Bridger hated Marlena with every fiber of his being, but she'd sold her soul to every devil she could find, every god seeking revenge, and it had been proven time and time again that she couldn't be stopped.

This curse would consume them all.

"It has to kill you, knowing that I can feel her." The muscles tensed in Bridger's jaw.

Marlena's cold stare was enough to turn mortal men to stone. "I love knowing that she can feel you, feel the pain of what you've done to her when she gets her memories back. But if you play nice, I'll break the bond before I kill them and spare you from unnecessary pain."

"I don't know why you continue to treat me like I'm one of them. Like I haven't fought by your side for forty years. Have I not proven myself to you? After all this time?" Marlena didn't answer. "You act as if I haven't killed her for you."

The air around them chilled, colder than any winter air had ever made him feel. In the blink of an eye, Marlena was so close to Bridger that her lips were on his ear, her breath sending chills down his spine. The hairs on the back of his neck stood up as he stiffened.

"You're still dreaming of her and denying me what I want. How is that supposed to make me feel?" she asked, her tone sour with envy.

Bridger knew she only wanted him to get one last dig in at Vega. "I don't want another Caelum sister. One was plenty for this lifetime," he sneered.

"That's too bad," Marlena purred. "If only I could've gotten to you first. You wouldn't be in this situation now, dreaming of a woman who's as good as dead."

"Why are you here, Marlena?" Bridger asked, taking a step back from her, putting space between them again.

"I'm requesting your presence in Stella. Bring Meyer. We have a lot to talk about to prepare for Vega's return this time." The feel of her on his skin lingered even after she'd vanished into thin air, and all that was left as proof that she was ever there was a billow of black smoke rising into the now calm night air.

Her powers had no limits.

Bridger let his breath loose, turning his attention back to the training arena around him. From the table, he grabbed the sword that answered to his soul, bonded to him and his powers, and sliced the punching bag in half.

5

Vega shook the wine bottle, coaxing the last drop of liquid out. She felt like a fiend, groaning when she realized she was officially out. "I can't believe this is my life."

The scar around her wrist hadn't lost its itch—it had worsened. Her skin was red and raw from her fingernails digging into the delicate skin.

She let the bottle hit the floor too hard, cringing until it stopped clattering and remained fully intact.

It had been over an hour since she'd gotten off the phone with the dispatch operator. Halfway through the bottle, she started hollering again, hoping that someone, anyone, would hear her on the other side. She felt like a prisoner in a cell.

A bottle of wine deep, she decided to press the Call button again. And again, and again, and again until her finger went numb. She wanted to cry, to scream, but what was the point?

She was alone. Truly and utterly alone.

Vega laid herself on the floor, sprawled out like a starfish. *One, two, three, four, five, six...* She began to count the lines in the ceiling tile until she had to go back to the beginning and start again.

A voice sounded on the other side of the elevator when she got to 995. "Hello?" Vega almost thought it was all in her head until the deep voice continued to talk. "This is the Chicago Fire Department. We're here to get you out. Can you hear me?"

Vega jumped up so quickly she made herself dizzy. "Yes! Thank you! Oh my god, thank you!" She rested her hand against the metal door, dreaming of the hero on the other side.

"Are you okay?" he asked.

What a fully loaded question.

Vega swallowed, closing her eyes. "I just want to get out of here."

"We've gotcha." There was movement behind the door. "What's your name? I'm Oliver." Poor Oliver had drawn the short stick and was tasked with keeping her calm while they broke her out.

"Vega." Her voice felt small.

"That's a pretty name. Okay, Vega, I'm going to need you to stand back. You're stuck in between floors." His voice came from above her head.

Vega nodded.

"You've got to give me a verbal confirmation that you understand before we start."

Duh, Vega! "Yes. I'm standing back." She stumbled backward. That bottle of wine had inebriated her, making her limbs feel heavy and slow.

"Good. We're going to get you out of there quickly. Promise," Oliver said, and she imagined him holding up his hand like a boy scout.

Vega did her best to keep her heart rate down—the visions she'd been having seemed to come whenever she couldn't keep herself from panicking.

"Vega?" The same voice was close to the door again. "You okay?"

This man was a complete 180 in personality to the woman on dispatch. "I'm okay. Are you almost done?" she asked, antsier by the passing second.

"We're going to pry the door open."

Those words made her squirm excitedly, her weight shifting from foot to foot.

Less than a minute later, the elevator's doors creaked open, forced apart by a crowbar. The opened doors revealed a dark wall with enough space in between the floor for Vega to fall to her death.

Heights weren't her favorite. Chase once surprised her with a bungee jumping excursion in the Bahamas for their honeymoon, and when she got to the top of the tower, she chickened out and ran as fast as she could to the bottom.

Maybe Jessica is more adventurous.

She choked back her fear, forcing her eyes up to the man splayed out on the floor above the dark abyss. His pretty amber eyes were clear even in the dim lighting. "Bobby's Diner?" he asked, noting her blue uniform with white, scuffed-up non-slip sneakers.

Vega stared, still dancing back and forth on her feet to avoid feeling antsy. *Words, Vega. You need to say words.* "Yeah. It's a really glamorous place." Maybe not those words, but it was better than staring blankly.

The handsome fireman smiled at her, reaching an arm down through the too-thin opening she was expected to slip through. "Pass your bags up to me, and I'll pull you out next." His fingers wiggled in wait.

After gathering her things off the floor, Vega reached up high to pass them over, realizing they were still soaked. "I swear it's not pee," she blurted out, biting her lip hard enough to cause a bit of pain as punishment for her stupid mouth. "A bottle of wine broke." *Definitely should have started with that.*

"Good to know," Oliver responded with a chuckle, putting her bag to the side. "Okay, your turn."

Scratch, scratch, scratch.

Her nails dug into her wrist again. Vega coaxed herself to the open door, willing her eyes not to look down—only up to the hero saving her. "Please don't drop me," she whispered, lifting her arms above her head.

"I promise I won't," he responded, wrapping his large hands around her forearms. "But I can't guarantee this is going to be a very comfortable position. I'm going to make it as quick as possible, okay?"

Vega's throat bobbed as she swallowed hard, giving him a single nod. "Okay." As soon as the word slipped through her lips, Oliver hoisted her up. It happened so fast Vega had no time to register she was even suspended in the air.

The dirty floors of her apartment building were underneath her quickly, and if she didn't know they'd never been cleaned a single time since living here, she would've kissed the fucking floor.

Oliver and another fireman helped her up. "You good?" His face was welcoming, a little stubble around his sharp jawline. *Damn it, Vega, you're married*—to a cheater. She threw those thoughts out of her head, focusing on the fact she was finally free.

"Great," she said with a small smile. "Thank you." Vega looked around at the other firefighters, thanking them as well.

"Our pleasure. The elevator repairman just got here, but I'm sure you're not interested in using this one ever again, huh?" His laugh was soft, his lips settling into a warm smile.

"This one or any other for that matter." Vega hoisted her bag over her shoulder and glanced up at the number outside the elevator door. Of course she'd gotten stuck a half floor away from her exit. "Thanks again," she said as her nails dug into her wrist for the umpteenth time.

Oliver's eyes grew wide. "You're hurt." He reached out to her with gentle hands, but Vega pulled away, burying her arm against her chest.

"Oh no, it's nothing. I..." Vega quickly searched her brain for an excuse. "The chemicals at work." She rolled her eyes, brushing off his worry. "Have a great night!" Vega turned on her heels, her shoes squeaking against the old, checkered linoleum.

She looked down at her wrist, where droplets of blood had started to dry and crust up.

As she slid her key into the door of her apartment, it flew open, and she was face-to-face with Chase.

His mocha eyes scanned her body, his short blond hair gelled back in his typical after-work style. "Vega." He sounded relieved, a sigh leaving his lips as he took in the scene behind her. "What the..." His round face was riddled with worry, dark bags clouding his under eyes, and for the first time in years, Chase had stubble forming on his jaw.

I can't do this right now. Without a single word, she turned around and padded away from her apartment and the man she'd once thought she might grow old with. Oliver, the handsome firefighter, and his co-workers watched in silence as she stomped past them. Their eyes flicked behind her, landing on the husband trying to keep up.

"Vega, we need to talk about this!"

She skidded to a stop, spinning around with her finger in Chase's face. "We'll talk when I'm ready. Until then, give me my space, leave me alone, and maybe go stay with your little *girlfriend*," Vega snarled.

Chase reached out and wrapped his hand around Vega's finger, pushing it down and away from his face. "Vega, please. This is all just a big misunderstand—"

Her hand connected with the side of his cheek, the crisp slap pulsating down the thin hallway. Vega pulled away from his touch. "A misunderstanding?" Her jaw dropped. "A misunderstanding?" Her voice grew shrill with each syllable. "What am I not understanding about finding your face between another woman's legs? Hmm? About finding out that you've been cheating on me for *over a year?*"

Chase's hand rested on his cheek, rubbing at the sting that was surely there. "Vega, lower your voice. People are listening."

She peeked over her shoulder and was surprised to see she felt no shame knowing there was an audience. Vega laughed, but the sound rang hollow. "Oh, am I supposed to try to protect your reputation?" She shook her head. "If you think for one second I care about your feelings right now or what anyone thinks of you, then you obviously don't know me as well as I thought." Vega ignored the looks lining the faces of each fireman as she walked by and slammed the stairwell door shut.

Vega hoped some fresh air would do her good after hours of feeling like she might suffocate to death inside an elevator.

The rain still dripping from the clouds above was finally starting to come to an end, turning into a cold mist, but the horizon was dark with more rain. This time of the year tended to be rainy, but the dark sky in the distance seemed heftier than typical spring showers.

There was a storm coming.

Storms always seemed to follow her worst days, clouding her like a blanket. Vega should find it ominous, but strangely enough, it felt calming.

Vega shifted her eyes down to her feet as they shuffled down the sidewalk—her body knew exactly where she wanted to go.

The lake was about a twenty-minute walk, but the sound of the waves rolling to shore was exactly what she felt she needed to help drown out the buzzing in her head.

Vega took a seat, the wind whipping her hair around as the storm started to churn the lake up. This bench ought to have a Vega-sized butt imprint by now. She had been coming to this spot since she moved to Chicago. Whenever Vega needed to clear her head or when she needed a moment to herself, this was her spot.

Staring out into the lake, Vega let her mind wander.

There were a lot of missing pieces in her memory. *Missing pieces? More like black holes.*

Vega couldn't remember anything before high school—nothing. Her therapist told her it was her way of coping with trauma, but did that really mean she fully couldn't remember a single memory before her mom's cancer diagnosis?

When her mom was alive, Vega used to ask about her childhood, about where they lived when she was born, or when they'd moved to Washington State—the pieces of information she had about her life weren't her own. They were implanted from someone else spoon-feeding her the answers.

Her memories always failed her, but she could remember a home with a lake view, a bedroom high on the side of a mountain, stars so close it felt like she could reach out of her window and grab them in her hand—a place so familiar it felt wrong to believe it was nothing more than a dream.

Her mom chalked it up to having a big imagination, and that must still be true today if she was genuinely considering Arlet's story.

But Arlet had been the only person in her life, ever, to give her any kind of insight as to where she was from—about who she might be. The only person to tell her the dreams were real.

The more she thought about the girl, the more her scar nagged at her. Vega rubbed her wrist, avoiding digging her nails into her skin still crusted with dried blood.

The itch wouldn't stop, no matter how hard she tried to disregard it. Vega groaned heavily, standing from the bench.

The dark clouds coming out of the east were getting closer. The colors of the lake were no longer blue like the Caribbean but stained with darkness from the waves churning up the bottom. Vega needed to take cover somewhere, but she didn't want to go home—she couldn't go home.

That apartment was no longer the safe space it once was.

Her feet guided her back the way she'd come, but when she got to the crossroads at the corner of her apartment building, something was telling her to go left instead of right.

She gave in to the incessant need to scratch her wrist.

Her mind kept wandering. What would it mean if this life was a mirage to keep her from knowing who she truly was?

Vega didn't know where she was going. She thoughtlessly followed the feeling growing inside her, like a string was tugging at her heart and she needed to find the end of it.

Maybe the feeling would go away when the rain washed her out to the lake, never to return to this life that didn't want her.

Perhaps she would walk until she collapsed from exhaustion.

Vega would walk until her feet fell off if it meant she could rid herself of this hollow mood that was starting to consume her.

The string in her chest tugged harder as she stood outside of a restored motel she'd never been to. Vega gawked at the neon sign above her head. It looked out of place in this part of the city, the sign flashing Vacancy in the window.

Her heart pushed her forward.

She took the stairs one at a time, thunder rumbling in the distance. The tug in her chest stopped, the itch of her wrist gone when she approached room number 444. A buzzing in her body told her to knock.

Her fingers rapped against the metal door.

The door opened, and there stood Arlet, leaning against the frame. She didn't say anything, but her face held an ear-to-ear grin.

"How the hell did I find you?" Vega felt that wave of unconsciousness settle into her and knew what was coming next.

Her vision went black at the same time Arlet stepped forward to catch her.

6

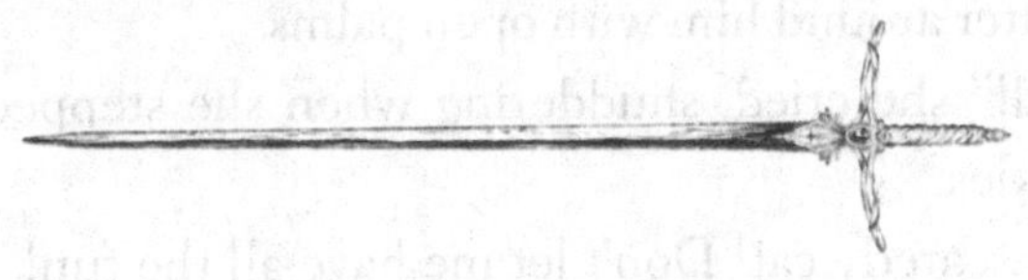

THE SUN HUNG LOW IN THE SKY, THE TEMPERATURE HIGH FOR this time of the year. The chilled, spring-fed water of Lake Mons passed over Bridger's hips as he walked backwards, taking small steps, his bare feet shuffling over the rocky bottom.

Bridger's gaze raked across Vega's bare skin while she pulled her tight midnight-blue dress off of her body, the light blue jewels around her neck settling between the valley of her breasts.

It had been his idea to skip the dinner their parents planned with the other Curia members and their children, sneaking into Vega's room before she had the chance to come downstairs and doom them to yet another boring night they didn't want to be a part of.

Vega looked up from her pool of clothing on the soft grass beneath her, eyes connecting with his. Her laugh was light and airy, filling Bridger's ears with the last sound he wanted to hear before he died.

She wasn't shy and didn't shatter under his gaze like most women did in his presence. She stood as tall as her short frame would allow, her dark brown hair flowing past her shoulder blades.

The setting sun illuminated her skin in purples and pinks, making her look every bit of the goddess Bridger believed her to be.

He licked his lips, hungry to get a taste—ready to relieve himself of the ache he'd been feeling since he'd laid eyes on Vega almost a full year ago. The muscles in his face twitched as a crooked smile spread across his lips. "What are you waiting for?" he bellowed, splashing water around him with open palms.

"It's cold!" she cried, shuddering when she stepped into water up to her ankles.

"C'mon, scaredy cat! Don't let me have all the fun!" Bridger fell backwards, plummeting beneath the water. When he surfaced, he shook his head and ran his hand down his face to clear it of excess water to find Vega had only taken a few steps further. "My little kitten afraid of some water?"

Her brows furrowed. "Oh, I'll show you scared!" The water splashed around her as Vega plunged herself into the chilled, crystal-clear water.

Vega stopped ahead of him, barely able to touch the bottom as Bridger swam further out with a lazy backstroke, keeping his eyes locked on her. "Give me your best."

The breeze turned into roaring winds, stirring up the lake's once calm surface. Dark clouds loomed in the distance, rolling in with cracks of thunder until they were directly overhead. Fat raindrops started to fall from the sky, stinging Bridger's face. The water churned, but the waves avoided Vega. The wind she controlled pushed them away, redirecting them to the shore with a crash.

Bridger blinked, astonishment lighting up his eyes from the middle of the lake while he continued treading water. He threw his invisible shield up, his power allowing the water in his circle to calm and protecting him from the wild waves of Vega's storm.

He'd never seen anyone like her—no one had.

She put on a show for him, lightning spidering across the sky with booms of thunder echoing off the mountains in the distance. If their parents didn't already know where they'd run off to, they did now.

Vega's smile lit up, her voice traveling through the wind. "Who's scared now?" When she winked at him, her storm started to die down, nothing left but a bit of rain and waves crashing across the lake's shore.

Bridger let his shield fall and swam until his feet touched the bottom, moving to close the distance between them. His chest was exposed, compared to Vega, where only the tops of her shoulders were flirting with the waterline.

Vega's chest swelled with an intake of air as he stepped against her. Bridger's fingers danced up her arms, skimming her skin and turning the tips of his fingers into individual infernos from the pulse of the electricity flowing underneath Vega's skin.

Her piercing eyes followed his hands like an artist admiring their greatest masterpiece.

Gently, Bridger placed his fingers under her chin and tilted it up to meet his gaze. "The only thing I'm scared of is returning to a life without you in it." How had he ever felt whole before meeting Vega? Why had they kept their relationship purely platonic since meeting when their chemistry burned hotter than the embers of a fire?

"Then make a move," Vega said with a breath, her voice a light caress.

His hands slid behind her head, tangling in her wet hair as the rain she created dulled to a steady drip. Bridger wasted no time pressing his lips to hers, starting off slow until they found their rhythm.

Vega's arms snaked around his neck, and she hiked herself up, wrapping her legs around his waist.

Bridger moved his hands to hold her tightly, squeezing roughly at the handfuls of her ass he now had a grip on. He moved his mouth from her lips, trailing kisses down the delicate skin of her neck to her chest, where he licked water droplets off.

He devoured every inch he could, getting the taste he'd been so desperately craving.

Vega drove her hips forward, grinding against Bridger's growing arousal. He groaned a primal sound from deep inside his chest.

Bridger inhaled the scent of her skin. Hydrangeas—honey and sweet vanilla. "You're going to be my undoing, Vega Caelum." His breath was hot on her neck as he licked from her collarbone to the edge of her jaw. He put his lips to her ear. "I have to have you. Let me show you what I've been wanting to do to you since the day we met."

Vega gave him permission with one single nod, followed by a whimpered, "Bridger, please."

But Bridger barely heard her words before he carried her out of the water.

Their lips met again as he laid her back against the warm, damp grass. He balanced his weight above her with one arm, the other pulling her out of what little clothing she had on.

He took a moment to take in the view—and it wasn't the far off snow-capped mountains wrapping around the capital city of Stella. "Gods, you're so fucking beautiful," Bridger panted.

Vega curled her fingers in the hair at the nape of his neck, pulling his mouth to hers in a wild kiss that set every nerve ending in Bridger's body ablaze. She let him take control, turning to putty in his hands.

"Bridger," she moaned against his lips. "Bridger," she said again. "Bridger." A third time. "Bridger," a voice said, but this time it wasn't hers, and he was no longer lying on the bank in Aeris, making love to Vega Caelum.

Bridger shot out of bed, coming face to face with Meyer Ignis, his best friend and the general of his army.

The blanket draped over his waist tripped him, tangling between his legs until he fell to the floor. He landed with a crash—not a graceful maneuver expected from a powerful war commander, let alone the most powerful warrior in all of Tolevarre. He groaned, pulling himself up to his elbows while his eyes adjusted to the darkness of his room.

The screeching of his alarm registered just as Meyer's hand slammed down on the button to silence it. "Your alarm has been going off for twenty fucking minutes." His baritone voice was even deeper with the grogginess of sleep. "I could hear it down the hall. You trying to wake the whole gods-damned wing up?"

Their rooms shared a wall, but the bathrooms separated their living spaces from being side-by-side.

Meyer approached, holding out his hand to help Bridger up.

He shooed him away, getting himself off the cold floor without assistance. "I must've been sleeping pretty good." Bridger ran a hand through his dark hair, sitting himself down on the corner of his ruffled bed. His elbows rested on the tops of his knees, head in his hands while he groaned.

"Ya think? Since when do you sleep past your alarm? It's been years since I've heard that—incredibly annoying, might I add— buzzing." Meyer scooped Bridger's charcoal comforter off the floor and tossed it to him before collapsing in a plush chair across the room. He lit a lamp with a simple snap of his fingers, fire dancing across the tips before disappearing.

The electricity in Tolevarre was powered by the natural elements around them. The running streams of Aeris, the solar power of Ardor. The intelligence of the people from Littera ensured their world had technological advances and machinery that assisted in making everyday life easier for its people, but Vincere didn't have the electricity the rest of the realm had—the ones who were powerful enough to have the luxury of well-lit homes, that is. The barracks and training facility saved whatever they could for their equipment and popular common areas.

"Since I started having dreams of Vega," Bridger admitted, lifting his head from his hands and wiping the look of longing from his face.

His feelings for Vega over the years had swelled from lust, to love, to longing, to hatred for the shell of a person she'd become—of what the curse had stripped her of.

"Ah." Meyer huffed.

The two didn't talk about her. They didn't talk about anything from before. Let bygones be bygones or whatever—that was how Bridger felt. Why bother when harping on the past wouldn't change anything?

"How many years has it been this time?" Meyer tipped his head, the flickering light illuminating the scar under his chin—a reminder of what Bridger had given up to save his best friend's life.

"Fifteen years," Bridger answered. "The longest time she's been gone so far."

"You think this means it's coming to an end? It's getting longer and longer every time she resets."

I hope not. "I hope so," Bridger said instead. "These dreams I'm having, they're not just dreams... They're memories. I'm dreaming of events in the order they happened before Marlena cursed Vega."

Meyer cocked his head. "Weird."

"Really weird," Bridger agreed, hoping he wouldn't push for more information.

"That's never happened before?" Meyer asked.

Bridger answered with a shake of his head. "I had dreams of her before I learned I could shield the memories and block the bond, but never of anything real." He'd never admitted that to anyone.

The shielding power of warriors typically only blocked outside forces. Bridger, over the years, had realized his powers were no longer just what he'd known them to be—nor were they only what he'd been born with. Already stronger than anyone their world had ever seen, Bridger somehow got *stronger*. The powers he'd gotten from his direct lineage to Mars had a long list: enhanced strength, hearing, the ability to bond with a weapon—allowing his powers to manifest within the object and become stronger when using it.

Mars's powers had given the people of his lineage everything they needed in order to be a skilled warrior—the soldiers of this realm meant to protect the people who called Tolevarre home.

The summoning made Bridger different, giving him powers he'd never imagined. He could play with the wind, manipulating it for his own use. He could heal small wounds—nothing like the real healers of this realm could do, but enough to assist in aiding his soldiers when they'd been hurt in battle.

It took years to uncover all the new things he could do.

There was also the bond he shared with the other three, the way he could feel them even when he didn't want to.

And if Bridger was strong before Remus linked him to them, then he could be damn near unstoppable now. It was why Marlena wanted him so badly—the two of them could take over this world and the next if he allowed it.

And then there was Vega, and their bond was...

"What did you dream about tonight?" Meyer interrupted Bridger's reverie.

Bridger's lips betrayed him, sliding into a slow smile at the memory of his hands on Vega's body. "You don't want to know."

Meyer almost laughed but shook his head instead. "It's got to be the curse breaking down. It'll be over soon."

Bridger didn't know what to respond with, so he didn't say anything, only nodded.

"Let's get a training session in before leaving for Aeris. Gods know you'll need it before whatever bomb Marlena's going to drop on us," Meyer said, pushing himself up from the chair by the armrests.

Marlena didn't personally invite Bridger to meetings—she didn't personally invite anyone to anything unless it was their execution.

Commanders of the army had an important job to do, having little time to lead a territory of their own, but they were still seen as part of the elite and included in every setting where a Curia member had been. And just because Marlena burned the Curia from the inside out almost fifty-five years ago didn't mean she threw out all of their traditions.

Bridger hated it.

He stayed out of the whole running of the realm business. That was what Marlena had fought so ruthlessly for. Bridger had never wanted to rule.

Let him punish.

Let him fight.

Let him kill.

Do not ask him what tax should be placed on the territories with less power.

"Bring your A-game. I've got some shields to put back into place, and I'm not going easy on you like I did last week." Bridger winked.

Meyer rolled his eyes and left Bridger alone to wonder if the shields he'd built inside his head had ever really been strong enough to keep Vega out forever.

7

Is that a disco ball?

Vega blinked the room into focus, the ceiling above her coming into full view after a few seconds. Her heart rattled in her chest as she shot up to a sitting position. She gasped, trying to remember where she was.

The walls were covered with fake wood panels better fitted for the 1970s, the carpet a red color that reminded Vega of her mom's old velvet car interior. The comforter underneath her was fuzzy and yellower than the sun on a hot summer's day.

Vega felt like she'd been sucked into a different decade.

She turned on the bed, eyes landing on the gorgeous stranger sitting at the end, watching her. *Oh. My. God. I found Arlet.*

"What did you see?" Arlet's brows furrowed, the confusion evident on her face. She held a glass of wine, and suddenly, that was all Vega could focus on.

"Oh good, wine." She wobbled when she stood, righting herself on the bedside table.

"Vega, what did you see?" Arlet asked her again.

Vega watched the red wine bleed into a paper cup made for to-

57

go coffee as she poured herself a hefty serving. She met it to her lips, the bitterness a welcome taste.

Vega held up her finger before Arlet had the chance to speak again. She chugged the wine down to the last drop, refilled the cup, and finally spoke. "I don't know. This one was fuzzy. It..." Vega paused, trying to gather her thoughts. "There was a fire. A house, a huge house, more like a mansion. It was engulfed, and there were little fires everywhere else in what looked like a city. I was looking down from a mountain." She turned her attention to Arlet. "That was my home, wasn't it? I remember that view. My bedroom overlooked a lake with snow-capped mountains in the distance."

Arlet gasped, her hand covering her mouth. Vega didn't know her, but it felt weird to see someone who seemed to be so sure of everything look so befuddled.

"What?" Vega barked, moving towards her, the wine bottle still in her hand.

"You're really remembering. I can't..." Arlet snatched the bottle from Vega and topped off her glass. Her plump lips met the rim, and she chugged with vigor like Vega. "This has never happened before. You've never had dreams of your life."

Vega hadn't taken her eyes off her—she watched Arlet's every move. "I need you to tell me everything. Starting with how the hell you can afford a bottle of wine this expensive."

Priorities.

Arlet's brows had yet to unfurrow. "Really? That's the first thing you decide to ask?" Vega shrugged her shoulders, waiting, and Arlet continued. "I stole it."

Vega choked on the wine in her mouth. *Am I supposed to trust anything this thief says?*

"Don't give me that look." Arlet pointed her finger, making Vega relax the muscles in her face. "I'm not here to get a job, settle down, and start a family. I'm here to get you and go home."

Home.

The word made Vega look down at the flimsy cup between her hands. She leaned against the old desk behind her. "What's it like?" She looked up. "I've seen it, or at least some of it, but I don't *know* it."

Arlet's face was so warm, her eyes had a way of looking right into Vega's soul. Arlet smiled at her, stare going distant while the world of Tolevarre came into focus.

"There are twelve territories. One for each original god."

Vega twirled her hair with one hand, the other gripping the paper cup like it would jump out if she didn't hold on for dear life. Her lips parted with a breath, ready to ask a question.

"Hold the questions for the end. I've done this speech a few times and can usually answer all of the questions you're about to ask."

Vega nodded, urging her to go on as she pulled herself up on the desk, legs swinging back and forth like a child on a too-tall chair. She was already mesmerized, and Arlet hadn't even started yet.

"How much do you know about the Roman gods this time around?"

Vega shrugged. "As much as anyone else knows about Roman mythology. That no one likes it as much as Greek mythology."

Arlet didn't hide her laugh, shaking her head as she shifted, pulling her legs underneath her. "What if I told you the gods were real?"

"Were?"

"Were. The tales have been misinterpreted here, but to this realm, they aren't real. To ours, it's the reason we exist. Remus and Romulus were sons of Mars, and like the silly men they were, they couldn't agree on where to put the Roman capital. Tragic, yes. How will they ever decide?" Arlet feigned worry, placing her hand over her heart. "Naturally, the answer was to kill the person who disagreed with you. Romulus plotted to kill Remus, but Remus found out. He knew he couldn't stop his death from happening, but what he could do was be one step ahead of his brother."

Vega sipped her wine, listening with intent like it was story time at the local library.

"Remus found a way to curse the gods when Romulus killed him, linking his life to theirs. When he died, they all died. Their powers had to go somewhere, and they ended up inside the mortals of Rome. Before the power completely dispersed itself, it created our realm, Tolevarre, a place where people like us can exist without worry." The fairytale continued. "It's been thousands of years since the beginning of our kind. We have powers as small as shifters who take the form of a bird, to a select few who can do things like control storms, manipulate what you see, turn into a dragon, or kill you with nothing but the air around you."

Vega shivered as the squall over Lake Michigan roared outside the motel window. "So who are we in the grand scheme of things?"

As if Arlet knew that question was coming, she smiled. "We're descendants of the original bloodlines. Our parents ruled the Curia. Our old government, remember?"

Vega nodded, recalling what she'd been told this morning.

Arlet kept going. "Their parents, aunts, uncles, so on and so forth, ruled before that. It's kind of like our version of royalty. The more power you have, the higher you rank in society."

Vega squinted. "Sounds kinda like here."

Without missing a beat, Arlet continued, "Not everyone believes that. There are plenty of us who are fighting against that ideology. But..." There was a slight pause. "No matter how strong someone might be, sometimes they still want more. Marlena wasn't the first to try and overthrow the Curia, just the first to succeed."

Vega didn't know what it was like to have a family, and it seemed she didn't have one to go back to either. "What happened to her?" That was Vega's luck—finding out she had a sister, something she'd always wished for, but she turned out to be evil.

Arlet shrugged her shoulders. The oversized sweater she wore engulfed her small frame. Her throat bobbed when she swallowed. "She was jealous."

"Of?"

"You."

Vega cocked her head. "Why?" She twirled the new ring on her finger aimlessly. Arlet watched her do it.

"Because you got to live carefree, go and do as you pleased. She's the oldest, the one who was destined to take over your parents' Curia seats. Both of your parents held seats from different families, and your sister was going to be the first to hold two. She's a conundrum because she was born with both of your parents' powers. Your father was Aeris-born, his power descending directly from Jupiter. He controlled the wind. Your mother was Amora-born, a descendant of Venus. Her power was invisibility. There aren't many people who get two powers, but Marlena got both."

Vega tried hard to control the look on her face, the one broadcasting her hesitancy like a billboard on a busy highway. "And somehow she was jealous of me?" Vega scoffed.

"She's not the only one who got two powers. You did too, and yours outshone hers. You somehow didn't get an ability from either of your parents. You got the control of lightning, a power our people haven't heard of in hundreds of years. And even before that, lightning wielders were rare. Later on, everyone thought you got your dad's wind too, just like Marlena, but it wasn't just that. You can control the weather—create it. There's never been a power like yours. But it wasn't just your powers. You got to have fun, grow up, live a normal life, and make most of your own decisions. She had structure, day in and day out. Her free time was few and far between. Your parents weren't as innocent as they made themselves seem, but they didn't deserve what she did to them."

Vega put the wine down, her palms starting to sweat. "What happened to them?"

Arlet averted her gaze. She was stalling—a bad sign.

She didn't wait for Arlet to speak, beating her to the punch. "She killed them, didn't she?"

Arlet looked up apologetically. "Yes." The word was a whisper.

"Hmm." It was all Vega knew to say. She couldn't remember any of this happening, and yet it sat heavily on her, a sadness creeping up for the girl who could. "Am I the only one who's cursed to forget?"

After taking the last sip, Arlet put her empty cup down on the nightstand. "Directly, yes, but it affects us all." There was hurt set deep into Arlet's face.

"I'm sorry for everything you've been through." Vega might not fully believe what Arlet was telling her, but it was clear Arlet held on to a lot of grief. She spoke about these events like she could remember every little detail.

Arlet chuckled. "You've been through it too."

She didn't want to feel sorry for herself—she'd done that enough in her life. She looked down at her hand, eyes landing on the new jewel sitting where her gorgeous emerald-cut engagement ring and matching wedding band used to be. "Whose ring is this?"

Arlet pushed herself off the bed and walked forward, grabbing Vega's hand. Vega stopped fidgeting with it when Arlet's fingers fluttered over the cool metal. "Yours."

"Did you give it to me?" Vega asked.

Arlet let go of her hand, shaking her head. "Someone else who used to love you very much gave it to you."

Vega glanced down at it, amazed at the way it looked in this light versus her apartment. The sparkles inside swirled, reminding her of the Milky Way. "Are they dead too?"

"Might as well be." The grumble reverberated off her chest, and Arlet's face changed, void of any emotion as she backed herself up to the bed.

"And the brand?" Vega took her eyes off the ring, lowering to the inner part of her wrist where the marking was most noticeable against her pale skin.

"There are four of us who have it from the night you summoned Remus."

"I'm sorry, I what?"

"Yeah, Remus, from tonight's history lesson? You summoned him. The demigod our people have to thank for their existence. It was badass. He bonded us. It's why I can find you." Arlet held her chin high, a big smile on her face.

"How is summoning a half-god even that cool?" Vega asked, unimpressed.

Arlet crossed her arms and ran her hands up and down softly, comforting herself from the memory. "Because you're smart. You knew he was our best chance at getting revenge. Marlena wanted the powers." Arlet tensed. "She summoned the twelve original gods. You know, Jupiter, Mars, Venus—the whole lot. We didn't know that then, not until later. Your sister was never stronger than you, but she's always been more cunning and willing to do whatever it takes to prove herself worthy, powerful. Your plan was never to get the powers from the other gods. You wanted the chance to bond the people closest to you, to fight together with whatever Remus was able to give us."

Vega raised a brow. "And what did Remus give us? Seems like we got the short end of the stick if Marlena is in power and we can't figure out how to break a curse after fifty-five years. And I mean, why even bother if she's going to win in the long run anyway?"

Thunder rattled the windows, shaking the pictures on the walls following her question.

"No." Arlet's voice was steady, sure of herself. "Remus knew what he was doing when he bonded us. He wouldn't have given us what was left of himself if he didn't think we could defeat her. All of us have different bonds. I can find you here. The others can't, but they can feel you when I make contact. That little tug you felt, we can all feel that. I was changed the most by the summoning. I never had an ability. My dad was from Vates, land of the seers. My siblings could see like him, but my mom was from a family of priests and priestesses in Oro, land of our temples. They're really into the whole live, laugh, love thing."

Arlet threw up a peace sign, lightening the mood a tad. "My mom could manipulate light, but she wasn't the most powerful in her family. I guess one of the kids was meant to be more like her." Her voice held a ghost of sadness. "But all I got from her was her beautiful hair."

Vega looked up from her scar. "But now?"

"Remus gave me a power no one has ever heard of. It's like he took whatever power I was supposed to get from my parents and combined it."

Vega was at the edge of the desk in anticipation.

"I can manipulate like my mom, but not light. I manipulate what is seen."

Vega's eyes grew a little wider. "You can make people see what you want them to see? Like, what's not actually real?"

"Yep," she said, popping the *p*.

"Are you doing that right now?"

She chuckled. "No. Our powers don't work here, or you'd be toasting people left and right."

Arlet poured the rest of the wine into their cups and threw the empty bottle into the trash. Vega could picture them sitting up all night, laughing while drunk on good wine. But maybe that was because she was lonely and wanted a friendship like Arlet painted all of her life.

Vega was still convinced this was all some fucked-up fever dream and she'd wake up wishing she could move to a realm far, far away from here. *But that doesn't explain the dreams.*

"There has to be a reason behind it all, huh?" If only Vega knew she was always the one trying to get to the bottom of everything, the one to ask the question, *Why?*

"Sometimes things just don't have a reason, Vega. They just are. I think this is one of those situations. Maybe Remus saw that. Maybe he knew something was coming and wanted us to have a fighting chance. There are so many reasons I've settled on over the years, but nothing with solid proof. I've given up worrying about *how* it happened, deciding to accept that it simply *did*."

There was so much she wanted to know—needed to know—but how could she in one night? Vega didn't even know where to begin with the torrent of questions floating around inside her head. "This is insane sounding, you know that, right?"

"Absolutely." The answer was honest and quick.

"You've been doing this for fifty years?"

"Fifty-five, almost. Minus a few weeks," Arlet corrected.

"How old are you?" Vega fired back.

"*We* are seventy-five. You're nearly three months older than me." Arlet winked.

She didn't let her mind rest too long on the age thing, *because what the fuck...*"Why?" *Why would someone risk their life for me?* Especially after being defeated continuously.

Arlet didn't ask what she meant—she knew. "Because you never would have given up on me if it were the other way around."

Vega's skin warmed, tingling with the honesty in her answer.

"What would happen if I said I didn't believe you and wanted to stay here?" Vega asked.

"You won't. You never have. If this weren't true, then how would you choose to explain the dreams, the tug at your heart that led you here?" Arlet's eyebrow raised.

That tug in Vega's chest made her get off the desk and abandon her cup of wine. She sat next to Arlet, their legs touching when the mattress shifted under the new weight.

Vega reached out and grabbed Arlet's right wrist, pushing up the sleeve of her sweater to inspect the raised brand on her wrist. Vega's fingers grazed over the skin gently. "Who are the others?" Vega was nervous to ask.

"Khort Fera and Bridger Dimico."

Bridger Dimico. "Bridger." Vega hadn't realized she'd said the name out loud until she watched Arlet's eyebrows draw together.

"You've dreamed of him." It wasn't a question.

"Yes, tonight before I came here when I got stuck in an elevator. I think I've seen him in dreams before—before meeting you. He just never had a name."

Arlet choked on her wine, coughing through a laugh. "You got stuck in an elevator?"

"I also slapped my husband across the face in front of a bunch of firemen, but I don't want to talk about it," Vega deadpanned.

"Oh honey, you poor thing. You're really going through it, huh?"

"Who is Bridger?" she asked, ignoring the pity in Arlet's eyes. "Please." *I have to know.*

"He's one of the bonded." Her reply was thought out, precise without giving too much away.

"Yes, I'm aware of that, but who is he to me?" Vega's throat tightened, her voice cracking.

Arlet drew a deep breath from her nose. "You and Bridger were together for seventeen years."

Were. Vega went pale. *I was taken away from not only a life with friends who have never given up on me but also a relationship—a seventeen-year relationship—with a man I can't remember.*

That realization hit her like a tidal wave. She wanted to ask more, but she was afraid of what Arlet might say.

"Vega?" Arlet broke through her haze.

"I'm fine." Vega let go of Arlet's hand, letting it fall gently back to her lap—but she didn't move from her spot next to her. Vega could count the freckles on Arlet's cheeks, see the green flecks in her eyes.

This close, she noticed the two scars that ran from her collarbone to underneath her right ear. "I want to believe you."

"I want that too." Arlet grabbed Vega's shoulder, giving it a comforting squeeze.

"How do we even get back?" Vega asked.

"There's a portal in Crescent City, California, deep inside Jedediah Smith Redwoods State Park."

Vega paled further at her response.

"What?" she asked.

"Chase and I used to go camping there with his friends during college," Vega whispered. Could it be a coincidence, or was this a detail Arlet knew and was using to make Vega feel safe around her?

There were too many unknowns.

"I just need some time to work through this. Last night, I found out my husband has been cheating on me, and today I'm not even from Earth." She barked a sad laugh. "It's a lot to take in."

Arlet nodded, picking at the hem of her sweater. "I would love to give you as much time as you need, but when I said time was running out, I meant it. The longer we wait, the closer you get to death."

Vega stood and started pacing the room in an attempt to process everything she'd learned tonight. "How do you know the curse is dying?"

"Because curses can't last forever. They run out of power, and when they do, if they haven't been broken, the cursed die with it... and there has to be a reason that you're starting to see bits and pieces of your life. From what I've seen of curses, they usually have a surge in power before it ends. I feel like that's what's happening with your dreams." Arlet watched her pace, eyes bouncing across the room with her.

"What if the curse's power runs out, and I'm on Earth? You said powers don't work here." Vega could ignore all of this, siding with the rational part of her brain reminding her that this woman could be on drugs or was out of her mind. *Right?*

"The curse is in your blood, your bones. It doesn't have to use any power to kill you." It scared her how relaxed Arlet was.

Vega groaned, running a hand through her hair, pausing at the base of her neck to take a deep breath. "So basically, what you're saying is if I stay here, I'll die? Probably alone. But if I go with you to this supposed realm, Tollybear—"

"Tolevarre," Arlet corrected.

"Whatever." Vega continued, "I still might die, but hey, I'll be a god with powers before that happens." Arlet looked at Vega like this wasn't earth-shattering news. "Why aren't you more worried about this?"

"I never said we were gods, just descendants of them. With powers, yes," Arlet replied with a calm coolness. "Because I've been worried about this for fifty-five years. The newness has worn off. Now you, you act like this every time you find out." Arlet flicked her wrist at Vega, who paced the room. "Twenty times now."

Every time. Every time. Every time.

Vega kept hearing those words, making her feel manic with jealousy for the people who didn't have fuzzy memories of their childhood. Jealous of those who weren't put in the position to choose to believe something this berserk or go back to living a life that was equally as pathetic.

"Fuck, I need some air." Vega headed for the door.

Arlet was up on her feet right behind her. "I'll come with you."

Vega turned around quickly, her hand resting on the door handle. "I think I need one more night alone." She'd had enough of them in her life. One more to decide the fate of her life wouldn't kill her.

But the curse might. Vega swallowed back a wave of nausea.

"I'll be here before noon tomorrow if I want to come. If I'm not, leave without me." Vega opened the door and marched herself into the storm outside.

8

8

THE SMELL OF THE STALE APARTMENT ENGULFED HER, ADDING to the long list of things she hated about the place she was at in her life. The landlord could fix all the leaks he wanted and would never be able to rid this place of its old musty smell.

Vega had never felt so alone, so forgotten that believing in what Arlet was telling her gave her something to hope for.

Something to lose herself in.

It was a distraction from the rock bottom she'd fallen to.

Vega had decided what she was going to do before making it back to her apartment, but she needed a night to say goodbye.

Goodbye to the grungy apartment that would never feel like a home.

Goodbye to the life that never wanted her.

Goodbye to the person she'd once been.

Vega's eyes shot up to the ticking clock on her wall.

10:36 a.m.

One last time she got out of the bed she used to share with Chase. She walked into the bathroom, which always felt damp no matter the time of year, and took a shower with the water on cold.

The chill ran through her, waking her up, and ignited something that felt like a wildfire inside her chest.

Dripping wet, foregoing a towel, Vega moved throughout her apartment naked. She took in the peeling wallpaper, the chip on the bedroom nightstand, and the crack in the bedroom window that always allowed the frigid winter air to seep in. Under the bed was a worn backpack—the one that carried her through all of her ups and downs in life.

The bag was small, perfect for the few things she cared enough about to take. Vega rummaged through her dresser for a pair of underwear that didn't have holes in them and maybe a bra where the wire didn't dig into her side.

Vega found her favorite band T-shirt on the floor, wadded up and discarded close to the hamper. She brought the black shirt with a circle and the letter *M* written inside to her nose, taking a whiff. Thankfully, she hadn't worn it in the rain or on a day when she might have needed a little extra deodorant.

Vega tied the excess fabric of the shirt into a knot at the front, her midriff showing above the leggings she'd chosen to travel in.

A toothbrush, toothpaste, and a hairbrush were all thrown into the bag haphazardly. She grabbed her wallet, passport, and birth certificate. The paper felt flimsy between her fingers.

The birth certificate read the name Arlet knew: Vega Caelum.

Chills ran down her spine. Vega shoved the documents in her bag.

Hopefully if I end up in a ditch somewhere, at least one of these will be found on me so they can identify my body.

Trafficking happened to people like her all the time, down on their luck, just trying to fit in or get by. Arlet didn't seem like the type, but she'd seen plenty of *Dateline* episodes... It usually was the people you least expected.

Who would come to her funeral? Would Chase play the doting

husband, riddled with sadness at the loss of his wife? Would Bobby come to give his condolences?

No one would miss you. The voice in her head was hard to ignore this morning.

Vega braided the strands of drying hair framing the front of her face in French braids, getting it out of her way like she always did. The rest of her hair fell down her back in loose waves.

Her gaze passed over the bedroom one last time. She slung her backpack over her shoulder and flicked the lights off.

Vega took a minute to sit down on the couch and glance at the memories scattered around the tiny apartment she was leaving behind—or at least what was left of them. Vega had destroyed most of the things that had once been a happy keepsake to her and Chase. The pictures from their wedding, their first date, and the day they moved to Chicago sat on the coffee table—Chase must have taken them out of their broken frames. Vega grabbed the picture of them from their first date and ran her finger over the image of herself. She still looked the exact same, hadn't aged a day since the picture was taken.

Chills shivered down her spine at the realization that she had always looked the same, even during high school. Vega chalked it up to maturing faster than everyone else... but if Arlet was telling the truth, that wasn't the case at all.

Vega pulled her phone out. Her finger hovered millimeters over the Call button by Chase's name.

Was she really going to do this? Was she leaving her life behind to dash across the country to a portal that probably didn't exist with some girl who might need to be seen by a mental health professional?

What do I have to lose?

The chances of her walking back into this apartment in a few days were still high—if she weren't killed. But there was still the "what if" that kept her intrigued enough to push forward—intrigued enough to, at the very least, take a break from the reality she was currently living.

Vega got off the couch and shoved her phone into the pocket of her leggings. *I can call Chase later.* When she knew what to tell him...

What shoes did one wear when about to step through a magic portal into a new realm? Vega scanned the slim pickings the closet by the front door had to offer. The black, beat-down combat boots called to her like they always did. They had moved around with her for as long as she could remember. Vega didn't know where they came from, only that she'd always had them.

They had taken her everywhere, so maybe they would finally take her home.

Vega gave one final goodbye to her dingy Chicago apartment after carving her initials into the center of the kitchen table.

Now every time Chase sat Jessica's naked ass on her table, they'd remember who bought it: VC.

The rain had finally stopped at some point during the night, and the sun was out for the first time in weeks. The universe seemed to be celebrating Vega's departure. She chose to believe it was a sign she was making the right decision.

Her feet pulled her forward, that tug at her heart becoming more noticeable the closer she got to Arlet's motel. A gleam of nervous sweat formed across her forehead as she climbed the stairs to room 444.

It was a minute until noon when the door opened to Arlet with a small, excited smile lighting up her beautiful face. "I thought you weren't coming."

"Against my better judgment, I told myself, 'Fuck it.'" Vega adjusted the strap of her backpack. "But just so you know, I took a six-week self-defense class when I moved to the city, so don't think I'm an easy target." Vega crossed her arms over her chest and popped her hip.

Arlet's smile widened. "Noted." She turned and grabbed the small bag sitting by the door. "Did you tell your friends you were leaving?"

"I have no friends, no family, no one. Just a cheating husband I can't seem to find the courage to talk to and a job I hate." She unfolded her arms, allowing Arlet by, and followed her down the stairs.

"Wanna call him now?" Arlet asked, peeking over her shoulder as she bobbed down the stairs, her curls bouncing in time with her steps.

"God, no. I'll deal with that later. Let's just figure out how we're getting to California. I might have enough money to get us some cheap flights into San Francisco." Vega hadn't owned a car in a few years, never finding the need for it with the abundance of public transport the city offered. She didn't notice that Arlet stopped at the bottom of the stairs and Vega ran into the back of her. She rubbed her nose, face scrunched. "What the fuck?"

Arlet raised a brow. "Vega, I don't have an ID. I don't have a passport. I'm not from this world. Flying isn't an option." She held up a finger, interrupting Vega's next suggestion. "And neither is a train. We've tried that before and got stranded in the middle of nowhere when I couldn't produce an ID halfway through our trip. I don't exist here." Arlet shrugged. "We're hitch-hiking."

Vega shook her head violently. "Absolutely not. That's where I draw the line."

"I thought you took self-defense classes?" Arlet's smile ticked up in the corner, as she fought back a laugh.

Vega rolled her eyes. "Yeah, but I've seen way too many murder mysteries, and that's how we end up dead in a cornfield. Wouldn't that put a little wreck in your portal plan?" She pulled her phone out.

Arlet watched the device light up. "They've somehow gotten

even bigger in the last fifteen years. How crazy." Her eyes were fixed on Vega's hands as she slid through apps.

"I guess this means we don't have cell phones?"

Arlet shook her head. "Our comm-devices aren't like this, no, but we're not some kind of third-world realm. Our technology is just different. And before you ask, no, we don't have *The Real World* or *Jersey Shore*... though sometimes I feel like Fraus could have a reality show of their own. Cheeky bastards."

"Sounds kinda boring," Vega confessed as the green Confirm button on her phone screen glowed and her request was processed. "Okay, I got us a rental car. I probably don't have enough money for all the gas on the way, but since you're so good at stealing things, I'll leave that up to you." Vega eyed her suspiciously.

Arlet's smile wasn't the sweet one Vega had become accustomed to seeing. It was full of deceit with a sparkle of elation. "Deal." The grin didn't die down until they were halfway down the street and Arlet had somehow managed to slip her hand inside a couple of purses and pockets unnoticed.

Vega couldn't help but continue to repeat the question over and over in her head. *What am I getting myself into?*

9

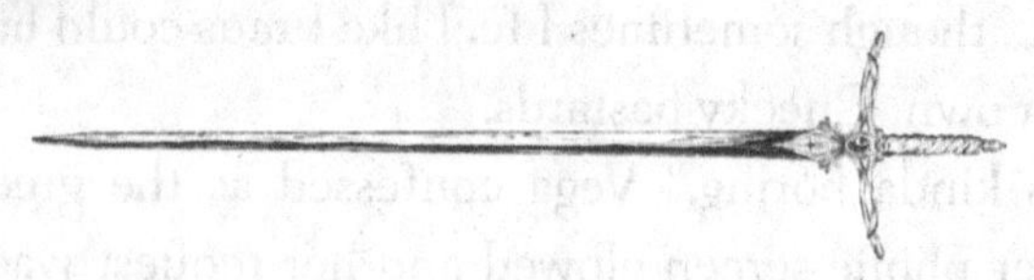

BRIDGER FORCED HIMSELF TO STAY AWAKE ON THE TRIP TO Aeris, afraid of the dreams that might torment him. Meyer dozed off early on, mumbling in his sleep.

Stella, the capital city of Tolevarre, sat above the clouds, and had once been the most peaceful place in the realm where every star outside the galaxy could be seen on a clear night. Now things were darker, the sun never seemed to peak as high as it once did during the warm season, and the stars had lost their sparkle a long time ago.

The nirvanic nights were no more, replaced with a chill that sat at the base of Bridger's spine at the mere mention of Aeris.

A welcome feeling for the Commander of Tolevarre whose life was no longer light and love but corruption and malice.

He was everything his parents hoped he would be and more.

Bridger had chosen this life. There was no going back. The darkness had consumed him.

Bridger kicked Meyer's boot to nudge him awake when Marlena's estate came into view, the sun setting behind the mountains with an ominous glow over the manor. "We're here."

This home always made Bridger antsy. Even with the original

building long gone, the ghosts of what happened here still lived somewhere deep inside him. Bridger would never forget Vega's scream when Marlena ripped her father's heart from his chest. Jonan's spirit would haunt this land until the end of time.

Some memories couldn't be suppressed, even with powers like his.

Marlena wanted to live here to remind everyone of what she'd done to her own family, of what she would do to them if they weren't careful.

The door to their vehicle opened as soon as it came to a rolling stop. Bridger expected to see one of his soldiers. Instead, they were greeted by the praefectus of Fortis—Bridger's homeland.

After burning almost all of Stella to the ground, Marlena implemented new rules and elected new rulers, whom she gave the title praefectus, to help her control those who were still alive. Their roles and titles were a tiny reminder they were only governors under Marlena and would always answer to her, always be below her.

"Oh, I wasn't expecting the two of you to ride together." Katrin dipped her head as a hello. "Meyer."

Meyer nodded, not saying a word as he shooed her away from the door with a flick of his wrist so they could exit.

Bridger met Katrin's gaze when he exited the vehicle, landing on a set of eyes the same dark color as his, her raven hair cut along her chin in a bob. "Hello, Mother." He stood to his full height, adjusting his cape.

"I think I'll go for a walk. I'll see you at dinner," Meyer said. As quickly as he'd exited the cab of their vehicle, Meyer disappeared into the garden of Marlena's home, leaving Bridger alone with his mother.

Fucking prick.

Bridger shut the door behind him. The matte black military machine roared to life with charcoal colored smoke puffing through the exhaust on top. Its four knobby tires meant for the rickety roads of the outlying territories grating against the clean cobblestone drive circling around the entrance of Marlena's home.

"What are you doing here?" he asked, striding up to the grand entrance of the estate.

Katrin kept up to his pace, her long legs meeting him step for step. "Can't a mother come see her only child? It's been months."

The look Bridger gave her was cold, his eyebrow shooting up as he waited for the real reason.

"Marlena invited me. She asked me to be here before the meeting. She sends her apologies for not being here upon your arrival." Katrin clasped her hands together at the front of her body. Poised. Raised to follow from a young age.

Bridger rolled his eyes. "You don't need to apologize for her. She doesn't mean it anyway." He was the only one who would outwardly say anything contentious about Marlena. She let him get away with it only because it helped build his image.

The angry, tortured, and fearful commander.

"Bridger," his mother hissed in warning.

"Please don't mock me by scolding me like a child. I'm not the boy I once was who could be easily swayed by your warnings." The doors opened into the luxurious foyer. The home was made of the finest materials from all over the realm. It was the perfect gothic dream house with deep emerald greens popping through midnight black, met with dark woods from the forests of Demuto. The home was too big for Marlena alone, but thankfully, she had a staff big enough to run an entire city and keep it clean, filling the corridors with noise.

Marlena had it rebuilt after her attack decades ago, but underneath the new floorboards, there was a small dungeon with ten cells and the old bones of the original home; every leader's home in Tolevarre included a small place to hold criminals for questioning and minor crimes.

The real criminals were locked away in Bridger's homeland of

Fortis—the land his mother now governed, despite it not being her birthplace.

Katrin was born a Viator, the original bloodline stemming from the dead god Mercury. She married Bridger's father as a young girl to link the Viator and Dimico line together—for power.

Katrin disappeared, gone in the blink of an eye as they ascended the stairs and reappeared outside of the room Bridger and Meyer shared while in Aeris. The black smoke of her traveler's power disappeared above her head.

Sometimes Bridger wished she would get stuck somewhere between time and space, never to return.

"I just don't understand how she hasn't taken a limb from you with the way you speak about her," Katrin commented as they entered the shared living quarters. A fire flickered to life in the hearth upon their arrival, illuminating the common room in a soft glow.

Bridger crossed the room quickly, and prepared himself a drink at the bar cart fully stocked with all of his and Meyer's favorites. He swirled the dark liquid before taking a sip. "In case you've forgotten, she spent two years of my life torturing me. I think she knows better than to cross that line again if she likes me where I am."

Katrin sighed, gliding over to her son. "Let's not talk about that." Her almost-black irises bored into Bridger's—he was a spitting image of the Viator line, but his powers were all Dimico. "You look tired. Are you not sleeping?" She reached out with her perfectly manicured hand and straightened the cape on his shoulders—the same design her husband wore during the entirety of their marriage.

Bridger's uniform was made of a tight material meant to withstand high blows, fire, or any other power that could harm him and was stronger than leather by tenfold. All the soldier's uniforms were made in the same style.

Bridger's accessories set him apart from the rest. His cape wrapped around his shoulders, clasped into place with the gold

Dimico insignia: a shield with an arrow stuck through both ends. Every original family had one as a tribute to the god their bloodline and abilities derived from. The material of the cape met the tops of his boots. It fluttered around his ankles as he stiffened like a board at his mother's touch.

"Sleeping as much as the commander of an army can," he said, taking an extra long swig of the drink in his short glass.

Katrin continued to fuss over Bridger, picking off a piece of lint from his shoulder.

"What are you doing?" Bridger's muscles wound tighter the longer his mother stood near him.

"Can't have the commander of our army walking around in an untidy uniform. I always used to get on your father about it. He would come in covered in dirt, soot, whatever he'd gotten into that day and think he could just parade around the rest of the night in filth. You have to remember people are always watching you."

He took a step back when he finally had enough of her preening. "Good advice. Thanks." Bridger didn't care for pleasantries when it came to Katrin. "It was a long trip, Mother. I'd like to rest up a bit before dinner." He unclipped his cape and draped it over the back of a chair by the crackling fire.

"Very well." Katrin sighed, but Bridger knew her well enough. She wasn't done. "Marlena mentioned Vega is stirring."

"And why would she tell you that?" He turned slowly. "Better yet, why do you think I need confirmation of that?" He cocked his head. "As if I couldn't tell," Bridger oozed with sarcasm, holding up his wrist with the brand.

She wouldn't answer him directly, choosing to dance around his question. "Eye on the prize, son. I have a feeling this time around you won't be able to avoid her like you have in the last few lives." Katrin reached the door, her hand resting on the knob.

A warning—what did Katrin know that he didn't?

Bridger chuckled, taking a sip of his drink. "Vega Caelum is at the bottom of my list of things to worry about." *But the dreams I'm having of her aren't.*

Meyer sat in his usual seat with a glass of wine, ignoring the chatter around him when Bridger stalked into the dining room.

"What have I missed?" Bridger asked as he slid into his seat next to Meyer, avoiding eye contact from the others around the table. Every praefecti of Tolevarre was here tonight—all but the three territories that were lost to the rebellion years before. As soon as Bridger sat, a servant sat a deep red glass of wine on the table beside him. Bridger didn't so much as acknowledge his existence.

In a room full of people who expected him to be the evil he believed himself to be, he must play the part. And Bridger was pretty good at it.

Leaning back in his chair, Meyer let his eyes drift around the table. "Nero and I argued about the age of enlistment and the idea of conscription now that the rebels are causing more trouble. He thinks we're wasting time and resources."

Bridger rolled his eyes, meeting the gaze of the praefectus of Littera. For a man with all the knowledge in the world, he sure knew how to put his nose in places it didn't belong. Nero glanced away.

Meyer continued, "Ivelle asked where you were."

Ivelle Fugere. If Marlena had a friend, she would be the only one.

Her long white dress flowed down to the floor, spilling around her gold heels with straps ascending as far as the eye could see up the slit of her dress.

She wiggled her fingers in a hello as Bridger's eyes scraped over her. With her ethereal beauty, she made it impossible to argue that the gods had once been real. It was her rotten heart that made Bridger recoil.

He returned his attention to his general, aware of Ivelle's continued stare. "Anything else?"

Meyer shook his head as the door to the room slammed open, rattling the hand-painted pictures hanging on the walls.

Marlena's bright blonde hair was pin-straight down her back, catching the wind as she strutted in like she was on a runway. Her leather pants were lined with knife holsters—adorned with blades she didn't need to strike any soul in this room dead. Her boots' heels were made for the dance floor and not a battlefield, clicking against the dark marble as she strode to her seat.

"Let's get started, shall we?" she asked, like she wasn't the one who always kept everyone waiting. "I have a lot to go over tonight." Marlena ran her glassy blue eyes over the people at the table as the servants came by to fill empty wine glasses, and she took her spot at the head of the table. A few members stood, welcoming her.

They didn't stand out of respect. They stood out of fear.

No one ever questioned why Bridger kept seated.

Marlena glanced around the long rectangular table. "As you know, we've almost passed the fifty-five-year mark of my sister's banishment, and every year, the rebels find new ways to corrupt the people of this realm. The uprisings are getting more frequent, and the amount of rebel camps in the outlying lands of your territories is growing." She waved her hands, motioning for everyone to sit back down. Chairs shuffled as they got comfortable again. "Commander Dimico and I talked last week. Each territory will be increasing their presence of soldiers. A new base will be set up outside of each city."

Bridger's eyes crept over the group of people at the table, watching their expressions at the news. Only one stuck out to him, his eyebrow raising when the youngest praefectus's gaze met his and then shot back to the table where he was staring a hole through the thick wood. The unmistakable redhead bounced his leg, shaking the rest of his body.

The meeting continued on, menial tasks being given to everyone to keep them sated with what little power Marlena allowed.

"Very well then." Marlena hummed. "Before we eat, there is one more thing that I'd like to bring to the table. Bridger was kind enough to take time out of his busy schedule to join us tonight, and for good reason." She moved the focus to him, heads at the table turning to follow her gaze.

Bridger stared her down, ready for the real reason they were all here tonight. He knew Marlena hadn't brought him all the way here for nothing—which is what this meeting had been thus far.

Marlena smiled at him, painting on a sweet face. "Khort Fera thinks he's found an ally in the form of a young traveler with a power we've never seen before. I'd love for you to meet him. He'd be a wonderful addition to your army."

Bridger's brow rose, face scrunched in confusion. "You brought me all this way to have me meet a recruit who's been assisting Khort in the rebellion?" Bridger huffed an annoyed laugh. "Seems like a waste of my time, don't you think? And trusting a traveler to do anything but look out for their own agenda is a mistake, Marlena. I shouldn't have to remind you of that." Out of the corner of his eye, Bridger saw Katrin tense.

Marlena stood from her seat at the head of the table and walked down the length, making eye contact with each member as she went.

"What is going on, Marlena?" Bridger asked through gritted teeth.

She quieted him with a finger over her lips before speaking. "I'm getting there. Let me have my moment." Marlena laughed. She ran her finger along an empty corner of the table and stopped when she reached the seat next to Ivelle. The redheaded woman smiled so hard her cheeks might pop.

Whatever secret she was about to expose was no secret to her.

"Almost a year ago, Arlet Videri was seen crossing through the portal to Earth." Marlena paused for dramatic effect, her eyes locked on Bridger. "She's been gone longer than ever, but she's there picking up an essential package, one that I have new plans for this time around." Marlena finished her stroll around the table, stopping behind Bridger's seat. Her hand slid onto Bridger's strong shoulder, slipping to his chest and then back up to the base of his neck

A chill ran down Bridger's spine as her fingers dug into his skin, and emerald-green fire danced from the tips of her crimson-painted fingernails. Bridger shot back, his chair crashing against the floor as he frantically got out of Marlena's grasp.

"So jumpy," she purred, her lips twitching upward into a smirk. Marlena was a tiger toying with a mouse.

Bridger's chest rose with deep breaths. The rest of the table watched, stunned. Marlena had done a lot to Bridger, but it had been many years since she'd publicly treated her commander this way.

Everyone's eyes were on him, undoubtedly waiting to see if the warrior retaliated.

"Halo, our new friend, will be here tomorrow morning to escort you and Meyer to the portal," Marlena told Bridger, her attention fixed on him.

Meyer finally broke the silence the room had fallen into. "What do you mean, to escort us?" He scoffed with irritation.

Marlena answered, "Halo can transport others. I've never seen it done before, but it was quite the discovery."

"Discovery?" Meyer asked, cocking his head. "How old is he?"

Marlena finally turned her focus from Bridger. "Nineteen. He can't even remember a life before my rule. A lost soul who found Khort and his band of rebels when he had no one else to guide him. A boy desperate for love, validation, looking to fit in somewhere. I used to know someone just like him, Bridger." A direct jab. "It didn't take much convincing to get him to agree to help me out." Bridger could relate on levels he never wished to speak about—how it felt when Marlena set her sights on something or someone she wanted. "He will continue to have an alliance with Khort and the rebellion. A perfectly placed spy with the ability to infiltrate whenever and wherever we might need."

Bridger closed the distance, his boots creating a thunderous rattle as the power he possessed bubbled with his anger. "Spit it out, Marlena." He had connected the dots, but Bridger wanted to hear her say the words, letting everyone in on the little mastermind plan that Ivelle and his mother already knew.

You won't be able to avoid her. His mother's words from earlier rang in his ears. Katrin could have warned Bridger, but she would never risk her own life—not for anyone, her son included.

"You and Meyer are going to Earth."

Bridger's jaw clenched.

"It's time to bring Vega straight to us this time. She's been gone too long. We don't have time to let her roam around Tolevarre, evoking the rebels further once she gets her memories back."

"Wouldn't it be easier to wait on this side of the portal?" Meyer asked.

"Wouldn't it be easier to sit down and shut up when the adults are talking?" Marlena barked back to the fire-wielder. "You will do as I say, and you will not question it, General."

He bowed his head, not another word coming from him about the matter as he sank into his seat.

Meyer could back down. Bridger wouldn't.

"You're risking us being trapped in another realm if something were to go wrong. Then what? If you had respected the leader of your fucking army enough to bring this to me first and not use it as hot gossip for your little friend over there"—Bridger gestured to Ivelle—"then you would know that I'm not willing to risk it."

Marlena's gaze turned to fire. "I don't answer to you, Bridger. *You* answer to *me*. Have you forgotten that?" The question didn't need a response. "You will be going to Earth, and you will be returning with my sister as your prisoner. That is an order." Without missing a beat, she strutted back to her seat and clapped her hands one time, cupping them together with a smile.

Pop. Pop. Pop. Pop.

Bridger's thumb moved over his fingers, cracking each joint as he loosened his fist for a fight.

"Who's hungry?" Marlena cooed.

The room instantly buzzed with commotion, servants moving around with trays of mouth-watering dishes, but Bridger didn't stay, and the force of his anger ripped the door off its hinges as he stormed out of the room.

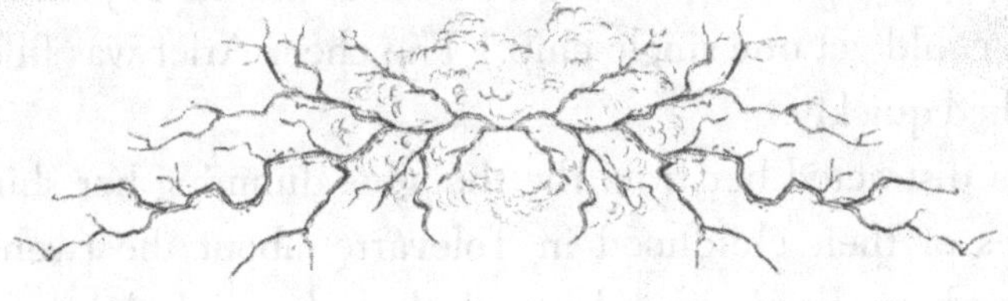

10

"Do I always drive the whole way?" Vega groaned, her eyes feeling grainy and tired, nearing twenty hours on the road. She rubbed her palm into her eyes, sighing at the temporary relief it gave her.

Vega didn't have a plan on when she'd need to stop for sleep. Arlet had stolen enough money to get them to California comfortably—which Vega tried not to feel bad about. Every time they stopped to fuel up, Vega grabbed a cup of coffee or an energy drink and rolled for as long as she could before needing to stop again.

With her feet up on the dash and a bag of Cool Ranch Doritos in her lap, Arlet stuck her fingers in her mouth to clean off the Dorito dust. "Duh. I don't have a license. How am I supposed to explain to the police that I'm not from Earth if we got stopped?"

Vega couldn't argue, shrugging with a nod of agreement.

"Plus, I've only driven a vehicle once, and it didn't go too well." She glanced over to Vega. "Don't ask. It scarred me for life."

The crinkle of the Doritos bag filled the compact-sized car. Vega held her hand out, wiggling her fingers.

"We don't have these in Tolevarre," Arlet told her as she filled her palm with chips. The crunch filled Vega's ears as she popped the first one into her mouth. "They were your favorite when you lived in Houston, and I've craved them ever since." Arlet laughed, recalling a memory. The way her face brightened gave Vega a peek of what she would have looked like ten years ago—as if she wasn't timeless enough already. "I brought a bag back once, and the boys devoured it before I could get one single chip." The cheer Arlet was filled with diminished quickly.

Vega distracted her from the thoughts dimming her shine with questions of their childhood in Tolevarre, about the twenty lives she'd lived on Earth, and learned that she and Arlet grew up together, becoming best friends instantaneously. Vega asked for more stories, and each time, Arlet delivered.

She learned about a man named Khort, who shifted into a dragon. Her brain couldn't wrap around the concept, but when Vega asked too many questions about him, Arlet replied, "Khort likes you to get to know him through him. He's picky—particular—just one of those guys who like things a certain way."

Vega knew the type.

"So, you said before that you never had a power before summoning Remus," Vega started, seeing Arlet nod out of the corner of her eye. "Are we usually born with our abilities then?"

Arlet twirled a curl between her fingers, staring out at the road ahead. "Yes and no. It's complicated. Yes, because we're born with whatever our power is inside us and no, because there's no telling what it's going to be until we've learned to manifest it. Before you can control what's inside you, you can always feel *something* though —a buzz in your mind, a trickle of power through your bloodstream. I never got that feeling until after the summoning. That night was the first time I understood what everyone had been talking about. We spend most of our adolescence in school, training our mind and body for the day we're strong enough to use it for the first time, and then we spend the rest of the time learning how to control it."

Vega didn't have to ask more questions because Arlet continued on. "Usually, your power is from the stronger parent, but that's not always the case. Sometimes a power can trickle down from generations before. Like you. You got lightning, and there hasn't been a lightning-wielder alive in your lineage for centuries. But I'm not so sure your lightning has ever been separate from your control of the weather. I think it was just all you knew how to control at first, and everyone assumed your lightning and wind were different powers." She shrugged.

The ping of Vega's phone interrupted her train of thought.

Arlet grabbed it before Vega could. "Bobby says you're fired." She flashed the screen to show her.

Vega rolled her eyes. "Susan is jumping for joy right now."

The sun moved through the sky, and the mountains started to peak in the distance. Vega turned the music up, attempting to drown out the silence surrounding them after finding out she'd lost yet another piece of her life back in Chicago. She didn't love her job at Bobby's, but it was another string snapped, disconnecting her from this life—from this world.

The radio began to skip, static hissing in the background as they got too far from whatever city station they were listening to. Vega reached for the dial and twisted until she found one that came through clearly. Songs from the early 2000s shuffled.

Arlet's bare feet began to tap against the dashboard, something Vega asked her not to do, worried that if they wrecked, her legs would go through her pelvis.

Arlet's reply had been, "Well, then don't wreck."

A song Vega hadn't heard in years came on, a smile forming on her lips at the same moment Arlet jumped forward to turn the volume up. Arlet squealed. "Oh my gods, I wish you could remember this, but in your last life, we listened to this on repeat for an entire three-day trip."

The happiness in Arlet's voice was like a warm blanket,

wrapping Vega in a tight hug as she began to sing the lyrics to "Over My Head (Cable Car)" by The Fray. Vega barely had time to wonder what happened to The Fray before Arlet started to bop on beat to the song.

Vega's smile grew, crinkling the corners of her eyes for the first time in what felt like an eternity.

Vega only watched Arlet for a few seconds—the throwback settling into her body, her hips wiggling in the seat while keeping her focus on the road. The highway was clear ahead, the other traffic moving at a leisurely pace.

From the outside looking in, they were two best friends singing along to their favorite song. Vega used the steering wheel as a drum pad, falling horribly off-beat, making them sing louder and more enthusiastically than before.

Vega didn't have a musical bone in her body, but Arlet had a voice she would consider a god-given gift. A couple of times, Vega found herself giving Arlet more solo time just to hear the melodic pull of her tone as she hit every note perfectly.

What if I'm already dead and this is my guardian angel escorting me to heaven?

Vega cracked up at Arlet's guitar solo. Her head bounced back and forth from the road to watching the performance Arlet was putting on, and a feeling of euphoria hit her. *This feels too right, too real to be fake.* What if they really were two best friends separated by a curse?

They sang over a fit of giggles, and for the first time since the road trip started, Vega felt like she was doing the right thing—that she was in the place she was meant to be, right here, right now.

When the song finally came to an end, without thinking, Vega reached over and held Arlet's hand as the next one came on.

Arlet squeezed it three times as she always had, but Vega didn't know that. She returned her hand to the steering wheel, fixing her eyes back on the road with a new feeling digging into her chest.

Hope.

Vega set her heart towards hope. Hope for a life she couldn't remember. Hope for people who loved her. Hope for being wanted. Hope for belonging.

That newfound hope kept her awake, driving her towards what might be the reason she'd never felt whole.

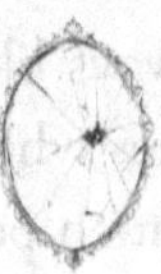

"Okay, so no Netflix, but there are TVs and radios?" Vega learned about their world and the beautiful gowns Tolevarre was known for —the balls, the holidays, how their world was up to date in technological advances but still didn't have nor need all the things Earth had.

Arlet took a sip of her coffee, preferring hers with cream and a single pack of sugar. Vega didn't want any of the extras—Arlet knew that, surprising her at their first stop with a large black, no frill coffee. Arlet chuckled, holding the coffee between her hands, her feet crossed underneath her lap. "Correct. We have TVs, but no shows or movies, nothing of the sort. They're called monitors, and they're used for official announcements, government stuff. If Marlena has an announcement, it'll be played on one of those. They're not something every household has. Most families in the outlying territories have to make their way into town for news." Arlet paused, blowing on the still-warm drink in her hands. "We have them at our camp, too, to keep an eye on whatever it is Marlena tells the people. Typically it's a bunch of brainwashing bullshit. She tells everyone she's keeping them safe from the rebels when really, she cares nothing about them, only what they can do for her. She throws them scraps when they behave and takes what little they have when they don't.

"As for radios, we have things similar to record players with prerecorded music, no live stations. The army uses comm-devices to keep in touch from across the realm, but again, those aren't attainable for most. Only the ones in control or the ones who can afford it."

Vega sipped her coffee. "Which is why it pays off to be powerful, huh?"

"Exactly, but it wasn't always like that. The Curia was created by the twelve original bloodlines when Tolevarre was born to ensure that not one person had too much power, that there was balance in leadership." Arlet told the history of this world without an ounce of hesitation, like it was fact and not still a complete tale to Vega.

"Until Marlena," Vega stated.

"Until Marlena," Arlet echoed.

Vega rubbed her temples with one hand, groaning. "My head hurts. This world doesn't sound any fun. I'm just leaving one messy life in exchange for what sounds like an even worse one." Vega let out a soft chuckle, trying to find the humor in this last history lesson.

From its place in Arlet's lap, Vega's phone rang with a familiar tone. Her head whipped over to see Arlet holding her phone up, Chase's name and a picture of him smiling while Vega planted a kiss on his cheek spread across the screen. "Fuck." She reached for the device and held it in one hand while she kept the other on the steering wheel.

"You can ignore him if that's what you want," Arlet reminded her.

Chase would call the cops—Vega knew he would. The last thing she wanted was to deal with what might come of having a missing persons report filed on her. *Ya know, if this ends up all being a figment of my imagination or a full-on hallucination from lack of sleep.*

Vega answered the phone, but before she could utter a word, Chase cut through.

"Vega? Vega, is that you?" His voice was panicked.

"Hi, Chase," Vega said with an exhale.

"Fuck. Where are you? Are you okay? What is going on?"

Vega rolled her eyes. "I'm fine, relax."

"Relax? *Relax?*" His voice raised to a shrill, ugly pitch. "You completely disappeared. Your passport is gone, your travel bag is gone, and you told no one you were leaving!"

"Who was I supposed to tell I was leaving, huh? You? Oh, maybe I should've called Jessica!" Vega didn't bother turning the volume down, allowing Arlet to lean over the center console to hear every word uttered.

"Jesus Christ, Vega! I am still your husband. We're still married!" Vega could hear him pacing, his footsteps echoing against creaky floors. "We can figure this out. We can get counseling. Just come home, and we'll talk about it."

"Counseling?" It was Vega's turn to have a screeched response. "I don't want counseling! I want a divorce."

"Don't say that," he interrupted, having the audacity to sound hurt.

"Don't you dare! Don't you *dare* play the victim here." Vega's speed picked up as her anger grew. "You did this. You caused me to leave! I have been through too much in my life to do this, Chase. I can't—I can't be with someone I don't trust. You were my person. *My* person... and you cheated on me when I was at my lowest. Why? Huh? Why." Vega waited for his response, unaware Arlet had settled back in her seat in an attempt to give Vega a little privacy.

"If you come home, we can talk about it. I'm so sorry. I broke it off with Jessica. I had a lapse in judgment."

"You know what? Shove that apology back down your throat and choke on it," Vega spat, leaning forward in her seat as if he were in front of her, not the open highway.

"I didn't call you to fight. I—"

Vega cut him off. "Oh, I'm not fighting. I'm telling you what you deserve to hear. You deserve to know what a shit person you are, how little of a man you are that you'd cheat on your wife because she lost her job and didn't fit into your pretty little picture anymore. How much of a coward you are that you couldn't just be honest with me about not loving me anymore." She choked out the last few words, biting on the inside of her cheek so hard she tasted blood, only to realize the feeling inside her chest wasn't sadness.

She forced the tears back and took a deep breath, calming herself enough to continue. "I should have told you this in person so I could see the look on your face, but I was too sad, too hurt. But guess what, Chase?"

There was silence on the other end.

"I'm not sad anymore. I'm pissed. Stop calling me. I'm done." Vega ended the call and tossed the phone into the cup holder with a clatter.

Seconds passed, maybe minutes, before Arlet spoke. "Damn."

Vega looked over at her to find Arlet grinning ear to ear. "What are you smiling like that for?"

"You're so you. You're really you this time, not some mousy duplicate. I've got my girl back." A tear slid down Arlet's cheek, but her smile didn't melt away.

11

"Mother," Bridger croaked, coming to a dead stop when she appeared in front of him out of thin air, billows of black smoke drifting to the high ceilings above. He reached out to grab her shoulders in his hands, bending at his knees to meet her dark, cold gaze. "Are you alright? Are you hurt? Where is Vega?"

"She's dead. The sooner you allow yourself to come to terms with it, the better off you'll be." Katrin reached for Bridger's cheek, but he was too fast, recoiling from her touch.

Bridger's already deep voice was racked with anguish, a rattle exiting his mouth as he stood back to his full height. "No. No, she's not dead. She can't be dead."

His mother's gaze hardened. "If she's not dead already, she will be, Bridger. It's time to stop playing house and stand beside your family where you belong. We've let this thing between you and Vega go on for too long, but it was a good distraction for a while."

The sound of an explosion shook the outside of the Aeris home, screams following the second blast. Bridger's nature was to protect. His instinct told him to run towards the sound of destruction, but his heart was begging him to find Vega—to make sure she was alive, to prove his mother the liar he knew her to be.

"You were behind this attack." The realization struck him like a blow, knocking the wind from his lungs. "You knew Marlena was going to kill her mother tonight, didn't you? You knew innocent people were going to lose their lives..."

Katrin's face showed no remorse, giving her away before she even had to admit it. "What do you think you've been training for your entire life? Marlena's betrayal to her family was just a nice little surprise—one that we needed to bring down her family and the rest of their loyalists."

Bridger's stomach rolled with nausea. This was planned under his nose, and he'd been too distracted with Vega to notice. "You evil bitch," he swore, taking another step back.

"This is your destiny. You were born to lead, to rule. You're no regular warrior." Katrin continued to talk, but Bridger heard none of it over the sound of footsteps looming in the distance.

He interrupted her. "I was born to protect my people, to help them rid the world of vile people like you." Bridger raised his sword, ready to strike, until a familiar voice cut through the anger.

"Dad? Dad! Where are you?" Vega was alive.

Bridger let out a breath, relief flooding his senses.

Katrin's head jerked toward the open door, but before she could move an inch, the tip of Bridger's sword dug into her throat. "If you so much as lay a finger on her, I will make you long for the mercy I'm showing you now. I'll gut you from the inside out and leave you on display as an example of what happens when you hurt the people I love."

She gasped. "How dare you threaten me?"

His laugh contained no humor, only hatred. "That's not a threat. It's a promise." Bridger stepped back and made a mistake he'd come to regret for the rest of his life: he let his mother go.

"Vega!" Bridger called, sprinting down the hall while slipping his sword into the scabbard on his back.

His eyes landed on Vega, her hair a tangled mess and the gorgeous gown she wore frayed and tattered from fighting. They'd been separated after Marlena's announcement, after she'd displayed her mother's decapitated head in front of the entire ballroom, and gave them the ultimatum of a lifetime: surrender or die.

"Bridger!" Her heels were in her hand, bare feet pattering across the marble floors until she was in his arms.

He wrapped her tightly against his chest, lifting her feet off the ground. "Are you okay?"

Vega didn't have to lie to Bridger. He didn't expect her to be strong all the time. "No. No, I'm not okay."

He set her down, keeping her close as he inhaled the scent of battle in her hair—the salt of her sweat and the smell of sulfur from her lightning mixed with the sweet scent of what was left of her perfume. "I'm sorry, baby. I'm so sorry, but we need to find Arlet and Khort and get out of here." He was already stepping away, pulling her by the hand in the direction from which she'd come.

"No. We have to find my dad." She pulled away from his grasp. "We can't leave him."

"Vega." Bridger's eyes widened with panic. "He might be dead too. We have to accept that and get ourselves out of here. Marlena isn't going to stop until she gets her hands on you." He said, trying to reverse the decision he knew she'd already made.

"I'm not leaving him." Vega darted off down the hall, running with speed Bridger had never seen from her.

"Vega!" *Jonan.*

Vega picked up her pace, Bridger a beat behind as they raced to her father's aid.

"Vega, Vega, help!" The voice was no longer the crying voice of her father, but the harsh voice of her sister—she didn't even sound the same, her tone haunted.

Vega and Bridger rounded the corner and there she sat, cross legged in a chair with their dad suspended in the air above her.

"Marlena," Vega said on a breath. She raced towards her sister, ready to shake her until the crazed look in her eyes disappeared. Flame licked up Marlena's arms. Vega's gasp reverberated off the walls of the grand meeting hall, and she was stunned into complete stillness. "Are you doing this? Oh my gods. Let him down."

"What? How?" Bridger stammered, his sword drawn.

"You want him down? Okay." Marlena beamed.

Whatever power was holding Jonan twenty feet over their heads died off, and he crashed to the floor. His body shattered, bones cracking when he hit. He didn't scream—didn't make a sound.

Vega ran to his side, hands roaming her dad's body for any sign of life. "What are you doing, Marlena? How do you have fire? What have you done?" The questions poured out of her mouth while she searched their father for a pulse.

Marlena's eyes were fixed on the new flames burning emerald at the ends of her fingertips with awe in her eyes. "I'm doing what everyone wanted me to do, what I was born to do. I'm ruling."

"This isn't ruling! You murdered our mom, their friends, our family!" Vega's tears stained her cheeks with mascara.

"Maybe you should have been paying closer attention to me, to what our *beloved parents* were putting me through instead of falling for my allies' son—instead of pushing me to the side like I was nothing to you. I told you you'd get hurt, but you didn't want to listen to me. The signs were all right there, but you missed every single one of them." Marlena pulled at the roots of her blood-stained hair. "Fuck, if you just would've *listened to me*, Vega... I wouldn't have to kill you."

Marlena moved with the speed of a Fortis-born warrior. Vega didn't see it coming, but Bridger did.

His hand tangled in Marlena's wild hair, throwing her to the ground with force strong enough to crack the marble flooring.

"You two are pathetic!" Marlena squawked. She pounced off the floor, leaping at Bridger, but he was ready again and shielded her blow for blow—she was faster than she should be, but Bridger would always be one step ahead in battle.

"Dad, please, we have to go." The broad man groaned, shifting under Vega's touch. "Please, please wake up."

Bridger's sword hissed, slicing through the air where Marlena had been. Her invisibility cloaked her, but Bridger could feel her, knew she was right behind him. Her arm wrapped around his neck, and he used that force against her, flipping her over his shoulder and sending her crashing to the ground again.

"Vega, get out of here!" Bridger heard her father screaming through labored breaths over the sound of Marlena's newfound fire soaring past his head. The flame scorched his arm before he rolled to the floor with a snarl, ducking out of Marlena's path.

"I'm not leaving you!" she yelled.

Bridger couldn't take his eyes off Marlena. He was holding her off, but it seemed that with his every move, she had a new power to surprise him with.

"Bridger!" Vega screamed, her voice pleading for help with her dad's blood-soaked body.

His forehead gleamed with sweat, and though he was stronger and lasted longer in a fight than anyone else in Tolevarre, Bridger would burn out eventually—the powers of their world weren't infinite.

This wasn't the Marlena he'd sparred with for fun, or the Marlena he'd been asked to train. She was quicker, more agile.

What had she done to herself?

"Kinda busy here, love!" He sliced at Marlena, forcing her to draw back.

Vega stood, keeping herself in front of her dad. Her lightning crackled at the base of her palm, ready to join the fight. "Marlena!" she called, distracting her long enough to steal the attention off Bridger. When her sister turned, Vega's lightning lurched forward.

Marlena moved like she'd seen the attack coming. "I've had enough!" She stomped her foot on the floor, and everything around them in the home shook. The walls cracked like spiderwebs, and the marble under them began to crumble to the level below.

Vega swayed, but she didn't stop, fighting more, pushing more. Marlena always moved just in time—no matter if the attack was from her, Bridger, or a combination of both.

"They're in here!" Voices rang from behind, and the second Vega heard them, a force shot up around her. Bridger's shield blocked them from the outside world.

"We have to go! We have to leave!" Bridger huffed.

"Please get him. I can't leave him!" Vega begged.

Bridger groaned in frustration, gripping at the dark strands of hair that fell out of the slicked-back look he wore tonight—his vexation grew, but it wasn't malicious. There was nothing he wouldn't do for her. He would burn all the worlds down for her if she asked. "Okay, we get out fast. My dad's whole army is on her side. They will not let us go if they get their hands on us. We grab your father and we go." Vega nodded. "You and me, Kitten."

"You and me," she repeated.

Bridger's shield dropped, but before they could reach Jonan, Marlena was standing over him. His eyes were open, staring directly into his eldest daughter's brutal gaze. His lips were moving, and a prayer was heard through a whisper.

"To the gods, please guide me to my afterlife. Let me fly with the ones of the past. Let me not fret death but welcome it."

The prayer of death—recited by soldiers who knew they weren't going to survive. Jonan had accepted his fate.

"Gods." Bridger exhaled, changing course. He grabbed Vega by the waist and hoisted her away from the path she was on.

Marlena plunged her hand into her father's chest and ripped his heart out. His eyes went cold before he had the chance to finish their people's death prayer.

Vega's wail pierced through the room. She kicked against Bridger, screaming incoherently.

Blood splattered Marlena's body, her father's still-beating heart in her hand. She had a smile so wicked on her face, Bridger felt chills race up his spine. "You can run, Vega, but you can't hide! I will find you, and I'm going to take everyone you love from you, one by one! Your perfect little life is going to crumble like the walls of this hollowed house will, like the Curia who underestimated me did!"

She cackled, and the echo of that sound would haunt this realm until the end of times.

There was nothing left of the girl who used to giggle with Vega when they snuck out to see their friends after curfew. This laugh was manic, crazed, and no longer carefree like it had been days before. "I'm going to make you feel as alone as you let me be!"

Bridger held on tight as he ran down the hall and took a turn into an alcove of the hallway, hiding from the soldiers who ran by. Vega thrashed, fighting to get back to Marlena. "Shhh, Vega!" His voice was muffled. "He's dead. There's nothing we can do about it, but what I can do is keep you alive. We have to leave. We have to find Arlet and Khort."

Vega sobbed. "She killed our parents. Oh my gods. She killed them."

Bridger watched, gutted, as her whole world crashed down around her. "Baby, I know. I know. I'm so sorry. Look at me." His hands cupped her cheeks. Tears pooled in his eyes. "There's nothing we can do. We have to run, okay? Pull yourself together." His words weren't harsh but firm. "We're not dying today. Do you understand me? We are making it out of here alive."

Vega's lips trembled, but no words came out. She nodded, and he wiped the tears off her cheeks.

"I love you," Bridger told her. "Let's find our friends and get the fuck out of here."

A knock on the bathroom door pulled Bridger out of the dream's daze. The reflection staring back at him didn't look like himself. His dark hair was longer than it had been in years, sweeping just above his eyebrows, still damp with sweat, and the bags under his eyes were darkening every night.

Meyer's voice on the other side was muddled with sleep. "Are you okay?" he asked.

Am I okay? Bridger didn't know the answer to that question.

"Yeah, had too much to drink," Bridger lied. He opened the door, meeting Meyer's suspicious gaze. "What?" he asked, leaning against the door frame to look as nonchalant as possible.

He couldn't—wouldn't show weakness. No one could find out his dreams were starting to eat away at the person he'd made himself become.

"You look like you haven't slept since level ten graduation," Meyer commented.

"Thanks, buddy, you're handsome too." Bridger winked, stepping around the tree-stump of a man Meyer was.

He turned around to find Meyer still staring at him. "You had another dream about Vega, didn't you?"

Bridger stood tall, his arms crossed over his much leaner frame compared to his general, but his eyes fell to the ground for a split second. Meyer was his best friend, the only friend he'd ever been allowed to have, and he knew him better than Bridger wanted anyone to.

"What was it this time?" he asked.

Bridger wanted to hold his tongue, but if he couldn't tell Meyer, who could he tell? He had no one else. Bridger answered before he decided against it, his voice a shred of a whisper. "It was the night Marlena took over. The night our world changed forever." He said the last part in a sing-song way—mocking a happy tone.

"You gonna be able to do this today?" Meyer's golden eyes softened in pity.

"You ask that like I would have another choice if I wanted it." Bridger straightened his posture, reminding himself that weakness was equivalent to death. "Stop acting like I'm some broken child, Meyer."

Meyer held a hand up, shaking his head. "I was just making sure you were—"

Bridger cut him off. "I'm getting sick of people assuming I'm one step away from running back into the arms of the woman who ruined my life." His voice deepened, mood flipping as he rammed that iron-clad shield back into place. "Vega is nothing to me. She will always be nothing to me." Though his words sounded fierce and sure of himself, something in the back of his mind whispered that he was wrong.

The dreams were making him feel things he had suppressed years ago. The pain of losing Vega, the anger of Marlena's curse taking the woman he'd once loved from him—those memories were meant to be subdued, locked away tight where the anguish couldn't reach him.

It was much easier to feel nothing at all.

Bridger turned around and started walking away. "Be ready to leave in two hours. I'm not waiting for this Halo kid if he's not here on time."

12

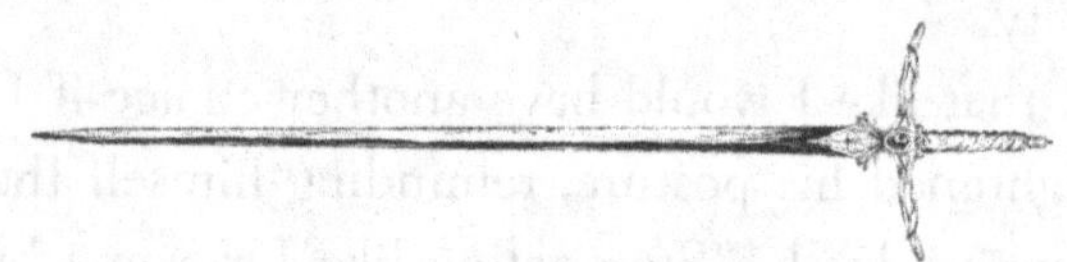

BRIDGER KEPT HIS HEAD UP AS HE MARCHED DOWN THE HALLS, dressed in his training suit with daggers of all shapes and sizes lining the holster on his leg. Stitched into place over his heart was the Dimico insignia, shiny and gold. No cape fluttered from his shoulders.

No one made eye contact with him, moving out of his way if they got too close. Bridger was never the friendliest commander, but he'd never been as outwardly brutal as his father.

Bridger stretched in the garden before taking off along the trail that led to a small lake outside of the city square. He took this run anytime he was in Stella. Meyer usually accompanied him—Bridger hadn't extended the offer today.

He pushed himself hard, his lungs filling with the crisp morning air. Athleticism was a trait of those with Mars's blood—the god of war. Bridger was who everyone strived to be when they were warrior-born.

Like a tidal wave, thoughts of last night's dream flooded his mind again, and he ran harder to push them away, his muscles tensing as he drove into the ground with strong strides. The memories stole his breath, constricted his airflow and caused a gasp to slip from his lips as he lost the pace he'd been keeping. The feel of Vega's ache, the cause of her turmoil in last night's dream, blacked-out his vision, and catapulted him back in time.

Bridger closed his eyes tightly, and against his instinct, he forced himself to slow to a stop. His hands rested on his knees as he hunched down to catch his breath. Bridger straightened his back to keep airflow coming in, breathing in through his nose, out through his mouth.

For so long he'd been able to forget how in love he'd been with Vega, how the thought of her was so all-consuming that he couldn't imagine a world without her. Remus had given him the power to block all of that out—to try and rid himself of the memory of her, of their life together before she became a shell of the person she'd once been. Bridger was able to pretend their relationship was something from another time, another world, because that was what it'd become.

Vega wasn't the same girl he'd fallen in love with, and he wasn't the same boy he'd been when he fell.

What the fuck is wrong with you? Get yourself together, Dimico.

He was miles away from the home harboring those wretched memories and made the run in record time until the panic of his thoughts halted him.

People trudged by on their morning walks around the capital, eyeing the commander discreetly.

He stood up tall and took in the view. Aeris used to hold a special place in his heart. These mountains were home to what used to be some of his fondest memories. Those memories were now the ones that haunted him, invading his dreams and stealing his sleep.

The mountains loomed, still capped with snow from the winter. Summer was in full bloom, but the very tip-top of Stella's mountain ranges would never fully melt.

The reminders of her burned, singeing his body. With a groan, he slammed his shields up and around his mind, forcing a calmness to ease into him.

Bridger's breathing steadied in time for the trees to rustle behind him with an unnatural wind. Everything Marlena did, everything she was, felt dark.

It didn't surprise him one bit she sought him out before he left today. In fact, he expected it. Part of him did hope she wouldn't, but Bridger knew her. He'd spent forty years working by her side.

"Good morning, Bridger." Her voice was gentle. It was easy to fall for her charm.

Bridger turned to see Marlena standing behind him on the shore of the lake. "Morning," he quipped.

Marlena's smile brightened as the people of Stella took notice of her, their eyes landing on her for only a split second before they shot back to the path ahead of them. People were afraid of her, no matter the power they might also possess—and in order to call Stella home, their powers had to be pretty significant.

"You missed a really wonderful dinner last night," she said with a sigh.

"Drop the fucking act. Do you play pretend like this around everyone all the time?" Bridger was exhausted by her constant charade.

Marlena chuckled, the sound sprinkling the air. Bridger threw a shield up, a silent bubble falling around them—it wasn't visible, but it was there, and Marlena knew it. Her tone changed, but her body language stayed the same. Tall, regal. Just because the people of Stella couldn't hear her didn't mean they weren't watching. "Of course not. I know I don't have to bluff around you." Her words were like poison, seeping through her tainted lips.

Her outfit today was a dark dress, crimson sparkles glittering in the daylight as she moved to stand in front of Bridger. Even clothed in a feminine dress, Marlena gave off a deadly edge—the one she'd killed for.

Bridger didn't dare move back from her. Once upon a time, he was afraid of Marlena, but that was a long time ago—a dream ago. "If that's the case, then tell me the real reason I'm going to get Vega instead of waiting until she's back here where there's less risk."

"I told you last night, I don't need her giving hope to the rebels this far into the curse. They're already a nuisance, and I'm growing tired of their false confidence." Marlena's eyes roamed Bridger's rigid stance.

"That's a load of shit." Bridger's face stayed hard as stone, his emotions locked away tight. "Tell me." He took a step closer to her, his gaze fixing on the muscle ticking in her jaw. "Or I'll send someone else. I'm a busy man, Marlena. I don't have time to play your games."

Marlena inhaled, her chest rising and falling before the words spilled from her red-painted lips. "I need something from her, and in order for me to get it, she's going to have to get her memories back." Her voice didn't falter. "And I want to be the one to return to her what I stole so she can see how forgiving I can be when I choose to."

Bridger's eyebrows drew together for a split second before realizing. Marlena caught the look, and a serpentine smile spread across her face.

She raised her hand, her index finger tracing the creased line forming between Bridger's brows. He batted her hand away, coaxing a chuckle deep from within Marlena's chest. "I can finally end this once and for all, and all I need is for Vega to give up one little piece of information, and to finally lose hope that she can ever beat me." She paused, cocking her head. "Do you think that sounds like something I should be telling everyone who works for me? The less they know, the better."

Bridger huffed, changing the subject to hide the shock of her disclosure. "I am not just *someone who works for you*. You made me look like a fool in front of your entire council last night."

Marlena painted on a remorseful look, making it look *almost* real. "I did not." It wasn't a power she possessed, but a skill she'd learned early on in her life to give people the side of her she knew they wanted.

Bridger snarled, shaking his head. "You did, and I thought we made an agreement a long time ago. You will not treat me like the dog you turned my father into. I am not left out of any decision that involves me. I don't care who or what it entails. Vega is your problem, not mine, and yet you're forcing her to become mine by cleaning up whatever mess it is that you can't handle yourself. You might not think you need me, but you do… and you've just made that so clear."

The air around them electrified with the shift in her mood. "I need no one," Marlena snapped.

"When will you stop lying to me?" Bridger had her backed into a corner, metaphorically. Marlena swallowed, but Bridger cut her off before she had the chance to speak. "If you didn't need me, I would've been dead a long time ago. You need me, Marlena—in more ways than one. The soldiers would have turned on you ages ago if it weren't for me. The relationships that I had to rebuild after my father's death, the work that I've done to make Tolevarre's army better than it's ever been, knowing that I keep them safe from your wrath is the only thing keeping them from joining the rebels. Just admit it, and I'll accept your apology for how dirty you did me last night, for keeping imperative information from me." Bridger smiled, his broad shoulders back and one brow raised knowingly.

Marlena's lips tightened. "Why must you push me?" she questioned, fists clenched.

"Because I'm the only one who can." His words struck a nerve, getting the reaction Bridger was hoping for. Fire trickled across Marlena's fingertips, making Bridger smile. "Ah-ah, your people are watching." Bridger shook his finger and nodded in the direction of a small group that had slowed to watch them.

"Fine. I need you. I need you because if you're not mine, then you're Vega's, and we know how that ended in the first few lives. You are the key to breaking her."

Bridger uttered a small laugh. "Good girl," he whispered as he leaned into her ear. "But everything after 'I need you' was unnecessary."

Marlena tensed, the fire gone from her hand. "I know what you're doing, Bridger. You're not as slick as you think you are."

"I know you know, but look at me, holding some power over you. It feels good." Bridger licked his lips, leaning away from her ear to catch her eye as the corners of his mouth ticked in the faintest upward tilt. "What you did to me last night will never happen again or I'll make you regret it. Know that you need me more than I need you."

Bridger dropped his shield and backed away from her, nodding a goodbye before he broke back into a run. Having the upper hand with Marlena was rare, and no matter the hatred that still bubbled in the pit of Bridger's stomach, he smiled, knowing that he'd gotten Marlena to admit what no one else ever had.

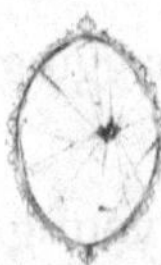

"It's nice to meet you, Commander," Halo said, his blond hair the color of snow in the sun.

Bridger nodded to him, giving him a once-over, but ignored the boy's greeting. "How does this work?" He straightened his scabbard, sliding his bonded sword in. Bonded weapons answered to their owner, making them stronger with that weapon than any other. They were made by blacksmiths in Ardor. He buckled the holster wrapped around his right thigh, ornamented with a few of his favorite daggers.

Bridger watched as Halo's eyes raked over his weapons with unease.

Meyer entered the room, dressed and ready for battle with his own assortment of weapons. Their powers wouldn't work once they stepped through the portal, and while they probably didn't need more than their bare hands to get the job done, Bridger wasn't taking any chances.

The boy's throat bobbed as he swallowed hard. "Um, I'm not entirely sure," he answered, fiddling with his hands in front of him.

Bridger raised a dark eyebrow. "We're off to a great start," he said under his breath to Meyer, his arms crossed over his chest.

Meyer wasn't born a warrior by blood, but he became one of the best from standing beside Bridger all his life.

The Fraus-born traveler shook his head. "I mean, I'm the only one of my specific kind that we know of, and I'd prefer not to end up an experiment so people get to understand how my ability works."

He had a point, to which Bridger nodded and said, "Fair."

Meyer patted Bridger on the back once. "Do you think the swords are really necessary?" he asked as he eyed them. Bridger cocked his head, ignoring the nagging presence of the young traveler across from him.

Arlet wasn't the helpless young girl she once was. She'd had fifty-five years to learn how to defend herself, and Bridger knew there was a power inside of her no one would understand—it was the one secret he'd kept from Marlena. He'd made mistakes in his life, but he felt like keeping Arlet safe from whatever Marlena might do if she found out was his final apology to the friend he'd crossed.

"Do you want to be caught facing a very angry Arlet with just a single dagger?" Bridger waited for his reply, watching him process the question with a raised brow.

"Absolutely not."

"Good choice," Bridger replied.

Bridger wasn't wearing his commander uniform, only his simple training suit with the gold insignia over his heart. Meyer's uniform mimicked his, though his family's insignia was a red flame.

Bridger's sword was pitch black, the dark metal sparkling like the night sky. It had been through everything with him, and not even a tiny chip near the hilt could get him to part with it. It was one of the two bonded items his power gave him at a young age, and while he could rebuild the sword and rematch the bond, there was an attachment to the chipped blade he'd yet to let go of.

"Alright, Halo. You ready?" Bridger asked the boy.

He was so young—too young to be siding with a woman who would suck him dry. Bridger wished he could warn him, but it was already too late. Marlena's corruption didn't take long to settle in— he knew that firsthand.

Halo's smile was sharp, aging him a few years. "I think the real question is, are you?" He reached forward too quickly for Bridger or Meyer to jump back. His hands wrapped around each of their wrists, and everything went black, a crushing feeling pressing into Bridger's whole being.

Bridger couldn't hear or see anything, but his senses were all on overdrive, ready to fight his way to the surface of this suffocating blackout. He was sure he was seconds from imploding, gravity squeezing him so tightly his breathing stopped completely.

He didn't implode, but when his feet touched the ground and the world was delivered back to him, Bridger bent over, dry heaving through the waves in his stomach. He stumbled, inhaling all the air he could get into his lungs as the world settled fully around him.

Panic seared his body. Bridger forced himself to assess his location, fighting through the sickness threatening to escape from the pit of his stomach.

They were in the deep forest of Vates, settled among a crumpled village—not just any village. *This is Arlet's village.*

At the end of this row of comfortable cottages, Arlet's former home sat deteriorated, vines engulfing the entire structure. Vates had been abandoned longer than any of the other territories.

The portal's new location was intended to be a mind game, another way for Marlena to slowly cripple Arlet if she made it back to Tolevarre alive.

Meyer was on his hands and knees, gasping for air. "What the *fuck!*" he screamed while jumping to his feet, charging for Halo. Fire danced above his hands.

Halo disappeared and then reappeared behind Meyer as a ball of fire blazed through where he'd been standing, burning a small shrub to a crisp. The boy was too quick, staying ahead of Meyer's every move.

"You get used to it," the boy said, smiling at Tolevarre's most notoriously vicious warriors trying to recover from a jump that took less than ten seconds.

"Never again," Meyer rasped, his fire simmering in his palms, but a hot ember still flickered behind his golden eyes.

Bridger's gaze landed on the trees, a shimmer between the two largest catching his eye. The portal appeared with Vega's curse, and only those who were tied to her could see it. To the rest of the world, it was just an out of place set of mangled tree branches. Halo and Meyer stared at Bridger as he marveled at the portal they couldn't see like it was his first time laying eyes on it.

"You brought us straight to the portal," Bridger commented, knowing how hard that was for a single traveler, let alone bringing two others in tow. "Some power you've got," Bridger gawked. Halo, a boy no more than nineteen years old, was able to do what no one before him could do. And so efficiently.

He was a force to be reckoned with.

"Thanks, Commander." Halo smiled, his shoulders pushing back with pride. "I'll leave you to it. Marlena told me to wait here for when you return." Halo traveled to the low-hanging tree above them, making himself comfortable on a branch. "I'll keep watch."

Bridger looked to Meyer, the color in his cheeks finally coming back. "Let's get this over with."

Meyer bowed his head in a nod, trusting Bridger fully, and cracked his fingers out in front of him with a quick snap. "Ready or not."

Here we come.

13

THE REDWOODS TOWERED OVER THEM, THEIR CAR FEELING smaller than an ant next to the enormous trees. "Do you think the curse brought me this close to the portal earlier in life as a joke?" Vega asked Arlet, choking back on the hatred bubbling inside.

"Probably." Arlet shrugged. "There have been a lot of weird things I don't understand about this life. I'm still mulling over the fact that this time you're remembering things before we can get your memories back to you." She pointed to a secluded area of the parking lot. "Park over there. We're going to need to walk the rest of the way."

Vega pulled the rental into a spot where it would eventually get towed for parking too long, abandoned like Vega's life on Earth. Her anxiety shot through the roof when she shifted the car into park. "How do I usually get my memories back?" she asked, talking to fill the silence and the roaring of her nerves.

The sun was beginning to set, the sky above the giant trees turning pink and orange. After the phone call with Chase, Arlet made Vega pull over for a couple hours to sleep, reminding her that their journey didn't end when they got to Tolevarre.

"We usually have to meet with a witch. We call them benders because their power isn't something that can be seen outwardly. It flows through their blood, and they're able to manipulate it into other things. Potions, curses. Marlena is the only one who can truly break your curse, but the memory block piece of it can be shifted." Arlet waited by the front of the car, watching Vega. "It took us about twenty years to figure out the best way to get them back to you. Trial and error, baby."

Vega went quiet as she stretched her stiff limbs. She reached into the back seat, sliding her backpack over her shoulder. Inside was a small pocketknife she'd kept hidden throughout the journey, waiting for the moment she needed to use it to fight for her life.

Do I even want to fight? What am I fighting for at this point?

Her thoughts lingered in her head, vision blurring as she stacked up all of the terrible possibilities that could happen while alone in the woods with Arlet—who, even though Vega felt a connection with her, was still a stranger.

"Did you hear me?" Arlet's voice broke through her fog.

"Hmm?" Vega hummed, yanking herself out of her head.

Arlet let out a puff of air, rummaging through her small bag. "Make sure whatever you want to bring from this life is something that can be connected directly to the body. The bag's gotta stay. The portal isn't great with excess belongings." Vega didn't want to ask how Arlet knew that.

Her nerves were already shot, and arguing about bringing a beat-up bag wasn't worth the energy she was trying to conserve.

The zipper on the bag needed a little coaxing to open fully. Vega made a mental list of the items she wanted to bring.

Passport: *in case I wind up dismembered, someone can identify my body.*

Pocketknife: *in case I need to dismember someone. Can you do that with a pocketknife?*

Vega shook her head, simultaneously shaking away the worry in the pit of her stomach.

She sifted through the bag and came across one more item she wasn't ready to part with. A picture. She held it by the corners. Dark eyes, full cheeks, and her mother caught mid-laugh with her hand on her chest stared back at her.

Vega looked nothing like her, their features almost complete opposites, with her long blonde hair, her slim and tall figure, and eyes as deep as dark chocolate. A tear slid down her cheek, but Vega wiped it away before it could drip or before Arlet could see.

Do not break down now.

She gulped down a steadying breath and slipped the picture into her pocket. Even if Gianna wasn't her real mother and Arlet proved to be right, Vega would love her forever, and the brief time she'd had with her in this life would always be her favorite memory.

"You ready?" Arlet asked. Vega nodded, slamming the car door. "This way." Arlet motioned in the direction of a far-off river flowing through the middle of the forest.

As they began their ascent into the depths of the redwoods, Vega pulled her arms into her thick black-and-white flannel to help with the chill from the setting sun. "I have another question."

Arlet peeked over her shoulder at her. "Yeah?"

Vega's nerves continued to spike, making her chattier than normal. "So, uh, if I've been here for fifteen years and I'm almost thirty, is that why my memories seem to start when I was fourteen? Sometimes it literally feels like I was just born as a teenager and can't remember anything before then. I did some therapy for a while, and they said it was trauma blocking."

Vega had no pictures of herself from childhood, nothing to prove her theory was wrong.

Arlet didn't turn around, keeping them at a steady pace. "Yeah, you're not going to remember what you never lived. Every life you have missing pieces. I'm surprised this life started you so young—

you're usually at least college age. We age a lot slower and live a lot longer than mortals, so it's not as if you've changed too much over the last fifty-five years. You can thank the gods' blood for that."

"Was my mom even real?" Vega asked.

"Of course she was, but if you don't want to know why she died, then don't ask the next question."

Vega couldn't help it. "Did she die because of me?"

"Yes," Arlet answered as gently as she could. "The curse caused her cancer. That's what it does. It sucks the life out of the people you love or forces them to push you away. Sometimes the relationship you were in was abusive. Once you were homeless. Your life is never happy here."

Vega never once felt guilty for what happened to her mom. Cancer took who it wanted, but knowing she was the cause of the kindest woman's death, that it was because of her curse Gianna died —Vega felt her regret crash on her shoulders like the weight of a thousand suns. Tears welled in her eyes, guilt shattering what was left of her heart.

Vega didn't hold back the sob. She could hide the hurt when it came to Chase's wrongdoings, the shame that came along with her sad life, but not the burden of knowing she was to blame for the death of someone so pure.

Arlet spun around so quickly, Vega didn't know what was happening until she grabbed Vega's shoulders and met her gaze with that same stare she felt the day in her apartment—like she saw deep inside her. "Vega, her death isn't your fault."

"Why wouldn't she remember not having a child? Like, one day she just woke up and had a teenager? It doesn't make any sense." Through the pain, Vega continued to ask questions—trying to distract herself from the throb in her chest.

Arlet scanned Vega, like she was looking for a reason not to answer her question. "The curse alters them too. No, it doesn't make sense, but no curse ever really does unless you're the one who made it. The curse didn't create your mother, but it chose someone who wouldn't miss a life outside of the one it made them believe." Arlet wiped a tear from Vega's cheek and rubbed her hands up and down her bicep for comfort. "It's okay to be sad, but do not let yourself believe this is your fault. You are a mere butterfly caught in the web of a deadly spider."

They traveled in silence for over an hour while Vega absorbed the new information she'd finally dared to ask for. The tears stopped on their own, but Vega knew her pain would outlast every tear she cried. "I don't want to sound like a child, but are we there yet? If you're gonna kill me, you've missed a lot of good places to hide my body." Vega groaned, her feet hurting worse than during a double at Bobby's.

"Five minutes." Arlet continued to trod through the thickening underbrush, giving her a breathy laugh.

"If there's really a portal out here, why aren't people going through it all the time?" Vega began to ask whatever the hell came to her mind.

"Because you must be from Tolevarre to get to Tolevarre. If a human tried to go through, they'd probably die, and I'm not even sure they'd be able to see it anyway."

Five minutes later, Arlet started to pay closer attention to the trees. She looked absolutely fucking insane. Vega almost laughed, but not at Arlet—at herself... for believing all of this.

"This way." Arlet pointed, the river they followed earlier a distant noise of rushing water in the background. She finally slowed, running her hand over a tree with familiarity. "There." Arlet gestured to a low hanging tree line, forming an arch between two of the biggest sequoias Vega had ever seen.

Vega walked closer, the moonlight causing a glimmer in the middle of the tree, a silver reflection catching her eye. For a moment she was convinced it was the moon playing tricks on her. She balled her hands into fists and rubbed her eyes. The glimmer was still there when she pulled her hands away, shimmering like a holographic card. "No. Fucking. Way." It wasn't just two trees with another falling too low in between. *It's real.* "Pinch me."

Arlet reached out and twisted at Vega's skin, getting a good grip through her clothing.

"Ow!"

"I told you," Arlet said.

Vega turned to face Arlet, her mouth slightly ajar. "You were telling the truth... all of it." Vega's heart raced as she processed everything she had learned over the last few days.

"I have a pretty decent imagination, but it's not that good." Arlet snickered. Vega caught the wistful smile on Arlet's face and the twinkle of longing in her eyes. "Are you ready to go home?"

"Yes. Please." Vega marveled at the way the portal's entrance flickered emerald and then back to silver. She cocked her head, a shadow forming in the middle. Vega took a step back, raising her hand to point. "Arlet, what's—"

She didn't have time to finish the question. Arlet snatched her back, away from the portal that led to a life she couldn't remember.

"Arlet," Vega said again, registering the horror creeping across Arlet's face.

"Vega, run." Her voice was soft, filled with a dreadful crack Vega would never be able to unhear.

Vega began to panic, her heart racing at whatever could possibly be passing through the portal that would frighten Arlet so bad.

"Go, Vega! Run!" Arlet screamed, pushing Vega in the opposite direction as a large male figure stepped through the portal and onto the sodden soil. He came into focus, and over Arlet's shoulder, Vega's eyes landed on the most dangerously handsome man she had ever seen.

Bridger.

Vega's breath caught in her throat at the realization, at the tingling feeling she got when his eyes settled on her. Her body was frozen, feet cemented to the ground, and shock unhinged her jaw.

He was more beautiful in person than he'd been in her dreams.

His broad shoulders flexed through the skintight suit he wore as he reached behind him and unsheathed a sword from his back. Another figure formed just behind him, coming into focus as Bridger's lips spread in a crooked smile so eerie it shot chills down Vega's spine.

She backed up, her heart hammering against her chest. *Do not fucking pass out,* she warned her body.

Bridger spun his long sword with terrifying grace. "Hello, Arlet, long time no see." His deep voice was like music to her ears, but something inside of her jarred to life, reanimating her body.

Run!

Vega darted away from the portal that would take her home, leaves kicking up around her as she ran with one goal in mind: live.

She should have asked more questions about Bridger because it was glaringly obvious that he wasn't here to assist in her safe return to Tolevarre.

14

"Not long enough" were the last words Vega heard Arlet speak before she was too far away to hear anything else.

Vega checked over her shoulder and took a tumble over a giant root. She collided with the dirt beneath her, the limited air from her constricted lungs whooshing through her lips.

She couldn't hear anything over the sound of her panting breaths and the heartbeat in her ears. Vega scrambled to her feet, and when she felt like she couldn't possibly run any further, she began to search for a downed tree to hide inside of.

After crawling into a log the size of a Volkswagen Bug, Vega hugged her knees against her chest, trying to keep the sound of her breathing low. She didn't have time to catch up with the knowledge that everything Arlet said was true. Vega was floored. The portal was real, and all of this was no longer some fairy tale that helped her escape the reality of her shitty life.

Vega really was being hunted by an evil sister who wanted her dead.

Her breathing didn't slow. Leaves rustled in the distance. "Come out, come out, wherever you are!" Vega didn't know the voice, but she did know it wasn't Bridger. This man's voice wasn't quite as deep and had a grit to it that didn't match Bridger's smooth tone—she'd remember his voice anywhere, even if her only reference until this moment was from her dreams.

Why is he here? What does he want from her? Fuck, you should have asked more questions, you idiot!

His footsteps got closer. "Save us a little time, Vega! It won't take long for Bridger to kill Arlet, and then it'll be two against one! And let's face it, you're useless right now." The crunching of leaves passed by the downed sequoia.

The idea of Arlet making it this far, this long, to die now sent Vega flying out of her hiding spot. *What am I doing?* She realized she'd made a mistake as soon as she came face to face with the huge man.

His skin was the color of dark umber, blending into the shadows, while his eyes glowed honey in the moonlight. He was tall, well over six feet, and broader, bulkier than Bridger's lean build. *Is everyone from this world hot?*

"Don't you fucking touch her." Vega kept her nerve, faking a calm she didn't actually feel as her heart continued to beat out of control.

"Ah, still the big, strong hero," he said, an unnerving smile sliding across his face. "You look good, Sparks. A little scrawny but still as pretty as ever."

"Fuck you." She scowled. Vega kept her distance, ready to run until her legs and lungs gave out. Though she was certain this man could likely outrun a cheetah—she didn't stand a chance.

"And she's got a temper? Bridger is *screwed*." He hacked a laugh, slapping his knee.

Vega took a step back, a twig snapping under her weight. She had to distract him. *I have to survive. Arlet has to survive.* She shot off, luring him back into the shadows.

"You did always love a good chase!" he called after her.

Vega didn't slow her pace, pushing herself faster than she thought possible, but she was fading fast. A year of at-home workouts hadn't prepared her for running through the forest being chased by two scary men—not to mention they were in better shape than nearly anyone Vega had ever seen in real life.

She puffed, backing herself up against a tree.

"C'mon, Vega! Don't delay the inevitable." He sounded close again. "We don't want to hurt you! We just gotta get you back so your sister can."

Vega closed her eyes and prayed to the god she didn't believe in. *I swear if you let me live, I'll start going to church.* It might be too late to pray herself out of hell.

"Where is she?" Bridger boomed, his voice echoing through the trees.

"She's playing a little hide-and-seek with us."

"Arlet's out here somewhere too," Bridger said.

Vega couldn't see either of them when her eyes snapped open—she'd given up asking God for any help. *Fuck, maybe I should pray to the Roman gods—no, wait, they're dead.* She was on her own here. Her muscles quivered from fear and fatigue, and her mouth was so dry she couldn't swallow.

"Are you bleeding?" the man whose name she didn't know asked.

"She broke my nose," Bridger growled.

The crack of a bone being reset echoed through the dark forest. Vega flinched at the sound.

"Find them and let's get the fuck out of here. Kill Arlet for all I care. Vega stays alive."

His words sent chills down Vega's spine. She wished she could see them and keep an eye on their movements, but all she could rely on was the sound of their footsteps against the fallen leaves.

Vega turned her head to the side, stretching to hear the retreating shuffle of footsteps when a hand clasped over her mouth.

Vega thrashed, a muffled scream vibrating against the hand. The person spun her around, and Vega's gaze landed on Arlet.

All the fear rushed from her body, and she gave Arlet a shove. "Fuck, I thought I was dead. I thought *you* were dead, oh my god," she sputtered in a hushed whisper. Vega wrapped her in a giant hug —it was the only way she could keep the tears at bay.

"We need to get to the portal, okay?" Arlet whispered.

Vega nodded, looking around. She'd gotten herself so badly turned around she'd never be able to find it again without Arlet.

"Stay close, and if I tell you to run, you run and you don't look back," Arlet said, peeking around the tree.

"They're going to kill you," Vega gasped.

"They can try." Her eyes twinkled with challenge. "Don't slow down. Keep running." Arlet didn't wait for Vega to agree—there was no time.

Arlet darted between a few trees, light on her feet. Vega crept forward to follow and took a giant breath, steadying her nerves. She'd barely taken three steps when a hand caught her by the collar of her flannel. Vega yelped as she flopped to the ground with enough force to knock the wind out of her.

Bridger stood over her. Shadows hid most of his face from view, making him look like a fallen angel with a disastrous plan.

She scurried back, trying to get out from underneath him. Darkness settled behind his gaze as he stepped into the moonlight, and when their eyes locked, Vega froze.

"Hi, Kitten." Confidence oozed through every pore of his body.

The air was back in her lungs with a frantic gasp. "It's you."

His forehead wrinkled as his brows creased together, but her comment didn't faze him for long. The look was gone in a blink. "Ah yes, your worst nightmare. Here to bring you home," Bridger declared.

"No, I—" She never got to admit she'd been dreaming of him because Arlet came out of nowhere, tackling Bridger like a linebacker on the hunt for a Super Bowl ring. The sound of Bridger's surprise rolled through the trees.

Arlet pinned Bridger, and hope filled Vega's chest when she saw her reach for a hidden dagger. But he didn't let her have the upper hand for long, flipping Arlet off like a sack of potatoes.

Vega jumped to her feet, ready to help her friend fight with the pocketknife she suddenly remembered having, when the man from earlier popped up in front of her with the smile of a devil on his lips.

"What's your plan, huh? It's best you stay out of this one." The warning rang in her ears.

"Let me guess. You're one of my sister's henchmen." Vega hated that she couldn't remember this man, that he knew all her secrets and she didn't even know his name.

"Not quite," he answered, starting to circle her like the prey she was. "But do go on. I'd love to hear who you think I am."

Vega kept her eyes on him. "Trash, obviously," she spat.

He distracted her with his circling, and Vega didn't expect him to lunge. She almost got herself out of the way, but he moved with unearthly speed. She was in his grasp, his arm sliding around her neck in a chokehold. He squeezed with enough force that black dots began to sprinkle into her vision almost immediately.

His breath tickled her ear. "Sleep tight."

Vega clawed at his arms, but he had her held tight with such little effort that Vega knew she was going to die. Blood seeped under her fingernails, but the man didn't loosen his grip.

Vega fought until she couldn't anymore, until the man choking the air from her lungs whacked her into a tree, knocking her out and into the abyss she'd come to know too well.

The real world floated away, and Vega settled into a world she'd never get the chance to see again.

The girls giggled, grabbing their light jackets and bounding down the stairs as quickly as they could.

Arlet fixed Vega's floral crown and from somewhere behind her back pulled out another to place on Marlena's perfectly styled updo. The dark red flowers popped against her bright blonde hair.

Marlena beamed as Arlet settled the crown onto her head. "Where did that come from?"

Arlet shrugged, a smile turning her cheeks pink. "I made an extra just in case."

Vega opened the front door of the Aeris estate, looking over her shoulder at her sisters—one by blood, the other by fate. Their faces fell when the door opened wide. "What's the..." Vega began, her words sticking in her throat when she turned to face her parents on the other side of the door. Their arms were crossed, expressions serious.

Arlet waved apprehensively from behind Vega. "Hi Ryanna. Hi Jonan."

"And where is it you think you're going?" Ryanna asked, eyes scanning the three girls dressed in bright colors.

Vega's brow furrowed in confusion at her mother's annoyed tone. "Uh, it's the last day of Floralia? We're going for the closing ceremony." The last day of the spring festival meant games, prizes, and baked goods at half the price.

Jonan strode his way through the door, plucking Marlena's crown from her head. "You two might be, but *she* isn't."

"Dad," Vega protested. "That's not fair. She hasn't been able to go all week, and you promised—"

Ryanna closed the front door. "We promised nothing, Vega. We said that *if* your sister catches up with all of her work this week, then *maybe* she could go."

Marlena huffed, throwing her arms up. "And I did!"

Arlet made herself small, sinking into the background as the Caelums argued.

"That's where you're wrong, daughter." Ryanna's voice was void of any warmth. "Your work as a leader of this realm is never done. Do you think your father and I have time to go meandering around the city during every festival? No. It's not becoming of a future seat holder to be seen partying through the night with her friends."

"Mom, we were just going for a few—"

"Vega, please. Stay out of this. You and Arlet go have a good time and say hello to Khort for us, would you?" Her mother reached out and brushed Vega's cheek, adjusting Arlet's crown of daisies in passing. "Marlena, go upstairs and change." She walked by without so much as a glance in her eldest daughter's direction.

"Mother, please, can I go for just an hour? All I want—"

Jonan's deep voice boomed. "If you ask one more time, you're going to regret it! Now do as your mother said and go change."

Vega flinched at her father's tone, eyes bouncing between Marlena and her parents. "Mar, I..." Her sister's gaze darted to her, a desperate plea hiding behind her eyes. "I'll bring you back your favorite berry tarte."

Arlet grabbed Vega's hand gently and pulled her through the doorway. Vega peered over her shoulder, watching Marlena's stare darken until the door to their home slammed shut.

15

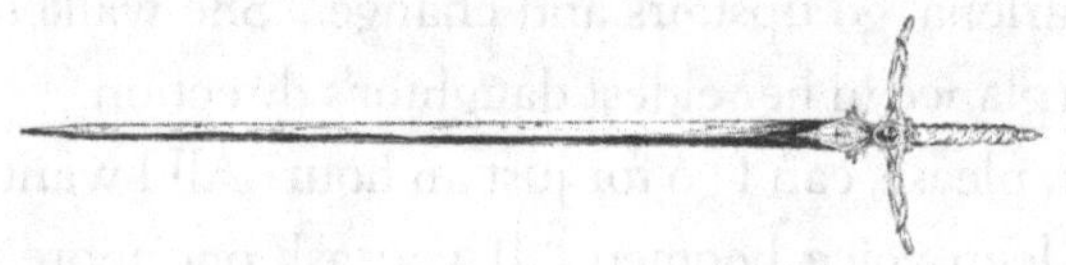

Vega's words distracted him, slowing his defensive moves as he tried to wrangle the dagger from Arlet's grasp. *What did Vega mean by that?*

"Someone's been practicing," he cooed sarcastically.

Meyer knew the plan: get Vega back to Tolevarre. Bridger would handle holding Arlet off until then. Or at least he thought he would, but Arlet was stronger and faster than he remembered.

Her dagger soared through the air and stuck its intended target. Bridger's leg.

"And you've slowed down."

His hand shot to the handle sticking out of the thick muscle of his thigh. Bridger hissed in pain, taking his eye off his opponent for a second too long—*rookie fucking move.* Arlet's heel met the hilt, tearing into Bridger's thigh before the handle snapped off.

Bridger came down onto his knee and bit his lip to keep from crying out.

Arlet vanished into the dark forest, leaving Bridger to deal with his leg. He inhaled through clenched teeth, and stuck his fingers inside the gaping wound to dig the blade out. Blood coated his hands, dripping down his leg. He looked up at the canopy of massive trees above him, his vision blurred from the pain.

The sound of Arlet's footsteps was covered by the wind dancing through the branches high above and the pounding of his pulse echoing in his ears. "Fuck," he exclaimed, throwing the ruined blade to the ground.

Bridger stumbled forward and fought through the fire in his leg. Being a warrior wasn't just about the fighting—it was about being well-rounded. And sometimes, being well-rounded meant needing to hunt. Tracking came second nature to Bridger. They wouldn't be too far ahead, but his new wound slowed him down.

He followed the direction of boot prints in a wet patch of mud until the sound of a scuffle east of him caught his attention. The voice of his general echoed through the trees. "When are you going to give up, huh? Vega won't survive this curse."

Bridger kicked himself into a higher gear, jogging through the pain to find Meyer and Arlet circling each other. Vega's limp body was on the ground behind them.

"I'm going to kill you with a smile on my face one day." Arlet wasn't letting them get away without a fight, that much was clear. She was a woman on a mission and fought like her world depended on it.

"You don't have it in you, Arlet Videri." Meyer's words made Arlet let out a gut-wrenching scream that sounded a lot like a battle cry.

Before he had the opportunity to reset and strike again, Arlet spun with the grace of a practiced fighter—an ease Bridger spent years training his soldiers to have. Her leg raised above her head in a roundhouse and kicked Meyer across the temple. His head snapped to the side, spit splattering the air, and his bright eyes rolled back into his head.

Meyer collided with the brush underneath his feet.

Arlet's attention turned to him, eyes wide with panic. "Enough, Bridger!" she shouted. "Please!"

Bridger drew his sword and spun it around his wrist as a habit. He laughed, a throaty, hoarse sound. "Please?" His eyes shot to Meyer and then back to Arlet. "Do you think if you ask nicely, I'll forgive you for stabbing me?"

Arlet was stronger than he'd ever seen her, with more determination burning behind her hazel eyes. She placed herself in front of Vega, and Bridger avoided looking at the woman he used to love. He didn't want to feel that tug he felt earlier when those two words slipped through her perfectly shaped lips—like a little heart.

It's you.

It's you.

It's you.

He backed Arlet up as far as she could go before she stepped on Vega, refusing to let his feelings resurface. *You have a job to do.*

"Don't do this again," Arlet pleaded, her attention focused on Bridger. Could she see the turmoil twisting behind his eyes?

A cough rattled through Vega's chest. Blood splattered out of her mouth and sprinkled her cheeks with crimson specks.

"Oh my gods." Arlet fell to the ground, and Bridger knew this was his chance. While Arlet cradled Vega's head on her lap, Bridger snaked his fingers into her curls, pulling her away from Vega's body.

She kicked, screamed, and clawed. "Bridger, no, please! Please! Let me get her to a healer! Let me save her," Arlet cried, tears staining her cheeks.

He stepped around to kneel in front of her on his good leg. "She's already dead." His voice was ice cold. "No matter what you do or how many times you save her, Vega will always be dead. She died that day in Aeris fifty-five years ago."

"No, no, you're wrong." Arlet wrapped her hands around Bridger's wrist, trying to pry herself free from his hold. "That's the Vega we know, right there. She's so her. Her spunk, her fight—it's really her, and she's about to die again. All this work, everything I've been doing will be for nothing if you don't let us go. Bridger, I know you're still in there somewhere. I know some part of you still loves her."

Bridger kept his hold on Arlet, eyes shifting focus between hers. "Loving her was my demise. It made me weak." Bridger threw Arlet to the ground with an angry force, trudging back over to Vega's bloodied body. With pain shooting through his leg and new blood seeping out of the wound, Bridger leaned down to lift Vega, but his eyes caught a twinkle on her finger reflecting off the full moon.

He knew instantly what it was.

It was the ring he'd given Vega in her second life. The one he forged out of the chip in his sword. The black metal was now a glimmering gem in the center of a gold band.

The promise he made to her in that life was simple.

I will never stop fighting for you. Not in this life or any that follow. My love for you is stronger than any darkness this realm can create. Me and you, forever.

Bridger hadn't seen it in decades.

Arlet scrambled to Vega's side, throwing herself over her best friend's lifeless body.

"Bridger." She caught where his gaze was fixed. "She's remembering you. She's seen you in dreams. It's happening without intervention, without breaking the curse. Her memories are breaking through."

Bridger felt like he'd been punched in the gut. Vega was remembering him before she'd been given her memories back. *What the fuck?* Was their bond strengthening again? Allowing her memories to travel down the chain linking them together? He ran a hand through his hair, fixated on the ring around Vega's finger as a pang of guilt shot through him—he'd lied when he made those promises to Vega, too scared to fight for what was right. *No.* He shook his head, pulling himself back into the present to lock his focus on Arlet's terrified gaze. Her eyes were wider than the moon peeking through the trees.

Over his shoulder, Meyer still lay flat on his back—out cold. Bridger's hands shook, his body felt cold, and he could still feel the throb pulsing in his leg like a drum in his ear. He returned his gaze to Arlet, and in a moment of weakness that shocked even himself, Bridger said, "Go."

He turned around and kicked at Meyer's leg, trying to jolt him awake. A moan slipped from the general's lips.

Arlet stood frozen, gaping at him.

"Get out of here before I change my fucking mind and kill you both."

Arlet scrambled to lift Vega and was gone from sight.

Bridger nudged Meyer with his boot a little harder this time. "Get up." Bridger winced at the movement of his leg, the muscle contracting. *Fuck, I hate this place, and its no-powers bullshit.* His leg would have been long healed by now if they were back in Tolevarre.

Meyer groaned, rolling to his side on the hard ground.

Bridger nudged him again. "Meyer, get the fuck up." Bridger tried to sound more urgent this time as his friend stirred and his hands shot to his head.

Meyer groaned, sitting up in a panic. "Where are they?" His eyes darted around, squinting into the shadows.

Bridger helped him to his feet. "She got away." He did his best to sound annoyed, like he hadn't just let them go. He felt the regret already sinking in, embarrassed with himself that he would so easily let Arlet get under his skin—that he would let this entire trip go to waste over a ring he'd given to a girl who was cursed to die.

"What do you mean, she got away?" Meyer was on full alert, spinning in circles and ready to attack.

Bridger wiped his bloody hands on the front of his suit. "She knocked you out, stabbed me, and then she got away."

Meyer eyeballed him. "What did you do?"

Bridger stood tall, having a few inches on his general's height. "What did *I* do?" Bridger scowled. "What are you insinuating?"

Meyer rubbed at his temples. "Tell me you didn't let her go."

"I didn't let her go." The lie rolled off his tongue.

Meyer walked the perimeter of the grounds, searching for any trace of the girls. "Gods, Marlena is going to skin us alive."

Bridger pretended to search too, knowing that Arlet was well beyond the portal by now.

"I hope she makes it quick for your sake." Meyer sent Bridger a death glare, his eyes landing on Bridger's wound that continued to drip blood and hadn't slowed at all. "You're going to die before she even finds out if we don't get you back home to heal."

Bridger looked down at his leg again, feeling a little lightheaded as the blood continued to pump out of his main artery. "Now we can say we've both been stabbed by the same woman." Bridger's lips quirked up in a smile despite his current condition, making a joke to pull Meyer's attention away from the lie he had to spin.

Meyer didn't laugh, only sighed. "Let's get you back before you bleed out in another world," he grumbled.

Bridger would take his new secret to the grave, allowing no one but Arlet to know that he'd let her go—that somehow that stupid ring worked against him. She'd gotten inside his head, twisted his emotions, and caused him to have a moment of weakness that would haunt him just like his dreams. Bridger's palms started to sweat, his heart racing in an unstable rhythm.

On the outside he kept his face set like stone, not allowing a break in his well-placed mask. But inside, a furnace of dismay lit, threatening to burn him alive. *You're gonna regret this, Dimico.*

16

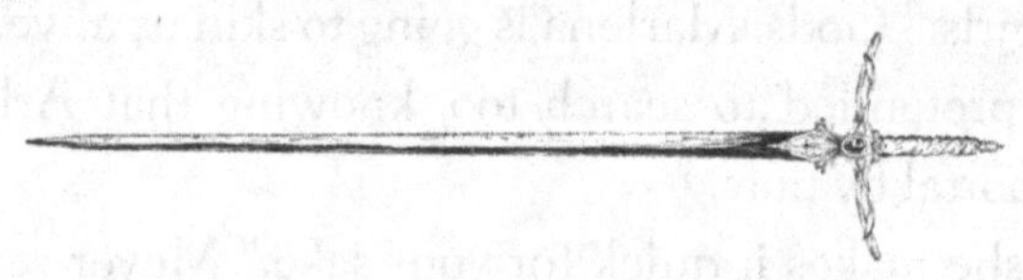

Halo was nowhere to be found when Bridger and Meyer came back through the portal to Tolevarre.

Meyer stomped, cursing the young kid loudly in the abandoned Vates forest.

"Relax. He couldn't let Arlet know that he was working with us. He probably took them back to wherever it is they're hiding." Bridger leaned against a tree, a small wince of discomfort drawn on his face at the burn in his leg while his muscles began to repair themselves from the stab wound.

Meyer continued to grumble, complaining that they would now have to find a way back to Aeris.

"Would you have rather traveled with Halo again?" Bridger asked.

Meyer leveled his gaze at Bridger. "No, but that doesn't mean I want to walk hundreds of miles back to the capital either." The grump really couldn't find a silver lining in anything.

"We just need to get to Pax. We can find transport there." Even while he healed, Bridger pushed them forward, giving his brain a task to avoid the looming reminder of what he'd done, of what he'd sacrificed by letting Vega and Arlet go.

It took hours to get to the border of Pax, a land known for its healers. Their gardens could be smelled from miles away, wafting the scent of fresh lilies and local blooms through the breeze as they approached a small village on the very northern border.

The smell of hydrangeas hit Bridger like a pack of wolves, ripping into him without warning. The scent wasn't what churned his stomach... They were Vega's favorite.

Meyer was ahead of him, keeping an eye out while Bridger fell a few paces behind. He blamed his speed on the slow healing of his leg when Meyer asked if he was okay, unwilling to bring up the smell of the flowers raging war inside his head.

Heads turned as they wandered the cobblestone streets, slick from a late afternoon rain shower. The homes in this border village were all different colors, their mismatched baskets with flowers on the windowsills standing out against the facades of their homes.

Bridger was still covered in blood and Meyer caked in mud. They were a sight to behold, strolling through the tidy streets of Pax.

Residents bowed their heads in respect as the commander and his general stalked through the streets, coming upon a barn stocked with horses and one gracious stable hand who was too afraid to say anything when asked to tack two horses up.

The vehicles used by the military and the families of power weren't available for those living in the outlying lands surrounding the bigger cities. Most of the advanced technology in this region was saved for Tolevarre's main hospital.

Each territory had its own healers, locals of Pax placed throughout the realm to assist in whatever the leaders might need, but Pax itself was riddled with the big and the small—healers who could fix a downed tree with just a touch or those who could stitch a wound with nothing but the flutter of their fingers over the skin.

Those with powers that didn't assist in bodily healing were

pushed to the side and seen as unimportant, but without them, the rest of the realm wouldn't be what it was.

Marlena and her followers forgot that a long time ago.

Bridger and Meyer picked up their pace on horseback, stopping just a couple hours outside of Stella to let the horses rest and hydrate at a runoff from the mountains.

Meyer broke the silence. "What are you going to tell Marlena? We should have our stories straight."

Bridger's eyes narrowed. "There's no story to tell. You got knocked out, I got stabbed, and Arlet got away with Vega." His lie came out with such ease that even he might have believed himself if he didn't know the truth.

That I'm a crumbling fucking liar.

The truth was that Arlet had won this round—he'd let her manipulation work, winning a battle she had no business walking out of unscathed.

Meyer knelt and cupped his hands together, bringing the fresh water to his lips before splashing it on his face to rinse the dirt and grime of the day away.

Bridger didn't bother cleaning up. He took a sip of water and stood back up.

"Don't you think she's going to find it hard to believe that the Videri without powers outsmarted us?" Meyer always had a way of asking questions Bridger didn't want to answer.

"I'm sick of caring about what Marlena thinks, Meyer." Bridger's annoyance turned to anger, raising the temperature of his blood. "Arlet Videri is stronger than any of us will ever understand, and she isn't the person she was fifty-five years ago. She knocked your ass out with ease... Are you embarrassed by that? Is that why you're so adamant that *I* did something wrong?"

Meyer bit the inside of his lip, frustration marring his features. He puffed air out of his pursed lips, scratching the back of his neck before speaking. "I'm just saying that maybe these dreams are getting to you and—"

The ground rumbled before Bridger exploded with his building irritation. His bonded dagger flew out of the holster on his leg and landed in his right hand. "And I'm telling you to drop it! Now!" Bridger dug his feet into the bank's grass, keeping his distance from Meyer because his fury was a risk to the safety of others—hurting Meyer wasn't something he'd ever considered, but Bridger felt himself slipping day by day, the torment of his dreams eating away at him. He couldn't trust himself not to mess up everything he'd sacrificed for.

Meyer's hands shot up in surrender, eyes wide. "Bridger," he said, barely breathing.

What the fuck is happening to me?

"Time to go," Bridger growled, resheathing his dagger. He mounted his horse and didn't turn back to make sure that Meyer was following.

Word traveled fast in Stella.

Marlena barged through the front door of her estate with her guards and Ivelle on her heels. "Where is she?" she roared.

Marlena's guards were for show—she hadn't needed them since the night she overthrew the Curia, since the night she summoned the twelve original gods and survived.

Bridger's horse shuttled back quickly, nostrils flaring as she picked her head up. He pulled back on the reins, settling her down in the face of danger. "She got away." Bridger looked down at Marlena from his mare, her hooves clacking against the stone drive in nervous steps.

"What do you mean?" Marlena's teeth were bared, eyes fixed on Bridger with intent to kill.

"Arlet stabbed me, knocked Meyer out. And. Got. A. Way." The last few words Bridger slowed down, really enunciating the last two he spoke.

Bridger dismounted, pulled the reins over the horse's head, and passed them to a servant. Meyer caught eyes with Bridger, sending him what was certainly a look of *good luck and don't die* as he put as much distance as possible between himself and the fire Marlena was about to rage.

Marlena's eyes fell to the blood soaking into Bridger's uniform. "You let Arlet beat you? Arlet, the Videri without an ounce of power." Her voice was seething.

"Marlena, don't be dim. Do you still believe Arlet went through the summoning just like the rest of us and came out of it completely unchanged?" He cocked his head, standing in front of the hot-headed blonde. Bridger wouldn't reveal Arlet's powers, even after being stabbed by her. "She's not the same Arlet who you used to—"

"Shut your fucking mouth," Marlena barked, grinding her teeth. "She's still a rat, and you're the strongest warrior our people have ever known. How am I supposed to believe she got away unscathed?" Marlena's growing anger raised the volume of her voice every time she spoke.

Marlena's staff started to pay closer attention, stalling their daily duties in hopes they could get a view of the argument going on between the commander and their ruler.

The gardener tending to Marlena's impeccable lawn of weeping willows and non-indigenous plants settled in a flowerbed to perk up some black bearded iris. They looked as if they'd already been taken care of, water droplets glistening in the sunlight.

"No, Marlena, I don't expect you to believe that. What I also don't expect you to understand is that you sent two men into a world they've never been to, against a woman who's pissed and has been traveling into said world for nearly half a century—she's prepared and not nearly as dumb as you want her to be."

Her fist clenched, and Bridger could feel the power bubbling between the two of them. Marlena was pushing him to break, but Bridger had been breaking for days. He didn't need her assistance.

The returning feelings he'd driven so far down inside himself and buried with a mound of concrete were now exposed and seeping through the cracks, and they pushed him farther away from Marlena.

"You better not be planning something, Bridger." Her voice was a whisper through a clenched jaw. "Vega is going to die. Forever." She grabbed Bridger's arm, nails digging into his forearm. Her touch was ice. "Don't make me regret keeping you alive."

"Imagine what would happen if you killed me now," Bridger countered, yanking his arm free and stepping around her, with the home in the background set in his sights.

Marlena's power boomed, shaking the ground underneath their feet as fire shot from her fingertips. "Find her, Bridger! Before I do it myself and burn this whole fucking realm down in the process!"

Her staff scattered, the gardener the first to hop to his feet and flee.

"Yes, Your Majesty." Bridger didn't turn back, but spoke loud enough for her to hear as he paved a path through the staff now trying to look busy.

He needed to get back to Vincere. There he would be able to regroup without Marlena breathing down his neck.

His dirty boots left tracks up the spotless stairs. He'd almost made it to his room when an ariose voice called from behind him. "Commander, wait!"

Bridger glanced over his shoulder to see Ivelle float up the last few stairs to meet him at the top. Her power rose her feet from the floor, and she floated towards him, her hips swaying as if she were walking. Her power was flight and she was inherently dangerous, but the praefectus of Amora had become lethal after years of standing beside Marlena.

"What do you want?" Bridger met her chartreuse eyes, his stare glacial and unwavering in his annoyance.

"Marlena is just looking out for you," she mused, coming to a stop in front of Bridger.

He scoffed, shaking his head as he ran his dirty fingers through his hair. He needed a shower and a shot, both of which he would wait until returning to Ardor for.

The sooner he got out of Marlena's wake, the better. Bridger knew she couldn't, but he was terrified that she might reach inside his head and pull out the knowledge of what he'd done on Earth.

"Ivelle, darling." He gritted his teeth, a vein throbbing in his neck. "You have no idea what you're talking about." He stepped forward, grabbing the beautiful redhead by her chin. Her long hair cascaded down her back, her fair skin glowing under the lighting. "Marlena doesn't care about anyone. The sooner you learn that, the better your life by her side will be."

Ivelle's mouth parted, a breathless gasp slipping through her plump lips. "I don't believe that. She just wants you to be happy, to let go of the past that is so clearly haunting you again." Bridger released her chin with a swift nudge, forcing her to take a step back. He turned away from her but could hear her footsteps following him. "Let me help you forget her."

Bridger stopped, his brain still stuck on the words Vega spoke today.

It's you.

Vega was dreaming of him too. *How? Why?*

Ivelle's touch radiated warmth up his arm, her hand wrapping around the brand that was a memento of the life he'd left behind—of the woman he'd chosen to walk away from. An everyday reminder of how much Vega hated him when she could remember him.

He was the villain in her story just like Marlena was, and that would never change.

Bridger looked down at Ivelle's hand before turning around. Her eyes promised lust, fun, and more importantly, an escape.

Snapping his wrist out from under hers, Bridger switched their hand placements, his now the one gripping her wrist. He pulled Ivelle into his chest, the other hand slipping to the small of her back.

She gasped, her head craning to meet Bridger's hard gaze as he leaned into her.

His lips were at her ear. "You want a first-class ride into darkness?"

The question lingered in the air as Ivelle took a singular breath, the inhale shaky. "Yes."

Bridger's crooked smile slid slowly over his lips, out of her view. "Then go fuck yourself, Ivelle."

17

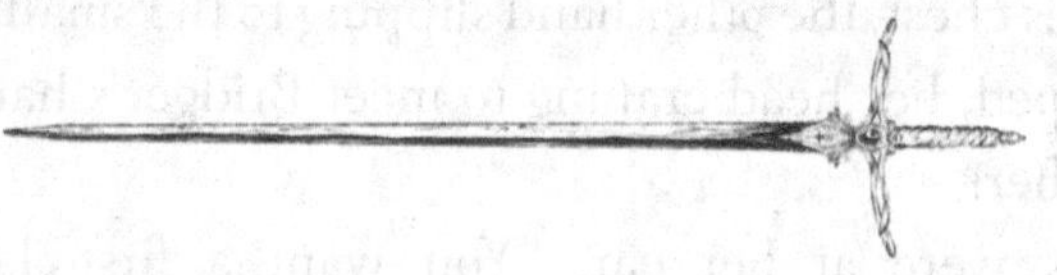

"Tell every single one of my soldiers they have ten minutes to meet in the indoor training center or I'll start removing limbs."

The soldier guarding the entrance to Vincere nodded, eyes wide. "Yes, Commander."

Bridger's threats were never taken lightly.

The trip back to Ardor was quiet and lonesome. Bridger chose to ride by himself, despite his general's never-ending warnings—*what if you're attacked?* He didn't want to talk to anyone, didn't want to be around anyone.

Bridger wanted silence to think about the decision he'd made.

His boots echoed through the halls as he descended further underground, taking only enough time to himself to slip into a tidy uniform.

Marlena's order had been clear: find Vega.

Bridger didn't plan on wasting any more time, spending the hours it took to get back to Vincere cursing himself for letting Arlet get inside his head in the first place—all letting Vega go did was make more work for himself. *Fucking idiot.* He needed to prepare for the inevitable pushback that was going to come from the people of Tolevarre with the new army presence in their lands, not spend his time tracking down his ex-girlfriend.

Bridger was running off little to no sleep, the dreams starting to take a toll on him while he was awake. Seeing Vega today hadn't helped with the emotions he'd been trying to smother. She looked so *alive*. Until she was on the brink of death—what would have happened if she'd died on Earth?

Ardor's temperatures sometimes dropped below freezing when the sun set, forcing Vincere to keep hearths burning with fires around the clock to chase away the brittle cold.

Bridger felt nothing as he pushed his way into the large room packed with some of the most dangerous soldiers in Tolevarre. The ceilings here were the highest in the underground bunker, giving plenty of room for powers to be used when sparring. In the center, there were five rings for hand-to-hand combat with soldiers lazing around them until they felt the mood their commander was in. Bridger's mood swings were flagrant, sending his men into a perfectly erect formation without the need for a direct order.

He stood in front of his soldiers, their attention focused solely on him. "Thank you for coming to meet with me on such short notice," he said as if they'd had a choice and he hadn't given them ten minutes to drop whatever they were doing to get here.

Over the years, he'd gained a reputation of his own. One of ruthlessness and unwavering loyalty to a world that had taken so much from him, but the men and women under him, they trusted him.

He was aware that most of them joined the army knowing Bridger might be the only protection they had from Marlena, blindly choosing to join without knowing if he was truly the man people said he was.

As he settled into the role of commander, his eyes grew darker, the room's temperature plummeting despite the roaring fire on the other side of the training center.

"I've called you here tonight because I need fifteen level tens for a highly important mission." Bridger liked to give his men and women the choice of stepping forward, but not before he told them the stakes.

If there was one promise Bridger kept himself, it was ensuring his soldiers' well-being and happiness... though he made it abundantly clear not to mistake his kindness for weakness. Some had made that miscalculation before and were no longer around to tell the tale.

Meyer stood in the crowd, raising his hand to volunteer.

Whenever Bridger took his place in front of his army, he did so alone—ripping a page out of Marlena's book to remind those under him he didn't need anyone to protect him, that he would always be the strongest warrior their world knew.

He shook his head. "General Ignis and a group of his choosing will be relocating to Solum to keep watch on the uprisings there since they're growing in number rapidly. I believe Praefectus Urban will be the next to fall to the rebellion's propaganda. I will need fifteen others to volunteer, or I'll be forced to pick you myself." At least fifty hands shot up. "I will allow the general to pick the group who will join me in the search for Vega."

Whispers began to break out through the group of soldiers at the drop of Vega's name.

"Tomorrow, my group leaves for Imber," Bridger continued, the boom of his voice drowning out the chatter.

Imber had been crushed to nothing by Marlena in the early days of her rule. The leader and his people were always clear allies of her parents, faltering at nothing. When she killed them, Marlena knew Imber had to be the first to go. It wasn't until she found out they were home to the rising rebellion that she flattened it to a pancake.

"I have reason to believe that somehow these rebels are hiding in plain sight." Bridger scanned the crowd, the mumbles getting louder. "Marlena doesn't want Vega out there imparting the rebels with hope, manipulating our innocent people to join a rebellion that will turn out to be nothing more than a suicide operation." Bridger didn't think about the words coming out of his mouth. "And they are going to feel like they've won after she and Arlet escaped from us on Earth."

Bridger's mouth opened to continue with his speech, but a grainy voice caught his attention as soon as the statement was out in the open.

"Yeah, I'm sure she just somehow *escaped*. Seems likely without any powers." Someone else chuckled, giving the boy courage to continue speaking. "Think she's still as good-looking as she was in her last life?" The words weren't meant to be heard, but there wasn't much Bridger missed with his increased sense of hearing—a warrior must hear all to stay one step ahead of their opponent.

Within the blink of an eye, Bridger was on him, hand fisting the training suit he wore. "What did you say?" he growled.

The boy stammered, trying to find his words. His face turned white, his breath coming out in short bursts. Bridger hoped he didn't piss himself. "I-it's—I-I'm sorry, sir. I just mean that it—it would be easy to find myself under her spell too."

Too.

The words made Bridger question what was going on behind his back—what his soldiers were muttering when he wasn't around.

It was time to remind those in this room what happened when they spoke out against the commander of Tolevarre.

The rumble of Bridger's power traveled through the young soldier's body. His face twisted in pain before his head caved in on itself. Bridger dropped the body. Blood sprinkled his cheeks, and when he flicked his wrist, brain matter splattered to the floor.

He wiped the remnants of the young boy off of his shoulder, his gaze returning to the crowd. Their eyes were wide with terror as

Bridger scanned the room. His height made it easy to look over his people without many meeting his gaze straight on or from above.

The room went completely still when Bridger walked to the middle of the room. "If anyone else has questions about where my loyalties lie, please speak up now." There wasn't a peep, not a single breath taken. No one moved—nothing. "Good," he said with gravel in his voice. "Fifteen of you, be ready by morning light."

The whole spectacle took no more than five minutes.

No one followed him as he took his exit. They were left cleaning up the mess Bridger made of their training room.

Taking someone's life wasn't new to Bridger, and the remorse that was supposed to come with it no longer did. There was no way to feel bad when he couldn't feel at all—when he'd buried his heart so deep in a pit, no one could reach it.

The darkness felt at home inside him. Bridger was right where everyone said he belonged.

The door to his room slammed shut from the sheer force of his anger, rattling the concrete walls around him.

His strength got away from him, especially at this stage of his anger. Bridger paced the room, the blood of the soldier still tainting his skin.

In the corner of his room was a small bar cart filled with bottles of different colored liquids. Bridger brought one to his mouth and chugged until it burned the pit of his stomach.

It wasn't the killing that made him want to escape—it was the way he felt listening to that young boy talk of Vega. The feeling of rage that bubbled inside of him when he'd objectified her. Vega had been dead to him for years, or at least the version of her that he'd been in love with—the version that caused him to bend to his knees, his loyalty to her as unrelenting as their romance.

The dreams were breaking into a part of his brain Bridger thought he'd long killed off.

"Fuck!" His scream was strangled and raw. The bottle in his

hand crashed against the wall before he registered he'd thrown it. The alcohol splattered across his room, the smell burning his eyes.

His room in Vincere didn't have many personal touches. Most of his belongings went up in flames with the childhood home in Fortis he'd burned to the ground after Vega was killed the first time. Before Arlet found her on Earth, Bridger sent a message in the form of fire to his family and everyone else who followed Marlena.

Bridger would have burned the world down if it meant he got Vega back. Everyone else was collateral damage he was willing to lose.

The heart of a true villain, even before he'd been damned.

Meyer stormed into the room hours later without so much as a tap on the door to announce his arrival. "What was that about?" he asked.

"The soldiers are getting too comfortable. They think they can talk however they want without consequences. I've been too nice." Bridger stood, unclasping his cape from his uniform and letting it flutter to the floor. He'd lost track of how much he'd drank, his only goal to free himself from the memories of Vega, of the ring, and seeing her today.

"I'm all for putting some of these smug bastards in their place, but that wasn't what tonight was," Meyer said.

"Enough. I've had enough of the fucking lectures from you. If you don't like how I reprimand my soldiers, then leave." Bridger wanted to be alone.

"I'm not here to argue or tell you that you're wrong. I'm here to make sure you're okay. I know this is a lot for you. The whole Vega thing..." Meyer's words trailed off. "It hasn't bothered you as much in the past. I thought you'd finally gotten over her, but now I'm not so sure, with the dreams and all. You're hiding things from me."

Bridger barked a laugh, turning to face his friend—the only friend he'd ever had, ever been allowed to have until he met Vega. "There are a lot of things you don't know, that I don't tell you, Meyer. Get used to it." Bridger sneered. "And since when are you so in touch with your emotions? Since when do you care about what I'm dealing with?" Bridger asked. The two had never been sentimental towards one another. "Tonight was a much-needed reminder that I have powers none of them could ever dream of, a reminder that I'm more than any of you will ever be." Bridger locked eyes with Meyer, sounding so much like Marlena he wanted to choke on the words as they left his mouth. His next statement was meant to strike, to drive a stake and draw blood. "I am your commander, Meyer. Not your friend." *Liar.* He turned around, heading to the bathroom where he would finally clean the blood and remnants of that soldier off his skin. "Get out and warn the others that I'm done being disrespected."

18

The scent of seawater came first, reminding her of the coastline of Washington. *Fuck, it was all a dream.*

The chill in her bones came next. *This is definitely a hospital. I've been admitted.*

Third was the tingle of her body, a low hum of warmth flowing through her blood like electricity buzzing through a live wire. *What is that?*

Vega's eyes shot open, and she darted into a seated position, heart pattering inside her chest loud enough to drown out the hum inside her body. A flickering light glowed in the corner, brightening the room enough to see every square inch.

One bare foot touched the floor, the other following as she moved slowly, trying not to make too much noise. Her muscles complained with the memories of the redwoods.

Chills ran down Vega's back, not because she felt fear, but because she was fucking cold. *Where the hell did I end up?* The walls were made of steel, the dark color of gunmetal casting a blue hue throughout the small space.

The last memory she had was of the man with the golden eyes, his arms wrapped around her neck until another vision—memory—embraced her.

Shit, shit! Did they take me?

A thin blanket lay on the bed. The scent of moss mixed with the deep smell of salt water surrounding her as she wrapped it around her shoulders.

In the corner, there was a small wooden desk with papers scattered across—a letter opener stuck out from under a pile of envelopes. *The perfect weapon.*

She could hear voices coming and going, passing by the door. Vega held the letter opener between her fingers and clutched to her chest. She reached for the door handle with her free hand, but as she pulled, someone from the other side pushed. The person crashed into her with such mass, Vega would have fallen back if they didn't reach out to steady her.

She squeaked, slashing out with the puny letter opener.

"Vega!" a male's voice cried, but she had no time to see much of the man before she was wrapped into a hug so tight it forced her muscles to relax and drop her makeshift weapon.

The smell of moss filled her nose again. "You're squishing me."

The man laughed, pulling back to hold her at arm's length while his eyes roamed over her body. "Sorry," he said. "What's that?" he asked, bending down to pick up the paperknife. "Really?" He held it up between them. "Who are you going to fight off with that?"

Vega's gaze met his green eyes—the color of a forest after a summer's rain. His face lit up in a charming smile. "You're Khort." It wasn't a question. Vega knew. She'd seen him in dreams, but his name had never been revealed like the others. She'd gotten to know him through what little Arlet would tell her.

"The one and only," he hummed.

Arlet got her back.

Whatever happened after Vega was knocked out, she'd probably never know, but what she did know was that Arlet made it... *right?* Arlet had to make it.

As if Khort could read her thoughts, he chuckled. "Arlet's okay."

Vega squished her brows together, puzzled, but relief flooded her chest.

"No, before you ask. I don't read minds. I just knew you'd ask if she was okay once you realized where you were."

Khort's stubble was more than a five o'clock shadow but not nearly a full beard like she'd been picturing. His hair was probably shoulder length if it were down, but he had a low, messy bun at the back of his head. His face had sharp edges and gorgeous angles, a sprinkle of freckles lining the bridge of his nose and the tips of his cheeks.

In this realm and any other, he would be considered devastatingly handsome.

"I know where we are... but, like, *where* are we?" Vega asked, her arms still covered in the blanket she'd stolen off the bed.

"About a mile under the Sea of Ros at the base of the rebel headquarters. Welcome to Castra." His response was so nonchalant that Vega wasn't sure she'd heard him right.

"A mile underwater?" Vega swallowed her fear. The dread of imploding was suddenly higher on her list than it'd ever been.

Khort shrugged. "It's home for now."

Home.

I'm home.

"I can show you around if you want," Khort said, stepping around Vega to get inside the room. He moved around with an ease that confirmed this was his room and not her own. *Do I even have a room here?*

The unknowns kept growing.

Vega took in the way his body shifted under the light. His clothing was casual, his loose cotton-white shirt stained at the edge with what looked to be oil.

Vega didn't know Khort, at least not this version of her.

"I'd like that. Can I see Arlet too?" Vega wanted to thank her and maybe give her a big hug—apologize for ever doubting her.

"Yeah, we can do that. She should be out of her meeting by the time we're done getting you some food and finishing up the tour." Khort came over with Vega's boots, a clean pair of socks stuffed inside. "Here, this'll help you warm up. You'll get used to the colder temps down here again soon."

"How long have I been here?" Vega asked, sitting back on the edge of the creaky bed while slipping into the beat-up boots she'd left Earth in.

"Almost four days," Khort replied, watching her from the other side of the room. Vega felt herself heat up under his soft gaze. He stared at her like he was smitten, so full of love Vega could physically feel it. She broke their gaze to tie her boots, needing to refocus her attention elsewhere.

"Shit," she muttered. "What have I missed?" Vega's mind wandered to the men, *to Bridger*, and worried if she was still being actively hunted.

"Nothing that you need to worry about just yet," Khort answered, reaching for a dark blue jacket on the back of a chair and handing it over to her. Vega didn't question its size and let the blanket fall to the bed, slipping into the large jacket.

"I don't like being kept in the dark for too long," she warned.

He met her words with a little laugh, his nose scrunching. "Oh, I know, but my biggest concern right now is getting you some food. I don't think talking to you about the things you can't remember will be of any help to us or you."

Vega agreed as her stomach rumbled. "Let me guess, fish is on the menu."

Khort nodded, strutting to the door with a sympathetic smile. "Breakfast, lunch, and dinner. Your favorite."

Vega had never liked fish, but at this point, she would eat a horse if it meant she could fill her stomach with something other than Doritos and gas station burritos. With the promise of a full stomach, Vega shuffled off the bed and followed Khort out of the safety of his room.

The hallways were narrow, doors lining up and down the cramped quarters. People slipped in and out of the rooms, nodding hellos to Khort. Vega couldn't miss the way people stopped and stared at her—the shock on their faces and the murmurs now fluttering through the hall were unmistakable.

Vega locked eyes with a woman, her dull brown hair drenched in what she assumed was sweat. She'd been entering a room until her eyes met Vega's, stopping her in her tracks to gawk in surprise. Vega noticed the suit the woman wore. It was similar to that of Bridger and the other man from the redwoods. Skintight, the fabric thick against her skin.

As they passed, the woman bowed her head, looking up through her lashes at Vega.

"Why are people staring?" Vega asked, speeding up her stride to position herself beside Khort instead of following close behind.

The smile on his face made her insides knot. "Because you're the face of hope."

Her memories failed her, and she was unable to wrap her head around why anyone would see her as anything more than a complete screw-up. In every memory she had of this life, nothing gave her the conception she was some savior who could help rid this land of Marlena and her tyranny.

Vega looked down as they passed another group of onlookers, afraid to see the same look in their eyes that she saw in the first woman.

A hand reached out, fingers grazing hers. Vega glanced over, catching Khort reaching out to offer her what little strength he could. Her eyes flicked up to him, his gaze still forward as they walked through the maze-like halls.

"Head up. They need you more than you need you."

Vega listened, straightening her shoulders, looking ahead—forward. It was an act. She wanted to fall into herself, but she wasn't allowed to fall apart.

Do not break down now. The words she'd always told herself started to feel more like something someone else had once told her... *but who?*

She'd been seen as weak for far too long. By herself, by Chase, by the people around her who constantly watched her fail. It was only the life on Earth she could remember and what few memories she'd been allowed to see, but Vega knew there were people in this world who doubted her too.

Would Tolevarre offer her the strength she needed?

"It's Vega."

"She's back."

"When did they find her?"

"Vega."

Muttering words filled her head. Vega couldn't look at them and wouldn't dare connect to the hope they felt when they saw her.

How many times had this moment happened over the last fifty-five years? How many times had she let the people here down?

Every loss stacked upon them was because she couldn't defeat a sister she had almost no memories of. Every loss came back to Vega not being enough.

Not strong enough.

Not smart enough.

Not enough.

She didn't need her memories to know that she had never succeeded at anything that mattered.

19

VEGA DEVOURED HER FIRST PLATE OF FISH AND WAS OFFERED A second. The pungent flavor was an afterthought to the rumbling in her stomach once she realized how starved she felt.

The only thing on Vega's mind was finishing the second plate of food until the door opened and Arlet walked in.

Vega's eyes fell to her outfit, which seemed to be a take on the training suits Vega saw the others in. The deep black contrasted against her golden skin. Arlet looked lethal—she was back where she belonged.

So far, it seemed like everyone was always dressed for battle in Castra—besides Khort, who she'd learned was working on the machine that kept their drinking water clear of salt, which would explain the oil stain.

Vega jumped from her seat and met Arlet halfway to wrap her in a hug that made the chill in Vega's bones melt away. "How? How did you get us here?" Vega breathed in, the smell of Arlet that of a summer's day. Sweet, warm, a scent of happiness.

Vega pulled back from their hug, eager to hear all about what happened. She had no idea what she'd done in any of her lives to deserve a friend like her.

Khort had taken Vega into a private room to eat, saving her from the prying eyes of the people of Castra. He promised it wouldn't always be like this, that people would get used to seeing her around again soon.

The large room was filled with more screens than a sports bar, and though there were still people in here, they were too preoccupied with their jobs to sit and stare for long.

This was the headquarters of Castra—where they kept an eye on the happenings of Tolevarre through hacked cameras, and only those with enough clearance were allowed inside.

Arlet looked over her shoulder, catching the gazes of a few people who looked away when they were caught staring at the pair's reunion.

"You done eating?" Arlet asked.

Vega hadn't finished her second helping, but the urgency in Arlet's tone made the last few bites on the plate seem insipid. "I am now."

"Let's go for a walk." Arlet motioned for the door.

She turned to see if Khort would be joining them, happy to see he was already striding over to her and Arlet. Even without her memories, the pull she felt towards Khort was strong.

Having the two of them close made whatever anxieties she felt about the unknown of her future settle. In this life she'd only known Khort for a couple hours, but it felt like a lifetime.

He felt like home.

And Arlet had proven herself as such long before Vega realized it.

Maybe home wasn't a place after all.

Vega followed Arlet through the winding halls, her ears popping as they descended further into the depths of Castra.

Vega hugged herself, the chill back in her bones. Khort grabbed her shoulders, squeezing lightly to remind her that he was right behind her.

Just like her hug with Arlet, Khort's touch sent tendrils of warmth through her body.

They arrived at a room shaped like a dome—glass walls rounding the ceiling in a way that made Vega feel like she was in a large reverse-fishbowl. Seats started at the bottom level and extended up against a thick glass wall like a large college lecture hall. A whiteboard on the opposite side of the room was clean, save for a small map of Tolevarre hanging to the right. Looking beyond the glass revived every fear Vega had about what the bottom of the ocean looked like and what monsters might be lurking in the depths.

Vega ogled for a few more moments, forcing herself to let go of the fears that would do her no good. "Why the secrecy?"

Khort and Arlet leaned against a long desk at the front of the room. Vega bit her lip, nibbling at the skin in anticipation.

Arlet met Vega's gaze, grounding her. "Because sometimes we need to talk as bonded friends with no one else around... and this is one of those times." Arlet steepled her fingers, looking down for only a second. "The men from the redwoods, they're the commander and general of Tolevarre's army."

Vega felt the blood rush to her head. "Bridger is the commander of Marlena's army?" He had been the one giving orders. Vega knew it wasn't the other way around. "What... what happened between us?"

Khort's lips pressed into a thin line. "I'm sorry. What did you just say?" He turned his head to Arlet. "I must be hearing things. How do you know his name?" he asked, pivoting back to Vega.

Arlet filled her cheeks with a bubble of air and deflated them slowly with a puff through her lips.

Vega's eyes bounced back and forth between them. "Um, I... Arlet?" Her eyes stayed on Arlet, looking for help. Arlet and Khort glanced at each other. His jaw was set, clenched as the muscles in his face danced. His anger was distinct.

"I mean, what did you expect when I told you she was seeing pieces of her life? That Bridger wouldn't be a part of that?" Arlet's eyebrows drew together.

Vega couldn't remember everything, but the things she could felt so real—even after years of telling herself they weren't, that her dreams were just a way to escape the past she couldn't remember.

Khort's jaw tensed more, and his mouth barely moved when he spoke. "You shouldn't have left that part out."

Arlet rolled her eyes so hard only the whites were visible. "Relax. I wanted time to process on my own why she was all of a sudden in this life getting her memories back naturally. Albeit slow and in small pieces, but still seeing bits... At first I thought it was the curse, but I don't think that's the case anymore. It's never allowed her to see her life before, so why would it start now? And wouldn't it do the opposite if it was the power running out? Wouldn't it *take* from her, not *give*? I think it's the bond. Our bond is unbreakable, the glue that holds us together. We've been changing, evolving over time since the bond was made. It's like it always knows what we need, when we need it. What makes you think it would suddenly stop after all these years? It's doing what it can to make us stronger." Arlet pushed herself off the desk, squeezing Khort's shoulder as if to give him a little warning to calm down.

"So having Vega remember Bridger is making us stronger?" Khort grumbled.

Her hand left his shoulder, her attention returning to Vega as she crossed the room to her. "Bridger is a bit of a sore subject around here, if ya can't already tell." Arlet spoke through the side of her mouth, eyeing Khort, whose lips were pursed in an unmistakable pout. She reached out to grab her hand, the same one with the brand around her wrist. Arlet's index finger went to the ring on Vega's hand. "He gave this to you in one of your earliest lives and promised to never give up on you." Her finger grazed over the gold band. "You threw it into the sea a while back. I had someone find it. I knew we could use it."

Vega watched as Arlet flipped her hand around to show her the underside of the ring. Arlet tapped the small band once with her finger. "His initials are inside if you look closely."

Vega took the ring off and noticed the engraving for the first time.

BD.

How did I miss that?

Vega's throat burned with bile as the ring fell to the cold floor with a *tink*. "Why would you give it back to me if you knew I didn't want it?" She stared at the ring until it stopped spinning, settling at the toe of her boot.

"We need Bridger to win this," Arlet told her, inciting a groan and the start of manic pacing from Khort.

"Bullshit," he muttered.

Arlet shot a look to Khort. "Whether you want to believe it or not, Khort, it's true. He's bonded to us, all of us. Remus wouldn't have included Bridger if he thought we could do it without him."

Khort scoffed, shaking his head. "We don't need him. We've never needed him."

Arlet sighed, a sound of exhaustion. Vega wondered when the last time she'd gotten a full night's sleep was. "Bridger back on our side cripples Marlena."

Khort fired back. "He can't be trusted. We knew that from the very beginning."

Vega listened to them pinball for a moment, taking in any bit of information she could.

Arlet stood up taller. "That's because Bridger never wanted to have *our* backs. It was always about Vega. He was with us *for Vega*. He became our family *because of Vega*. Once she was gone, once he'd been broken down enough, tortured enough, of course he was easily manipulated. Marlena wanted him. She *needed* him. She knew what breaking the four of us up would do. I hate him for what he's done to her, *to us*, but you can't be blinded by your own anger enough to deny that Remus didn't plan for us to be apart. To win, we need Bridger."

"Wait, stop." Vega took a step towards the two bickering friends. "Hey." Their argument drowned out her meek interruption.

"Exactly! We don't need someone so selfish on our side. Someone who's only looking out for himself. Let him dig his own grave. Leave him where he belongs—with Marlena, where his soul will continue to rot until there's nothing left of him." Khort flicked his wrist, the one with his matching brand.

"We can use him, Khort."

"Hello?" Vega waved her hands at them. The two continued to go at it, unaware she was even there. Vega picked up a ruler from the whiteboard's rim, then slammed it against the board with a whack that echoed through the room. The flimsy wood snapped in two, splintering down the middle from strength Vega didn't know she had.

Khort and Arlet jumped, their argument ceasing instantly.

"Thank you." Vega smiled as she dropped the useless ruler to the floor, glad to have their attention. "Just because I can't remember anything doesn't mean either of you is going to make decisions for me." Her eyes bounced between them now that she had their undivided attention. "Stop arguing and answer my question. Why did you give the ring back to me?"

The ring still sat on the floor.

Arlet glanced at it and then back to Vega. "Because I hoped that if Bridger saw it, he'd falter, that something in him might crack... and it did." Arlet crossed her arms across her chest.

"What?" Vega felt like she'd worn this question dry—like a child constantly asking her mom, "What?" and "Why?"

"When you went unconscious, I had to fight them both. I

managed to stab Bridger and knock Meyer out long enough to get under Bridger's skin." Vega listened intently, her hands starting to shake. "He saw the ring. I told him you'd been seeing him, and then he let us go. That's how I got you back here. Bridger let us go." Arlet lost confidence when she admitted that, her posture slacking. "I'm strong, I know that, but I didn't stand a chance against him. Bridger is the strongest warrior this realm has ever seen. With or without his powers, he was going to tire me out and kill me. The ring saved us."

Khort's jaw dropped—apparently, Arlet had been keeping a few secrets from him.

"I got back through the portal with you, and you started seizing. Somehow Halo, a Fraus-born you haven't met yet, found us. He got us back before I lost you. We don't have another fifteen years for me to find you again. I can't be gone for another six months, a year. We have to get this right this time, Vega."

"Why wouldn't you tell me Bridger let you two go?" Khort asked, hurt breaking through his anger.

"In case you haven't noticed, you're not Bridger's number one fan, so I don't particularly like talking about him with you. And I wanted Vega to know before you, or at least tell you both at the same time."

Khort rolled his eyes. "Don't think that him having a little moment of weakness means he's back on our side."

"No shit," Arlet conceded.

Khort's nostrils flared, and Vega knew he was going to let Arlet have it later. "We've been keeping you in my room, only allowing our closest healers to work on you. We weren't ready for the rumor mill to start. Our people need to see you strong, ready to fight. They're getting tired, beat down."

Vega's head started to pound. "Don't you think our people should give me a little grace? I'm being put through the wringer here." Vega was exhausted, and it was only the beginning... Again. "What is this? My twentieth life?" Vega chuckled, but the air around her turned serious. "I've got a lot to catch up on. Starting with why the man who used to love me is working with the sister who's trying to kill me."

"He gave up on you," Khort clipped, changing the subject quickly. "This is all new to you for now, but to them, to our people, you've had plenty of time, and now it's running out. There is no more time for grace. They're getting antsy. I told you earlier you're the face of hope, but not everyone feels that way. Fifty-five years is a long time to have hope for something, for someone who never delivers." His posture was stiff, every muscle in his body rippling with tension.

"Ouch." Vega's voice sagged along with her shoulders.

Arlet frowned, staying quiet, but Khort stepped forward and reached for her. "I'm sor—"

Vega held a hand up. The pounding in her head grew between her temples. She didn't need to hear apologies just for the sake of her feelings. "Save it."

Khort's hand fell.

"I guess I better figure it out this time then, huh?" The laugh that sawed out of her mouth was sad. She'd gone from a loser on Earth to an even bigger disappointment here in Tolevarre.

Arlet gave Khort another look—they were really good at communicating silently. "You're not in this alone. We've all failed, but we're on the right side of this. It's not over yet."

Yet.

The word hung over the three of them like a sinking ship ready to disappear below the water for the last time. Vega would eventually be that ship, gone forever, along with the hope of the people who were rooting for her—who needed her.

Without her memories, Vega couldn't remember the love she felt for these people and the realm she'd been fighting tirelessly for.

"Before we do anything, before I smite anyone, I need my memories back so I can make this choice for myself." Vega was terrified. For what? She didn't know. Those memories were hers to have.

Vega had lived so many lives—who had she been in the last life? The one before that? Who was she in her original life? Arlet had commented on how much like herself Vega was in this life, but what if she were more now? All of her lives had to add up to something.

Khort nodded in response.

Arlet grinned. "Memories, here we come!"

20

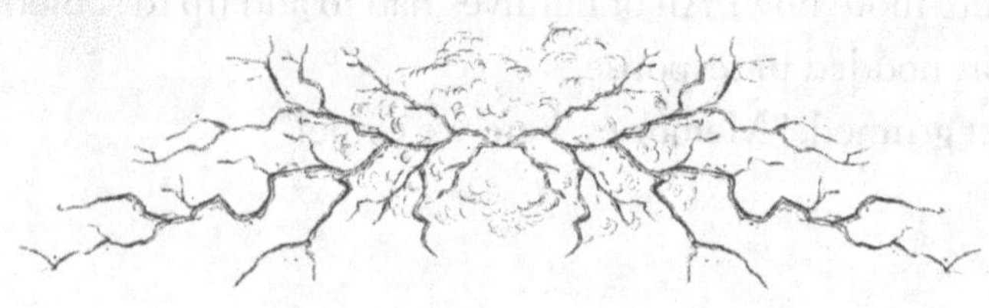

It had been days since Vega woke up from her mini coma. Days of learning that the buzzing through her veins would start to feel natural again soon. Days of learning about herself through someone else's stories. Days with Khort while he taught her how to use the fizzle of electricity sparking at her fingertips and palms whenever her emotions flared.

Vega groaned, shoulders sagging as Khort stood across the training room from her.

"Try again," he told her.

"I can't do it. We've been trying for hours, Khort." They'd been spending a lot of time together while Arlet slipped back into her role here in Tolevarre. On Earth, Vega had felt like Arlet could convince her to follow her anywhere, and it seemed the rebels of Tolevarre felt the same. She could rule any world, and Vega would believe that was exactly where she belonged.

Arlet woke up every morning to meet with the other leaders of Castra, planning their next attack, their next move. It left little time for Arlet to train Vega or even spend much time with her now that she was back after being gone for a year.

"You're not giving up. Try again." Khort, who she'd learned was the leader of their tiny rebel army, was relentless in their training. The respect the people of Castra had for Khort could be seen in the way they bowed their heads when he walked by and how they lit up when he held a conversation with them.

Vega found herself curious if there was someone to keep his bed warm at night—*stop it, you idiot. He might be hot, but he's supposed to be your best friend*—but those thoughts soon faded when he didn't let up on her, forcing her to work through the fatigue. "Won't I just remember how to do this when I get my memories back?" Vega puffed, returning to the fighting stance Khort kept forcing her to start in. One foot in front of the other, feet spread the width of the hips.

Today they were trying to will her lightning out of hiding. There were so many more powers Vega held under her skin, but this was the easiest for her to control—this was the power that came first, meaning she'd wielded it the longest and it should be the simplest to control... but the sweat pouring down Vega's face proved otherwise.

She was struggling.

"Your brain will, but your body won't if you don't allow it time to remember how to react. And you certainly aren't in fighting shape," he replied. Everything Khort said made perfect sense, but Vega still rolled her eyes and mocked the last part of the sentence. "If you stop mocking me I'll make this your last time."

Vega took a deep breath and closed her eyes, focusing on the center of her body, where she could feel the zapping power rise. Warmth trickled down her arms, bubbling around her wrists until she could feel the tingle of her lightning at the ends of her fingertips.

When she opened her eyes, blue sparks danced in her hands. *I did it!* Her smile was huge, and while she felt cocky enough to try it, she pushed with all her strength, forcing her lightning towards the target wall on the opposite side of the room. A single bolt shot out and struck the large target, barely. "Ah-ha!" Vega exclaimed, jumping with a spring in her step out of pure excitement.

Khort's arms crossed tightly across his muscular chest, but he couldn't fully contain his smile. Vega saw the little muscle twitch at the corner of his mouth—he was trying to be the ever-strong dragon shifter everyone expected him to be, but Vega saw right through him.

"Oh, come on! I know this isn't new to you, but it is for me. Right now, this brain doesn't remember all the cool things I can do." Vega pointed to her head, her hair up in a high ponytail with braids roping the shorter layers together. The braids didn't keep all of her flyaways subdued, especially with the static of her power fizzing beneath her skin. Vega let go of the swelling power, allowing it to slink back inside of her body as she crossed the room to Khort.

"It was one bolt of lightning, Vega. You can create storms out of thin air. You've got more inside of you than even your original brain could comprehend," Khort said.

Vega smiled, feeling his words flutter in her stomach. *Fuck.* She hadn't forgotten his comment about their people losing hope, but she'd gotten over the hurt that came along with it. He hadn't said it to be an ass—he said it because it was true. "I don't actually get new brains every time, right?" She shook at the thought, grossed out by the visual.

Khort laughed, shaking his head. "No, no new brains. That's still you in there somewhere." He reached out and placed his large palms on either side of her head, giving her a little shake.

Vega smiled, giggling along with him. The bliss of finally feeling the power she'd been fighting to take hold of let her relax a tiny bit.

When Khort's hands fell away from her head, she reached forward and grabbed his right palm. Her eyes landed on the matching ring around their wrists. Her fingers glided over it delicately, the raised skin soft to the touch like hers and Arlet's.

When Vega peeked up at Khort, his eyes weren't on their branded wrists—they were on her. Vega's face hardened with a frown, glancing back down at the skin under her fingers. "Is this why I feel so close to you and Arlet? Even without my memories? It's like… I can't explain it." Her voice was soft as she rotated his wrist to look at the whole scar.

"It's like you can feel our hearts beating? You know where we are even without having to think about it?" Khort said the words she'd been trying to find.

"Yes," Vega said, exhaling.

Khort nodded.

"I can feel Bridger too." Vega kept her voice low. The words leaving her lips felt like a secret. A muscle in Khort's jaw ticked at the mere mention of Bridger. "Can you and Arlet still feel him?" she questioned, finally letting his arm go.

"No," Khort admitted through gritted teeth. "We haven't been able to sense him since he became commander."

"He's strong?" Vega asked. Learning more about the man she used to be in love with felt important, even if she knew she would get those memories back eventually. *Soon, so soon, you'll feel whole,* she hoped.

"The strongest warrior our people have ever seen. More so than Mars himself."

Mars, the god of war. Vega's knowledge of the Roman gods was minimal at best, but she could at least follow along with the names and what their powers were—Arlet's brief history lesson was proving to be more helpful than she'd realized it would be.

"Do you think he knows that I can feel him or is it an oversight since I've just gotten back?" Vega knew Arlet would be the better person to ask about Bridger, but if she didn't ask as the questions arose, Vega would have a list longer than the deepest point of the Sea of Ros.

"He knows. Bridger and Marlena don't have oversights. Bridger might have had a moment of weakness when he saw that ring and let you go, but he knows what that brand on his wrist can do. The sooner you remember that, the safer you'll be." Khort stiffened, signaling the end of this conversation. He took a breath before speaking again. "I need to put a couple more safety measures in order before we take you to Fraus to get your memories back, but it's coming soon. I promise." He took a step back and nodded toward the other end of the room. "Let's go again."

She could feel anger bubbling inside of her, threatening to blow. Vega had been back in Tolevarre for nearly a week, and all she kept hearing was that they were working on making sure it was safe to get her memories back—like she hadn't traveled through another realm and almost died with the promise of no longer feeling lost inside her own body. "Khort," Vega said, stepping towards him. She was exhausted.

"Again." His voice was deep, ringing with finality.

Vega wanted to keep digging, but she could see Bridger was a touchy subject with him—she wasn't naive. In this world or any other, jealousy was easy to pick up on. "Khort," Vega said again, not allowing him to fold into himself and hide behind a mask. Were he and Bridger ever actually friends? The frustration of not knowing was starting to wear on her.

"I said again," Khort spat, his tone that of a man talking to his dog.

His words pushed her over the edge. Thunder rumbled inside the room as Vega's blood felt like it might boil over. "You're not going to talk to me like that." One of the old versions of herself might have listened and followed along like a lost puppy, but this new Vega, the one who couldn't remember those variations of herself yet, wasn't going to put up with being talked down to.

On Earth, she'd embraced the sad and worn-down girl she'd become, but here she felt the fight she'd lost. Vega was sick of people thinking she was too weak to care for herself.

Chase.

Bridger.

Marlena.

She wanted to prove all of them wrong.

The walls rattled with the booming thunder. The fact they were miles under the sea never crossed her mind. All Vega could feel was the power flooding her senses. When she closed her eyes, behind her eyelids she could see the swell of the sea above them, the rising waves crashing against the coast of Imber. *Am I doing that?* Her eyes shot open.

Khort circled her in the room. Vega spun slowly, never allowing him to get behind her like he'd been teaching her. Like she'd allowed Meyer to do... Her breathing was ragged, sweat prickling her skin as her agitation grew. Khort shuffled his feet with the next boom of thunder, a little smile forming on his face.

Vega caught on to what he was doing, egging her agitation on to get a rise out of her powers.

"You feel that? That raw anger?" His smile made Vega even crankier—the lightning sparked and grew between her palms as she flexed her hands. The warmth building in her palm pulled her gaze to the source. Her eyes matched the color of the crackling power in her hand. She stared at it in amazement. "Use it." Khort's words were barely a whisper. "Remind everyone who you are and what you can do because they're forgetting." The words sank inside Vega. They weren't meant to make her mad; they were meant to make her strong.

Khort knew Vega didn't want to let anyone down—that she always wanted to be the hero to her sister's villain.

Vega wanted good to prevail in a world where evil loomed around every corner.

The wind in the small training center started to swirl, the thunder rumbling more as her lightning continued to crackle, making Khort's loose pieces of hair stand on end from the static in the air.

"Rein it in. Control the downfall. Don't let it consume you when you're mad. You will battle angry, tired, and feel more defeated than you've ever been, and that doesn't stop the fact that you have to continue on in order to survive. If you can't think while you control those powers, it'll consume you. You will end up like some of your other lives: dead before you even get the chance to fight for your life," Khort continued circling her.

Vega allowed herself to close her eyes again and feel the way her body tingled, the way her brain seemed to thrum along with the beat of the thunder. "Am I making those waves?" she asked, clenching her jaw while she watched the water above them settle.

"With your wind, yes. The water isn't yours to control. It's a reaction to the ability you do have."

Vega strained, her teeth grinding as she fought to control the storm brewing thousands of feet above.

"When those memories come flooding back, you're going to be mad. You're going to feel hatred, betrayal, sadness, all of it, all at once." Vega listened to Khort's words, grasping for the control she wanted, telling herself to bring her power back to a simmer and not a dangerous boil. "You have to be ready to remember everything, Vega. It's not all pretty." He was much closer now. Vega's eyes shot open when she sensed his proximity. Her breath caught in her throat as his dazzling eyes fixed on hers. "Do not falter this time."

Vega didn't flinch, only marveled at the calmness of the room around them now. There was no wind, no blue lightning nipping at her hands, no thunder rumbling the walls, and the sea above was back to flat waters. It was as if none of it had ever happened.

"Once you remember, don't forgive what he's done to you. Use that anger but never lose control, or you and everyone else will be dead." Khort stepped back.

Vega felt like her air was her own again, not a shared space, warm with emotions. She took a large gulp to steady her racing heart.

"That's enough for the day," Khort declared. "I'll see you at dinner."

She stood in the middle of the room, shaking from the release of power she'd exerted—from the realization she was needed here.

That finally, she was wanted.

Vega fell to the floor and rested her back against the bench in the outer corner of the ring. She was so tired, her muscles screaming from overuse.

You're not alone here.

As tired as she was, a smile still spread across her lips. Vega's head rested against the bench, and she stared up at the ceiling.

You were never alone. They were always with you.

21

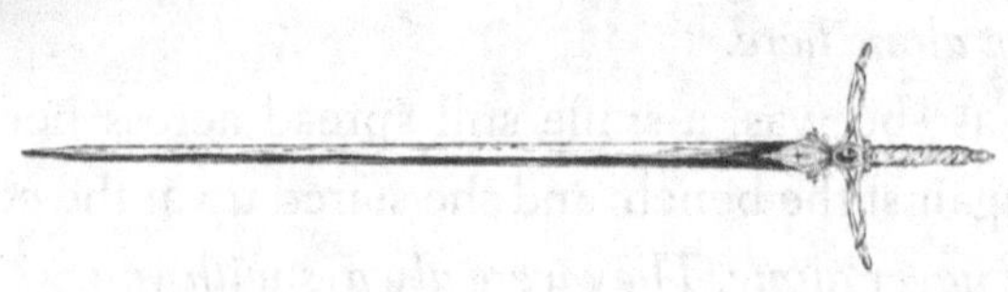

Blood stained the water swirling down the sink's drain, the candlelight in the room flickering against the wooden walls.

Bridger wasn't sure whose blood he was cleaning off his face, from his hair, and scrubbing from underneath his fingernails. It could be his, the soldiers of Tolevarre's, Vega's father's, or the blood from the other three sharing the dilapidated cabin with him—the blood from their successful summoning of Remus.

There had been no way to prepare for Marlena's attack. There were rumors of an uprising within some of the families, but it seemed like their parents were handling it well enough. Little did they know, Marlena had been planning to give herself a promotion, and all it took was murdering her parents and anyone else who opposed her—all while betraying everyone who loved her.

Once the blood from their fight out of the capital was wiped from his skin, Bridger shut the water off and headed back into the main room slowly and silently. The others hadn't heard him approach, allowing him the time to overhear their conversation.

"Imber is on our side. Emil would never betray my father. That much I know for sure." Vega sat in the middle of the room, a fire crackling beside her. The fireplace might have once been gorgeous, but now the stone was caving in, and the chimney was falling through the ceiling.

A map sat in the middle of the floor. Vega's black fingernails pointed at the island off the coast of Solum. "They're going to be our biggest ally. This is where we start."

Khort leaned forward, motioning towards another spot on the map of Tolevarre. "Good luck getting through Littera. We don't need to hear from them to know Nero's going to follow Marlena." He tensed when he spoke her name out loud.

Arlet had her back to the musty couch, arms hugged around her legs to make herself as small as possible. Out of the four, she was most outside her comfort zone.

Arlet's family fled years ago when the Curia divide became more prominent. The Caelums took her in, shielding her from the outside world until she was ready to flourish on her own. Her eyes were tired, and her gaze was lost in the flames while Vega and Khort threw ideas out into the open.

Bridger wondered if this was the first time she'd been back in Vates—her homeland—since her parents had disappeared.

He made an intentional move, letting the others know he was in the room with them now. Vega's eyes shot up from the map, meeting his. Bridger gave her a wink as he pushed himself off the door frame, uncrossing his arms. Her smile felt like a lighthouse, guiding him home when he felt lost and alone.

Bridger walked to Vega and crouched down next to her as he took in the map of their world—a map he could draw from memory. He'd spent most of his life studying all things Tolevarre; he knew this realm better than he knew himself. "There's a passage through the Solum hills straight to the Sea of Ros." Bridger ran his finger along the brittle paper, tracing the route.

Arlet had finally stopped staring into the fire. "Khort, do you still have shifter friends living in Solum?"

Vega rested her hand on Bridger's leg, then rubbed her fingers aimlessly along the lines of his muscles. Heat soared inside him at the simple touch. He placed his hand over hers, rubbing his thumb over the newly branded skin on the back of her wrist.

Khort shook his head. "I don't know. I can't bank on it, not when we've lost communication with Demuto. I'm assuming any shifter who was left in other territories fled, or they were killed."

Khort's family had been in Stella for Marlena's Curia induction ceremony tonight, but he'd been unable to find them when Marlena's attack on the capital began. There was no telling if his family had made it far before being killed or captured.

"Then we need to get in touch with your family," Bridger stated evenly. "I don't think Marlena had the manpower to send armies all over the realm. This first attack was opportunistic, planned at the right time in the right setting. It could have gotten messy if she had her best men out searching for one lone family while the rest were infiltrating and overthrowing the Curia."

Bridger was right. He knew they knew it by the look in their eyes. The rest of them weren't trained for war and death. Bridger was.

Arlet let her legs loose, uncurling herself. "So we head to Imber?" Her voice was quiet as she asked.

"To get to Solum's boats, we still need to cut through Littera, and as I said, we all know Nero will side with whoever he knows will keep him alive longest," Khort pointed out, looking at Bridger with unease.

Nowhere felt safe.

"No, we go through Oro," Bridger told them. "Their people won't side as quickly as Littera will. Gaia will do her best to stay in the middle as long as she can. Same with Pax. They're going to hold on to peace for as long as Marlena will let them. As for the Silvas and the people of Solum..." He paused, shrugging. "Our government just fell after over two thousand years of Curia rule. There's no telling what's going to happen next."

The room fell into silence for a moment while the four of them mulled over what was to happen in the coming hours.

"It's late." Arlet was the one to point at the ticking clock on the wall. "We need rest. We've been up for thirty hours. We aren't getting in touch with anyone tonight." She stood up, stretching her limbs.

Bridger looked up at her, giving her a slight nod along with a tight smile. "You're right. Let's clean ourselves up, get a little rest, and we can start again at dawn." He followed Arlet in standing, holding his hand out to help Vega off the dirty floor. He pulled her into his chest, wrapping her in a quick hug, and placed a kiss on the top of her head.

Dawn would be here in just a few hours, but at least they could try to get what fleeting rest they could. Bridger nodded to the back bedroom. "There are two small beds in there. You two take them. I'll take first watch out here."

Vega had already found an extra pillow and blanket in a closet filled with dust to set a spot up on the couch. This tiny home hadn't been lived in in what seemed like hundreds of years. Everything was dated, with no updated appliances from the modern era.

After setting up a makeshift bed on the couch, Vega hugged Khort first, his broad arms engulfing her. Bridger looked away, giving them their privacy. He distracted himself with a goodnight hug of his own from Arlet. "We're going to be okay," Bridger told her.

"I hope you're right," Arlet said, rubbing at the new brand on her wrist. "Did you hear what he said?" she asked, whispering so only Bridger could hear.

His eyes grew wide. "You heard it too."

At the same time they both said, "I saved her. Do not waste this opportunity."

"What do you think it means?" Arlet asked.

Khort filed into the bedroom on heavy feet. Arlet's worry came apart when Vega walked up, her sister in every right but blood. She put on a fake smile. Bridger knew it was to protect her from any more worry.

"It's been one hell of a day, huh?" Arlet did a pretty good job deflecting, but Bridger was certain Vega would see right through her.

Vega slid into Bridger's side again, her arm snaking around his waist. "I'd say." Vega reached out her free hand and took Arlet's in hers. "Get some sleep. I'll see you in the morning." Without another word, Arlet squeezed Vega's hand before slipping behind the door of the bedroom.

Vega looked up at Bridger the second they were alone. He positioned her in front of him, and she wrapped her arms around his midsection. She was short enough to lay her head on his chest as he pulled her against him.

It was the first time they'd been able to have a moment to themselves since they found Arlet and Khort in Aeris. "How could she do this?" The question was spoken into his chest. Vega's ordinarily soft voice was filled with rasp, strained from the last thirty hours.

"I don't know," he replied honestly. Bridger had been asking himself that too. Marlena had him fooled. From the second he'd met her, she'd been calculating her attack like the spiteful creature she was.

Vega tensed in his arms as she held back a sob.

"Hey." Bridger's hand shot to her face, lifting her head by the underside of her chin. "Do not break down now."

Vega's eyes were clouded with tears. She had been so strong all night, but Bridger needed her to hold on to that strength for a little longer. He needed her to keep her head in the fight until he was able to get her to safety. Then she could break down, scream, kick—burn the whole fucking world down if she wanted. But not yet.

"You heard her. She's going to take everyone I love from me."

Her promise echoed down the halls and still sat at the forefront of their minds.

"She'll never take me from you, Vega. Do you hear me? I am yours from now until my last breath." Bridger rested his forehead against hers.

Vega reached up, cupping his cheek in her palm. "Don't make promises you can't keep." Her thumb brushed over the stubble forming on his face.

"She'll have to destroy me before I give up on you. On us."

Bridger removed what little space was left between them, their lips meeting with such intensity the fire roared in response, reacting to the heat in the room. Bridger's hand tangled in Vega's dark hair. It fell down her back in loose, wild curls—worn from the fighting, from the running.

She opened her mouth as he slid his tongue over her bottom lip.

Bridger was going to devour her.

His other arm snaked around as he picked her up with the ease of lifting a feather.

A tiny gasp escaped her lips, the sound muffled against Bridger's. Vega wrapped her legs around his body for stability, her back resting against the warm stone wall of the cottage as Bridger's hand detangled from her hair.

Bridger pulled his lips from hers only to place them on new parts of her body—kissing down her jawline to her neck, where he nibbled softly enough to elicit goosebumps on her soft skin.

Vega wiggled under his lips, arching into him with a soft gasp. "You better shield this room from sound if you don't want the others to hear the noises I'm about to make." Her voice was breathless, full of lust.

Bridger laughed, the sound deep and husky. "Way ahead of you, Kitten." He didn't take his mouth off her body, his lips continuing to explore the soft skin around the spot on her neck that he loved so much.

Her head lay back against the wall, giving in to Bridger entirely as he continued to move his way down to the collarbone peeking through her tank top. Vega arched forward, yanking her shirt off with one swift movement, tossing it haphazardly to the floor.

Bridger's length bulged, pressing into the apex of her legs. He thrust his hips, giving her the friction she craved.

"Oh gods," she sang, the need inside her building with the darkening of her gaze.

Neither spoke it out loud—they didn't have to. This might be the last time they ever had a moment like this together. Their fear, want, need, hope, and despair melted altogether.

Vega worked Bridger out of his shirt, her hands running down his toned chest.

His lips only left her body long enough to slide his shirt the rest of the way off. Bridger met her lips when his shirt hit the floor, the kiss deepening with desperation he'd never felt before.

Their tongues fought for dominance as Bridger slid his hand into the front of Vega's skintight pants. His thumb found her clit, rubbing tight circles while he slipped two fingers inside.

Her nails dug into his back hard enough to break the skin, tight walls constricting around his fingers as soon as he pressed into the spot that would make her lose control in *three, two, one...*

"Bridger, I'm gonna..." Vega's breath hitched, her eyes fluttering with the promise of release.

"That's it. Eyes on me while you come undone for me, baby." Bridger pressed a quick kiss on her whimpering lips. She was right there. *So close.*

His hand started to travel to the clasp on Vega's bra, but it never made it there.

"I hate to break up this moment, but I'm going to need to talk to Bridger."

His shield hadn't only kept those on the outside from hearing them, but it'd distracted him from paying attention to what was going on outside it too.

Vega gasped, her eyes jolting open with panic. Gods, she'd been right there—so close Bridger could almost taste her pleasure on his fingertips... and he would have if it weren't for the intrusion.

Vega slid down the wall, feet meeting the floor as Bridger turned at the familiar voice. His dark gaze landed on the golden eyes of his best friend. "Meyer." Bridger would have sighed in relief if it weren't for the flames dancing in Meyer's free hand, the other wrapped in Arlet's hair to hold her in place next to him.

"Let her go!" Vega lunged forward, wasting no time with crackles of lightning sputtering to life in her palms. Meyer used Arlet as a shield, putting her between him and Vega.

"Call off your shirtless guard dog, B." His voice gave away the smile forming on his lips.

Bridger bent down, grabbing his black shirt off the floor to toss to Vega. "Let her go, Meyer." Bridger stepped forward, shifting closer to Vega in case she decided to lunge for Meyer's throat next. It wouldn't be the first time.

"I just came here to talk, and this little bitch"—he spat the word —"stabbed me."

Bridger finally noticed the blood on his shirt, right under his ribcage. The wound was almost completely healed already.

Pride swelled in Bridger's chest at the idea of Arlet using the skills he'd been slowly training her in over the last few years.

"And I'd do it again for what you did to Khort," Arlet yelped, twisting in his grasp. Her hands were around Meyer's wrist, trying to pry his grip off.

"Oh, relax, I only knocked him out. He'll be back up and ready to choke me out again in no time." Meyer tightened his grip on her hair.

Vega moved before Bridger had the time to react, making his move closer to her completely useless when it mattered. Bridger didn't reach for Vega first; Meyer could hold his own for a bit. Bridger helped steady Arlet, who'd been dropped like a ragdoll in Meyer's attempt to get ahead of Vega.

A bolt of Vega's ice-blue lightning shot across the room and burned an already ragged curtain to ash. Meyer ducked with less than a second to spare.

"Go check on Khort. I've got these two," Bridger told Arlet after assuring she was unharmed. He turned to the scuffling fools in the living area, the room rising to an uncomfortable degree from the swell of Meyer's ability. "Meyer, you better apologize, or she's going to kill you." Bridger crossed his arms over his bare chest lazily.

The two had never seen eye to eye, differing on too many topics to keep track of, but recently, it felt like Vega and Meyer might be turning over a new leaf—that had gone to shit quickly.

"I don't want an apology. I want to stab him too." Vega had turned into a vengeful little thing over the last thirty hours. Bridger smiled, watching her in awe.

"Bring it on." Meyer didn't know when to stop sometimes.

Vega ducked to the floor, her leg sweeping out in front of her with a spin, knocking Meyer onto his back. Vega stood over him, her control of storms cracking a thunderous rumble through the cabin, mixing with Meyer's blaze. Their powers made the room feel like a summer day before a thunderstorm.

"Okay, Kitten. I think you've proven your point." Bridger moved forward, standing behind her, his hand hovering over her shoulder. He didn't dare touch her while her lightning prickled over her skin— she was a live wire.

Vega looked back at Bridger. "You heard what he said he did to Khort, and he called Arlet a bitch." She talked through gritted teeth.

Meyer sat up, rubbing the back of his head where it had knocked against the wooden floors. "That's because she is."

"You're pushing your luck," Bridger said, holding his hand out to help his friend up. Vega's death glare had yet to fade. "You better get to talking before she fries you, or worse, stabs you and leaves you to bleed out this time."

Vega sported a promising smile.

"I'm not going to be the only one gutted if you don't cut this shit out, Bridger." Meyer kept his eyes on Vega, only shooting his attention to Bridger once her sparks of lightning fizzled out.

Khort and Arlet started stirring in the bedroom, and Vega gave in —for now. "You better hope he's okay, or I'll feed your corpse to the wolves." Her eyes flicked to Bridger, who nodded for her to give him and Meyer a minute alone.

"What do you mean?" Bridger asked, still standing with his arms crossed.

"You know where you belong during a war, and it's not with them," Meyer scolded.

Bridger's eyebrows rose, jaw dropping slightly. "You can't be serious."

"We've been training for this our entire lives. We knew something like this would happen. We knew the role we would play."

"This is not what we were training for. Not for the slaughter of good people," Bridger scoffed.

Meyer blew a laugh from his nose. "You think becoming your father's replacement would come without bloodshed? You think he'd give up his position, step down, to what? To live out the rest of his life in peace? Come on, Bridger. You know he wanted more power. Don't tell me you didn't see this coming."

"Not like this." Bridger's response sagged out of his chest, remorse rising.

A crash echoed through the cabin, glass shattering in the back bedroom. Bridger spun around in time to see Arlet standing in the bedroom doorway, her eyes wide, face painted in horror. "Run!"

The front door blew open seconds after Arlet's warning,

splintering wood soaring through the room. Meyer dodged a shard before it could pierce through his eye.

"And how would you have preferred I handle this situation, son?" With his sword drawn, Lucius Dimico strode into the cabin with his blond hair full of ash from the burning capital.

"Father," Bridger said with a deep breath.

Bridger awoke with a pounding headache, his vision blurry from the pain and his skin tingling from the memory of Vega's body against his. He sat up in bed, rubbing at the ache between his temples. "When will this end?" he asked himself.

He'd been searching for Vega and the rebels for almost an entire week. Bridger took his troop of soldiers to Imber multiple times, sniffing around the ruined territory for any signs of life. They found nothing, and neither did anyone else who Bridger tasked with finding Vega.

Marlena was eerily quiet during his search, staying out of his way like she knew it was best to leave him alone.

Vega's touch wasn't the only thing that stuck with him when he woke. Seeing the ghost of his father was also the reason Bridger couldn't allow himself to fall back asleep tonight—he knew what dream was up next, and he wasn't sure he could stand to relive it.

Bridger groaned in frustration at the exhaustion setting in, throwing himself back against his mattress with a thud. The brand on his wrist itched, and no amount of scratching would sate it. Bridger snagged one of the extra pillows from his bed, pulled it to his face, and screamed. He had a sound shield around the perimeter of his room, but this felt better.

He longed for the days he slept through the night, waking before his alarm, well-rested and ready to take on whatever challenge the day threw his way.

A beep from the comm-device on his bedside table caught his attention. Bridger rolled to his side, peeking from under the pillow to bring the small device to his face. A message rolled across the dull screen:

Commander, we've received word back from Halo Apsens. He will be here tomorrow morning to meet with you.

Bridger breathed a sigh of relief. "Finally."

He dropped the handheld back on his nightstand and rolled onto his back. Bridger hadn't heard from Halo since returning from Earth, assuming he was lying low after getting caught by Arlet at the portal.

Tomorrow, he could finally end this hunt and work on returning to his normal life, focusing on rebuilding his shields and ridding himself of the memories he didn't want to remember.

If he couldn't rebuild his shields, Bridger knew the dreams would be his downfall—Vega would be his downfall, like she always had been.

The memories of her, the love he'd once had, would end him... but Bridger wasn't going down without a fight.

OVER THE LAST WEEK, VEGA SLEPT BETTER THAN SHE HAD IN years, but she wasn't sure if it was the training or the fact she somehow felt safe—even though she was in more danger here than she'd ever been in any life on Earth.

They would be leaving to meet with a witch in Fraus tomorrow morning. Vega was hours from getting her memories back.

Her room was small, similar to all of the bedrooms in Castra. There was barely anything of importance in it, which led Vega to ask why she had nothing from her original life—or any others for that matter.

It was Marlena's ultimate goal to make sure Vega had nothing, even if that meant she took the pictures her sister tried to hold on to.

The small bed creaked as she tossed and turned. Tonight, sleep eluded her. The anticipation of what was to come kept her brain from slipping into the deep slumber she'd been spoiled with lately.

Vega huffed, giving up. Her memories would just have to excuse the sleepless brain they were re-entering.

The brand on her wrist itched, an inkling of pain slipping

through here and there, like one of the other three was trying to scratch the damn thing off. She knew the others could feel it too.

Vega opened her small closet and let her fingers dance over the clothing hanging inside. There was an extra training uniform, the flannel she'd worn on her trek back from Earth, and a few other odds and ends that didn't strike a memory. These pieces were all she had from her lives over the years—outfits she was sure had meaning, big or small.

Vega gripped a dress, velvety black with a dramatic slit up the leg. She pulled it out of the closet and held it up, taking in the low-cut V down the chest. She'd never owned anything so beautiful.

She had to try it on.

Quickly, she stripped out of her sleepwear, and it pooled under her feet as she stepped into the gown. The sleeves were long, cutting just along the wrist. Parts of the fabric were singed with lightning-like marks.

Vega lightly traced the outline of the streaks, feeling the roughness under her fingertips. The mirror in her room allowed for a full view of the dress. She gaped at the reflection staring back.

The fabric was slightly baggy on her, her body not filling it out like it might have once. Over the last year, she'd been fighting demons she hadn't even let her husband see.

A wave of sadness washed over her.

Chase.

Shouldn't she still be grieving over that loss? Grieving the life she'd once loved? *That wasn't your real life.*

Vega had no idea what to feel anymore, not when her life took a turn she couldn't have made up in her wildest dreams. She wrapped her arms around herself, meeting her gaze in the mirror at the same time someone tapped on the metal door to her bedroom. It rattled, a familiar voice coming from the other side.

"Vega." Khort had been avoiding her, going as far as to have

Arlet take over her training the last few days—excusing himself while he handled an issue in another territory.

An issue no one seemed to want to tell her about.

"Shit," Vega muttered to herself. "One sec!" Vega spun in circles, gathering her pajamas on the floor and holding them against her chest. She bumped her hip against the bed frame and dropped the clothes with a hiss of pain. *Fuck, that's gonna bruise.* She bit her lip to keep from cursing out loud.

"Is everything okay?"

Vega didn't answer, continuing to spin in circles like a dog chasing its tail. The handle turned, and it was too late to hide.

"Ve—" Khort's eyes landed on her.

Her cheeks burned red, embarrassment canceling out the feeling of sadness consuming her moments earlier. "I couldn't sleep," she admitted. Vega watched as his eyes roamed over her body, wishing she could disappear forever.

"I remember the night you wore that like it was yesterday." Khort stepped into the room and closed the door behind him. His Adam's apple bobbed as he swallowed, his hands behind his back. "I, uh—I..." He paused, and Vega wasn't sure she'd ever seen him so flustered. Khort cleared his throat. "I had a little itch that you weren't able to sleep."

Khort brought his hands from behind his back, holding up a couple crystal glasses and a bottle of deep red wine with no label. "Your favorite wine from Solum."

Vega forgot all about the dress and smiled, grabbing the bottle from him. The dress rustled as she walked. She couldn't remember the taste, but any wine was better than none on a night like tonight when her friend insomnia came back to visit. "Come to Mama," she cooed, rummaging through drawers for a bottle opener.

Khort cleared his throat. "Vega." She paused, turning to look at him. "Come here." He nodded his way.

She closed the distance between them. Vega held out the bottle, but he shook his head and placed his hands around hers on the neck. She met his gaze.

"This was always your favorite party trick." He glanced at their hands. "Focus on the air at the very top of the bottle."

Vega groaned. "No training! My brain hurts."

Khort chuckled. "It's easy, c'mon. Focus."

She huffed, closing her eyes. The air in the bottle was the same temperature as the air outside, and when Vega's mind wrapped around it, the pressure built. A breath whizzed through her teeth as she focused, and it only took seconds for the cork to shoot out with a pop. Vega jumped, almost dropping the wine.

Thankfully, Khort still had a hold over her hands. "There you go!" He picked up the glasses and poured them both a fair share.

Vega swirled the dark wine in the glass, taking a whiff once it settled. The notes of tobacco and black currant hit her like a sucker punch. Her mouth watered, and she was unable to hold off any longer from taking a sip. "Mmmm." She held the glass close. "Glad to know I've always had good taste."

Khort smiled, taking a seat in the plush chair in the corner. "Arlet and I crack a bottle of this every year on the anniversary of your first death." His radiant smile faded as he spoke.

Well, that's morbid. Vega wanted to tell him so until she realized what he was saying. "Today?" she asked, biting her lip.

Khort nodded in silence.

"Oh," Vega said, slinking to the bed. She sat on the edge, staring at the glass in her hand. "Fifty-five years?"

Khort nodded again, lips meeting his glass. He didn't need to look at Vega for her to see the sorrow etching the lines of his face.

She moved over to the chair with Khort, lowering herself onto the arm. "Cheers to fifty-five years." Vega held her glass out, waiting.

"That's morbid," Khort said, plucking the same thought from earlier out of her brain.

Vega took a sip, raising her brow playfully. "So is popping my favorite wine every year on my death-iversary."

"Touché." Khort's laugh was light, though his eyes showed a lingering sadness.

"You said you remember the night I wore this?" Vega gestured to the dress she wore. "What was it for?" She still asked questions, even though she'd get all her memories back soon.

Khort looked like he didn't want to answer, taking a long sip from his glass to stall. But whatever he saw on Vega's face made him sigh.

"You wore it the night your sister overthrew the Curia. The same night she'd been inducted and took over your mother's seat in Amora," Khort admitted while his eyes dragged from the bottom of the dress, lapping up her exposed leg draped over the chair's arm. His gaze made it to hers, and Vega did her best to hide the feeling boiling inside—his stare felt like a heater, scorching every inch of skin it touched.

Vega wasn't drunk enough to blame it on the wine yet. She licked her lips and shifted her focus back to the conversation, not Khort's wandering eyes. "Were you there?" she asked as he ran a hand through his shoulder-length hair. It was down today, freshly washed and still damp at the ends.

"Of course. The four of us were inseparable then." Khort showed zero emotion.

"So you two *were* friends?" Vega asked, pushing for more information. Everyone liked to dance around the topic of the man who broke her heart.

"Eventually. It took some time," Khort answered as he finished his first glass. When he moved to get up, Vega placed her hand on his chest.

"I'll get it." She popped up, the glass in her hand still half full. Vega's attention had been on Khort, not the wine. She topped hers anyway after filling his. "Why?" she pushed, putting the bottle down within reach before settling back into place on the arm of the chair.

Right now, hearing stories of her life felt like just that: a story. Something she didn't have to believe but chose to dive into anyway. Her memories were the stories that kept her moving across the country with Arlet, but anytime she'd asked about Khort, Arlet gave her the bare minimum.

It was time he got the chance to tell her what Arlet wouldn't.

Khort hesitated, choosing his words wisely. "I lived in a fantasy world before he came into the picture."

Vega rolled her eyes. "This is all a fantasy world to me right now." She chuckled, brushing her hand against his arm as she spoke. Khort stiffened but leaned into her touch. Vega watched his eyebrows twitch as his hand fluttered above her exposed thigh before finally settling down. His touch didn't feel odd or misplaced—it comforted her.

"Why do I feel like you're trying to tell me he got the girl?"

"Because he did," Khort answered quickly.

"Oh." Vega was joking, and Khort's response made this conversation a little more serious than she intended. "Khort, I-I don't —" Vega stammered.

"Stop. We don't have to get into this." He squeezed her thigh before returning his hand to his bubble.

Vega felt an emptiness in her chest with his hand gone. "You have to let me make my own decisions. I know you're trying to protect me. You have serious golden retriever energy."

Khort's eyebrows creased. "What's a golden retr—"

Vega interrupted him before he could finish. "Shit, forgot about the whole different world thing. A dog. You know what a dog is, right?"

"Yes, Vega... I know what a dog is." His badgered tone was enough to make Vega smile cheekily as an apology. "I just meant we don't need to get into this before you get your memories back. There's more to this than I have time for," Khort said.

More to this.

What did their shared past look like? Vega glanced at the dress, finally noticing the shorter sleeve on her left side. "I wore this when I summoned Remus, huh?" Vega changed the subject, willing to give Khort the space from this conversation he needed. *For now.*

"Yeah, it was in better condition when the night started. We danced all night under the moonlight. Your parents knew how to throw a party."

Vega offered him a smile as she asked, "Will you tell me about it?"

"It doesn't have a happy ending." His tone was laced with warning.

"That's okay. Sometimes the best stories don't end how we want them to."

Vega did her best to keep her expression soft, understanding. He nodded and drew in a breath before starting off the story.

Vega closed her eyes and leaned away from Khort, her back resting against the wall beside the chair. If she concentrated, Vega could pretend she was there—that she remembered.

The music from the band beat against Khort's chest, the current song loud and rowdy. Everything about tonight had started off slow. The Curia swearing in the next generation of leaders always dragged on for hours longer than it needed to.

As of tonight, Marlena had taken over her mother's position as the seat of Amora, and in a few years, she would take over her father's too, becoming the first in Tolevarre's history to rule over two territories. Her mother stepped down early, allowing Marlena a jump start while Ryanna enjoyed an early retirement.

"And to hopefully plan a wedding!" She'd beamed, eyes on Vega and Bridger during her farewell speech. Ryanna had finally accepted Vega and Bridger were in it for the long haul. Her father had yet to come around.

Khort twirled Vega in a circle, her black velvet dress rustling against his leg. Her smile lit up the whole room while she laughed the happiest sound Khort had ever heard. Vega moved along to the beat perfectly, backing into Arlet, who danced with Bridger. The girls turned to each other, singing along to the song without missing a word.

They took breaks from the dance floor every so often to grab glasses of wine from around the realm—Vega always choosing the red from Solum. Her lips were stained, giving her succulent pout an unmistakable lift.

Vega leaned against the bar, her dress sparkling under the moonlight. "Have you seen Marlena?" She cuddled into Bridger's side, her arm wrapped around his hip as she leaned in to hear Khort's and Arlet's no's.

Vega pouted. Not having Marlena celebrating with them was bumming Vega out whenever she stopped dancing long enough to think about it. She would have to learn to accept the fact Marlena wouldn't be able to be around as much—it had been a hard transition for her since her sister began to pull away over the last year.

"I'm sure she's being hounded, getting all the attention she loves," Arlet answered, reaching out to tap Vega's hand comfortingly.

"Sure," Vega said as Bridger kissed the top of her head.

"C'mon, baby. Smile. She'll find us as soon as she can," Bridger told Vega, his fingers tilting her chin to catch her gaze.

The sisters were always close, more like best friends than siblings, but as Marlena was exposed to more responsibility, it took a toll on their friendship. And everyone around them could sense it.

Khort looked away just before their lips touched. When he turned his head, a certain redhead caught his eyes, her pale skin reflecting the moonlight while her red lips spread over her face in a smile laced with lust.

Ivelle Fugere. The Caelums' cousin. Easily one of the most beautiful women in Tolevarre.

"Excuse me. I'll be right back." Khort's lips twitched in a smile, crossing the dance floor to her. Bridger and Arlet led in the hooting and hollering as he beelined for the woman who'd become his distraction while Vega fell deeper in love with someone else.

Before he reached her, a scream pierced through the room, echoing against the courtyard—the sound got lost in the mountains. Khort jumped on defense, his eyes turning to slits as his dragon form prepared to launch into the sky. His eyes shot over to Vega and Arlet. Vega's lightning sparked, dancing between her hands. Arlet stood behind Bridger, who was somehow already armed with two daggers.

Everyone in the room froze, new screams traveling through the air as their eyes landed on the spectacle on the balcony above.

Blood was splattered across Marlena's face, and she held her mother's head by the hair.

Just her head.

Vega's lightning fizzed out as her knees buckled. She crashed to the ground, her jaw distended as far as it would go. Not a peep escaped, the disbelief choking her to silence. Vega's eyes brimmed with tears.

Marlena's stare was fixed on Vega, her index finger sliding across her throat as her lips ticked up in a wicked smile.

The room broke into complete madness. A woman barreled past Khort, knocking into his shoulder with enough force to snap him out of his trance.

He locked eyes with Bridger from across the room, and with the nod of their heads, they dove into action.

When Khort finished his retelling, the bottle of wine was finished, and their glasses were almost empty.

"So. Ivelle?" Vega asked, wiggling her eyebrows as an attempt to deflect from the pain on Khort's face.

"She was behind it all with Marlena."

"Of course she was. Let me guess... there was a promise of power in it for her?"

Khort nodded and then finished his glass. "Listen, I came here to apologize for how I acted at our last training session. I shouldn't have pushed you like that. I'm just tired of losing you."

Vega held the last sip of wine in the glass, the rim resting against her bottom lip. Her mind was lost in the story, imagining the shock of seeing her mother's head hanging over the people of her land.

"I'm sure I'm sick of leaving," she finally replied, meeting his eyes again. "I want to experience something for the first time tonight before I get my memories back."

Khort hesitated. "What?"

Vega laughed, shaking her head. "Get your head outta the gutter, Fera!" She popped him on the shoulder, giving him a playful shove. "I want to see you shift."

Khort's eyebrow rose. "Why?" His hand was back on her leg, empty glass in the other.

"I want to feel the wonder of this world one last time. When I get my memories back, it won't be new to me anymore. This brain cannot comprehend a man turning into a dragon. I bet it's exhilarating."

Khort removed his hand from her leg to push himself up. "There's nowhere for me to show you down here. I'm a little too big for any of the rooms we have here in Castra." He was trying to dismiss her request.

Vega shot up, her butt numb from sitting in an uncomfortable position. "Then let's go up. I could use some fresh air tonight." Her face was warm from the wine.

He shook his head, putting the glass down on the table by Vega's door. "It's not safe. Bridger and his soldiers have been sniffing around Imber lately, no doubt looking for you."

"Fuck him. I'll fry him to a crisp. Please, Khort." Vega batted her eyelashes, giving him her best set of puppy dog eyes. "I want one more piece of excitement in this life before it all gets serious."

He ran a large hand over his handsome face. "Fine, but if Arlet finds out, I'm blaming you."

Vega squealed, jumping once, trying to keep quiet so she didn't wake the mother and son who lived next door.

"I'm only agreeing because my wings could use a good stretch."

23

On their way up, the elevator screeched with rusted gears. The nerves from her most recent elevator ordeal caused a tightening in her chest, her breaths shallow, and not even the wine could wash the memory away.

The elevator shook, and without thinking, Vega hit the button that read Kitchen.

"Detour," she commented as she stepped through the opening door.

Khort followed with quiet footsteps.

Vega searched through cabinets. "I know you know what I'm looking for. It might be easier if you tell me where it's kept."

Khort's warm laugh heated the air, impelling Vega to adjust her attention to him hoisting himself onto the counter. His strong legs dangled off the counter, boot heels bouncing against the wood with a hollow thud. "Sometimes you have to ask for help."

Vega scrunched her nose. "No thanks." She continued to rummage on her own.

"Four cabinets to the left, top shelf."

Vega didn't move, staring at the shelf he was talking about. "Are you fucking serious?"

"Gotta keep it away from the kids." Vega could hear the smile on his lips without looking back.

"Some of the kids here can fly. Do you think this is stopping them?" Vega swiveled to find Khort hopping off the counter with a playful smile on his face.

"Don't go giving them ideas." Khort's eyes crinkled in suspicion. She could almost see the memories welling behind them.

"Don't give me that look. I bet you weren't innocent either." Vega caught the way his shirt rose as he reached for the top shelf effortlessly. When he only brought one down, her eyes turned to slits.

That look was all Khort needed to burst into a cackle. "Vega! One, you need to slow down on the drinking thing. Arlet told me about your drinking habits on Earth." He closed the cabinet, turning to face her. "And two, we have a pretty important day tomorrow. I'm not letting you wake up with any regrets."

She groaned, rolling her eyes. "One," she emphasized by holding her finger up, "my drinking habits were almost nonexistent until walking in on my husband with his face between another woman's legs." Vega held up a second finger. "And two, let me remind you I have had the craziest two weeks of my entire fucking life... lives...?" She paused, wondering how to continue. "Whatever! I deserve to have a fun last night of ignorant bliss." Vega stared him down.

"I didn't know about the husband thing. I'm sorry. We wo—" He paused, placing the bottle on the counter nearby.

"Worry about me, I know. I know. It's just the more I think about all this, the more I realize this isn't the first time I've felt this way, and I can't imagine what it's going to feel like to remember all of it. I've been warned, but that doesn't prepare me." She was rambling, finally letting her inner thoughts out. "Does it hurt?" she asked. This was the question she'd been fearing the most.

"You handle it well." Khort skirted by the truth. Vega knew without a doubt whatever was happening tomorrow would be unlike anything she'd ever felt... or that she could remember.

Vega began to sink into worry, her arms wrapping around her torso as she imagined herself inside the stories she'd heard.

"Come on." Khort grabbed her by the hand and tugged her towards the elevator.

"Can we take the stairs?" She shivered at the thought of getting back into that creaky contraption.

"This is faster. You're not spending your last night sulking about tomorrow's worries or fretting about an elevator I've only been stuck in once." With his free hand, Khort pressed the button for the top floor.

"What do you mean, only been stuck in once, Khort?!" Vega hadn't been outside her new underwater home since arriving, but now all she could picture was dying inside the elevator.

"Relax, please." Khort threw his arm around Vega's shoulders and pulled her into his side.

"I can't relax. My whole life is a mystery," she said through gritted teeth. The awaiting scent of salty air was enough to snag her out of her funk and force her to block out the squawking of the machine box she was ascending in.

The smell hit her before the shrieking stopped. Vega filled her lungs with the briny air, exhaling with a heavy huff. "How do you stay down here for so long?" she asked as the elevator slowed.

"I don't think about it much anymore."

The door slid painfully slow, opening to a round staircase. Vega quickly removed herself from the death trap and looked up, leaning against the beginning of the handrail.

"This is the exit?" Vega asked, looking up, dizzying herself at the height.

Khort started up the stairs and didn't turn while he answered. "One of them. We wouldn't limit ourselves to a single exit."

Vega followed, his long legs taking two stairs at a time. She was nearly wheezing by the time they got to the top. "I should've exercised more in this life." A hatch loomed above her head. Vega caught her breath, annoyed that Khort didn't look fazed by the climb at all.

"We'll keep training."

Vega held up her middle finger while she gasped for breath. "Open. I need air."

Khort climbed the small ladder and turned the wheel on the ceiling. It clicked as gears she couldn't see unlocked. He gave the hatch a strong shove, and it heaved open, sucking in fresh air with a howl. Vega followed him up the rungs into the deep night sky.

Khort emerged first, holding the door open. When she cleared the opening, she gasped at the landscape surrounding them. A crumbled building wrapped around the entrance they had appeared through, but beyond that, the land was a complete waste—like a bomb went off and destroyed everything in its wake. Khort closed the hatch, and in the exact moment the door became flush with the entrance, it disappeared.

Vega's jaw dropped. "Where did it go?"

Khort handed her the bottle. "Open."

This time Vega didn't have to focus as hard to get the air to push the cork out. The pop didn't startle her either. She took a long swig right from the bottle.

"You can thank Arlet for that." Khort kept his eyes on Vega as she marveled at the door no longer there. The walls around them were destroyed, stone sitting on its side, the night sky twinkling overhead with no light pollution.

"She's actively concealing this all the time?" Vega asked.

"We've been lucky enough to have some people from Littera help out. They've built a few machines that mimic her ability and help keep us hidden. When we first built Castra, though a lot smaller back then, it was all her. It was just impossible for her to go to Earth and keep a hold on her powers here," Khort admitted.

This rebellion sacrifices too much for me... "She's fucking incredible," Vega said instead.

"That she is," Khort agreed.

Vega hadn't changed out of the dress, kicking herself now that they were crawling through rubble to get to the open land outside of the abandoned stone home. "You could've warned me I'd be trudging through an old war zone," Vega mumbled.

Castra was nestled deep under the sea, but this hidden exit tunneled through the core of the crumbled remains of what was once Imber.

Now, there was nothing left of the buildings or their people. All that lay present to the eye was a ruined territory destroyed for standing against Marlena.

Khort laughed gently, standing in the clearing as Vega slid down the last pile of rubble to her feet. "You've done worse in a dress. Stop complaining." He looked up at the night sky as the wind blew tendrils of his blond hair around his face.

Vega groaned, pulling the skirt of her dress up above her knees to avoid the mud. The land around them reminded her of pictures she'd seen of Ireland with jagged cliffs and homes that might have once resembled castles. "Not this body."

Khort reached out and grabbed the bottle of wine, then took his own sip. "Don't be so hard on yourself. You've been through a lot."

The reminder sat heavy on her chest. "I've had enough time to figure it out. You said so yourself. I don't need to be babied. It's time to shit or get off the pot."

The serious air hanging over them shattered as Khort's laugh bellowed from deep inside his chest. The wine in his mouth sprayed onto Vega, covering her hands, chest, and exposed leg. "Oh my gods," he said between laughs. "I'm so sorry." He wiped his mouth on his arm before reaching out for Vega.

Her mouth was open wide, a smile still pulling at her lips as she began to laugh freely like Khort was.

This might be the last time I get a laugh like this.

"Khort!" she whined, drawing out his name while shaking her leg to clean off the red wine sprinkling her skin.

"Shit or get off the pot?" He still laughed, holding her by the arms as they both continued to cackle like a couple drunk friends at the bar. "Do people *really* say that on Earth? That's awful."

Vega nodded as he pulled away from her, wiping at the stubble on his face. "The convenience store owner down the street from my place loved using it when his customers were taking too long. He was a delight." It felt odd reminiscing about Gregor, a man who used to seem so evil before she knew what evil actually looked like.

"I hate that one," Khort replied. The smile on his face gave Vega butterflies. She looked away, using the dress as a napkin to wipe the rest of the wine from her body.

"There's plenty more where that came from," she promised, wiggling her eyebrows.

"Great." He chuckled, rolling his eyes snarkily.

Vega snatched the wine from him and stepped back, leaning against the rubble she'd just climbed. She pointed to the open landscape. "Show me what you've got, dragon boy."

"Pushy," he said, beginning to unbutton his white shirt. "And it's dragon *man* to you."

Vega's eyes wandered to his chest as he stripped. His muscles rippled with his movements, and Vega couldn't keep her eyes off the pulsing veins running down his forearms.

Khort caught her watching him. "This isn't shifting material." The shirt fluttered to the ground. She cleared her throat, her gaze dropping low before it shot to meet his. His lips spread in a smug smile.

"And the pants?" Her mouth went dry.

Get it together, Vega.

Khort stretched his arms over his head, swinging them in a couple big circles. "Those *are* shifting material, but I can take them off if you want." His fingers hovered over the button.

Vega's cheeks burned, and she hoped she was far enough away he couldn't see the way they flushed. "What would old Vega say about that?" Her eyes settled on his with heavy focus as she forced herself to push any thoughts away that would get her in trouble.

I'm just drunk. That's all. No big deal.

"She would've hit me," he said with a goofy grin.

"Good to know. Better keep those on then." She held up her fist and wiggled it as a warning.

"Terrifying," he cooed.

"Enough stalling. Show me what you've got."

"You run your mouth a lot for someone about to be in the presence of a dragon." And before Vega could respond with some new sarcastic comeback, black wings shot from his back, and the rest of his body followed suit.

He morphed so quickly, Vega didn't have time to see his bones shift as they grew to new lengths and sizes. The sound of whooshing wings masked the sound of cracking bones.

Vega's hand gripped the bottle, the other digging into the stone behind her as Khort's new face landed inches from hers. She took a gulp of air, catching her breath in a lump.

Standing before her was no longer the handsome blond without a shirt. Replacing him was a black dragon, scales twinkling iridescent green like the color of his eyes. Vega didn't budge, waiting for Khort to make the first move.

He turned his head for her to see directly into one of his eyes. Vega filled her lungs with air, propping the bottle against the dismantled wall, and took a few steps closer to Khort—*to a fucking dragon.*

"Holy shit." She breathed, reaching her hand out to run across his scales. They didn't feel as snake-like as Vega imagined. They were rough, pointed, and sharp in areas if she pushed with too much pressure. He huffed, smoke puffing through his nostrils. "Can you hear me in there?" she asked. He nodded his large head up, then down smoothly. Khort's legs were folded underneath him, keeping himself low to the ground, but Vega didn't even reach his shoulder.

The fairy tales she'd grown up reading and watching spoke of a dragon's size, but never had she imagined she'd stand next to one. She began to walk around him, his head moving in a serpentine motion as he followed her movements.

Khort stood with his claws digging into the ground beneath him. He stretched his wings from behind his back and took off into the sky. The wind off his wings sent Vega's hair flying behind her, and she gasped, watching him soar. The way his large figure moved so effortlessly took her breath away. She could see his inhale before fire poured from his mouth and lit up the night. Vega couldn't take her eyes off him catching wind and disappearing behind a small patch of clouds.

It could have been minutes or hours. Vega lost track of time as she stared up at Khort in wonder. She didn't move until his back legs touched the ground and his wings tucked against his sides. The beast stalked up to Vega, nose to nose with her again.

She reached her hand out, and as her palm landed on Khort's scales, he shifted back before her eyes. The wings seemed to retract into his back as the rest of his body shifted like a breath of air. The only bit of dragon left was the smoke exiting his nostrils as they shaped back into his button nose, and Khort returned to the man he was before.

Her hand rested on his cheek, a gleam of awe still fluttering behind her eyes. "Thank you," she whispered, worried she might ruin the moment by speaking too loudly.

Khort smiled, reaching up to place his hand over hers. "You'll come to find that I would do just about anything for you," he said, his voice matching her volume. He pulled her hand to his lips, nuzzling a kiss into her palm—his lips were still warm from his fire. Khort turned her hand around, placing a lingering kiss over the brand they shared. "Let's get you to bed." Khort went to move, but Vega grabbed his bicep as he tried to walk by.

"Can we stay out here a little longer? Please. I'm not ready to go back under," Vega admitted. The people of Castra might be used to the claustrophobia of their home, but Vega wasn't. The night air filled her lungs like a drug, begging her to stay.

"Sure." Khort turned towards her. "But we can't stay long. You're the most wanted woman in Tolevarre."

"When did you shift for the first time?" Vega asked, distracting herself from the thoughts of his bare chest before he slipped back into his shirt. *It's the wine.*

"I was thirteen," Khort answered.

Vega sat in the lush grass, leaning on her elbows to look up at the stars as Khort sat down beside her. She was buzzing from the wine and adrenaline.

"You were there," Khort said, his smile reminiscent of the memory.

Vega glanced over at him, taking in the way the moonlight seemed to glow off his skin. He finished the wine, tossing the empty bottle to the side to retrieve later. She waited for him to continue.

"My sister had been shifting for a year. She was seven years younger than me, and I was so scared that her getting the dragon gene meant I wouldn't."

Was.

Everyone had lost someone they loved.

"I was so mad she beat me to it, that a six-year-old, which is very young to shift for the first time, by the way, was learning to perfect her ability while I sat around hoping to fly one day too." His gaze was straightforward as he continued to recall the memory. "Dad was a phoenix shifter. Mom came from the dragons. There wasn't a lot of either left, and it wasn't guaranteed I would get either of their forms. It happens sometimes—a kid won't get their parents' powers. I wasn't showing any signs, and Mom and Dad were starting to whisper that maybe I wouldn't be the powerful one. That maybe Delori would take my parents' seat instead."

As he spoke, Vega could see the anger he tried to hide.

"And whatever, it wasn't the power I was after. I think I just wanted to be the strong older brother, ya know? To be able to protect Delori from the ugly in our world. Being weak back then, hell, even now, isn't something that plays out well." Khort glanced at Vega before continuing. She reached out and laid her hand over his to urge him on. "You and I were playing in the woods behind my home. It happened so fast. I complained of a burning in my gut for a couple days, which was brushed off as indigestion." He snickered. "I almost burned the forest in my backyard down when I shifted. It's not a pleasant feeling the first time, so as soon as it began, I screamed... and what came out of my mouth? Fire." He shook his head, meeting her eyes. "You clapped the entire time, only excited that I finally came into my form. You didn't shut up about it for weeks."

Vega laughed. "Baby Vega, your biggest fan."

They sat outside for longer than they should have, enjoying the night air and each other's company. The silence wasn't awkward— Vega welcomed the leaves rustling in the distance and the sound of the water crashing against the cliffs.

The back of Vega's head rested in her linked hands, face turned towards the moon, eyes closed like she was soaking in the beams.

"Vega?"

"Hmm?" she hummed, opening her eyes and turning her head to face Khort, his eyes waiting for hers already.

"I want you to know, even before you get your memories back, that I love you. I don't think that's ever been much of a secret." He wet his lips, and Vega's eyes focused on the movement. "You're my best friend and the girl that got away, yes, but that doesn't change anything for me. I will fight with you, for you... always."

The words didn't startle her, only made her sad she couldn't return those sentiments—at least not right now. "Have you tried fighting for yourself yet?" Her question came out before her brain could process it, catching her by surprise.

"Fighting for you is fighting for me. You're the key to the end of this," Khort said.

Vega frowned. "That's a lot of pressure to put on one person." Her voice was quiet as she took in the magnitude of what he'd said. Khort didn't say anything in return, just turned his head to look back up at the sky. Vega sat up, staring at her hands. "What if I can't stop her? What if all this is for nothing and Marlena wins anyway?" The what-ifs could be never-ending.

"Then we all die." Khort's answer was curt.

Vega swallowed the lump in her throat. "Did you have to say it like that?" she asked. The laugh slipping through her lips was dry, nerves jumping to the surface.

"There's no sense in hiding the truth from you, Vega. If we lose, we die. That's it." Khort sat up too, resting his arms on his knees. "It might be the easy way out, but you've never been a quitter. Well, in a couple lives you were, but that wasn't your fault. That was what those lives had dealt you. This Vega..." He reached out and put his hand on her chest, over her heart. "This one isn't a quitter."

"Okay, so you're not the sugar coater... Noted." She gave a single nod but smiled faintly at what his words meant.

This Vega can do hard things. She has done hard things. *I will not let these people down—they've given too much for me.*

"I used to be, but a lot has happened since then." Khort stood up and held his hand out. Vega took it, letting him help her off the dewy grass.

"What happened to Delori?" Vega asked as they climbed back over the rubble.

Khort paused for the briefest of seconds, reaching down to open the hatch to Castra even though it wasn't visible to the naked eye. "She got stuck in Demuto by a curse Marlena put on the territory for siding with the rebels. Del had gone back to get people out, but it was too late. The curse on Demuto locked the shifters inside the borders, and eventually, without contact to the outside world, they started going mad, losing themselves inside their beast and animal forms. After a while, Delori was one of them, and it must have become too much for her because she took her own life."

He let Vega climb down first—she was careful not to lose her footing on the metal ladder. Khort shut the hatch and locked it with a loud scrape against metal.

"I'm sorry I asked," Vega whispered, horror nipping at the edges of her emotions. How many more had to die because Marlena wanted revenge?

Khort reached out and brushed Vega's cheek. "It's okay." His lips dipped in a frown, and he dropped his hand to his side. "She loved you and Arlet. Always trying to weasel her way into whatever it was the three of us were doing so she could hang out with the two of you."

The halls back to her room were quiet, most people tucking themselves into bed hours ago when the main lights went out for the night. Vega had no idea what time it was, nor did time have much meaning to her these days.

Vega put her back to the door and smiled at Khort. Her voice was low when she spoke. "Thanks again."

"Next time, when there's no wine involved, I'll give you a ride. You used to love that when we were young."

Vega's cheeks grew pink as her mind went to a place it shouldn't. *Bad Vega!*

Khort's eyes grew wide. "Not like th—"

Vega laughed softly, reaching out to touch his forearm. "I know. I just..." She paused, biting her lip. "You were my type in this life, so

I'm trying to push that away and not ruin whatever it is you and I have."

"Blonds? No way." His smile was soft. "That's not very Vega-like."

She nodded. "Oh yeah, blonds." She wiggled playfully. "My husband... ex-husband..." She tripped over the words, because what was he now that she was an entire realm away? "Was a blond. He didn't look half as good as you with a man-bun though."

What are you doing?

Vega didn't have memories of what their relationship was like in her other lives, but she could tell he wasn't used to her seeing him in any other way than her friend.

"Noted" was all he said as Vega's hand fell off his arm. "Goodnight, Vega."

Vega's lips pursed together in a tight line. "Night, Khort."

He turned on his heels, and Vega knew she should go inside her room and go to bed... but she didn't.

"Khort." Her voice was barely a whisper, but he heard her. He spun around too quickly, locking eyes with her immediately. "Tell me I'm crazy and that you don't want to kiss me."

The wine. It had to be the wine or maybe she was still so lonely that the craving was overriding the little voice in the back of her head telling her to stop. She'd come all this way in hopes she would instantly feel at home, and while she felt welcomed, Vega still didn't feel whole yet.

Getting her memories back would help. They had to.

Vega knew he was going to lie by the inferno burning behind his eyes. "I don't want to kiss you," he muttered, half choking out the words.

Before she could stop herself, she closed the distance between them in seconds. Khort didn't move away, push her off, or tell her any more lies. As soon as her hands slid up to his shoulders and locked behind his neck, he hoisted her up with ease and their lips met for what Vega knew was the first time.

His hands grazed her body delicately, like if he moved too fast, she might come to her senses and stop. The kiss started slowly, allowing them both time to get to know each other's movements. Khort backed them up into Vega's door, one hand turning the handle to move them inside.

Smart. They didn't need prying eyes catching them in the middle of what surely would be a mistake. Vega was good at mistakes in this life—she racked them up like a punch card with a free coffee after ten stamps.

The door closed, and Vega opened her mouth, letting Khort's tongue slip inside and consume her. He tasted like a campfire—warm and smoky.

She was lost in the moment, completely unaware of the pull in her mind telling her to stop, over and over and over again. Wasn't it too late? If she stopped now, she couldn't take it back anyway. She missed the touch of another human, the way it felt to be wanted.

She wiggled her way out of his arms and slid down his body, never once allowing their lips to part. Her hunger for his touch only grew as a groan slipped through his lips and vibrated against hers. Vega could feel his want, his hunger matching her own. He took a large step back, sitting himself down on the squeaky bed. Vega climbed into his lap, straddling him. The long dress hiked up to her hips, cinching around her waist and exposing the sheer underwear she wore.

As Khort's hands slid up her thighs, she finally broke their kiss, throwing her head back. Her hair fell over her shoulder. She could feel his erection underneath, pressing into her center. Vega rolled her hips, grinding against him. That evoked another deep growl from Khort, sounding like the rumble of a dragon.

"Vega." Khort's voice was full of gravel, kissing her neck as his hand slid up the back of her head. He forced her face close to his.

"We can't." The words stopped her hips, her body begging for more friction.

She breathed heavily, letting his words settle in. "Why?" she asked, still lost in the moment.

"Because this means something more to me than it does to you."

Vega hauled herself off of his lap, all of the blood rushing to her head and causing her to go cold. The hem of her dress fell, pooling around her feet. "Fuck, Khort. I'm sorry. You're right." She ran a hand through her hair, pushing it away from her face while she looked at him, wide-eyed, from across the cramped room. "I'm so sorry. I don't know what I was thinking. I just wanted to feel something." She let her hair fall back into place. "I got lost in the night. I-I wasn't thinking."

"It's okay." He stood up, closing the distance as he grabbed her face in his hands. "Don't be sorry. I just know who you are when you're not lost in that pretty head of yours, and this isn't what you would want."

Vega nodded. "But it's what I want right now." Her icy gaze held him. "And just because I can't remember our past doesn't mean I haven't been thinking about kissing you all week."

Khort ran his hand over his face and started to pace the room. "Gods, Vega. I want to. Believe me, I've wanted this—us. Fuck. We can't do this. Not right now." He stopped pacing in front of the door, hand resting on the doorknob. "Get some sleep. I'll see you in the morning." He twisted the handle and slipped out, shutting the door behind him.

Vega stared after him, the small clock on her bedside table ticking on the second. The realization of what she'd just done churned her stomach. This time it wasn't the wine causing her to feel like she would upend the contents.

Vega slumped onto her bed, putting her head in her hands. "Fuck, Vega. Fuck, fuck, fuck." She cursed at herself, her chest tightening with an overwhelming sadness. Vega, in this life and every other, was a glutton for punishment. *God, if for once in your life you could just get it together!*

How long would it take for the people she loved here to give up on her too? It happened on Earth. Why wouldn't it begin to happen here?

So much for not letting me wake up with any regrets.

24

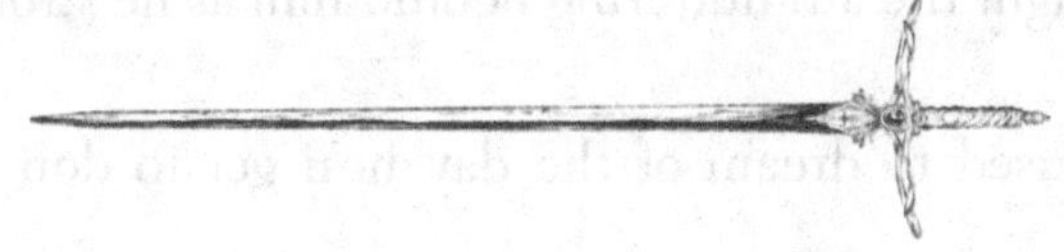

His hands were bloody again, this time from the hours he'd been banging on the door of the empty room that had become his cell. He and the others were knocked out and separated, making it impossible for Bridger to know where they were taken.

Bridger didn't need to see the outside of this room to know he was in Ardor—Meyer's homeland. The walls were made of orange clay with stucco textures; nowhere else in their realm would this adobe material be used.

Bridger paced, his dirty boots scuffing against the ceramic tile flooring. He scratched at the brand on his forearm that stifled his powers, begging the dead gods to give them back—to let him get to Vega.

Power benders from Fraus were a special kind of people, and the worst part of their power was their ability to stop others from using theirs. Bridger was in deep shit. They had made the brand on his forearm, which was outlawed for use outside the Curia's control. It turned him into nothing more than a powerless human.

A sound rattled from the other side of the door, causing Bridger to stand at attention in the middle of the room.

His broad shoulders rolled back, preparing for a physical fight if needed. When the door opened, his parents entered. His mother was clothed in a long black dress flowing to the floor around her feet. Her hair was sharp, the cut tight to the edge of her chin, not a strand out of place as usual.

His father wore a clean commander's uniform, completely black. His cape caught the air, fluttering behind him as he strolled into the lonely room.

Bridger used to dream of the day he'd get to don the suit his father wore.

"Where is she?" Bridger stormed toward them both, but his father held his hand up, his powers still intact. Bridger slammed into the wall of his shield, one he could usually bend to his will if his powers weren't being smothered.

"Knock it off, Bridger." His mother's voice sounded as if she'd run out of patience. "You need to snap out of this." She stood on the other side of the invisible wall Lucius had up, not a lick of concern for her son on her face. She was annoyed, even slightly bored, as she watched her only child pace the length of the shield, looking for a hole in his father's power.

He wouldn't find one.

Bridger was stronger than his father, but he wasn't as experienced, which would always be his fatal flaw.

"I swear to the gods, if you've hurt her, I will rip your throats out." Bridger's voice was a growl, his pacing more like that of a beast trapped in a cage than a young man talking to his parents. He stopped directly in front of them, close enough to reach out and grab them by the necks.

If only he could.

His father finally spoke up. "She's alive... for now." The smile lingering on his face shouldn't be there—not when talking about the woman his son loved. Bridger wanted to snap him in half for finding the idea of Vega's death humorous.

"You need to listen to us." His mother began to sneak into her doting mother tone she used when someone was listening. "A war is coming, and we need to prepare. We cannot present a divided front in this family."

Bridger spat at the feet of his parents. "We are not family."

His father sighed, stepping through his shield with the grace of a warrior only years of practice could earn.

Bridger didn't stand down. He stepped forward, ready to go toe-to-toe with the man who'd taught him everything he knew.

"I've had enough of this." With a swift kick, Lucius had his son on his knees, knocking his legs out from underneath him.

Bridger reacted quickly once on the cold floor, grabbing his father's leg with one arm and bringing him to the floor beside him. Bridger was able to wrangle himself on top of his father thanks to his unexpected retaliation.

He went to wrap his hands around his father's throat, but the man didn't let him get that close. Without anything more than the power inside him, Lucius flung his son across the room like a piece of paper. Bridger skidded across the floor, hitting the wall with a boom that stole the breath from his lungs. Gasping for air, Bridger popped up, hunched over and bleeding from the corner of his mouth when three guards grabbed him from behind.

"Take him to Marlena," Lucius barked. His men obeyed, dragging Bridger as he tried to fight them off. These men had trained beside him—had they known what was to come? Or were they just as blindsided as Bridger was and were now forced to follow along because of the oath they took to their realm?

He fought the whole way, not willing to make this easy on anyone. One of his father's men thrust him through a double door at the end of a long hallway.

Where was Meyer? Did he know what they were doing to Bridger?

Years of hostage training made Bridger focus on his location and where his most accessible escape might be—the easiest escape to slip away with Vega.

He cared about Arlet and Khort, but not in the way he loved Vega—they knew that. There was no hiding behind a facade with Bridger.

Inside the large meeting hall, Bridger searched the room for Vega first, then Arlet and Khort. He was alone except for the guards and his parents. It was him against five others and he was powerless, but that didn't mean he was ready to give up—he didn't give up.

His dad was at his side again, freeing him from the harsh grip of his soldiers. "If you touch me again, I will snap your neck."

Bridger knew he wasn't kidding.

"You're a sick man. Fucking pathetic! Look at who you're following. She's a monster. Marlena is killing her loved ones, killing innocent people all around her!" Bridger knew his father had never been a caring man, had witnessed his harshness first hand—he'd always lived up to the dark reputation the Dimicos had despite the fair, angelic features he possessed.

"You act like you have any idea what's going on. If you only knew the half of it, you'd shut your fucking mouth." Lucius Dimico, commander of Tolevarre's army, was nose to nose with his son, teeth gritted.

Bridger was about to give his father a quick headbutt when the door swung open again and a voice cut him like a knife, spilling his guts all over the lovely Ardor flooring. "It might do you well to listen to your father, Bridgey."

The pet name Marlena used to tease him with on nights he thought they were friends ripped him open. Marlena came strolling in, covered in soot and blood. It had been days since the initial attack in Aeris—had she showered or was her killing spree so never-ending that it didn't matter how many times she washed herself clean?

His gaze locked on hers, her lips curled in an insolent smile.

Gone was the girl with flowers in her hair. In her place was darkness set free.

"Quiet now, are we?" Marlena stalked, circling the room with him in her sights. "Come on. I know you have something you'd like to say to me." Her grin could rattle even the bravest of soldiers.

"Where is Vega?" It was the only question he wanted answered.

Marlena sighed. "It's always about her." Was this all because of a sister's jealousy? Marlena was always going to have the power, the title. Vega didn't even want it—her parents' plan for her was always to marry another Curia member's kid. Vega would be the bride, Marlena the ruler.

"She's alive... for now." Her words echoed his father's, and it was in that moment he realized how far involved his parents were in all of this. Marlena had them wrapped around her wicked little finger.

Vega was okay. Bridger had to get to her. Almost as if his muscles reacted before his brain did, he surged towards Marlena.

Bridger got within inches of her, but a power like nothing he'd ever felt before slammed into him. Marlena didn't even flinch. The only muscle in her body moving was a twitch at the corner of her mouth.

The sinister smile she'd started to adorn pulled at her cheeks, never leaving her beautiful face.

Bridger was hovering in the air, just like Vega's dad had been, not able to move an inch.

Marlena marveled at him, *no*, at what she was doing. "Wow," she said, exhaling. Bridger watched her test her newfound powers as he observed her in horror.

What the fuck has she done?

She flicked her wrist, and Bridger slammed into the wall, the adobe clay splintering from the force as his ribs cracked, collapsing a lung. A guttural noise ripped from his mouth at the pain.

"Bring them in." Marlena marveled at her hands. The emerald flame Bridger saw before she killed her father swirled in her palm.

Bridger forced himself to a seated position, gasping to fill his one working lung with oxygen. Three doors opened around the room at the same time, all from different directions. Dragged by men in his father's army were Khort, Arlet, and Vega.

Khort's face was black and blue, his blond hair coated in blood from the cuts all over his face. With their powers stripped, they wouldn't heal at a rapid rate.

Arlet didn't seem to be conscious.

Vega was screaming, flailing against the hold on her, covered in blood and beaten. But fighting. "You rotten bitch! Tell me why! Why!" Her screams echoed off the tall ceilings.

The guards threw Khort and Arlet onto the hard floor. Khort was hardly able to catch himself, holding his tattered body up with one arm. The wrist on his opposite arm was bent in the wrong direction. Arlet hit the ground with a *thwack*. If she wasn't unconscious before, she was now.

"Shut her up, or I'll do it for her, Bridger." Marlena meant it as a threat, but Bridger took it as a command. With everything inside him, broken bones and all, Bridger crawled towards Vega.

The guards were still holding her, but she was fighting with everything she had left.

"Vega..." he choked.

Her name from his lips stopped Vega in her tracks, her attention snapping to Bridger on the floor, battered and broken.

"Bridger," she gulped, finally aware someone other than her, the guards, and her sister were here. Her eyes fluttered to the others. "Oh my gods, Bridger. What did you do to him?" Anger bubbled behind Vega's eyes. Marlena motioned for the guards to let her go. Vega tumbled forward, collapsing to the ground beside Bridger. "Are you okay? Look at me." She grasped his face gently between her hands.

"I'm okay," Bridger croaked.

Marlena growled. "Your love has blinded you."

Marlena had been planning this for years. *Years.* And none of them saw it coming. She played them like fools, plotting with his own parents and other Curia members behind their backs at night and then meeting them all as friends for breakfast the following morning.

The time for talking was over. Vega could ask why as much as she wanted. It wouldn't change a thing.

"How could you do this to me? To us?" Vega looked around the room at the friends she and Marlena grew up with. "Answer me. Give me something." Vega led with her heart, and Marlena had utterly crushed it.

"You want a reason?" Marlena snapped her head up. She was by Khort, who hadn't said a word and wouldn't make eye contact with anyone.

She prowled over to Vega and Bridger, the boots on her feet leaving smudges of blood and mud behind her. Marlena grabbed her sister by the hair. Vega clawed at her, nicking her with one of her nails. Marlena tossed her back to the ground in the middle of the room where everyone could see.

Bridger felt broken and useless.

Marlena towered over Vega, always taller but now more confident and lethal than she'd ever been. She leaned down to get within inches of her sister's face. Vega's wide eyes didn't show fear, but pain—despair. She'd been betrayed by her own flesh and blood; she had every right to feel agony.

"I did this because someone had to, and the last one they would have expected was me. Perfectly poised, ready-to-lead Marlena. Always-following-the-rules Marlena. Never-biting-back Marlena! Guess what I realized, sister... Why would I settle for just two seats when I could have them all?"

Power.

Marlena wanted more than she was allotted.

Vega choked. "You killed our parents. Slaughtered them. What happened to you?"

Marlena grabbed her sister's face. "Maybe I should have been watched a little closer." She rose, the room's electricity flashing. "Our parents raised a powerful woman. One meant to rule, and yet you're surprised when I finally do?"

"It wasn't supposed to be like this!" Vega wailed.

Marlena laughed. "This is always how it was going to be. You just couldn't see it because you accidentally fell in love with my future commander."

Vega looked at Bridger, defeat settling on her face.

"It worked in my favor. You would have done anything for him. You even went as far as to summon a dead god—I'm sorry, a *demigod* —to protect him. Them." She pointed to Arlet and Khort.

Marlena looked at Vega with longing, with the eyes of someone who'd been forgotten, of someone who just wanted to come first to someone... anyone. "You picked them."

Bridger's physical pain worsened while watching the interaction between the Caelum sisters, his heart running amok in his chest.

"You're my sister, Mar, my best friend. I would have picked you. Always." Marlena still towered over Vega, cowering on the floor, looking smaller than she'd ever been. Bridger had never seen her shrink for anything, under anyone.

"You're a liar." The hatred bled through, tarnishing every ounce of who Marlena once was.

Vega shook her head, sitting up on her knees, looking as if she might reach out and touch her sister.

"You were oblivious, lost in your perfect little world. You never even stopped to see what I was going through." It seemed Vega might be getting to her, that if she kept pushing, she might be able to have a breakthrough. "You didn't care."

"That's not true," Vega countered, reaching out to grab her sister's hand. Marlena let her have it, taking the time to look down at their connected bodies. Vega was covered in blood, her hair tangled around her face. She wore Bridger's shirt still, drowning in its size. "Whatever you were going through—whatever you're going through, we can fix this. It's not too late. We can do this together."

The Caelum sisters both looked like they had fought for their lives.

Only one had.

The other completed her tasks with zero remorse, zero regrets. It was written all over her face, easily seen even under the mask of vulnerability she currently wore.

"You let them beat me. You ignored the bruises, the nights I was locked away. You never stopped to see what was happening to me right in front of you. It didn't have to be like this. I could've saved you."

Bridger watched from his position on the cold floor, ignoring the fire of pain lapping up his side, a familiar hand on his shoulder. His mother finally decided to check on her son, the one who had been lying on the floor in a heap in front of her for longer than any mother should allow. Bridger tried to push her away, but she held on with a vise-like grip, forcing him to a standing position.

Katrin Dimico leaned in, whispering her simple order. "Stand tall. Don't let them see you fall apart." At least her hands were kinder than his father's would have been.

Bridger felt like he was watching this unfold from outside his body. He could see his mother hoisting him up, sliding her shoulder under his to help support most of his weight. He watched as Arlet blinked, coming to and finding her surroundings. When she realized where she was and who was around her, she froze. He could see Khort cave into himself, accepting their deaths.

Bridger refused to do that. He'd promised he would fight with Vega, side by side.

Until his dying breath.

Marlena's mood shifted. Vega's hand was still in hers, the sisters in what might be their last calm physical touch. Marlena's gaze moved from their hands to Vega's identical eyes.

And her sinister smile came back.

Without another moment of hesitation, Marlena yanked Vega up from the floor, snapping her wrist. Vega yelped in pain.

Bridger stumbled forward, pulling away from his mother.

"Stop," she hissed.

"Marlena, please, let us go," Bridger begged, something that was drilled into him not to do since he was a child—Dimicos don't beg. But he would.

For Vega, he would do worse.

Marlena couldn't hear him. Her hand was around Vega's throat, holding her at arm's length, her head cocking as she took in the gurgling noises coming from her sister. Vega scratched at Marlena's arms, unable to get her plea out.

Water pooled around their feet. Bridger looked down, the room filling with dark seawater, warm from the Caldor Ocean. He couldn't keep his eyes off Marlena and Vega, fear dulling the pain.

Lucius stepped forward, and with the help of his father, Bridger was contained, going nowhere. His mother picked him up, reminding him not to embarrass their family, but his father had always thought he was a disgrace—long before Vega. It didn't matter he was the strongest warrior their world had ever seen. Bridger wasn't his father, and that fact drove Lucius mad. Lucius's brutality wasn't a trait Bridger ever wanted to bear. He didn't want to lose the humanity inside him to impress a man who mistreated everyone just because he could.

Bridger was good. He was fair. He wanted to change the way the army operated one day. Bridger dreamed of the day his father stepped down and he got to make a difference... but that day would never come. Instead, he'd die because he wasn't the son his father wanted him to be.

Lucius threw him to the floor again. "If you're going to act like one of them, you can die like one of them." He slammed a boot to the side of Bridger's head. The water splashed in his face, salt burning his eyes and turning them bloodshot. Even through the physical pain he felt, he still tried to fight himself free.

"I'll do anything, Marlena. Please, let her go." Bridger's words were garbled, the water beginning to pool over half his face.

Marlena whispered, speaking to no one but herself. "It's too late." She raised her other hand, emerald electricity crackling in her open palm. Another new power. This was no longer the Marlena who could hide herself with invisibility and create a dangerous gust of wind. Lightning crackled from somewhere inside her, and she turned her head to admire it before she looked back to her sister. "You think you're the only one who can summon dead gods, sister?"

Vega's eyes were red, vessels bursting and staining her irises with blood. Marlena eased up, and Vega choked out, inhaling with a wheeze. The look of shock she should have was stolen by the need to breathe.

Marlena laughed, taking in the rest of the room's reaction. She was enjoying this, the power, the upper hand.

"How?" Vega squawked, her vocal cords sustaining damage from the hold Marlena had on her. Marlena didn't let go. She yanked her by the neck, bringing them back face to face.

"Where do you think you got the idea from? It wasn't yours. I've been planting the idea of summoning a god for help in your brain for years. It was so easy." Marlena's voice heightened, mimicking a conversation they must have had privately. "Could you imagine if we summoned one to fix the problems inside the Curia? We could change the world." Her laugh was uneven, her voice returning to its normal tone. "We could have. Together. But you made your choice, and I can't do anything to save you now. I won't. How hopeful you were. You've always been so easily manipulated, so easy to crush... and yet you got the better powers. It should have been me." Marlena let go of Vega's throat but switched her hold to the newly branded wrist the four of them shared.

Marlena was strong. *Too* strong.

The water continued to rush in. Bridger fought his way upright enough not to drown. His father let him, but only because he was as bewitched by Marlena as the rest of the room.

"I bet my twelve murdered gods are a lot angrier than your one vengeful demi," Marlena divulged, finally revealing her secret. "You may have been stronger, Vega, but I've always been smarter." Ardor's building shuddered. The water suddenly stopped rushing in, falling to a stillness around their feet.

Arlet made it to Khort, holding on to her friend in what was bound to be their last moments. Bridger looked over to them from his spot on the floor. Arlet and Khort nodded, tears streaming down their cheeks.

Marlena had summoned the twelve original gods, their powers now all hers.

And they didn't stand a chance.

"What are you?" Vega asked, not moving.

Marlena leaned forward, sharing a secret with her sister the rest of them couldn't hear. Vega's eyes went wide, jaw nearly unhinging from how quickly it fell open.

Marlena drew a blade from a holster. Khort lunged forward. "No!"

Arlet went with him, standing zero chance against whatever power consumed Marlena. Her attention was all on Vega. She didn't have to look at the two bodies coming towards her to stop them.

Water splashed up around Arlet, cocooning her inside an impenetrable force field. The saltwater slid down her throat, drowning her where she stood.

A gust of wind picked up, suspending Khort in midair. He couldn't move, eyes opened wide as he was forced to watch while his best friend drowned—while the girl he'd been in love with since childhood was held at knifepoint by her sister.

Bridger's ears rang. He heard no sound, only knew he was screaming and trying to yank free from his parents.

Bridger fought.

Until the end.

Marlena sneered, "Je te verrai." *I'll be seeing you.* And then she plunged her knife into Vega's chest, piercing through her heart.

Vega didn't have time to scream before the life drained from her eyes.

"Vega! No! Vega!" Bridger didn't know if those were his words, or if they came from Khort or Arlet. His heart broke, shattered, tears spilling over as he fought with all his might. His elbow slammed into his father's nose, breaking it with a crunch—blood gushed, and he let go of Bridger long enough for him to overpower the guards with polished punches and warrior-like grace.

The pain in his side didn't matter. His uneven breathing didn't matter—nothing mattered anymore.

Marlena let Vega's body crash to the floor and released whatever power she had on Khort and Arlet. Khort fell twenty feet to the floor, and yet somehow, he still managed to get to Vega's lifeless body. Khort shuddered with wails of physical and emotional pain.

Arlet couldn't move, coughing up all the Caldor Ocean from her lungs.

Marlena looked to them, head held high. "She'll be back." Vega's body disappeared, snatched from Khort's hold. "Go find her."

Marlena left with a puff of black smoke. The water on the floor disappeared, evaporating like the villain of their story had.

Bridger's tears mixed with the water dripping from his hair. He slammed his fist into the flooring, shattering the tile and his knuckles. His cry wasn't from the pain, but from the hole the size of their realm inside his chest.

Bridger knew from that moment on he would never feel complete again.

The cold toilet seat against his cheek pulled Bridger back to reality, awakening his senses. He could *feel* the cool porcelain, could *see* the light from underneath his bathroom door, could *hear* the thrum of his heart in his ears, could *taste* the bile on his tongue, could *smell* the contents of his stomach he'd retched up until his entire body hurt.

Bridger used the tactics he'd learned when being trained by his father for surviving torture. *Use your senses to stay alive.* He heard the echo of his crisp voice in his head as if he were standing over him in the bathroom.

He hadn't meant to fall back asleep after receiving word about Halo, but his exhaustion was hard to ignore, and sleep, no matter how restless it was, was hard to fight.

These dreams were his own personal form of torture.

It took a curse that wasn't even his only a few weeks to begin deconstructing the walls of his mental shield block by block. A shield that had been fortified over forty years.

Each night was a new reminder of all it had taken from him.

Watching Vega's first death play out inside his mind would stick with him. Bridger wasn't sure he'd ever be able to rebuild the walls he'd once had. Waking up this morning felt like the first morning without her.

Hollow.

Bridger spit into the toilet and wiped his mouth across his forearm, flushing one last time before hoisting himself off the cold bathroom floor. He could not let this consume him—he wouldn't. He looked at his reflection in the mirror, at the sticky sweat on his face. The bags under his eyes were more noticeable than they'd ever been.

Bridger had taken all his memories of Vega, good and bad, and burned them from his mind, ridding himself of the guilt he felt when he thought of the things he had done to her and their friends.

Nothing any of them had been through was easy, and they had all found ways to cope with the misery they felt, but Arlet and Khort had yet to give up on Vega.

Bridger had.

Marlena knew breaking Bridger would be breaking Vega—their relationship had always been more than just love. After the summoning, their bond was unlike anything Bridger had ever felt. He could sense her mood shifts, felt like he could hear her thoughts before she spoke them, and their powers—gods, they were so strong together.

Being tortured by Marlena for two years, locked under the home she'd rebuilt in Aeris, changed him. In some ways, it made him sharper, but in others... he'd never be the same.

Bridger could only imagine what it felt like for Vega to remember everything all at once. At least the rest of them got the time to heal slowly, becoming whatever person it made them along the way.

Sometimes he wondered if she would rather be dead forever than have to do this over and over and over again.

Death could be peaceful, but Death wasn't kind.

Bridger didn't have the luxury of forgetting, of wishing for death. Today, he had to swallow his pain and hunt down the very woman he'd promised to fight for until the end.

25

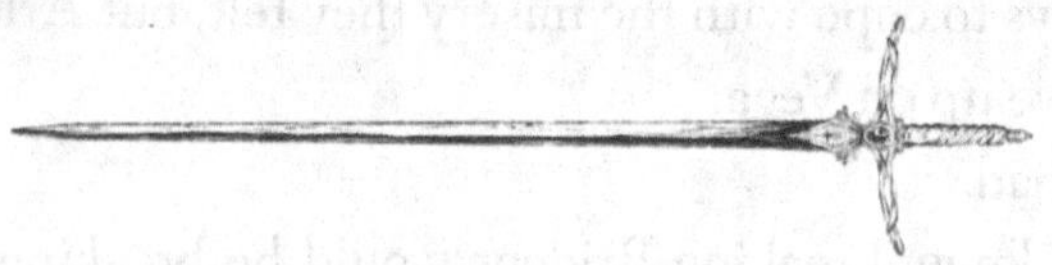

THE ELEVATOR DOORS OPENED INTO HIS OFFICE WHERE HALO waited. Bridger's brows creased. "Do you often find yourself snooping in places you don't belong just because you're able?" The fact he could materialize in and out, wherever it was he wanted to be, set Bridger on edge.

He had to remind himself no matter how young Halo was, he was still Fraus-born, and just because he was helping at the moment didn't mean his assistance would be granted in the future.

"Commander!" Halo startled, hands shooting to his side. "I apologize. I was just looking at the map you have here. It's old." Halo backed away from the table as Bridger moved closer, putting himself in between the young man and the map.

"Yes, great observation skills." Bridger smiled, leaning against the table. He folded his hands in front of himself. "It's been passed down the Dimico line since the beginning of our time. Something no one outside my inner circle gets to see." *And it holds secrets I can't trust you with.* Bridger met the young boy's eyes, watching them grow wider as he nodded his head.

"Understood. I didn't see anything. Promise." Halo shrugged it off, but Bridger wouldn't let his guard down. "What was it you wanted to talk to me about?" Halo asked, eager to change the subject.

Bridger pushed himself off the table, the map rolled up behind him now. Wind control came in handy in more ways than one.

"I'm curious about a couple things." Bridger stood much taller than Halo, the young boy still growing into himself. "One, why is it you disappeared after dropping us at the portal?"

Halo shifted on his feet. "When Arlet came through with Vega and saw me, I had to come up with a reason as to why I was there. I couldn't let her think I was with you. I spun the story that I'd seen you two sneaking around and knew the portal needed to be moved to throw you off if you made it back with Vega and Arlet was left behind."

Bridger replied, "Good." He crossed his arms over his chest. "And did she seem suspicious?"

Halo shook his head. "No, she was too busy worrying about the Caelum girl."

Bridger watched the way Halo moved, the way his eyes shifted to the left when he spoke and the way he rubbed his hands together when he started to get nervous. There was a lot to take in about the boy, who was the same age Bridger had been when he met Marlena and Vega.

Halo was from a land where gangs and villains ran rampant, where the people didn't care about their neighbors or families. Every move made was to better oneself, worrying about no one else in the process—some would argue if they cared for no one, nothing could hurt them. Everyone learned to hate the people of Fraus, but no one more than Bridger—no one more than the boy he'd been when he'd needed a mother to protect him from the abuse of his father.

"Her name's Vega," Bridger said impassively. "Marlena is also a Caelum girl, and we'd hate to get them mixed up." Marlena wasn't partial to being compared to her younger sister.

Halo nodded, looking down at his boots.

"Eyes up," Bridger commanded. He sounded like the fearsome commander he was rumored to be.

"Sorry." The boy's eyes were piercing green, and he wore his emotions all over his face.

"Don't apologize. Learn. If you want to be part of this army, which is what it seems you're interested in...?" Bridger paused.

Halo nodded quickly, an earnest look of excitement glittering in his eyes. "Yes, sir. More than anything."

Bridger watched this hopeful young boy turn from someone so sure of his odd power to one who looked for praise in places he shouldn't. There was no one like him in all of their realm—he could go anywhere, be anything, and yet he'd allowed Marlena to sink her teeth into him.

Bridger nodded, studying his lanky build. His eyes flicked up his body and then back down. He continued where he left off. "Then you're going to have to change parts of yourself that feel wrong. Parts of you that you don't think you can live without. You'll have to do things that make you feel as if you're going to crawl out of your skin, things you can't just wash away in the shower or with a strong drink."

The glitter in Halo's eyes was part wonder, part fear—it was precisely what Bridger wanted. The excitement of something scary, unknown, and out of the ordinary was what most of his best soldiers were looking for when they joined him after his father was murdered.

Bridger wasn't his father. He believed in the souls who laid down their lives for this realm, and in return, he had thousands of warriors standing behind him, ready to attack at any given moment.

A war was brewing between the rebels and those who followed Marlena. The rebels' numbers were rising every year with the mistreatment of those with lesser powers. The people who helped grow their food, kept their rivers flowing with clean water, cared for the homes of the powerful—the people whom Marlena had always seen as insignificant.

Bridger wanted to be on the winning side of this war.

"Why do you want to join Tolevarre's army?" Bridger's posture oozed power.

"Because I want to belong somewhere," Halo responded, his voice cracking with honesty. Bridger felt a tug at his iron heart—those were words he'd spoken before too.

"Then prove it." As much as he felt for this boy, Bridger knew better. Though he was partially Fraus-born himself, thanks to his mother, he was Fortis-bred and would always protect the soft underbelly of himself and his people.

Marlena had taught him to always be one step ahead.

"What do you need?" Halo asked.

"Do you know where Vega's hiding?"

"No. I mean, yes. Somewhere under the Sea of Ros off the coast of Imber, but I've never been allowed inside. Khort never lets me in," Halo answered with a solemn expression, his eyebrows knitted together.

"Under the Sea of Ros?"

"Yes, they keep it hidden somehow. I don't know how or with what, but I do know Vega and the others aren't there. They left this morning to meet with a witch in Fraus to get Vega's memories back." Halo's face drooped around his mouth, his frown hanging low.

"Even better. Why don't you go pay the witch a visit? Tell her Commander Dimico will be by to get Vega, who is a fugitive in this realm, and if she does anything to warn them I'm coming, I'll kill her nice and slow."

Halo smiled. "I'll report back with her location. Anything else I can do for you, Commander?" He was so eager to please—almost too eager.

"Yes, as a matter of fact..." Bridger grabbed the sword on his back from its sheath with a speed so quick the move might've been missed if Halo blinked. The tip pressed against the lump on Halo's neck. "If you tell anyone you're running my errands or make a peep about where the rebel headquarters is located until I have a chance to look into it, I will add you to the growing list of kills I've made this week for speaking out against me."

Halo backed against the bookcase, the tip of Bridger's sword pricking through his skin. A trickle of blood slid down the front of his neck. He couldn't move, nod, or speak without the sword sinking deeper.

"Understood?" Bridger drew far enough away to allow Halo to answer.

"Of course, Commander. I would nev—"

Bridger cut him off. "That includes Marlena. She doesn't need to know every detail about how I run my show here."

The boy nodded now that he had room to without piercing his jugular. Bridger returned his sword to his scabbard and stepped away, flicking his wrist in dismissal. "I'll be waiting for you at the border of Fraus in three hours. Do not be late."

Halo said nothing, and when Bridger blinked, he was gone.

Bridger stood alone in the room, a smile that would bring chills upon any who saw it spreading across his face as he basked in the silence surrounding him. He'd planted his seed.

Slowly but surely, he would break down the trust Marlena was building with people like Halo, with the ones whose powers couldn't be understood—the ones who Marlena was trying to take hold of like a parasite.

He would protect those who would protect him.

Bridger wasn't stupid. The more control he had over his soldiers, the less Marlena had... and that was worth more than anything in this world.

The dreams about Vega were wearing on him, breaking him down while he relived some of the hardest moments of his life, and even so, he still held on to the hope inside that one day, Marlena would crumble on the very throne she'd built through blood and death.

All things came to an end, and Bridger knew when Marlena's reign finally shattered, he'd go down with her.

But he could leave a legacy within the people whose lives he changed. Not all the people of Tolevarre believed him to be the unforgiving commander he painted himself to be.

His soldiers were waiting when he arrived, jostling about the training center. Some warmed up their muscles, others chatted with their comrades. Meyer sat in a corner, staring blankly at nothing.

Their fight still felt fresh after Bridger's mutilation of one of their soldiers. They hadn't talked since that night.

"Is the new base ready in Solum?" Bridger asked as he approached his right-hand man.

Meyer sat up straight when he realized Bridger was beside him. "Yeah, my group and I are leaving in a few minutes." Meyer's usual demeanor was strong and assured. Right now, he sounded withdrawn and laden with unspoken anger.

Neither of them had time to hash out whatever was building between them.

They had orders. Orders from a woman who better get what she wanted if they wanted their heads safely on their shoulders.

"Good," Bridger said, nodding for Meyer to stand. He did without hesitation. "I need you in this." An order from his commander.

"I am."

"No. I need you level-headed with no animosity blinding you." Bridger could see right through him.

"If you're talking about the other night, I've forgotten all about it," Meyer bluffed.

Bridger sighed. "Do you think I don't know when you're lying to me?"

Meyer scowled, trying to avert his gaze. "We're not friends, remember? What does it matter?"

Bridger wouldn't apologize for what he'd said, always too afraid to seem weak. "I spoke without thinking. You should know I'm good at that by now."

There was a moment of silence between the two before a soldier came up behind them, bowing her head before speaking. "Commander Dimico. General Ignis. Both troops are ready to go."

Meyer spoke before Bridger had the chance. "We'll be there shortly. Start loading up."

The woman nodded, leaving the two in silence again.

"Keep an eye out for rebels today as you travel into Solum. They're going to be on high alert and ready to attack," Bridger said, fixing his cape before leaning against a wall casually, an air of ease around him.

"More so than any other day?" Meyer asked.

"I met with Halo early this morning." Meyer's brow raised in piqued interest. Bridger could see his mood shifting. "Vega will be in Fraus today visiting a witch to get her memories restored. We're going to intercept."

Meyer's hard face broke into a cruel smile. "You sneaky bastard."

Bridger knew he wasn't forgiven for the way he'd acted, but at least for now, Meyer would forget why he was angry. "So yes, watch your back a little more than usual today. I suspect Khort will be acting out of rage instead of using his lizard-sized brain."

Meyer backed away. "It's been a while since I got the chance to go toe-to-toe with the shifter. Send him my way, would ya?"

Bridger chuckled. "Only if he doesn't come for me first." He watched Meyer turn to leave, but after reliving the night Meyer barged into the cabin before he and the bonded were taken prisoner, Bridger had been dying to ask him a question.

"Hey, Meyer," Bridger called, waiting for him to turn around.

He faced his commander. "Yeah?"

"The night you found me in that cabin with Vega and the others, did you know my father was following you?" Bridger didn't allow his voice to rise much above a whisper. He'd never asked, choosing to avoid questions he might not want honest answers to.

Meyer took a moment to respond, which Bridger took as admission in itself. But then he spoke. "No." He paused momentarily. "I picked my side before coming to you that night, but you deserved to have that choice too."

Bridger stared at Meyer, his best friend, his brother. He didn't expect the next piece of information to fall from his lips.

"They were going to let you stay with them, with Vega. Our parents were going to name me commander, but Marlena wouldn't allow it. That was the night she killed your father, a week before she captured you for torture."

26

Is THAT SOMEONE AT THE DOOR? VEGA PULLED THE THICK COVER over her head when the noise echoed through the room again. "Five more minutes." The door creaked open and then closed with a click before someone crossed the room and dove on top of her.

"Arlet," Vega groaned, drawing out her name.

"How did you know it was me?" she asked, pulling the covers off Vega's face to peek at her.

"Because who else in their right mind would jump on a girl with electricity coursing through her veins this early in the morning?" Vega responded, her voice deep with sleep.

"Good thing I'm not in my right mind." Arlet poked at Vega, making her wiggle. "Come on, it's memory day. Get up!" She ripped the covers off, revealing the dress Vega fell asleep in. "Man, it's been a long time since I've seen this thing." Arlet reached out to feel the velvety material, a pang of sadness dancing across her face.

"I got bored and played dress-up and got caught by Khort." The memories of last night flooded in as Vega's mind started to wake from her sleepy fog. She went pale when she remembered the kiss.

"Fuck..." She buried her face in her hands. "I think I did something stupid," Vega whined, peeking through her fingers.

Arlet's eyebrow raised. "What did you do?"

Vega propped her back against the metal bed frame, pulling her knees to her chest. "Promise you won't get mad?"

"No," Arlet answered candidly. "But now you have to tell me or I won't let you leave this room."

Vega let out a long sigh and tattled on herself. She even shared the little detail of how Khort told her he loved her.

"Oh, Khort," Arlet said with the release of a breath.

"And he walked me back to the room... and I, uh, I kissed him." Vega watched Arlet's jaw drop in slow motion.

"You *what?!*" Arlet jolted upright, sitting on her knees. "Please tell me it was, like, a cute little peck kiss! A thanks-for-taking-me-outside-when-you-know-Arlet-would-kill-you-for-it kinda kiss!"

Vega shook her head. "Tongue. Groping. Hands in hair. Romance novel level kiss."

"Fuck, Vega." Arlet's sigh made Vega feel about the size of an ant. "Why would you do that?"

"Because I'm a glutton for punishment!" Vega pulled a pillow up and pressed it to her face. "Don't yell at me. I'm sorry. I know it was stupid, but I was drunk and he's so good-looking... and he's been all strong and commanding during our training sessions that I just... I don't know. I kinda wanted it?" She continued to hide behind the pillow until Arlet snatched it out of her hands and tossed it across the room.

"No. No. You're not allowed to do that to Khort. You can't use him as a play toy."

Vega felt as if she were being scolded by a parent. "That wasn't my intention. I'm not some kind of temptress luring him to his death. It was a kiss. I'm sure he understands it was a drunken mistake."

Arlet stood, eyebrows pressed inward. "Vega," she said with an exasperated huff. "The man confessed his love for you. He's been in love with you since we were ten."

Vega stood too, feeling silly in the ballgown next to Arlet in her gear. "It was a mistake, and it won't happen again. It's not like I have any memories of who he is to me yet. I was drunk and horny."

"You need to use better judgment with him, and I'm not saying you can't be with him if that's what you *want*, but that's a decision you need to make when you know the full truth of your relationships in this realm. Not after a drunk night where your adrenaline's high from sneaking out."

Vega puffed air through her lips. "You're right. I know you're right. He stopped me. Said it would mean more to him than it does to me."

"He's right." The sadness in Arlet's tone stood out against the silence in the room.

"I'm sorry."

"I don't think it's me who deserves an apology."

She's right, you fucking idiot. Vega nodded. "Yeah."

"Get dressed. We're leaving in half an hour." The door clicked shut, leaving Vega alone in her room to sulk into the shower.

After she was dry, Vega wiggled into her suit. The clothing was starting to feel tight around her legs and hips. The training putting some weight back on her body, filling her out in places Vega had always envied on other women.

Looking at herself in the mirror while she braided a few strands of wet hair seemed harder than usual. There was shame hidden behind those bright eyes of hers this morning—she couldn't stop imagining what it would feel like when she got her memories back and the full effect of kissing Khort set in.

Along with everything else.

The braids held the hair out of her eyes, the rest drying in waves behind her back. Vega opened her door, looking behind her in hopes this wouldn't be the last time she was in her room. Vega shook her head, knowing she'd be back tonight—a whole new person.

Would she be happy with the Vega she saw in the mirror then?

She closed the consuming thoughts inside with the rest of her worries.

There were people in the halls, going about their lives like any other day. They nodded, waved, stared—some going as far as to stop and watch as she went by.

I'll never get used to this. Being watched.

Vega heard his voice before she saw him.

"We'll be back before dinner. Don't worry." Khort had a mellow smile on his face, a blonde girl with dark roots smiling up at him with a gleam in her midnight blue eyes. "We used this witch last time, and everything went smoothly." As if he could feel Vega's presence, his head snapped forward, and all of his attention shifted to her. "Vega!" he called, waving her over.

Shit. Vega bit her lip, forcing a smile to hide the awkwardness simmering beneath the surface. Their eyes met, and her stomach fluttered at the memory of her lips on his.

"Morning!" Her reply sounded overly chipper and forced. *It's going to be a long day.*

"How did you sleep?" he asked as Vega closed the distance between them.

"Good," she hummed.

The girl next to Khort cleared her throat, stepping forward to draw attention to herself. "Hi, I'm Quinley." She held her hand out.

Vega took it, giving her a solid handshake. "Vega. Nice to meet you." There was a palpable thread of tension pulling at the air between the three.

Quinley chuckled. "I know. I mean, we all know who you are."

"Of course." Vega looked down at her feet, her hair shifting in front of her shoulders. "Still getting used to the whole everyone knowing me thing."

"I'm sure it's hard to adjust." She bowed her head quickly and then turned to face Khort. "I should get going. Lots to do." Quinley stood on her tiptoes and placed a quick kiss on Khort's cheek. "See you tonight. Be safe."

Vega looked away, keeping her jaw clenched to hide the shock shifting through her chest. Khort never once mentioned he was dating anyone—nor did anyone else. "You didn't tell me..." She trailed off, not knowing what to say.

Khort bit the inside of his cheek. "I, um, it's not serious."

Vega scoffed at his response and wanted to laugh at herself for being so silly. She had too much going on to care about what he had been doing for the last fifteen years of his life. *You also have absolutely no right to be jealous.*

Vega scooted past, choosing not to say anything and beelining for the door down the hall where they wouldn't be alone to talk about this.

"Let me explain." In just a few strides, Khort was beside her.

"There's nothing to explain." Vega tried to brush off the conversation before it could even start.

"Yes, there is." Khort reached out and grabbed her hand, stopping her before she opened the door.

"No, Khort, there isn't. What I did... what I said last night was out of line, and I'm sorry. I'm lost, tired, and in a world I thought would feel like home, but right now it just feels like more wasted time." The truth slipped out, and Vega saw the hurt on Khort's face.

"I don't want you to feel that way."

"We don't always get what we want." *The truth hurts.* Vega didn't want to be mad about Quinley—she had no right to be, but somewhere inside she felt a little fit of anger bubbling. "You said it yourself, we don't need to talk about this. Let's just let it die and never talk about it again." With finality, Vega opened the doors and stepped into the training center, where the start of today's journey would begin. All eyes were on her as she strode in for the last time with no memories of who she was. *Fingers crossed.*

Arlet's eyes followed Vega, then bounced to Khort for a split second.

Vega stopped in the center of the room and pulled a large breath in for encouragement. "I appreciate you all for coming with me. Again," Vega said, forcing herself not to look down at the floor. A few mumbled their responses, but most of them stared like they'd seen a ghost.

She was in a tight black training suit with a black embroidered lightning bolt shooting up both of her sides. It blended in and looked like a seam to someone who didn't know it was there. It trailed from the curve of her hip to under her arm, where it disappeared. It clung to a body that was starting to feel stronger than ever.

There wasn't much talking as they each grabbed a small bag to travel with. Vega stayed out of everyone's way and dreamed of the day she would feel useful.

Khort completely ignored any eye contact with her, and Arlet kept her distance from both of them. Leave it to Vega to piss off the only two people who ever cared for her. Would they realize how exhausted they were eventually and give up on her completely?

The boat they were taking appeared out of thin air, another object being concealed by Arlet. The trip would take under three hours. They would travel from the southern tip of Imber to the northern part of Fraus—close to Fortis's territory line.

Vega hadn't spent much time on boats when she was on Earth, but she always lived around the water, and the ones here in Tolevarre weren't much different. This one was similar to the military boats she'd seen near Seattle's naval base, except it was all black instead of a dull gray.

The boat wasn't huge, only fitting ten people comfortably underneath.

"We're almost there." The interruption drew Vega from her

deep thoughts. Her head shot up, and Arlet sent smiled from her standing position, pointing at the open seat beside Vega. "Mind if I sit?"

"Of course not." Vega scooted over to give Arlet more room. "This trip isn't as fun as our road trip," she jeered.

Arlet smiled softly. "You're right. Maybe we should sing to lighten the mood."

Vega grimaced. "Maybe you should. They definitely don't want to hear me sing." Vega couldn't help herself. She reached out and grabbed Arlet's hand. "I'm scared," she whispered.

"It's okay to be scared." Arlet squeezed in the same pattern she'd done back in Chicago when they were sitting on the cheap motel bed together and in the car after their singalong. "I'd be worried if you weren't."

Vega's eyes fell to their connected hands and she changed the subject. "You didn't tell me that he was seeing someone," Vega said in a hushed tone.

"Who, Khort? He's not. Not really. It's casual. He's been honest with her about that, but Quinley wants more. Everyone knows he'll never really be available. Not until he's ready to be."

"She kissed him in front of me this morning, so I just assumed."

Arlet cackled. "She what?!" She kept laughing, a few heads turning to look their way when she snorted. Arlet threw a hand over her mouth.

Vega's eyebrows drew together in confusion. "I mean, it was on the cheek, but she looked pretty cozy doing it."

Arlet wagged her head. "She was marking her territory." A giggle slipped through her lips. "She's from Amora, and she shares the invisibility power with your sister. She's only met you in one life. She's been spying for us for a while and has been crushing on Khort since the beginning. I've hoped he would take it more seriously, but he won't."

Vega felt a pain of regret in her chest. "Why didn't I choose him?"

Arlet let go of her hand and looked out the porthole window at the waves crashing around the boat as they slowed. "You loved Bridger from the very moment you saw him. Watching you two fall in love was like watching two destined souls finally find each other. He was taboo for you, wild, dangerous. Khort was safe, and you've never been one to choose the easy way." Arlet elbowed her playfully.

"Great," Vega mumbled.

"We're approaching the port," Khort called down from the top deck.

Arlet stood and held out her hand to Vega. "Let's go up."

Vega took it again, and the two walked hand in hand to the deck. She needed Arlet. Her guide, her protector, and the only friend Vega had ever been able to count on—in this life and all the ones before. If she never got her memories back, she would still consider her the best friend a girl could hope for.

Vega's boots hit the wooden deck, and she ogled at the land surrounding her. The weather here felt damp, causing a chill to settle on Vega's skin.

Fraus's buildings were pointed at the top, made out of large stones. The roads were cobbled, and the people on the docks reminded her of the pirates she'd seen in movies. Vega looked behind her and noticed their boat no longer looked like a war ship, but like the *Black Pearl* from *Pirates of the Caribbean*. She scrunched her eyebrows, confused.

Khort noticed. "The people of this land don't have the advances we have. Only those in governing positions, the army, the rich. Our boat can't look like one if we want to stay incognito."

Her eyes wandered over the gothic city—Fraus seemed to have a perpetual fog hanging over the peaks of its tall buildings.

"How do—"

"Shhhh!" Arlet was at her other side, finger over her lips.

"People know who you are, and there's a pretty big bounty on your head right now. I can control what people see, not what they hear. You need to keep it down through the town. No one will see us. Khort is the only one the people won't be suspicious of. He deals here often."

Deals here? The closer she got to her memories, the more questions she had.

They walked through the cobblestone streets, Vega and Arlet dodging bodies like bullets so they wouldn't blow their cover. The streets were alive with vendors by the harbor, residents going to and from shops and their homes.

The air smelled salty with a tinge of simmering coals. Vega quickly realized the fog was actually a haze of smoke as she watched people disappear from their doorsteps in a heartbeat. Tufts of tar-colored smoke covered them before they disappeared.

"They're like Halo." Vega had only met the young boy once since waking up in Castra on a day Khort agreed to let her go up top with him. Khort had figuratively taken Halo under his wing, but Vega still wasn't too sure about him. She'd gotten a spine-tingling chill when his eyes met hers for the first time—his frosted green irises felt like windows into another dimension.

"Somewhat," Arlet replied. "He's the only traveler we know of that can transport others too."

The streets started to grow smaller, turning into dark dirt as they moved through the city. Once out of the prying eyes of the busy city, Arlet let go of their shield. Vega felt exposed, bringing her power to a bubble beneath her skin. She didn't understand it fully, not yet, but it was *there*, and God did it feel *good*.

Thirty minutes passed, and Khort knocked on a small black cabin deep in the woods. Vines grew up the sides of the home, smoke rising from the chimney from a lit fire. A frail older woman with dark circles under her eyes opened the door. Her hair was darker than the night sky with a blue hue. "Come in." Her voice was high-pitched and whiny—exactly how Vega expected someone compared to a witch to sound.

The five of them—two rebel guards from Solum, herself, Arlet, and Khort—entered through the door. A stifling feeling wrapped around Vega.

Something isn't right. Her power felt like a static ball in her hands, her heartbeat spiking. *You're fine. Breathe.*

The woman led them into a back room, where vials lined the walls, the smell of herbs strong. "Have a seat." She pointed to a small pillow on the floor beside a cauldron. The sound of bubbling liquid inside grabbed Vega's attention. She crossed her legs as she made herself as comfortable as she could. Her heart thudded so hard in her chest, she was sure everyone else could hear. "Did you bring the payment?" she asked, turning to Khort.

"Yes. You'll receive it after Vega has gotten her memories returned." Khort crossed his arms, and the Solum guards left the cabin to post outside.

The witch grumbled, moving about the room to collect vials of liquid and baggies of herbs.

"This isn't the first time we've worked together, Flavia. I haven't done you wrong yet. Why would I start now?" His eyes rolled in annoyance.

Vega twiddled her thumbs, chewing on the inside of her cheek while her eyes bounced back and forth during Khort's intense interaction with Flavia. The decrepit woman quickly mixed the herbs and liquids into a hot cup of water from the bubbling cauldron. "Drink this," she croaked.

Vega took the warm mug in her hands, looking around the room. This was it—she was about to *remember*.

"All of it."

Vega tipped the mug back and chugged the contents. The tingle of her lightning overwhelmed her senses. A burning agony shot through her body, so strong words couldn't form into anything coherent. Her eyes squeezed shut, and when she opened them, the corners of her vision started to go fuzzy. *No, no, no. Not this again.*

"Halo?" Out of the corner of her darkening vision, Vega saw the young blond traveler. *Trouble. We're in trouble.*

There was that chill Vega felt the last time Halo was around. She stood without thinking. Flavia's hands were on the sides of Vega's head. *When did those get there?*

"What are you doing here, Halo?" That was Khort.

The room went black.

27

"I asked you a question, Halo! Why are you here?" Khort got louder. Vega could barely comprehend what was happening, her vision not fully back yet after blacking out—she relied on her hearing to piece together the world around her.

This was the first time she hadn't seen anything when blacking out—had it been the witch who'd caused it?

"I wanted to make sure you guys were safe. That no one in Fraus had stopped you." This was his homeland—he knew it better than any of them, but his words and tone faltered.

Vega's vision started to blur into focus, the ring of black pushing out to the corner of her eyesight.

Khort's nostrils flared when he was within reach of the blond boy. "You liar," Khort said on an inhale. "I can smell him on you." A dragon with heightened senses—there wasn't much you could get past him.

"No," the boy said, taking a step back and putting his hands up. "I wouldn't—I didn't," he sputtered, trying to backtrack.

Vega's world came into full focus, but the pain never completely subsided. A dull ache pounded at the base of her skull, and her eyes burned like she'd opened them underwater. Her back rested against the wall behind her, but Flavia's arms slid under Vega's, hoisting her up.

"Come along, girl."

Vega shook her head, still unsure if she was able to speak.

"Fine," the witch sneered.

A surge of Vega's power shot through her body by no control of her own. She screamed, but nothing came out. She was frozen in shock from her lightning working against her. *This witch is going to kill me.*

The rest of the group was focused on Halo and the betrayal unraveling.

"My payday will be much better from Marlena anyway." Flavia's voice came out like a snake ready to strike her in the jugular. The old woman pinned Vega inside herself, her body fighting for release from the hold on her power.

No, no, no. I'm not giving up. I'm not dying again. Fight, Vega! Flavia's power continued to strain her own, turning the static of her veins into a current of energy Vega couldn't harvest. *Focus.*

Flavia dragged her backward, her hands still beneath Vega's underarms. Vega's heels dragged on the ground. "Walk."

Vega wanted to scream for help, for anyone to turn around and save her from the havoc being wreaked on her body and mind. *Arlet. Where is Arlet?*

Everything moved in slow motion. "Walk or I'll kill you." Those words jarred something inside Vega.

I am not the weak girl I used to be. Anger fizzled inside, and Vega could feel her lightning come back to her core. The scream finally came, ripping through her vocal cords. Her vision darkened again, but this time she felt the spark of her power—her power in her control.

Vega dug her nails into the witch's thighs, surely drawing blood as the lightning zapped through her fingertips. There was nowhere for the blue lightning to go other than straight into Flavia.

The only noise the woman made was the sound of her body hitting the rickety cabin floor. Her body convulsed, cracking against the plank flooring again and again until eventually she went limp. The whites of her eyes were visible through the slits of her eyelids.

"No." The word slipped off of her lips in a whisper. "No, no."

Arlet came rushing into the cabin, the front door crashing against the wall. Vega couldn't remember her going outside.

"Shit." Arlet rushed over to Vega. "Oh gods. What happened?"

Vega fell to her knees, taking Flavia by the shoulders. "No, no," she repeated. "I killed her. Oh my god. I killed her." Vega gasped, on the verge of hyperventilating as she held the dead woman's body.

Arlet's hands gripped her shoulders gently. "She's gone."

Vega recoiled. "Stop it! Don't touch me!" She scrambled, pushing herself farther from Arlet and pulling the woman's lifeless form into her lap. "She can't be dead. I can't have killed her. Someone do something! I didn't mean to. I just—I wanted to get her off me." Her eyes were wild with fear, as wide as a deer in the path of an oncoming car.

"Fucking shit!" Khort's voice roared over her own pleading. "Vega!" He crossed the room in large strides. "What did you do?"

"She was going to take me to Marlena. She said..." Tears streamed down Vega's face. "She said she could get a better payday by giving me to her."

"We don't kill innocents!" His eyes clouded as he lost his temper.

"Did you not hear her? The bitch was going to turn her over to the *enemy*. She wasn't an innocent!" Arlet stood in between Vega and Khort.

"I killed her," Vega repeated. She'd taken someone's life. It wasn't the first she'd killed, but it was the only one she could remember.

"Do you know how long it took me to find her? To find someone with her kind of power who would work with us?" Khort's voice wasn't kind anymore—the friendly edge that made her melt into their kiss the night before gone. "Years! I risked everything to get her memories back!"

"We'll find another way!" Arlet reached out and shoved Khort back. "We always find another way. She was going to kill Vega, or worse, turn her over to Marlena, Khort! *Marlena!* Bury that nasty pride of yours and open your fucking eyes."

Vega quivered as she sobbed, shaking Flavia's body. She was about to turn Vega over to the enemy, maybe kill her, but she still cried for the woman—for the life she'd taken.

Khort turned his anger to the traveler still standing on the opposite side of the room, frozen in fear. "Halo, you piece of shit! Get over here!" Khort wasn't worried about Vega's current state. "You're working with them," he growled like the angry beast he could shift into.

"No! No! I came here to warn you. They're here." Khort lunged for him, but Halo was gone in a cloud of dark smoke.

"Fuck!" Khort screamed. throwing his arms in the air, storming back to Vega. "Get up. We have to go." He reached out for her, but she twisted away from his touch.

"Don't touch me!" Vega screamed again. "I killed her! I killed her, and I don't know how I did it. She had a hold on my power. She was using it against me. I killed her. I stole it back and killed her." She sounded like a broken record, but it was the only way she could process what she'd done.

"We have to do things we don't like sometimes. You did what you needed to do to keep yourself alive, to protect yourself." Arlet knelt, and Vega allowed her to get close but not to touch her. Her skin blazed with heat from her lightning flickering, and she wasn't sure she knew how to turn it off.

A rumble of thunder sounded outside. Arlet glanced at the

window as the wind whistled through the cracks of the home. "You have to calm down," she told Vega. The guards moved inside, standing by the front door. One looked out of the door's tiny window for movement. "You don't have control over your storms yet." The house rattled.

"We're supposed to be the good guys, right? We are supposed to protect these people! Not go around killing them." A bolt of lightning cracked outside, making the old home shudder.

"We are the good guys. We are. We have to protect ourselves too. Even if that means doing something we don't want to do." Her head shot to the window as it rattled again. "Vega, please. We can't let all of Tolevarre know we're here," she begged, the sound of panic distorting her usually melodic tone.

Vega didn't know how much time had passed when she finally let Arlet grab her by the shoulders. Her touch made Vega jump, still worried she would zap anyone who came in contact with her.

"I didn't mean to," she gasped, swiping at her face with her palms as her storm outside began to calm.

"I know you didn't. I know that. You were protecting yourself." Arlet sat on the floor, wrapping her arms around Vega. She smoothed her hair away from her face, soothing the sobs wracking Vega's body as she lost herself to the pain of taking a life.

28

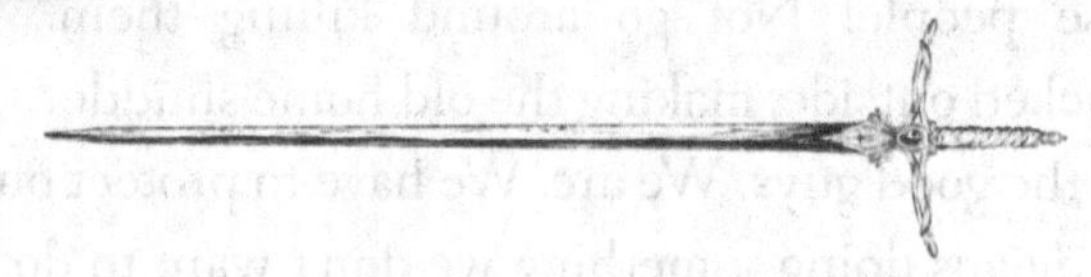

His men hid in the shadows of the Fraus woods. Bridger bounced his leg, eyes forward. The large rock he used for a seat dug into his thighs.

Halo was late.

Something was wrong—Bridger could feel it in the way the wind picked up. He shot to his feet when ice-blue lightning lit up the sky. *Vega.*

Black smoke wafted in his direction, and Halo choked on his breath as his body came into view.

"What happened?" Bridger boomed.

"I got the time wrong. They were already there when I arrived," he rasped. "Khort knows. He knows I betrayed them. She killed her."

Bridger's stomach dropped, and he felt the weight of a thousand stones sitting in the pit of his gut. He hadn't felt her die—he hadn't felt Vega die.

"I couldn't talk my way out of it. He said he could smell you all over me." The way his eyes grew and his panic spread, Bridger could see Halo's age for the first time. He wasn't ready to be a spy.

Bridger fucked up. "Who killed Vega?" His mouth felt dry.

"What?" Halo stopped his pacing. "No, not Vega. The witch. Vega killed her by accident. She wasn't okay after, started crying. Did you hear the thunder? The lightning... Gods, she's so strong. What the fuck." The boy shook his head, his blond hair falling into his eyes.

Vega's alive.

"Where are they?" Bridger grabbed Halo by the shoulders, forcing him to look in his eyes.

Bridger's soldiers readied themselves for a fight, grabbing their weapons off the ground, but most were already equipped—their weapons the abilities streaming through their blood.

He watched as Halo's eyes darted around, waiting for punishment. "Halo, focus. Take a breath. This mission isn't over. You didn't fail, not yet. But if you don't take me to them, then we lose and they win. We have time to come out on top here. You have to relax and take me there. Now."

"Okay," Halo said, exhaling.

Bridger turned around and pointed to two soldiers. "With us." He hoped Halo could get all of them there in one piece. He took a deep breath. "Steady yourselves and get ready. Do not close your eyes. It helps." Though he didn't promise they wouldn't absolutely hate what it felt like to slip through time and space. "The rest of you wait here. We'll bring the fight to you if one unfolds." Bridger turned back to Halo, happy to see the look of panic he'd worn before was disappearing now that a structured plan was formed.

His confidence would grow later—everything came with time.

"Ready?" Halo asked, his voice even. He looked around the circle. "Keep your hand on me at all times."

"Or what?" one of the soldiers asked.

"You'll die." His smile told Bridger he was no longer nervous— put the boy in his traveling element, and he was strong. It was battle and spying he wasn't ready for. *That* Bridger could work with.

Bridger returned his smile with a soft, grounding one of his own. "Take us to a location close by so we have a moment to regroup." And just like that, Bridger felt like he was falling, shredding into nothing and reforming into a new location.

Bridger and the small group stood outside of a house in the middle of the woods. He sank down, forcing the rest of them behind a row of bushes to allow them enough time to fight the nausea of traveling. Junie's eyes looked as though they might bug out of her head, and Jak was lying on his back, eyes shut tightly.

Junie and her twin brother were both from Imber. They were children when their land was destroyed, having no memories of their lives before Marlena's rule. Jak was a water-wielder able to pull his power from the moisture in the air. He made quick work of drowning someone with a single drop of water.

Junie took after their mother's line—the people of Littera bred two types of powers. The power of infinite knowledge, complete know-it-alls... and then there were the powers like Junie had, rare and now outlawed under Marlena's rule—another group of people who'd been killed if they didn't pledge their allegiance to the new governing system and turn themselves into a weapon for the military to use.

Mind control. Junie could slip into someone's mind if she got her hands on them—Bridger had seen her make men do terrible things for putting their hands where they didn't belong.

"Ground yourself," Bridger barked, reaching out to steady Junie as she swayed. "It's over. Connect to your core, feel your power, and don't let his linger too long." Junie turned her head and puked, retching on her boots.

The air around the clearing felt colder than it had been outside of town. The front lawn was a mess with branches and shingles. A downed tree leaned against a shed behind the house. Vega had lost control.

When Bridger looked back from the shed, the house was gone.

Arlet. It had been years since he'd seen her power in action. She could hide buildings now... Bridger didn't know his jaw was agape.

"It's Arlet. She can manipulate what you see," Halo said.

"Magnificent," he marveled.

Halo kept his voice low, pointing straight ahead. "Do you see that large branch?" he asked Bridger.

"Yes."

"Look at the glimmer behind that." The second Bridger caught the change in what he thought he saw, it was gone. He focused on the big picture, catching another shimmer at the top of the tree line. "The door is right behind that branch."

"Fucking Arlet," Bridger said with a smile on his face. An old part of him felt a swell of pride for the girl who used to feel so inconsiderable compared to her friends and their abilities. The feeling was gone before he could register what it was. Bridger turned his attention to Halo. "Stay here. We will come to you when it's time to go. Understood?"

"Yes, sir."

Bridger nodded to Junie and Jak, who were finally coming down from their first traveling experience, signaling them to get ready.

"How many bodies?" Bridger asked Halo.

"Five. Khort, Arlet, Vega, and two guards. I don't know who or what they have waiting on the outskirts."

Five. It was five against three, but Bridger wasn't worried about that. Khort was strong, but he'd never beaten Bridger in hand-to-hand combat. Vega didn't have her memories back, which made her immensely weaker than she would be—but never weak. Bridger knew better than to underestimate her in any life. Proof of her power lay around the clearing. Arlet was one hell of a fighter now, and if she could manipulate visions as well as she could now, Bridger considered her their biggest threat.

The two guards Bridger didn't know about—but he knew what

he and the twins could do when on a team. They would be nearly unstoppable if Meyer were here.

"Perfect. Jak, drown the guards. Junie, grab Vega. I'll take care of the others."

The twins nodded in unison.

"Let's go." Bridger moved them across the lawn, head held high as he eerily glided to the front door of the old, cobbled cottage.

The door opened as they approached, one guard stepping through. Jak used the water from a bird feeder to drown him before the man even had a moment to realize he was going to die.

Bridger's powers concealed the echoes of their footsteps, giving them a muted entry into the main room, where voices traveled through the open door at the back of the cottage.

"We have to leave right now," Khort bellowed.

Bridger held up his hand, his soldiers slowing to a stop behind him. He pointed to his left and right, sending them to the shadows of the room where he would let them hide until it was time to pounce.

"If Marlena knows we're here, it's already too late, Khort." Arlet was calm, talking the hot-headed shifter down. "If we run, we won't see them coming. If we stay, we can hold our ground. It'll give me time to get Vega out of here."

Bridger made his entrance, lowering his shields as he cleared his throat and leaned into the doorframe.

But Vega's eyes were on him long before that, glued to his presence.

"I agree with Arlet. I think you're already too late." Bridger looked around, watching Khort jump in front of Vega. Smoke came out of his nose, making Bridger chuckle as he pushed himself upright. "It's a bit small in here for your wings, buddy." He motioned to the low ceilings. "Chill."

Bridger's air of cool, calm, and collected rattled everyone around him. His eyes landed on Vega as he circled the room. She moved from being slumped on the floor, her eyes puffy from crying, to standing tall when he'd come into the room.

Khort huffed. "Get your eyes off her or—"

Bridger didn't let him finish, the blade of his dagger sliding through his fingers with a smile. "Or what, Khort? You'll soar off into the night sky and roar because I took the girl? Again." Bridger's laugh was dark.

Vega stepped out from behind Khort, her fingers dancing with her captivating electricity. "Are you always such a dick?" Her voice floated through the room, always so easy to listen to, even when she was being snarky.

"Oh, hello, Kitten." His gaze darkened as he looked her up and down. Bridger licked his lips for effect. And to get under Khort's skin.

"Don't fucking call her that." *Hook, line, sinker.* Bridger's distraction was working, allowing his soldiers to get into their places behind them in the corners of the room.

"But why not? She used to love it when I called her that. I have a few more nicknames I can try out. Should I use a different one?" Bridger provoked Khort, hoping for a fight before he snuck out of here with the one thing that he couldn't stand to lose.

Vega.

A bolt of lightning struck where Bridger had been standing seconds earlier. He moved too quickly for her. Without the memories of her power control, she was predictable. "You're going to have to be quicker than that, baby," he purred, his dagger whipping out of his hand, soaring over his shoulder, and slicing through the air towards the guard who thought he was sneaking up behind him. It struck home between his eyes without Bridger having to turn around. "And so will your guards."

Arlet and Khort jumped into action. Arlet grabbed Vega and disappeared right in front of Bridger's eyes. The shock of their disappearance lasted only long enough to allow Khort a blow—the punch landed right between Bridger's eyes, cracking his nose.

A quick and easy break that would heal itself in no time. Bridger was getting really sick of broken noses from these two.

The blood dripped down his sharp features, mixing with the wry smile on his lips. Bridger wiped the blood dripping down his chin with the back of his hand. His laugh was feral as he reached behind his back and unsheathed his sword. "Think you can hold up in a fight with me as an actual man, Fera? Or should we take this outside so I can let you hide behind your overgrown lizard body?"

Khort lunged for him again as Bridger struck out with his sword. Khort swung and dove, maneuvering to the corner of the room to grab his own weapon. His move was swift, but when Khort made his move, Bridger forced his shield up. Khort's blade struck air as thick as a brick wall, breaking the tip clean off.

Khort laughed, shaking his head. "I thought you wanted to fight me like a real man. If I don't get to use my powers to outdo you, then neither do you."

Bridger allowed his wall down, beckoning Khort with two fingers. "If you insist."

Khort threw his useless sword to the ground with a clank. The twitch of Bridger's lips welcomed the chaos of a brawl. He sheathed his sword between his shoulder blades and brought his fists up in front of his face. Khort watched his every move but took his eyes off Bridger's legs as they settled on his hands.

It was exactly what Bridger hoped he'd do. Bridger knocked Khort off his feet with a kick, but he landed smoother than expected, crouching as Bridger attempted a blow to his face with his knee. Khort used the momentum to push himself up and landed beside a wooden chair he picked up to wield against Bridger's next blow. The chair splintered, pieces soaring through the small room.

Bridger caught a piece mid-air and spun it in his hand like he would a dagger. He threw it in a straight line, and it nicked Khort's arm. He hissed in pain, a hand hurtling to cup the wound. He pulled his hand back, blood covering his palm. Khort let anger get to him—he'd always been quick to throw off, forgetting he needed to focus on the moves he made physically and not mentally.

Bridger grabbed him by the arm as he charged in his direction and flipped Khort to the ground, vibrating the floorboards with the force of his fall. He put his boot on his neck, pressing down hard enough to block his airway but not to kill.

Bridger smiled down at him, triumphant. "Checkmate." He was about to crush Khort's windpipe, adding more force, when a scream erupted through the house.

Bridger didn't give Khort the option to move, turning his head to find Vega in Junie's grip, writhing in pain. "Enough," Bridger snarled. Junie complied, keeping her grip on Vega to remind her what she could do if she decided to fight back.

"Get your hands off her!" Khort gargled underneath Bridger, his hands fighting against Bridger's boot to free himself. Bridger pressed down harder.

"The more you fight, the harder I push," Bridger purred, the pain he caused to Khort working like a calming drink. "Come on out, Arlet. Or I kill them both."

Arlet answered by letting her power's cloak down, stepping over the threshold into the main room. Her fists were clenched, eyes bouncing between Khort under Bridger's boot, Vega in Junie's hold, and Bridger, his menacing grin in place.

Vega breathed heavily, standing as still as she possibly could to avoid Junie's torture.

"What do you want, Bridger? You want us to surrender? To back down? We'll never do what you did to Vega!" Arlet's eyes met his. "You might as well kill us all if that's what you expect. Reset Vega and let her wither away on Earth. At least she'd be free of you. Finally."

Bridger ground his teeth, his jaw clenching at her words.

There was no one to blame but himself for turning his back on Vega—turning his back on their relationship and the ascendancy they would have had together.

"Tell your gecko to back down." Bridger looked down at Khort, his face red from struggling to breathe. "And stop fighting back. I'm taking Vega."

"No!" Khort scratched at his boots still, attempting to use his feet to kick out from under Bridger.

Bridger pinned Khort down with his shield, holding him completely still. The boot on his throat wasn't needed anymore, but Bridger liked the feeling it gave him.

Bridger's grin spread across his face when Arlet dove towards him with a dagger in hand. He moved out of the way, finally releasing his boot from Khort's throat just in time for Arlet's momentum to keep throwing her forward. She stumbled over Khort, catching herself before taking a full tumble.

Someone groaned from behind, causing Bridger to jerk his head to see Junie falling to the floor and Vega barreling towards him with lightning the color of her eyes. Bridger threw up his shield. Vega crashed into it, unable to remember any of his easiest moves. "It's too bad you couldn't get your memories back in time to remember how to fight me." Junie twitched on the floor from the electric jolt Vega sent through her. *Gods, it would be a shame if she's dead.*

Vega didn't react to his words, only stared him down. The hatred in her eyes simmered, a cold chill traveling up his spine. He showed no reaction, only forced the feeling away.

"I've had enough." Bridger faked a yawn when he saw Junie open her eyes. "Put Vega to sleep." She was up, dazed but alive. She drew no attention to herself as she crept behind Vega. Arlet was too busy trying to free Khort from Bridger's power to notice.

"Goodnight, love," Bridger said, looking into the eyes of the woman he once would've done anything for as Junie gripped her shoulders. Vega slumped in her arms, head dipping back. Jak walked in with Halo. "Take her to Aeris." Bridger allowed his shield to drop and released his power on Khort, who popped off the ground instantly.

"You traitor!" Khort almost had his hands on Halo before he stepped through thin air, taking Vega's body and the twins with him. Bridger was now alone with Khort and Arlet for the first time in nearly forty years.

"Looks like you both lost again." Bridger reveled in the way their hatred could be seen in the lines of their faces. "Aren't you tired of it yet?"

Arlet sneered. "What happened to you? I don't even recognize you." She'd lost her best friend again, and for that, Bridger felt a tiny pang of remorse.

"I got tired of losing. No one is worth this type of pain." Bridger pointed at her and then at Khort. "Maybe one day you'll see that too." Bridger backed out of the room, the two of them stalking around him now that he was alone. He looked like the mouse, but they all knew he was the lion.

Halo was back, materializing beside Bridger—officially choosing sides. "Commander, let's go." Halo's gaze averted from Khort's ice-cold stare.

"Look at him, Halo," Bridger growled. "It's too late to go back now. There is no forgiveness for what you've done. Own your choice."

Halo lifted his head, locking eyes with Khort, who only had one question. "Why?"

"Because I'm not a hero. I want to be on the winning side, not fighting a losing battle."

Bridger spit out a laugh as he leaned down and pulled his dagger out of the dead guard's head. "Everyone can see it now. You're losing your own people. They don't believe you can win. Let that sink in."

Bridger put his hand on Halo's shoulder, a triumphant smile on his face. "And now, I'm going to torture your girl. Bye-bye!"

Halo traveled them straight into Marlena's home as Khort shifted into the black dragon he should have been from the start.

29

VEGA'S EYES OPENED, AND PANIC TWISTED HER GUT INTO A thousand knots. Her last memories swirled in her head, where a splitting headache took hold. Having Junie inside her mind was a feeling she never wanted to experience again. It was like someone tied her to puppet strings and did whatever they wanted while she had to sit back and watch. And then Flavia's manipulation...

I killed Flavia.

Bile pooled at the back of her throat. Vega jumped to her feet. Her vision blurred, but she didn't stumble, only searched for the power inside to ground herself.

Focus.

The panic made it hard to feel the electric pulse that had become second nature to her since returning to Tolevarre.

"Fucking focus, Vega. Fuck." She kept her voice low as her eyes scanned the room. There was nothing special about it—no hints as to where she was. The walls were a deep green, the flooring sturdy planks of dark brown wood. It didn't creak as she walked across it. No pictures hung on the walls, and there was minimal furniture. She knew she was in Aeris, that much she could remember from before Junie got her hands on her, but she had a sinking feeling this might be the home of someone she wasn't ready to meet.

Vega kept calling on her powers, scared when nothing bubbled inside of her. "No, no, no." Tears welled in her eyes as her panic turned to fear. The enemy had taken her, and now she had no way to defend herself.

The hollow feeling inside was unwelcome. She hadn't had her abilities back for long, but after having them returned and then stolen from her so soon, Vega felt empty.

There was a door on the far wall. Vega sprinted to it, her footsteps echoing through the room, and she jostled the handle. It didn't budge. Her heart rate spiked as dread crawled through her body. There were no windows, no exit.

I'm trapped.

Vega wouldn't turn her back to the door, leaving the only out she had in her sight. The suit she'd been dressed in was torn, and half of her left sleeve was ripped off. A new brand on her forearm caught her attention—it was a small circle with an X through the middle, its edges spilling out the sides like it had bled through. Vega ran her fingers over it, and when they reached the center of the X, the mark burned her. She hissed, jerking her fingers away.

This new brand had to be why her powers weren't answering when called, why she could no longer feel the tingle underneath her skin.

Vega took a breath and tried to talk herself down. *It's okay. They will come for you. They always come for you.* She hoped she was right as her chest tightened. Vega wanted to cry, realizing she might be in the most danger she'd ever been in, right at this very moment.

She didn't want to break down, scared of how that would make her look. She knew who would walk into the room next. It had been fifteen years since her sister laid eyes on her, and regardless of her memories being wiped from her head, Vega knew Marlena would be eager to see that she'd won... again.

Vega wanted to show no weakness. As badly as she wanted to fall to the floor and bawl her eyes out, she didn't. She stood, her back to the wall for what would end up being hours until the door handle turned. Her eyes felt heavy, and a large bruise was beginning to form around her left cheek.

When the door opened, it wasn't the blonde sister she'd seen in pieces of memories. It was Bridger. The scowl on her face couldn't have been more definitive. "Where is she?" Vega asked, rolling her shoulders and faking confidence.

Bridger held a hand over where his heart would be—if he had one. No one with a soul could act the way he did. "It's always about her," he said, his smile sharp, showing off his perfect set of teeth.

How can someone so rotten be so fucking handsome?

"You should be used to being second best. You're the one who traded me in for the other sister with power." Vega's back stiffened as he got closer. He reached out and grabbed her chin, forcing her to look up at him, directly into the eyes she thought were much darker in the witch's cottage. In the new light, she could see swirls of copper around his irises.

"You shouldn't speak about what you don't know, Kitten."

Vega spat in his face. She took advantage of his eyes being closed and shoved him as hard as she could. He stumbled but didn't fall, his feet too quick. "Call me that one more time." Vega stared him down, and if her powers weren't being kept from her, her fingers would be dancing with those blue sparks she'd become accustomed to.

Bridger wiped the spit from his face and prowled back to her when the door swung open with a loud bang. The voice that came through was one Vega had heard in all her nightmares.

"Hello, sister." Marlena's smile spread across her face like wildfire. Her graceful walk came to a stop beside Bridger. She rested a perfectly manicured hand on his forearm, the touch so delicate Vega couldn't help the feeling welling inside her gut. *There's no way.* "Have you been having a good time with Bridger? He hasn't done anything to get himself into too much trouble, has he?"

Vega backtracked, taking a large step away while she took Marlena in fully for the first time. The dress she wore was the color of blood, a rich satin fabric that hugged her curvy waist in places Vega only hoped to thicken up. Her bodice was tight, pushing her breasts up to make them the center of attention. Her hair was wrapped around her head in a braided coronet—seated atop the beautiful braid was a thin halo made of black iron.

A crown.

Simply banded and dark as coal.

The color of her eyes made Vega feel like she was looking in a mirror. The blue was the color of water frozen by winter's chill. Marlena's matching set bore right into Vega's, sending ice down her spine.

Her sister stalked towards her. "Am I as you remember?" Marlena asked, looking down at her. She had to be over half a foot taller than Vega in her heels. "Oh, that's right. You can't." Her laugh was eerie, high-pitched in all the wrong ways.

"Do my memories make me too powerful?" Vega retorted, her stare turning as cold as her core felt. She clenched her jaw tight to keep her teeth from rattling. Marlena was every bit as terrifying as she'd expected and more gorgeous than anyone could have prepared her for.

Vega noticed the hint of a smile Bridger tried to hide. She couldn't wait to wipe that smug look off his face. *One day.*

"You've never been more powerful than me, no matter what those little friends of yours have said, what lies they've gotten you to believe." Marlena's smile faltered an inch. "But there is a reason I brought you here this time instead of ordering you to be killed like all the lives before." Marlena began to circle Vega, examining her like a cow for slaughter. "There's information I need from you, and you'll need your memories back in order for me to get what I want."

Vega kept her eyes on Marlena, trying to hold back her shock. "Am I as you remember?" Vega didn't falter when she realized she'd thrown her sister's words back at her.

Marlena reached out and grabbed Vega by the nape of her neck, coiling her fingers in her hair. "Funny," she sneered while tightening her already unyielding grip. Vega gasped, pain radiating up the back of her neck and into her skull. A jolt went through her body, darker than her own electric shock. It forced her eyes open, gaze locking with Marlena's. "You'll learn quickly that I don't like your cocky attitude." Marlena gave Vega a shove, and she tumbled to the floor.

She let out a gargled moan when bone snapped, her wrist giving out and sending her hurling to the hardwood floor, where her head hit with a crack.

Marlena's heeled footsteps echoed through the empty room. Vega's eyes landed on her boots first before dragging up her body. She cradled her newly broken wrist against her chest, gritting her teeth to keep the cries of pain back.

Do not let her see you cry. The voice inside her head was stronger than she was right now.

Vega kept telling herself to stand tall, but if this was just the beginning of her torture, there was no way she'd last more than twenty-four hours.

Marlena knelt down in front of Vega, a sneer painted on her lips. "You won't be so tough when I lock you in the dungeons and torture you for days on end. I want you to beg for death so when you finally decide to tell me what I need to know, you'll break. You won't have the hope you've been holding on to for fifty-five years."

"I can't imagine what I did to make you hate me so much." Vega breathed through the pain.

She was ready to feel whole again. There had been an ache in

Vega's chest since the moment she woke up in Tolevarre, a missing piece of herself that still left her feeling hollow and lonely.

Marlena's gaze made her feel insignificant. "You'll remember eventually, and when you do, I want you to cry for the forgiveness I'll never give you." Marlena backed away from Vega. "Lock her up, Bridger."

I should have stayed on Earth.

30

"Get up." The words were distant, even through his ears. Vega peered at Bridger through her eyelashes. The pain in her eyes was recognizable to him despite how well she was attempting to hide it. She set her lips, and his eyes flicked to them for a bit longer than they should've.

The fire behind her eyes sizzled, and if looks could kill... *I'd be dead.* "Please don't make me tell you twice." Bridger crossed his arms and tapped the toe of his boot on the floor, bouncing it impatiently as he waited.

Vega rasped, standing. "Shove it."

She stumbled when she took her first step, and Bridger shot forward to keep her upright. The realization of what he was doing set in, so he changed course. Instead of gently steadying her, he shoved his hand under her arm and yanked her upright.

It'd been two lifetimes since he'd touched her.

He jerked his hand away and shoved it into his pocket. The feeling he used to get when they were together tingled up his arm—her touch feeling as electric as it ever had, even with her powers choked out from the branded spell on her arm. "You complain when

267

I'm an asshole and you complain when I'm nice. I can never win with you." He pointed to the open door. "Walk." Vega didn't budge, her face paler than before she stood. "Are you going to puke?"

Vega's unease turned to anger, her eyes turning to slits. "I can see why everyone hates you." She finally took a step, her footing more stable.

Bridger stayed close but kept enough distance to ensure he didn't touch her again. "Do you think it's any news to me that people don't like me, Vega?" He said her name like he was keeping a secret—deep and savory to the ears. "No one ever really liked me. You're going to have to get better at your comebacks." They continued through the long hall and took the stairs down at an infuriatingly slow pace.

"Maybe when I get my memories back and I remember all the fucked-up shit you've done to me, it'll help with my comebacks."

"Such language." Bridger's abdomen pulsed with a hint of laughter. "I think I liked it better when you kept that pretty little mouth of yours shut. You were so peaceful when you were asleep."

Vega held up her middle finger, not speaking another word. Bridger noticed the fresh black polish on her nails. *And the ring.* His heart dropped, but he recovered quickly, and he returned her sentiment with a wink before burying himself inside his mind.

Her fingernails are painted black and she's wearing the ring still. Bridger immediately forced his focus to the back of her head, where her dark wavy hair was down, braids keeping the hair out of her face. Another detail reminding him of the Vega from fifty-five years ago.

These details hadn't always been there. Sometimes the person Vega became in these other lives didn't even feel like her—so different from the person she'd been before the curse.

That wasn't the case here. From the fingernails to the sass, this was the Vega he fell in love with. *My Vega.* He swallowed the lump in his throat as they approached the bottom of the stairs. "Left," he ordered, happy to have something to focus on other than the woman in front of him.

There was no one around Marlena's estate to see the sister who'd returned from the dead. The halls were empty and hauntingly quiet as they began to descend into the belly of Marlena's home—into the original dungeon. Nothing had changed down here in thousands of years. It was cold and damp, with iron bars and cages crammed in.

Vega came to a sudden stop. Bridger almost collided with her as she spun around, eyes wide with panic.

"Don't make this worse than it needs to be," Bridger warned. The Vega he'd known once wouldn't go down without a fight. His gaze fell to her legs, catching the twitch in her muscle.

Vega's leg swept out, attempting to collide with Bridger's and take him down like he'd done with Khort. He sighed heavily as his hand shot out and caught her by the calf, tripping her up. Bridger snatched her by the bad wrist, never letting her hit the ground. She yelped when he wrapped his hand tightly around the broken bone.

Vega was bound up like a pretzel. "Nice try." Bridger hoisted her over his shoulder like she weighed nothing.

Vega kicked and screamed, pounding her fists into his back. "Help! Help! Let me go!" she screeched.

"No one can hear you down here." Bridger dropped her in a cell lightly.

She exploded off her feet, chasing after him. He closed the cell door, a piercing scrape echoing down the hall as he locked her in. This dungeon hadn't been used in years and smelled like mold and mildew.

The walls were made out of old stone, crumbling around the corners. The cell doors' thick black iron rods were rusted with age, flaking off in chunks.

Bridger, Vega, and Khort had spent seventeen nights here during Vega's second life.

"You can't leave me down here!" she belted, clutching the bars and shaking them as if they might break with her anger. She looked down at both hands, her bad wrist no longer limp. She calmed and wiggled it, her eyes shooting up to him. "When you grabbed my wrist back there..."

Bridger's crooked smile pulled at his lips as he watched the recognition sink in. "You can thank me by being a good girl down here tonight. Don't give your guard too hard of a time, and maybe I'll see to it that your breakfast isn't cold."

"Fuck you, Bridger!" Vega screamed, rattling the cell bars.

"You have, actually." He laughed like the sound of a bell ringing. "See you tomorrow, Kitten."

"You're going to hell!"

Bridger knew Vega was picturing him burning for eternity.

"Newsflash, we're already in hell!" His voice echoed off the empty cell walls. She was the only prisoner down here.

Vega continued to scream until Bridger was out of earshot. When he could no longer hear her cursed promises, he let out a breath.

31

THE SILENCE WAS DEAFENING. VEGA'S EARS RANG WITH THE echoes of her gargled screams. She'd finally given up hours ago—she'd screamed until she could taste blood. Her throat felt like sandpaper had torn it to shreds piece by piece until her jugular was exposed.

Her fingertips were burned from the brand on her forearm. Vega had tried to claw the nasty mark off her body in hopes it would release her powers back to her.

It didn't work, only leaving her more wounded.

Vega curled into a corner to try and find what little bit of warmth was hiding in the shadows. The suit she was in did help with being exposed to the elements, but not enough to stop the goosebumps from forming over the new brand on her arm.

The brand was small, covering only a quarter-size space on her forearm. Vega tried to peel the skin off, digging her nails underneath until the pain was too much to handle.

She rested her head on the hard wall, her knees pulled up to her chest. A sob made her chest heave. After hours of playing tough,

Vega let the sorrow and fear take over. The floodgates opened, and tears poured from her eyes.

All her life—this life—she'd found a way to pick up the pieces and move on, however reluctant she might have felt. How was she supposed to do that now?

Footsteps sounded through the quiet hall. Vega jumped up, readying herself to fight.

Come on, lightning! What good are you if you can be taken from me so easily? The brand on her arm seared when she tried to call on her abilities.

A hand popped through the cell bars. "Here." A man appeared on the other side seconds after. His vacant stare was cold, annoyed.

Vega honed in on the container of water he was holding. "No." She scowled. Vega knew better than to trust the food and water given to her down here.

The man rolled his eyes and let it fall to the ground. "Suit yourself. I'm here to babysit, not to make sure you don't die from dehydration." The dented canteen rolled to a stop next to her feet, the metal clanging against the stones.

The guard leaned against a beam with his back towards her, staring at the stairwell down the hall—not a single threat to worry about. Vega fizzled with anger, not just from this but from everything that happened today. Getting herself into this position, pushing to get her memories back as fast as she could, the entire interaction with Bridger—had he felt the jolt that went through them when he touched her upstairs?

She thought about the sensation that rocked her body the entire way down to the dungeon, barely giving herself time to look around as he marched her to her new personal version of hell.

Vega should have been paying more attention to how she could escape, not her captor ex-lover's touch.

She snatched the full container from the floor and lofted it in the guard's direction through the bars. Her aim wasn't any good, so when it cracked him in the back of the head, Vega might have been more surprised than the guard. "Tell Bridger to suck my dick!" Her sister wouldn't have been the one to send her the water, that much she knew for sure.

Her smile slipped when the guard turned around and icicles sprouted from his hands.

Vega skidded away from the bars as an ice missile shot from his hand and pierced through her calf, sending her sailing to the ground. She caught herself, wailing at the pain in her leg.

The cell door creaked with a warning. Vega had no time to prepare herself for a fight. His hands were frigid against her skin, the material of her suit wrapped up in his fist as he heaved her from her seated position.

"Listen here, you little bitch!" His voice was loud in Vega's ear, his breath hot against her cheek as he spat his words. "You're supposed to be long dead already, and that little stunt you pulled might have cost you another life with no memories." He shook her, her head whacking against the stone wall.

Vega thought her head might explode, stars scattering across her vision. *I'm not ready to die.* She did the only thing she could think of to save herself and drove her thumbs into his eyes like every true crime podcast on Earth told her to do during an attack.

Only one thumb sank in, and the pop his left eyeball made when she pushed against the inside of his socket made acid rise in the back of her throat.

A piercing scream erupted from his chest, his icy grip releasing. Vega didn't have time to waste. As she hobbled away, wincing in pain, she ripped the icicle from her leg, and a scream of her own bubbled out as blood poured from the open wound.

Vega tried to focus on the task at hand: escaping. But the pain slowed her down to a hobbled jog.

The guard roared behind her, his heavy steps exiting the cell. "You're dead!" The voice was close. *Too close.*

Her breathing was heavy, her heart threatening to beat outside her chest as she took the first three steps too slowly. *He's going to kill you if you don't MOVE FASTER!* Vega wanted to cry out in frustration, but she forced herself to pick up the pace, ignoring the pain threatening to slow her down.

Ice exploded on the wall by her head, but Vega didn't are to look over her shoulder. All her momentum pushed her up, praying to any god, dead or alive, who would listen—*let me get out of here.* A hand tangling in the hair at the back of her scalp interrupted her prayer, tugging her down, down, down.

Vega felt every step dig into her on the descent, her shoulder taking the brunt of the final fall. There was no time to catch her breath, no time to get off the floor. Air never reentered her lungs, her chest seizing when the guard's heel pressed into her breastbone. Vega felt a rib pop inward, sending a new wave of pain up her side.

The guard's bloody hand covered her mouth, stifling her scream. Hot tears spilled from her eyes, her breathing shallow, and every inhale felt like fire charring her lungs.

"It's too late for crying. You should have thought about that earlier. I'm going to enjoy this next part."

Vega heard the knife before she saw it, the swish of the blade leaving its sheath. Out of pure fear, she chomped down, biting his finger straight to the bone. *Definitely harder than biting through a carrot.* The guard retaliated quickly, driving his dagger into her shoulder blade.

This was it. She was going to die at the hands of some guard with an ego problem. She would have to start over, making this life and all the others before it a complete waste. Vega didn't feel bad for herself—she felt for the friends who kept fighting for someone who never won.

Dying for good might be the best thing I can do for them. Would this be the final thought she ever had?

The guard pulled the knife out and recentered his aim, arm raised for the killing strike.

Vega couldn't stop him, the pain growing too strong. No matter how much the voice in her head told her to fight back, she couldn't. *I'm going to die.*

A new voice sliced through the room. "Grimes, what the fuck?"

The guard, Grimes, didn't move, but he no longer held the knife over Vega's heart.

"The bitch started it, and I'm going to show her what it means to finish something. Look at what she did to my eye!" His hand with the blade rose again, but before the knife struck, the other guard snatched it from his grip and knocked him to the side.

"Commander will have your head. What were you thinking?"

Vega heard them talking but had nothing left. All she could do was focus on the short rasps of her breathing.

"Your eye will heal." The man took a breath, pausing. "Maybe. That looks fucked up."

Grimes turned back to Vega with veins popping on his neck from rage, rushing towards her again. "I'm going to kill her."

The new guy jumped in front of his path. "If she's gone in the morning, your life won't reset like hers. Gods, Grimes, you're foolish." He stood over Vega, taking in her battered body. "I came here to relieve you for the night. Commander wants all level sevens ready to leave for Ardor in the morning." There was no movement. "Now! Before I summon him myself."

Footsteps and mumbled grumbles faded as Grimes took his leave. "Felix, you fucking kiss-ass."

The new guard looked at Vega, eyes scanning her body. He reached down and scooped her up, gentler than expected. "I'm sorry about him." His words were soft like a warm blanket. He sat her down in her cell, and Vega chirped at the discomfort.

"Please. Get. Me. Out. Of. Here." She dragged a breath between each word.

"No can do, Sweets, but you're still in luck. I'm a healer before a soldier, and I'm going to get you fixed up. You won't be good as new, but I guarantee you'll feel better than you do now." The man's voice was honeyed, unlike any enemy Vega had met yet. He continued to talk to her as his warm hands, so much warmer than the hands that had just defiled her, worked over her body.

Vega cried out when her rib popped back into place.

The man spoke up. "Take a deep breath. You're going to be okay."

"No, I'm not. I'm going to die," Vega cried.

Destined to die.

A welcome feeling followed her words—the out-of-body experience of the curse giving her back a memory. Typically, she would panic and fight the inevitable blackout... but as the pain seared through her, Vega closed her eyes and slipped into her mind, where at least she wouldn't feel anything—where her memories held her tightly and made her believe she was less alone.

An older woman's face floated into view, her jaw falling open while her hand outstretched to help Vega off the cold marble underneath her.

"Miss Vega, I'm so sorry." Her doe eyes fluttered to someone standing behind Vega, panic fluttering across her face.

"Oh, please, I—" Vega started, pushing herself off the ground.

"Gods, watch where you're going! You could have hurt her!" Marlena said from behind her.

She looked over Vega, grabbing her by the shoulders to check her inch by inch as if she'd been to battle and not taken a small tumble to the floor.

"I'm so sorry, Miss Marlena. Of course," the older woman croaked, bending down to gather the winter decorations that crashed to the floor when she'd collided with Vega.

"Marlena, I'm fine," Vega said, but Marlena continued to check her over. "I said I'm fine!" Vega snatched herself out of her sister's grasp, meeting her matching eyes with a glare.

"You're lucky she's fine, or—" Vega didn't let Marlena finish.

"It was my fault. I was walking backwards, not looking where I was going. She didn't mean to. Calm down." Vega's dark hair was pulled back from her face with braids while the rest tumbled past her shoulders.

"No, my apologies. Your sister is right. I should have been paying attention."

"It was an accident. It's okay." Vega had long forgotten about her bumped elbow, bending down to help gather the scattered decor.

"Miss Vega," the woman began again.

"Please, just Vega," she interrupted. "Your name is Della, right?" Vega smiled softly.

"Yes." The maid's smile was huge, a sparkle in her eye.

"How is your granddaughter? She shifted for the first time last month, didn't she?" Vega asked as she picked up the last of the decorations and put them in the brown box.

"She did. You remembered," Della cooed.

"Of course. I remember the first time Khort shifted. It's such an important moment for your people. Do you mind me asking what form she took?" Vega lifted the box off the floor and held it close to her chest.

Della couldn't hold back her smile. "A sparrow, like her father."

"I bet she's loving her new wings!" Vega's voice rang through the busy hallway with excitement. "Will you tell her congratulations for me?"

The woman grabbed the box from Vega and nodded—her smile had yet to fade.

"Of course, Mi—" Vega gave her a look. "Vega. Of course I will. She's going to be so excited to hear you remembered."

The woman hurried off to finish her duties, and Vega watched until she rounded the corner. Her emotions switched when she was alone with Marlena again. "What was that all about?"

"The help needs to learn to be more careful." Marlena stood by what she said, her spine straightening as she looked down her nose at Vega. Compared to Vega's loose curls and lazy braids, Marlena's hair was pinned up tight, not a piece out of place.

For the first time, Vega saw what Marlena would become—the ruler she had been schooled to be. She scoffed. "It's like I don't even know who you are these days." Vega shook her head. "What's gotten into you?"

Marlena crossed her arms, closing herself off. "Nothing, Vega. Jeez, I didn't think you'd get this upset about me trying to protect you."

Vega shook her head. "That's not protecting me. That's you treating the people beneath you like they're less important. She didn't do anything wrong."

Marlena let out a laugh, motioning towards where the maid ran off to. "Oh, c'mon! Get a grip. She is lesser than us. She shifts into a deer. A deer! That's why she works for *us*, Vega, not the other way around."

Vega's cheeks heated with anger. "Oh my gods! How dare you say that! That's not how we were raised, Marlena!" Their argument was starting to turn the heads of the help roaming through the halls of their home, readying the Caelums for their annual Saturnalia Ball. "Because if what you're saying is true, remember that I'm stronger than you. Does that make me better? Do I deserve more than you do?"

"You have no idea how I was raised! How our parents are raising me!" Marlena's entire demeanor changed, her temper palpable. "You've been sheltered inside a tiny bubble and have never taken a moment to see what it's been like for me!" The girls were nose to nose, Marlena swift on her toes to close the distance. "You live inside your own world. Don't pretend to know what I've been through, what they do behind closed doors to me you know nothing of. Because if you'd open your eyes, just a little, you'd see the differences. You'd see that you might be more gods-blessed in your abilities than me, but I have always, will always, be smarter than you."

Vega stepped back, stammering, "What are you saying, Marlena?"

Marlena took her own step back, creating space between them. "I have been raised to rule, not you, and the next time you forget that, I'll happily remind you."

A door slammed, and the vision was over. But this time Vega didn't startle awake—her body continued to float into nothingness.

32

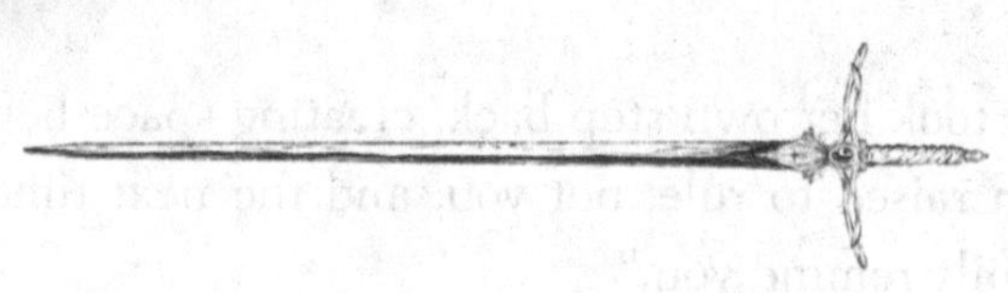

"ARE YOU AWAKE?" VEGA'S VOICE TRAVELED THROUGH THE room, filling Bridger's ears. His smile was weak, but the sound of her voice—the fact she was still alive—sent a wave of happiness through him.

His eyes fluttered open. "Barely." After seventeen days with little to no food and just enough water to keep them alive, Bridger, Khort, and Vega could barely find it in themselves to move from their sleeping spots.

The crumbling stone under their bodies was all they had in their cells. No beds, no bathrooms—they were caged like abused animals. Khort had stopped talking ten hours ago and only grunted to let them know he was alive.

"I want to touch you."

Bridger could tell Vega was crying, her voice cracking as he pictured the way her lip quivered.

He pushed himself off the floor, his body feeling heavier than ever. "Come to the corner of your cell." Bridger reached his hand out, waiting for hers to slip into his. The two did this every night, willing the other to last one more night—just one more night, and he'd figure out a way to get them out of here—to stay strong, to think of the future they would have together when they made it out of this alive. "I love you," Bridger whispered, wrapping his hand around what little bit of hers he could.

"I love you too." Her response was soft. "I don't know how much longer of this I can take."

Bridger shut his eyes tightly. "Hold on just a little longer. I'll get us out of here, I swear." Who was he if he couldn't keep Vega safe?

They'd been fighting every single day for the last year and a half. Arlet and Khort had found a way to get Vega's memories back to her. They came in pieces, but they were back. Marlena killed the Fraus-born who'd helped them and then used the information she'd beaten out of her to track them down. Vega only had three days of mental freedom before being thrown into the dungeon of her childhood home.

The two fell asleep hand in hand, but their slumber didn't last long.

"How cute."

A heeled boot tapped against their connected hands, jarring them both awake. Startled, Bridger jumped back, stumbling under his weak body. Marlena stood in front of them through their closed cells.

The cell across from him was empty—the one Khort had been in. "Where's Khort? What did you do to him?" Bridger raced to the edge of his cage and gripped the bars.

Marlena stared him down, her eyes glimmering like ice. "If you two weren't so busy cuddling, you'd know what was going on." The sneer on her lips was always there when she looked at them, but it slowly faded when the familiar scream echoed down the stairs.

"What are you doing to him?" Vega's voice broke, her outcry rattling off the walls and down the hollow halls. "Marlena! Marlena, look at me! What are you doing to Khort?"

Marlena's eyes never left Bridger as her sinister smile formed. "I won't do anything if your boyfriend here does what he's asked to do." There was always a trade-off with Marlena—except she could never be trusted to follow through on her end. The locks on their cells clicked open with the flick of Marlena's wrist, and at the same time, Bridger and Vega bolted out—free for the first time in seventeen days. Bridger hurled himself at Marlena, while Vega dashed down the hall after Khort.

Neither one made it to their destination. Marlena used her power to trap them in place, slamming a shield over and around them. Vega screamed in frustration.

"Vega! Bridger!" Khort's voice echoed down the stairway from above. His voice strained as the sounds of a fight followed. "They found Arlet! They have Arlet!" Khort roared in pain, and then the echoes of his voice died.

Marlena let her power drop, taking one large step back from Bridger. "Both of you are too weak to fight me, let alone win. We can do this the easy way or the hard way. You choose." Marlena's arms crossed over her chest, head cocked to the side.

Vega crashed into Bridger's side. "Don't fight. Hear her out. She has Arlet. We give her what she wants to ensure she's safe... that Khort's safe." Her voice was panicked, pleading. Vega was still trying to hang on to the hope that Marlena would snap out of it and return to the sister she grew up with—Vega couldn't see she was gone and was never coming back.

Marlena looked bored when Bridger forced his eyes away from Vega, who was so beaten and broken that she hardly looked like herself anymore. "Whatever she has to say isn't going to be what we want, Vega. Marlena will never let us have what we want."

Marlena smiled at his words. "Ever the smart warrior."

She took a step forward, and Bridger noticed she had no weapons on her. Marlena didn't see them as a threat...

Vega clung to Bridger, half using him for support.

"What more could you possibly want from us?" Bridger rasped.

Amusement rippled through Marlena's cackle. "Everything. This isn't even close to over. We're just getting started. I am going to break you both down until you have nothing left in you, until you're too tired to keep fighting, until Vega is nothing more than a shadow of the person you knew. A memory."

Bridger spoke before Vega could find the words. "You'll never get away with this."

"I already have. Who's going to stop me? The people of Tolevarre that matter are on my side, leaving you with no one. Other than maybe the people Vega tried so dearly to protect, with their sad little abilities. Where are they now, huh?" Marlena made a point to look around the room. "I see no one on your side. Not a mouse, not a deer, not a sparrow."

Vega's face fell, sorrow filling her soft features. "What did you do to them?"

Bridger didn't know what was going on, his eyes darting between the sisters. Their mirrored eyes had vastly different emotions pooling in them. One sad, the other filled with pleasure.

"They're dead. Just like everyone else who conspires with you will be. Just like you're about to be for the second time in your sad, pathetic existence." Marlena said the last words with excitement.

"No," Bridger growled, standing in front of Vega. "You won't lay another finger on her."

Marlena's smile stayed lethal. "You're right. *I* won't."

The world seemed to stand still, her words and their meaning sinking in.

A dagger appeared out of thin air, and Marlena tossed it at Bridger. It clattered against the cold and cobbled floor until it landed at his bare feet. "But you will."

"No," Bridger said again. The dagger was his. He could feel the draw to it, a thread pulling at the inner connection with his bonded blade.

"Yes," Marlena replied, staring at the couple. "And since I know you're going to give me a hard time..." She turned her attention to the stairs, and on cue, the sound of a body tumbled down until an almost unrecognizable woman hit the bottom. "If you don't, she dies too."

Olenor Fera... Khort's mother.

The woman groaned as she came to a stop at the bottom of the staircase. Her body convulsed with a wet cough, blood splattering from her mouth.

"How can you do this to the people who love us?" Vega asked, the tears still pouring out. She didn't dare move from Bridger's grasp.

Marlena cackled. "Those people never loved me. They loved the idea of the power they could have if I continued to be their lapdog for the rest of my life."

Bridger reached for the dagger, the pull between him and the bonded blade the only thing he could feel of his powers.

"Kill her, Bridger," Marlena hissed when the blade settled in his grip.

"No!" he bellowed. Slower than normal but still with smooth warrior grace, the blade flew across the room—straight at Marlena's head. It was aimed perfectly at where the center of her head should have been, but it wasn't.

Marlena was on the other side of the room, her hand gripping Olenor by the throat, dangling in mid-air. Her sandy blonde hair was matted with blood, and her eyes were slits from how badly she'd been beaten. Every part of her body with exposed flesh was littered with a rainbow of bruises.

"The clock is ticking, Dimico." She squeezed Olenor's throat harder, the woman coherent enough to claw at Marlena's hand.

"Bridger," Vega cried, forcing his eyes away from Marlena and Olenor. "You have to."

"Are you insane? No!" Bridger jerked away from Vega like she had two heads.

"We cannot let Khort lose his mother. Khort can't lose his family too... not because of me. Please, Bridger." Vega looked at Marlena, who watched the scene impatiently.

"Think faster." She dropped Olenor, her head hitting the ground with a pop—her body was too mangled to catch herself.

"I don't care about Khort! I care about you. I'm not killing you!" Bile sloshed a blistering trail up his throat.

Vega retrieved the dagger from the floor and hobbled back to Bridger.

He couldn't do this—he couldn't lose Vega again. There had to be a way out of this.

Bridger's throat tightened when she pressed his dagger to his chest, the hilt flush against his skin.

"You have to do this. You promised to help me, to fight with me. That means keeping our people safe too, not just me." Vega spoke through her tears.

Hot tears burned his eyes as he brought his dirty hand to his chest and covered hers, feeling the warmth of his blade through their palms. "I can't lose you." The first tear fell. "Not again."

Vega let go of the dagger. "It's okay." She reached up to wipe a falling tear from Bridger's filthy cheek, but he looked away. He didn't want her to see him break down.

Bridger could hear his mother's voice in his head. *Stand tall. Don't let them see you fall apart.*

Vega brushed her fingers against his face, the sensation pulling his attention back to her as she pressed a kiss to Bridger's lips. He wanted to melt away, just the two of them, somewhere far off where nothing could get them—where all of this was just a distant nightmare.

The kiss hadn't lasted long enough but long enough for Marlena to notice. "You have thirty seconds, or I'll kill all three of you."

Bridger wanted to watch the life escape Marlena's eyes, but he couldn't—not without his powers. A part of him was beginning to believe even then he wouldn't be able to take her down.

"One, two, three..." Marlena began to count.

"Fuck!" he screamed, pushing away from Vega. His hands tangled into the hair at the side of his head, the dagger still in his grasp. "Baby, I can't. I can't kill you. I'd rather die with you."

Vega cupped both sides of his jaw, gently forcing him to meet her tear-soaked gaze. "Hey, look at me." She bit down on her bottom lip to stop it from trembling. "It's okay. I won't really feel it. Not for long. I'll just wake up in a different life... and you'll find me again." Was Vega saying this to convince herself or to comfort him? "You will always find me."

"Eighteen, nineteen," Marlena continued.

Vega tugged his hands down. "I love you, Bridger. I have since that first Saturnalia. I trust you. There's no one else I'd rather see before death."

"I love you so much. I'm sorry." He heaved the words out.

Bridger shook his head, tears still streaming down his own face. Vega guided his hand with the dagger to her chest, pressing the point into the skin directly above her heart.

"Twenty-one." Marlena's voice felt so far away.

"I'll see you in the next life."

Those were the last words Vega spoke before Bridger slammed the dagger through her heart. Her blue eyes lit up like ice, jaw dropping as she gasped for air that would never come. Vega's body sagged against Bridger, lifeless. He pulled the dagger out, and Vega's body vanished as the curse whisked her away from their world.

"Thirty."

Bridger could hear the smile on her lips long before he looked up. Marlena wasn't good at keeping promises, so when she drove her hand through Olenor's chest and ripped her heart out, Bridger didn't even flinch.

"I've always wanted a dragon heart to add to my collection." Her hand covered in shifter blood, Marlena turned her focus to Bridger. "All that work for nothing. How long can you handle losing her for?

Five years, ten? A lifetime? How long until you realize that I'll never let you be with her, that being with her makes you weak? How long until her friends no longer trust you?" Marlena's eyebrow rose. "How long until you're no longer the person she loves? Because I will torture you slowly, painfully, until the Bridger she knows is gone. Until you're the commander I need."

Bridger blinked, one last tear escaping.

"You're free to go, but remember, as soon as she's back, so is your torture." Marlena's laugh could be heard echoing through the dungeon halls long after she'd vanished.

Deep below the ruined home of the Caelums' estate, no one could hear his screams, but when he finally made it up the stairs, he was met with an unharmed Arlet and Khort.

Bridger looked at his hands—Vega's blood coated them, and his vision went bleary. "I killed Vega. Your mom's dead." His words were quipped in a short staccato.

He couldn't hear Arlet's and Khort's screams as he lost consciousness and collapsed to the ground.

His brand had ached all night, sending waves of pain spidering down his arm. It grew unbearable enough this morning that he finally gave in to the nagging pull tugging him towards the dungeon.

Bridger didn't allow anyone to hear him when he didn't want to be heard, causing his guard to jump in fright when he suddenly appeared next to him.

"Commander." Felix's hand was over his heart. "You scared me half to death."

"Has she eaten?" Bridger asked without thinking.

"No, sir, and she won't drink anything, either."

Bridger exhaled loudly. "Go fetch breakfast. I'll keep watch until then."

Felix protested, "Sir."

"Go." Bridger pointed up the stairs, watching as the soldier turned without another word. He waited until he couldn't hear his footsteps anymore before moving from the doorway. "Not eating or drinking isn't going to make you grow big and strong," he said as he approached Vega's cell door.

Vega didn't respond. Her back rested against the wall, legs kicked out in front, with her head back on the hard stone. She twisted her neck to meet his stare when she heard him approach.

He opened his mouth to speak, but the words were stolen when he saw the shape Vega was in after a single night in captivity. This was why he'd felt pain last night... His hand gripped the iron door and ripped it off its hinges.

Vega's eye was swollen shut, blood caked on her hands and along her chin. Her suit was ripped from her collarbone to just above her breasts. Bridger squatted down to her level, but her eyes fell to the floor, averting his gaze. He reached for her, but she flinched away from his touch.

"Vega." His voice was a low growl. He moved slower this time, grabbing her by the chin to force her to look at him. Bridger ground his teeth together at the way his skin tingled when he touched her, at the ring on her finger glinting in the low light of the dungeon. "Who did this to you?"

Her eyes were cold, and Bridger saw a flash of his dream from last night—Vega's inanimate eyes after he drove the dagger through her heart. His hand fell from her face.

Vega didn't answer.

"Who. Did this. To you." He asked again, and this time his tone left no room for her to ignore him.

"Isn't this what I'm down here for? To be beaten?" she asked.

Bridger's blood boiled. "Not by my men. Tell me who hurt you."

Vega's jaw stayed locked in place, her eyes fixated on Bridger's with scorn. "Aren't you the one who sent the guard down here with water last night? Shouldn't you be able to put two and two together?" she sneered, not a single muscle moving other than her lips. Her eyes stared straight into what was left of his soul, pulling strings he thought he'd cut, burned, and destroyed.

The pound of the guard's boots hitting the stone stairs echoed down the empty halls. Bridger's attention turned from Vega and her eyes full of hatred to Felix carrying a tray of food down the stairs.

"I want to hear you say his name, and if you don't, I'll beat it out of him instead." Bridger stood slowly, nodding to the sound of Felix's footsteps getting closer.

"No," Vega said with a breath, her eyes darting to the hall outside her cell.

"Felix," Bridger called, beckoning the soldier his way.

"Yes, sir?" He shuffled into view, the tray clattering to the ground when his eyes landed on the mangled cell door.

Bridger turned with eerie stillness, his hand reaching behind him to unsheathe his sword. "Can you tell me who laid their hands on Vega last night?"

"I..." he stammered.

"Grimes!" Vega interrupted, worried for his soldier. "His name was Grimes. He beat me until I couldn't breathe—until I thought I was going to die again. Felix is the reason I'm alive. He stopped him and then healed my fatal wounds. You should be thanking him, not threatening his life."

Bridger looked over his shoulder at Vega. "Now, how hard was that?"

"If you hurt him, I swear to every dead god, in this life or my next, I will kill you." Vega stood, rolling her shoulders with a wince. No matter how battered, no matter the memories she didn't have, Vega still defended others. Why did she care so much about people? After everything she'd been put through, why continue to care?

Bridger's smile slid across his face, slow and sultry, while he put his sword back in its place. He felt relief from Vega's attitude—if she was running her mouth, she wasn't fully defeated yet.

My Vega.

"Lock Vega in a new cell," Bridger commanded, winking at her as he strode from the cell and up the dungeon stairs. She called him every name in the book as he disappeared from her view.

33

Felix gathered the fallen food and placed it back on the tray. The bread was stale, and Vega was sure the discoloration on the cheese wasn't from the grimy dungeon.

She grabbed the tray through the slit in the bars. "Should I be worried about poison?"

"I think that should be the least of your worries right now. Keep your strength up." He disappeared too, and Vega felt the sudden loneliness sink in as the silence took over again.

Her eyes darted to the tray in her hands, and her stomach rumbled at the sight of the unappetizing selection. *I would kill for some stinky, fresh fish right about now.*

Vega gasped at the sting in her side as she sank down against the wall. Felix had done what he could for her broken ribs, but he'd been honest about his skillset. She scarfed down the dry bread and picked around the molded cheese. Her stomach growled when the food was gone, her body begging for more.

Would this be the rest of her life? Eating last week's discarded scraps on a cold floor with the fear of her next beating looming over her?

A new canteen of water was untouched near the door to her cell. Vega crawled and gave the liquid inside a sniff after twisting the cap off. There wasn't a scent, but she wouldn't be able to tell if something was wrong with it anyway—she didn't know how to sniff out poisons in this life.

Vega chugged every last drop in one go.

"Your issue is that you don't listen." Bridger's voice cut through the silence, along with the sound of muffled pleading. "So let me show you how."

Vega moved to press her face between the cold bars, her knees digging into the rough stone. Bridger came into view with Grimes dragging behind by the collar of his uniform. Her heart began to thunder with anticipation.

"Commander," Grimes pleaded, not as tough as he'd sounded the night before when he promised to kill Vega. "I lost control. It won't happen again."

"You're right. It won't." Bridger yanked the door to her cell open. She scuffled back as he flung Grimes into the cell with her.

"Apologize," Bridger growled, the sound reverberating through Vega's chest.

"Why should I have to apologize to a prisoner? I said it won't happen again. Isn't that enough?" Grimes attempted to stand, but Bridger's boot dug into his shoulder, shoving him down until his chest was flush with the floor.

Bridger leaned down, his mouth hovering near Grimes's ear. He spoke loudly enough for both him and Vega to hear. "I suggest you do as I say. After all, that's the reason you're in this position in the first place... for not listening to your commander. There is no other option. It's apologize or die." The words rang as a promise.

Vega's eyes went wide, bouncing between Grimes, who had nearly taken her life twelve hours ago, and Bridger—he looked every bit as intimidating as one would expect the strongest warrior in history to look. His dark hair was ruffled out of place, a strand falling over his brow.

If Vega weren't terrified for Grimes's life, she might take more time to enjoy the features of Bridger's unfairly attractive face. *This man almost killed you. You shouldn't care about his life, and you also shouldn't be admiring Commander Dickhead!*

"I'm sorry." Grimes's apology wasn't sincere, the words forced.

"It's fine." Vega felt like she was hearing the words coming from someone else. She couldn't remember saying them herself.

"Actually, it's not. He doesn't mean it." Bridger's boot pressed harder into his back. Grimes gasped as the air began to leave his lungs. "Stand." Vega's gaze left Grimes, shooting up to Bridger. Her confusion was evident in the way her eyebrows scrunched together. "Stand, Vega." His voice softened, catching her off guard.

She did as she was told, swallowing a yelp from the throb in her side. "He apologized." Her voice still didn't feel like hers.

"And he's going to do it again." Bridger got down on his knees, removing his boot from Grimes's back long enough to switch his hold. His hand gripped the back of his neck, clutching tightly to keep Grimes in his place, his cheek against the floor. Grimes shook in fear as Bridger leaned in to speak through gritted teeth. "One more time... and this time you better mean it. I'm not giving you another chance to disobey my orders."

Vega looked down from her position above, Bridger on his knees and Grimes underneath his hold. When Grimes spoke again, Vega's eyes weren't fixed on him—they were glued to Bridger's stone-cold gaze. *Why is he doing this?*

"I'm sorry, Vega. Truly." Grimes's voice quaked, his breathing as ragged as hers had been the night before.

"When I get out of here, because I will get out of here, don't let me find you." Vega wasn't sure where the sudden boost in confidence came from, but it sparked something inside her. "I'll make you regret putting your hands on me." Vega's eyes were no longer on Bridger, but out of the corner of her eye, she caught his mouth twitch into his crooked smirk—the one Vega had seen in every memory he plagued.

"Up to your knees." Bridger stood, releasing his grip as his soldier followed directions. Grimes's eyes were on Bridger as he took in big breaths, allowing his lungs to refill with the stale dungeon air. "As the commander of Tolevarre's army..." He said the words and they didn't sound cocky—they sounded confident. "When I give you an order, you will listen. If I get a single complaint about you or your smug-ass attitude again, I'll butcher you in front of everyone."

Vega would never forget the sound of Bridger's boot cracking against Grimes's head. She had only a split second to see his lopsided nose before he let out a bloodcurdling wail and a hand shot to his face. Blood gushed and overflowed into his palm.

Bridger wasn't done—he seemed to have a very specific way of forcing his men to fall in line when they disobeyed direct orders.

The stone walls shook with power as Bridger reached behind him and unsheathed his sparkling black sword. In a single motion, he twirled the long blade and sliced it through Grimes's arm at the wrist. If the soldier's scream pierced Vega's ears before, this time the sound that filled the room was his soul leaving his body.

Hysteria unraveled inside Vega, stealing any ounce of confidence she'd felt seconds earlier as images of the dead witch flashed into her head.

"I said I was sorry!" Grimes wailed.

With grace, Bridger slid his sword back into its resting place between his shoulders. "Great."

Vega tried to keep her eyes off the blood spewing from Grimes's nub—that meant she had to watch Bridger.

How was this man so calm after cutting someone's hand off? And why did he look like he enjoyed it?

"Felix." Back to the composed Bridger who Vega had come to know. It didn't matter if he was cutting someone's hand off or chasing down his soon-to-be prisoner in a world he didn't belong—he never seemed to waver.

The other guard made quick work of getting to his side. "Yes?"

"Heal him." Bridger left the cell too casually, turning on his heels to look back at the mess he'd made.

"I can't regrow his hand," Felix stuttered from fear of disappointing his commander.

"Well aware. I want him to have a reminder every single day of what happens when people defy me. I want everyone to see what I did to him and ask themselves if it's worth crossing me."

34

A NEW GUARD WAS ASSIGNED TO VEGA AFTER FELIX FINISHED healing Grimes. Vega sat in the back of her cell, eyes closed, with hands cupped over her ears while Grimes was healed only feet from her.

Had she ever been used to the slaughter this world deemed acceptable?

Vega finally drifted off into a dreamless sleep when the screaming ended and Grimes was cleared from her cell. There was no telling how long she'd been asleep when Vega's eyes shot open, her arms wrapped around herself to keep warm.

Marlena stood over her, kicking at Vega's boot. "Morning, sweet sister." The smile on her face made the chill in Vega's spine travel up her back. "We're going on a little field trip." She yanked Vega off the floor by her shoulder.

Marlena walked in front, never looking back as they climbed the stairs. A sinking feeling eased its way into Vega's stomach at the realization she wasn't a threat, and she was beginning to wonder if she ever had been.

Her lungs burned by the time they got to the top. Marlena only picked up her speed.

The house was empty, not a soul in sight as they moved through the halls. "When we were children, we used to walk the halls of the original home, hiding behind doors to jump out and scare one another," Marlena recalled, peering over her shoulder. "One day, I slipped behind one, and you looked for me for hours until you finally found me. I was sitting in a room you'd never been in, staring at a wall of mirrors. That room was used to force me to hone my original power. Our parents locked me in there for six days with no food until I could fully disappear from every angle. I was nine, and you slept soundly in your bed on the floor above, never once asking where I was." Abruptly, Marlena stopped outside a door, wind rustling her hair as she spun to face Vega. "I didn't know it then, but years later I decided I wanted a trophy for every time I beat you, and since these mirrors were a present from the parents you so dearly loved, what better way to cause you anguish than with the very objects they began my torture with?"

Marlena pushed the door open, revealing the room of mirrors, and then disappeared. Vega could still feel her. She reappeared behind her, proving the six days she'd spent locked in the room perfected the ability as it was meant to.

"Is that what they are to you now then? Trophies?" Vega questioned, eyes ticking between the mirrors and her sister. Marlena shut the door and a lock clicked into place.

"They're more than that. Do you know I am the only one in our world who can curse inanimate objects? That's what these mirrors are: little pieces of your curse that stem from you. They're your memories, your lives. Everything you've had taken from you." Marlena's footsteps didn't make a sound as she circled the room. "They're my windows into your lives, how I stay one step ahead— because I know it all. Your curse is mine, made of our shared blood. It makes sure I know all that you can't remember."

Marlena chuckled, glancing at the mirrors with a happy spark. Her smile made her look *giddy*. "Except there's one missing piece, and it comes from the pathetic demi you summoned." Vega watched her as Marlena's focus shifted from the mirrors to her. "I don't usually admit when I'm wrong, but I've run into a bit of an issue, and you're the only one who can help me." She rolled her eyes. "Imagine that."

Vega didn't move a muscle.

Marlena floated down the aisle of mirrors, her index finger dragging along each frame. She snapped her head to the side, motioning towards a mirror. "In this one, I snapped your neck the second you stepped through the portal." Another mirror grabbed her attention at the end of the room. "There." She pointed to one with a dark brown frame, cracks splintering the wood. "That one there is from the first time Bridger killed you. It happened downstairs, outside the very cell you're in now."

"And let me guess. Here"—Vega pointed, beating her sister to it —"you killed me. And then in that one, you had someone else kill me. It's a never-ending cycle. So why don't you just get it over with already and kill me for good? What's with a curse that draws the inevitable out?"

Marlena's lips split into a poisonous smile. "That's where you come in."

Vega scoffed. "You really think I'll ever feel inclined to help you?"

Marlena ignored the question. "When we were children, your powers outshone mine. Everyone wondered if our parents would break the Curia's eldest child decree and let you rule both seats instead. They had an entire meeting about it while having me in attendance. That night I snuck away to Littera and started my research on summoning gods." Jealousy oozed through Marlena's tone—she nearly turned green with envy. "At first, I wasn't going to involve you, not in the way you are now. I chose to ignore the fact you were overlooking what was right in front of you. I chose to believe you would choose me over the parents who had made my life miserable." Marlena began to walk towards her. Vega crept back, keeping herself out of reach.

Their matching eyes made Vega reel with fear. *You're not her. You're good, you're good, you're good.*

"Why are you telling me all this?" Before Vega knew it, her back was against the largest mirror in the room stretching floor to ceiling. Even through the thick material of her suit, she could feel the ebbs of power inside the reflective glass.

Marlena stalked towards her, wafting the scent of her perfume into Vega like a tidal wave—roses with a spice she couldn't place. If Vega closed her eyes, she could visualize a meadow of roses on fire, smoke encapsulating her until she could no longer breathe.

"Have you not figured it out yet? This is how I give you your memories back. I could do it the easy way. Let you drink a potion and move my powers through you to break the memory block of the curse. But that would be too easy, not painful enough. The mirrors don't let your memories seep back into you. They cram them all in at once. The process is quicker, but it won't feel that way. Your pain will last for days." The blonde took her last step forward and pressed her hands into the mirror on either side of Vega's head.

Vega didn't wane, reminding herself of the person everyone told her she'd been. Even in the face of the sister who had spent the last fifty-five years tormenting her for fun, she told herself she wasn't afraid.

She wasn't scared of the sister who wanted her dead.

She wasn't scared of what it would feel like to get her memories back.

She wasn't scared to die.

Not anymore. Vega took a deep breath.

"So brave." Marlena was much taller than Vega, forcing her to crane her neck to hold the gaze of fire Marlena wore behind her dead eyes. "Your courage is fleeting. I can see it." Marlena leaned down.

Vega gasped. "You can't break me."

Marlena chortled an off-putting sound. She kept her hands on the mirror, boxing Vega in with no hopes of escaping. "You're wrong. I've been breaking you this entire time. I've been taking the people you love from you, taking your life, taking your memories. You're a shell of who you once were... and it's time you see that."

Vega's back began to burn, scorching the fabric of her suit. Parts of it melted into her skin, and when she went to scream, nothing came out. Marlena no longer stood in front of her and was too far out of reach for Vega to drag into the oblivion she was falling into.

The darkness engulfed her, consuming her inside and out. There were no feelings at first, only the burn of the mirror swallowing her whole. Vega wasn't sure where she was or if the place she was in even existed outside her own mind. The first jolt of pain shot through her brain with such ferocity Vega was sure her head would explode. She clutched her skull and tried to scream, but no sound came out—there was no sound, no light, no movement.

The first memory squeezed in, erupting into her vision. The dark void was gone, and in its place was the face of the man she'd fallen head over heels for the second they'd met.

Bridger's smile was radiating, warming Vega to the core. Her laugh echoed in her ears, the sound happier than she'd ever remembered it being. Vega backed into a tiny coat closet, her spine pressing against a shelf. "We're going to get caught." Her smile spread from ear to ear as the door clicked shut, and Bridger's hands were on her.

"Mm, let them watch." His voice was so deep and riddled with lust she could feel it in her chest.

His toned arm slid around Vega's body, pulling her against him as he pressed his lips to hers in a desperate kiss—like he was starving for air and she was the only one who could save him. He tasted like her favorite wine, remnants of it coating his tongue. Bridger trailed kisses down Vega's jaw, moving to her neck.

Vega's breath caught in her throat. "Oh my gods," she gasped, throwing her head back and rolling her body against his.

"No, Kitten, it's just me. The gods aren't here with us." Bridger sank to his knees, pushing the skirt of her dress to her hips, pinning it there. He placed sloppy kisses on Vega's thighs, his hands slipping between her legs to pull her lace panties to the side. "Fuck." His eyes rolled back in his head, an animalistic look on his face at the sight of her completely bare in front of him. "Spread your legs and let me have a taste."

Vega did as she was told, moaning the second his tongue touched her. One hand tangled in his tousled hair, the other freeing his hand from the hold on her dress.

Bridger's groan of approval vibrated against her while his tongue racked her body with little bolts of pleasure. "Bridger," Vega moaned, thrusting her hips into his face for more friction.

Two large fingers slid inside her, and when they massaged the spot that would bring Vega to her knees, the scene melted away and she was thrown into another.

A sharp pain erupted through her chest as the darkness built a new memory around her. When she looked up, there stood Bridger, his eyes no longer glazed with lust.

Her sister's feral laugh rang in her ears. "So much has happened since your last life, dear sister. Poor Bridger has been under my watch for most of it, spending his time locked away in my dungeon with no one to talk to but the ghosts in his head... and me. Do you know what happens to people when they spend too much time with me?"

Vega shook her head, swallowing hard. "No."

She was different in this life—so unlike the woman she used to be. This Vega was timid, unsure of herself and everything around her—her last life on Earth left lasting effects she couldn't shake.

"They break," Marlena answered.

"I'm sorry, Kitt—Vega. I'm so sorry." Bridger's lip quivered at his correction. "It wasn't supposed to be like this."

"Why?" Vega gulped, her hands pressed against the wall behind her.

"I'm doing this for you. For them. For us," Bridger whispered. "She's never going to let us win. She's never going to let us be together. I can keep people safe this way." His voice shuddered as he stared into her eyes. "You knew I was destined for darkness."

Tears flowed down Vega's cheeks. "Don't let her get into your head."

"Too late," Marlena cooed sweetly.

"I can't let the people we love die just for us to be together. Marlena was right. Our love has blinded us."

Bridger's eyes wandered over to Meyer. Bridger's sword levitated under his chin by Marlena's power.

Him or me. It's him or me.

"Tick-tock, Bridger. Choose or I'll choose for you." Marlena dug the blade in deeper.

"We can save him!" Vega cried, fighting against Bridger's hold on her, and trying to free herself from the clutches of fate.

"Please don't kill Meyer." Bridger's voice sounded so weak.

"You know what you need to do." Her sister nodded towards her, forcing the tip of Bridger's sword further into the underside of Meyer's chin. Blood started to trickle down the blade.

"This will be easier for us next time," Bridger promised as he closed his eyes and took a sharp inhale. He plunged the dagger through Vega's heart, and even though it was a memory, Vega could feel the ache in her chest.

The memories kept coming, pouring back into her one by one—so painstakingly slowly Vega felt every ebb and flow of the curse releasing them to her.

Even though some of them were happy, they all reminded Vega of everything she'd lost.

Over and over and over and over—Marlena always won.

35

Vega's eyes fluttered open, eyelashes tickling her cheeks. She was back in the cell, the pounding in her head intensifying as she slowly sat up. "Gods." The curse left her mouth, and the pain in her head became an afterthought.

Vega jumped to her feet, her vision spotting. She bent down, her hands resting on her knees, to inhale a breath of stale air. At first, she thought it had all been a dream, the memories, but when she started to ignore the pounding in her head, she realized something...

She remembered.

Everything.

"Oh my gods." Vega stood up straight, a hand over her heart, the other over her open mouth.

She remembered the first time Arlet skinned her knee outside her house and how Marlena snuck into the infirmary to steal bandages so the girls wouldn't get in trouble for being outside when they were supposed to be studying.

She remembered the sound of her mother's voice and the smell of her home burning to the ground.

She remembered the stories Arlet and Khort told her. They were no longer fairy tales from someone else's head—they were hers.

"I remember." Vega choked out a sob. "I remember."

Tears rushed down her face, and she didn't care about anything going on around her. Nothing mattered except for one thing: the hollow feeling in her chest was gone.

Vega had her memories back, and if she died for good soon, at least she got to remember one more time. There was so much pain in her life, and the memories weren't all happy—but they were hers.

I'm whole again.

Vega didn't care she was locked underground in the Aeris chambers. Maybe she would find a way out, and maybe she wouldn't. There was so much she could be angry about. The pain, the longing feeling she'd become so used to, the loneliness she'd been forced to feel, the curse. All of it would eventually make her blood boil, but for now, Vega just wanted to revel in the beauty of what it felt like to be whole—of what it felt like to be *her.*

She sat down with her back to the wall and smiled up at the ceiling. Vega was locked in a prison with a smile on her face. Her head no longer felt like a whoosh of radio static.

All of her lives on Earth were there too, spinning around with the lives she had here in Tolevarre. Over her last twenty years, Vega had learned a lot about herself. Fifteen of those years had been on Earth, where she was shaped more than she'd ever been. This last life on Earth wouldn't leave her. None of them would—because they made her stronger, despite how weak she'd felt then.

Marlena meant for last night to be another moment that beat Vega down, but she'd been wrong.

It only made her stronger.

36

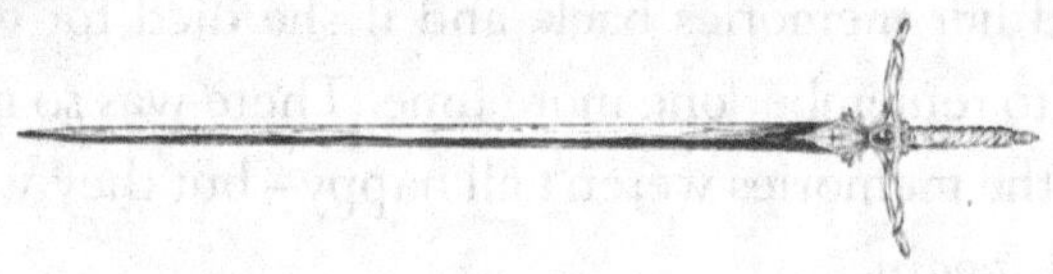

Carts rumbled over Fortis's streets, their wheels bobbing over the cobblestone roads as merchants packed up their wares from today's market. Fortis might have been Bridger's birthplace, but it hadn't felt like home in decades.

Vega has her memories back. He could feel it down the bond, just like he'd always been able to. It wasn't the first time, and it might not be the last time she'd get them back, but for the first time in almost forty years, Bridger felt anxious knowing Vega would remember it all —worried how her remembering his betrayals would affect *him*.

This trip to Fortis was meant to be short—*thank the gods*. After he punished Grimes for his behavior, Bridger's mind hadn't felt like his own, like the one he'd conditioned to forget.

Before he could make it up the driveway and into the home, his mother filed down the front steps with two guards flanking her. "Darling." Katrin reached for Bridger when she was close enough. "You're home." She kissed the side of his cheeks with an exaggerated *pop*.

"Not for long," he answered.

Katrin frowned. "What is it?"

"Why don't we head inside?" Bridger motioned to the house.

She looked him over, a glimmer in her dark eyes. She nodded and strode back to her home. Katrin's guards never left her side, putting themselves in between the commander and his mother as they approached her study, but Bridger's power blocked their access. They turned on quick heels, ready to defend.

"You two are to stay outside the door," Bridger announced.

"We have been given orders to—" one of the guards started to chatter.

"Orders to keep my mother safe from danger, yes. I'm aware. I'm the one who gave the orders." The two men stepped out of Bridger's way as he crossed into the room. He turned around to face the men, speaking to them before shutting the door with a small gust of wind. "I assure you, Katrin isn't in as much danger as she could be."

His mother stood on the other side of the room. "Bridger." Her face scrunched with unease.

Bridger turned slowly to face the woman who'd raised him beside a father who never actually loved him. It had always been obvious to him. Lucius looked at having children as a job, a way to train the next generation of rulers. It was why he only had one. Bridger was nothing but an obligation to his realm.

"They can't hear us. I have a question for you."

"Son, are you okay?" Sometimes it seemed as if his mother cared —maybe losing her husband had forced her to sit back and see what she had left in her life. Her husband was dead, her family in Fraus saw her as a traitor for choosing to rule over a territory that wasn't hers, and her son kept her on the outside of his life.

"Fine," he insisted.

Bridger watched her lean against the front of her desk. Her black dress sat at the top of her black shoes, gold soles the only color on her. "You don't seem it. Are you sleeping?"

Again with the fucking sleeping thing. Bridger rolled his eyes. "Who has time for sleep?" he asked her, dismissing her question with another. "I'm not here to talk about my sleeping patterns, Mother. I want to know what happened the day Father was murdered—the day Marlena killed him." His dreams were consumed by Vega, but the few times his father made an appearance stuck with him, reminding him of all the things he'd forced himself to forget about the man.

Her face went pale, her spine rigid. "I've told you I don't want to talk about that." She straightened and moved to the other side of her desk, pretending to busy herself with the paperwork scattered around.

"I don't care about how he was killed. You and I both know he wasn't worth saving." They'd never talked about the way his father acted towards them, how he'd beat them when they didn't fall in line or how he belittled Katrin for not being the strongest of her line. His mom wasn't a saint, and she liked to wreak more havoc than help, but she didn't deserve the abuse.

"Bridger!" Katrin scolded, her eyes wide and mouth ajar.

Bridger hadn't moved from his spot across the room, his posture stone-like as he ignored her reaction. "He was dead. You could've saved me."

Katrin huffed but stayed quiet for a beat too long—to come up with her next excuse. "From what? Your destiny?" She continued to ruffle through the stacks of papers.

Bridger flicked his wrist, and a tiny gust of wind knocked them to the floor. "Look at me." He pleaded. This wasn't the Commander of Tolevarre talking. This was Katrin's son.

Katrin cleared her throat and forced herself to meet his gaze. "What is this about?"

"You and the choices you made." Bridger's face fell. "You and the Ignises were going to make Meyer commander. You were going to let me stay with them, with Vega."

His mother's expression became unreadable. "Who told you that?"

It's true... Not that Bridger thought Meyer would lie to him, but he held out hope—hope that he'd been wrong.

He felt smaller than ever. "It doesn't matter who told me. It matters that I know." Bridger felt like a teenage boy again, telling his parents he was in love with Vega and not Marlena—the wrong sister. The sister who hadn't promised them endless power.

"You were never meant to be with Vega, Bridger." Katrin's voice didn't waver.

"I don't think you truly believe that." His words shocked her. "I think you were afraid of what it would mean for you if you didn't side with Father."

"How dare you!" she fumed, her lip curling at the edge.

He saw tears, *real tears* in her eyes. Bridger had never seen her shed a single tear in his entire life. She cried for a man who'd never truly loved her but wouldn't cry for the son who lost everything he cared about.

"When Marlena killed him, why didn't you leave? Why would you stay and assist her in my capture? Assist her in my torture until I broke?" Bridger's teeth gritted together.

"I..." She couldn't find the words. "I owed it to your father to make sure you followed in his legacy. In your bloodline's legacy." Her words were the script she'd created, the one she'd been repeating for decades.

"I don't believe you." He'd come all this way to hear his mom say what he knew to be true, what she had never admitted to anyone before—he had to hear her say it.

"What do you want me to say, Bridger?" Katrin's voice was rising. He'd gotten under her skin.

"Tell me how afraid you were to die. Tell me that you were so afraid of dying like your husband that you would rather your only son be tied up, beaten for years, *years*, Mother... and tortured until he was no longer himself. Say it."

"No, that's not—" she stuttered.

"Liar," Bridger growled, the room rumbling with his growing anger.

The guards pounded on the door the instant they felt Bridger's powers spike.

"Fine!" She stomped her foot down and traveled across the room, disappearing to only reappear directly in front of Bridger. "I was afraid to die, yes, and I knew that I could save myself by turning you in. All I needed to survive was to bring you home where you belonged!"

Bridger chuckled, no humor detected. "There it is." He backed up, having come there to hear those words. "You knew all you had to do was allow your son's life to be ruined to save yourself."

Her face was red. "Your life was never ruined. You just fell off track for a bit."

"I loved her!" he howled. "I have done unspeakable things to a person who has wanted nothing more than to keep her people safe!"

The same thing he'd been trying to do with the men and women in his army—keeping them safe from the world outside of his control. If they didn't answer to him, they'd answer to Marlena.

And he might blur the lines between good and evil, but he'd never be Marlena. *Never be Marlena. Never be Marlena.*

"You were destined to rule. Lucius and I knew the power you'd possess... and then you gained more, becoming stronger than we ever could have hoped." She kept trying to reel him back in. "I wasn't going to let you give that up for a girl who was destined to die."

Bridger gaped at her. "I became stronger because Vega was able to summon Remus. I didn't become who I am because of you or my piece of shit father... I am this way because of her, because of her tenacity and determination to kill her sister."

"Oh, please—"

He cut her off. "You've never loved me."

"Bridger, you're my son." A tear fell finally, but Bridger saw right through the act.

"I was nothing but a pawn to keep you in a life of luxury. You sold my soul to the devil for power. Power I didn't want—you wanted it."

"I did what I had to do because I love you."

"You've never loved anyone more than you love yourself. Fraus-born, through and through."

The knocking on the door got louder, but his shield was still up, and the men outside the room couldn't hear what was happening inside—only silence and the rumble of the house around them. They'd never be able to break through the hold Bridger held on the door, trapping himself and Katrin inside until he was ready to let go.

His mother took a step toward him. "You wouldn't understand why I've—"

On instinct, he took his dagger out and pressed it against his mother's neck—for the second time in his life, he held a blade to her throat. "If you tell a soul about our conversation, I'll make sure you're the next one destined to die."

That was a promise he planned to keep this time.

Bridger was done here. He let down the shield, and the guards came in with their weapons drawn. Bridger unsheathed his own bonded sword and decapitated them both with one fell swoop.

"Bridger!"

His mother kept calling his name as he stormed through her home, but he wouldn't look back.

He couldn't look back.

37

HER SCREAM VIBRATED AGAINST HER EARS. VEGA CLAWED AT them, hoping she could rip them from her body and stop the high-pitched ringing. She hadn't begun to beg. *Not yet.*

"Stop." Her sister's voice was monotone, telling Junie to pull back on her current method of torture. "Are you ready to talk, Vega? I can go all day." Marlena sat in a chair in the corner of Vega's cell, making herself comfortable. She kicked her feet back against the wall, inspecting her fingernails.

Dried blood caked under Vega's nails from the trickle out of her ears. "I don't know how Remus did it! I've told you that!" Vega screamed, anger replacing her pain.

"Wrong answer. Junie." Marlena didn't look up from her hands, only motioned for the girl to begin again.

The pain restarted, and Vega plummeted to the floor. She wished she could go back to her blissful morning, where she sat and thought about the things in her life that made her happy—distracting from the fact she was the prisoner of a sister who wanted her dead. Junie kept going, kept clawing at her brain with the ability to peel her apart, layer by layer inside her own mind. Junie reached inside the part of her brain in control of pain, and it was like she pushed the On button until Marlena told her to stop again. Junie removed her hands from Vega, taking a step back with a blank expression.

Vega was beginning to see stars, nearing the point of blackout. She retched on the floor from the buzz still bouncing around inside her head. There was almost nothing inside to throw up.

"One last time, Vega... How did Remus curse Romulus and the original gods? You summoned Remus. I know the answer is inside of you somewhere. Think harder."

This was the information Marlena had given Vega her memories back for... knowledge that she'd never known. *Why does she want to know? What could she possibly need that information for?*

Vega screamed, incoherent to herself, trying to drown out the pain still bubbling inside even without Junie's powers dancing around. "I don't know, Marlena! I. DO. NOT. KNOW!" Vega knew what it felt like to go mad—having Junie inside her head was unlike any torture Marlena had ever subjected her to. She didn't know how much she could put up with Junie using her brain against her. *Where did they find this bitch?*

Marlena sighed and pushed herself up from the chair. "I'll give you the night to soul-search. We'll be back tomorrow."

Vega stayed on the floor, chained to the wall. When she could no longer hear their footsteps, she let herself cry. The tears wouldn't solve anything, but after everything—all the duress she'd been forced to live through—Vega deserved to cry for all she'd lost, for all she'd become.

Her new guard didn't speak or bring her food. The last time she'd had anything to eat was when Felix was on guard, and she ate moldy cheese and stale bread like they were a greasy burger from her favorite fast-food place in Chicago. Her stomach growled with a hunger she'd never known.

Her fingernails were chewed down to bloody nail beds—it was all she could do to distract herself from the endless torture.

Nothing felt right, *but hey, at least I have my memories...*

The chains were tight around her ankles, keeping her confined to a small corner of the already tiny cell. She'd officially lost track of time and was beginning to give up hope that her friends were going to be able to save her. How long had she been here? Four, five days? A week? When would time mean nothing at all?

Vega spun the ring on her finger, fidgeting to keep her mind off the loneliness in her chest. Her cell smelled of puke, keeping a constant wave of nausea rolling in her gut.

She didn't hear the footsteps until they were right outside her cell—irreparable damage in her eardrums might surely be the cause of her delayed sense.

"What did you do to deserve no food tonight?"

Bridger.

Whenever her memories took her to the past with Bridger, laying out his never-ending list of betrayals, she ignored the hurt like Khort told her to do. Instead, she focused on the pit of anger bubbling like lava in her chest.

Remembering him drove a stake through her already depleted heart. "Go away, Bridger. Please." Even her own voice sounded muffled through her ears. She continued to stare at the wall, hoping he would get the hint. Vega didn't have it in her to have it out with him.

"That's all you have to say? 'Go away, Bridger?' That's a little tame for the Vega I know."

She coughed out a laugh, the pain in her throat stinging. It was raw again, drops of blood seeping down the back of her throat when she talked. "You don't know me."

"I beg to differ. The Vega I know would be cussing up a storm, pulling at the chains until her ankles bled, and she certainly wouldn't have said 'please' when telling me to go away. In fact, the Vega you were days ago was ready to send me straight to the underworld."

Vega shot up, head spinning, but she ignored it. "Maybe I'm finally giving up. That's what you both want, right? For me to finally come to terms with my inevitable death?" She walked to the end of her chains, meeting Bridger's eyes for the first time since remembering who he was, who she was. "The last thing I want to do before I die is look at you, at the sad, pathetic excuse for a man you've become." She'd once told him differently.

"There she is," Bridger said.

"Here I am." Vega rolled her eyes, and the chains rattled as she pulled against them. "What do you want, hmm? To rub it in my face that you're winning?"

"Winning?" Bridger barked. Vega felt power slip around her, the chains at her feet falling off. He'd thrown a shield around them, keeping their conversation private—Vega could feel his power brimming, making the brand on her wrist tingle. "What makes you think I'm winning?"

Her body pushed her forward, free of the restraints that kept her in the corner, struggling to hear. "Did you hit your head on the way in?" she asked before continuing. "Look at you, hiding behind that commander's uniform. You did it so you could win, right? Traded me in for the bigger, badder, and better Caelum sister. Traded me so you could wear the warrior's wardrobe you'd dreamed of since childhood."

Bridger looked her up and down, his lip curled in disgust. She could only imagine what she looked like to him—his clean-cut hair, longer in the front than it'd been in her last life, his facial hair growing into a five o'clock shadow, his perfectly pressed uniform. *Clean and as handsome as ever.* Compared to her own blood-stained body, dirty hair, and the fact she couldn't remember the last time she'd been able to bathe or use a real bathroom—Vega knew she was an eyesore at best.

"You have no idea what you're talking about."

They stood directly in front of each other. The only thing separating them was the iron bars.

"Don't I? I have my memories back now, and everything is so clear. You chose Marlena because you thought I wasn't strong enough to beat her. Maybe I'm not, but at least I'll be on the right side of history. You'll always be remembered as nothing more than her sad little pet she walked all over," Vega sneered, returning his look of abhorrence.

Bridger clenched his fists. "You don't know what I've been through, Vega. Assuming to know only makes you ignorant."

She huffed a laugh. "Poor Bridger got everything he ever wanted. An army, power, respect. But wait, do they respect you? Or are they just afraid of you like they're afraid of Marlena?"

Vega was close enough to slip her hands through the bars and strangle him—but she couldn't. She had no powers, no strength, and she knew he would cut his losses and kill her before she could finish.

I will not start over. Not again. Something inside her was still trying to fight.

"Get a grip, Vega! I did what I had to do. I made the best of the cards I was dealt! You weren't there—you have no idea what I went through and what I've done to get here." His voice raised, that deep baritone rumbling against her chest.

"Sure, you're right... but I bet it wasn't as bad as being killed twenty times, feeling the memories stolen from your mind as you take your last breath. Or falling in love with someone who promised to fight for you and then being stabbed in the heart by them. Multiple times. Or how about—"

Bridger cut her off, his temper flaring. "Do you think I need reminders of the last fifty-five years? I was there! While you got to forget, I lived this life, with these memories haunting me until I learned how to escape them!" Their voices matched decibels, echoing inside the sound bubble Bridger trapped them in.

"And how did you escape? By lying to yourself that what we had wasn't real? You left me! You left me, and you stand here like none of it mattered to you!" Vega refused to cry. Instead, she gritted her teeth until she felt like her jaw might shatter.

"Forgetting is easy! It's remembering everything, every grueling detail, that's the hard part!" Bridger slammed the palm of his hand into an iron bar, the structure swaying under his strength. "You're not the only one of us who has been through shit! This curse isn't just on you—it affects all of us."

Vega balled her bloody fists, clenching hard to keep herself from rearing back and punching Bridger through the bars. *If only I had my lightning, my storms.* She would turn him into a pile of ash... But there was still a piece of Vega deep down inside that wanted to reach out and touch his beautiful face, to feel his lips on hers. To feel the way she felt when he *loved her.*

Pathetic, pathetic, pathetic. Get a fucking grip on yourself! The Bridger you loved is gone.

Vega's smile was meant to kill. "The only part of the curse still haunting you is the memories of us you'll never be able to shield yourself from. No one has ever loved you like I did, and they never will again. People can see right through that cold heart of yours. This ruthless personality is a work of art, and all it took to get was a curse and manipulation so deep, you hurt the only people who would've fought for you." Bridger went to say something but clipped his mouth shut. "Now you're alone, and you always will be. Your mother doesn't love you, your best friend would never choose you over the crippling fear of disappointing his parents, your father is dead, and Marlena won't save you in the end. As soon as you no longer serve a purpose to her, she'll dispose of you too." Vega took a step away from the bars, her eyes never leaving Bridger's.

"I'm so glad you know everything. Everything except how to save yourself from this." He pointed to the bars keeping her caged in. "Too smart for her own good," he mused.

Cocky son of a— "Go fuck yourself, Bridger."

"I don't have to do that anymore. My bed is nice and warm... And look at you. You don't even have one." He moved away from her cell, his cape floating around his legs. "All you had to do was play nice, and you might have gotten dinner tonight. How ever will you beat us if you're skin and bones?"

The question didn't need a reply, and Bridger didn't give her time to respond or retaliate before he fled the room.

Vega liked to believe he did so with his metaphorical tail between his legs.

38

SLEEP. IT WAS ALL VEGA COULD DO. NO FOOD OR WATER WAS brought to her overnight, and Bridger was the last person to have a conversation with her.

The cell was impenetrable. Vega knew that from this life and the ones before it where she'd spent countless nights locked away. There was nothing more she could do... so sleep would become her friend, the only solace to be found.

Pain seared up her arms, and Vega's eyes flung open, still blurred with sleep. Marlena wrapped her hands around Vega's wrists, glowing an unnatural emerald green from the flames licking at her palms.

Marlena had always liked to play with fire—it was no surprise it was one of her favorite abilities now.

"Oh, good morning. How did you sleep?" Marlena released her grip, shoving away from Vega to stand above her. "And how did you get those chains off?"

Vega glanced at her wrists, taking in the damage from her sister's wrath. Her left wrist still donned the original brand from Remus, but the other now bubbled with third-degree burns. Her suit was held together by threads, exposing the places her body was marred by her sister.

"I have an admirer," Vega responded candidly.

"You still seem so lively. I didn't think you'd have much left in you after yesterday. I guess I'll have to try harder today."

"When will you bore of this?" Vega asked, pushing herself to stand with a wince as the newly formed blister stretched over her skin.

"Never." As an extension of her reply, Marlena disappeared.

There was no time to brace herself before Marlena came back into view and slammed her fist into Vega's face. *No, not a fist...* She felt the blood running down her face at the same time she saw the animal-like claws protruding from the tips of Marlena's fingers.

Vega's head rolled back and through the stars in her eyes, she caught the lightning trickling from her sister's fingertips—green for the color of her envy. *She's teasing me.*

Blood poured into Vega's left eye, blurring her vision. With the back of her hand, she wiped away the excess, scowling at the pain.

It would scar without her powers.

Vega longed for the fizzle of her lightning, the boom of her thunder, the wind and storms that swirled inside her body. She wanted to unleash it on Marlena—on this place and everyone inside until they were buried underneath the rubble.

She watched her sister bounce the unnaturally green lightning between her hands. "I guess you're not jealous of my powers anymore," Vega said, clenching her injured eye shut.

"I was never jealous of you, Vega." Marlena moved too quickly, snatching Vega by the neck.

Liar. Vega couldn't speak, but if she could, she'd call her bluff.

"I was hurt." She tightened her grip and continued to speak. "Pissed that my sister, my best friend, would have done anything for anyone but me. I needed you more than they did." Her voice was a hiss, venom leaking from fangs.

Vega gasped, her eyes turning scarlet from blood vessels popping. "I. Loved. You. So. Much," she somehow managed to squeak out.

"Shut up," Marlena growled, releasing her throat. "I'm here for one thing and one thing only... Tell me how Remus cursed the gods to die."

Vega struggled to get her breath back, her voice hoarse. "I told you I don't know."

"I don't believe you, not when you've been keeping an important secret from your friends for a very long time." Vega's blood ran cold. Marlena's grin terrified her. "Did you think I'd forget what I told you?"

Vega had kept a secret in every life—one even now she'd been mulling over since her memories were returned. Sometimes the words her sister whispered into her ear before she'd killed her the first time felt like a dream. How could she be sure they were real? *They were real. Marlena wouldn't lie about something so big, something that made her the most powerf—*

Marlena interrupted her thoughts. "What do you think happened the night you summoned Remus?"

The words swirled around her head, polluting her thoughts as she replaced the air in her lungs. "I can't trust you."

Marlena shrugged. "You don't have to trust me to know the truth. You know I wouldn't lie to you about what I've done and why we're able to do the things we can do."

She stalked closer to Vega, a bucket of water appearing from thin air—Marlena had always been able to conceal things from sight. It was why Vega'd never been able to find her Saturnalia gifts, no matter how hard she snooped.

The night we summoned Remus I became...

Marlena sighed. "It's going to be a long night for you."

Vega began to pray to the dead gods of Tolevarre as Marlena used the bucket of water to torture her for hours—drowning her until life nearly left her, only to allow her to live and start all over again. Vega lost count of the hours, and every time her sister asked about Remus, she slowly stopped replying.

The only company Vega had was the voice in her head, the voice of a demigod long dead. Words Vega heard before she became what Marlena never planned for her to be...

"I saved you. Do not waste this opportunity."

39

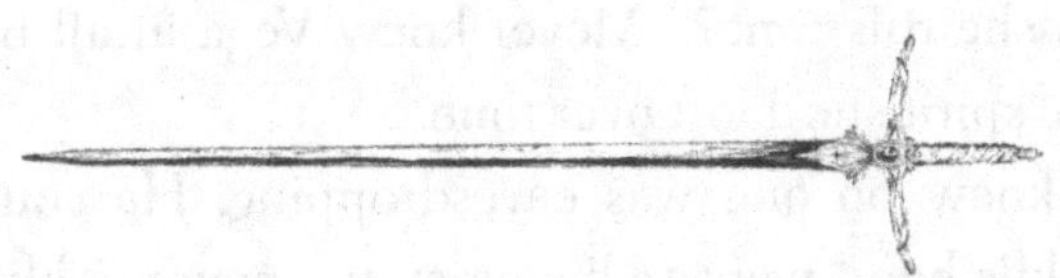

The smell of fresh linens, usually so prominent in Solum, no longer lingered in the air—little fires were burning everywhere, and Bridger wasn't sure they'd be able to put them all out in time. It wasn't the physical fires; it was the ones burning inside the people of Tolevarre, the torches of new rebellion camps popping up all over their realm.

It didn't matter Bridger had some of his best people in Solum. They would never stand a chance against a raging rebellion and the anger they felt now that Vega wasn't with them safe and sound. They would never stand a chance against those who would rather fight to the death than continue to live the life they'd been forced into under Marlena's rule.

Bridger could see Marlena's empire cracking, splintering like ice over a body of water, but he knew that meant he would fall with it.

"Bridger." Meyer snuck up behind him.

"Gods." Bridger spun, his pulse spiking uncharacteristically high for someone who never spooked. He chuckled at himself, but Meyer's brows pinched together. Bridger waved his hand in dismissal. "Got a lot on my mind."

Meyer sat on a freshly cut tree stump, joining Bridger in looking over their soldiers going about their day from the top of a hill. "She remembers." It wasn't a question.

Bridger gave a quick nod, his hair slicked back and out from his face. "Yes." He didn't meet Meyer's gaze, keeping his eyes out on the horizon. "She remembers."

"Who is she this time?" Meyer knew Vega in all her past lives too, knew the spirit she'd lost over time.

Bridger knew no one was eavesdropping. He could feel they were alone. His hand went to his wrist, the new prickling sensation since Vega got her memories back hard to ignore. "She's Vega."

My Vega.

He hadn't said those words out loud yet, but it was true, whether he was ready to admit it or not. The girl inside the deteriorating body was wholly Vega. But she wouldn't be for long if Marlena continued her torture. He knew firsthand what her tactics did to someone.

Meyer sighed. "I hope you know if that's true, she's going to burn this whole fucking world down to kill her sister."

"I know" was all Bridger knew to say.

They sat in silence for a while, watching the horizon as the sun rolled in and out of the moving clouds. Meyer finally spoke up. "I came up here to make sure you were okay. You aren't sleeping. I hear you in the training room every night. You're killing and maiming your own soldiers, and you're avoiding everyone. Me included."

He glanced over at Meyer, amber eyes wandering over Bridger's tired face.

"I'm fine," Bridger lied, finding it hard to meet the general's gaze.

"Why don't you trust me?" Meyer asked, his eyes flickering with a sadness he forced into hiding. He and Bridger had always had a different relationship, never exposing their emotions to one another because their parents taught them to always keep their underbellies covered—even from the ones they loved.

Old habits die hard.

Bridger's mouth opened and then shut as he tried to find the words. It felt like hours before he finally spoke. His posture changed, a breath releasing from deep in his lungs. "I trust you. I don't trust myself with what happens after if I admit out loud the toll these dreams are taking on me. If I tell you, I can't control what comes next, and that terrifies me." Bridger sounded more depleted as the days passed. "And then if I admit what these dreams are doing to me, what they're making me feel... then it's real." Bridger rested his head in his hands. "I don't want it to be real because then I'll have to live with losing her a second time."

Meyer was quiet for what felt like an eternity. "You still love her." Another statement, not a question.

Bridger threw his hands up in frustration. "No." It felt more like a lie than he wanted to admit. He started to pace, his boots pressing into the firm Solum soil. He caught himself and stopped abruptly.

Pacing was a trait of Khort's that had always driven Bridger crazy.

I'm letting them back in.

"I really did want her to die, to end the torment I felt every time I looked into those fucking *blue eyes*." Bridger growled the last words, a low rumble. "But I've recently started to wonder what happens if one of the bonded dies. *Really* dies. Do the rest go with them?" Bridger faced Meyer.

"What can I do to help?"

"Nothing," Bridger answered. "I'm sure it'll be over soon." *I hope.*

There was nothing else to say. Bridger wasn't interested in delving deeper into a conversation he already hadn't wanted to have.

"Are you staying here for the night?" Meyer asked, standing from the stump he still sat on.

Bridger uncrossed his arms from his chest. "No. I think I'll head back to Aeris. I have some business there in the morning."

Meyer stood. "I'll keep an eye out here then. Would you like me to prepare a caravan for you?"

"I think I'll take a horse. I could use some fresh air." Bridger loosened his stance, forcing himself to relax and pull himself out of his head.

"I'll get a group of guards."

"No," Bridger commanded. "I'm going alone." He didn't want an entourage.

"Arlet, Khort, and the rebels are out there somewhere, looking for Vega. I am not letting you go alone. Gods knows what they would do if they caught you." Meyer was thinking smart, planning ahead like he always did.

"I can handle a shifter and his misfits." Bridger's tone shifted slightly. "I'll be traveling alone. Please get a horse ready."

Meyer nodded, taking his order. He began to pad away on heavy feet but stopped suddenly to turn and look over his shoulder. "Don't do anything stupid."

Bridger didn't reply until he was out of earshot. "I make no promises."

40

The burning in her lungs surpassed any of the lingering pain she felt from her sister's other torture tactics. Vega's wheezes echoed off the cell walls, her cough shooting pain through her chest.

After hours of attempting to get comfortable, Vega resorted to standing in the corner of her cell. Her feet burned, but she shifted her weight between both to ease the pins and needles radiating up to her hips.

She still hadn't eaten. Vega couldn't keep her days straight anymore and decided to stop trying. She was ready to give up, to call it quits, but even if she did die, the curse wouldn't let her rest. Her memories were back, but Vega didn't feel full of hope that she could beat Marlena. *Evil will win.*

Her mind weighed on the secret she'd kept from her friends. She never thought about it in some lives, unable to wrap her head around what it meant; in this life it hit her harder than most.

Had she told her friends, would they have been able to continue looking into it while she was gone? Had she damned them all with her selfishness?

The weakness of hunger finally set in, and her legs gave out. The muscles she'd built by training with Khort were gone too quickly. *Gods, what I would do to see his face—to hug Arlet one more time and know who she is. To say goodbye to my best friends...* Footsteps down the hall did nothing to stir her from her new position on the ground—Vega was sure she would stay here until they got sick of her and killed her, starting the cycle over again.

"Have you had a lapse in memory? I'm growing tired of waiting." Marlena came into view through the cell door.

Vega's voice sounded nothing like her own after the hours of near-drowning Marlena had carried out. "I told you I don't know. Don't you think I'd have told you by now?"

She didn't know how to break her curse. She didn't know how Remus cursed Romulus and the original gods, but Vega'd had an epiphany during her last round of torture. A detail she'd missed in every other life...

"No, I don't. That's why you're still alive." The cell door creaked open, and Vega flinched away from Marlena. "It's a pity because I'm ready to be rid of you for good."

Marlena lifted Vega with one arm by what was left of the suit she wore. Holes lined the gear, her chest barely covered from the newest rips in the seams. She studied Vega's face with a hint of a smile. "Your healer friend, what was his name?"

Was. Vega's stomach toppled to the floor. "Felix." She could hardly hear her voice.

The smirk on Marlena's face grew. "When I found your wounds healed after hearing what your first guard did to you, I decided to look into both of them. Grimes is from a family in Imber, a family your rebellion got killed. Felix, well, he knew our parents. I couldn't let a rebel sympathizer live, Vega. And I surely couldn't let him back down here to fix any more of the scars I plan to give you. Bridger won't be happy, but he'll understand. Sometimes we have to do things we don't like. I'm sure he's reeling over the decision he had to make to delimb Grimes. All because he didn't follow the rules.

While I don't agree with his decision, I get it. He's come a long way since he let you go. So strong. He's everything his parents wanted him to be and more." With a gentleness Vega didn't know Marlena could possess, her sister ran two fingers over the wound on Vega's left eye. "If only you could see the mess I've made of your pretty little face."

"Fuck you."

How many people had to die simply because they were kind to Vega? Marlena's palm connected with Vega's cheek. The hit was meant to sting.

"Watch how you talk to me, dear sister." The pet name held no affection.

"You can scar every inch of my body, beat me until I'm black and blue, kill everyone I love, but that'll never save you from the hatred you have for yourself." The twitch in Marlena's eye gave Vega the energy to continue. "Our parents might have mistreated you, hell, they probably did abuse you like you claim, but what better are you? Taking it out on those below you who can't fight back is cowardly. You're not as strong as you think. I see right through you. You look just like the sad sister I remember who couldn't believe people liked her baby sister more than her, couldn't believe people *chose me* over someone so vile."

Marlena gripped her tighter, green flames burning behind her eyes.

"You think you're so much better than everyone, but look at you! You still need me!" Vega boasted, her laugh booming through her chest as she ignored the ache. "You can't figure out how to end this, end me. Summoning Remus messed up your curse. You hadn't planned for me to become like you. You made a curse for a *demigod* who can die, a curse for what we used to be. Want to know something I've come to realize, *dear sister?*" Vega sneered, the final piece clicking into place.

The blonde slammed Vega up against the wall, the stone

thwacking the back of her head. She saw stars but was able to get the words out before Marlena did worse. "My curse can't run out. That's another lie you've created to buy yourself time. A curse can't kill what can't die, and I'm no longer the demi you originally cursed. That's why you need to figure out how Remus cursed his brother and the rest of the gods... You're trying to curse a curse or this will never be over. I'll just keep resetting forever." Vega laughed, sounding manic, but she never broke eye contact with her sister. "You let your lust for power get in the way. You planted the idea of summoning gods in my head, and what? Didn't think I'd do it to get my revenge on you for killing the people I love?"

Another slam against the wall made her vision spotted. Marlena let out a feral cry of desperate frustration. Vega's eyes rolled to the back of her head, but she held on to what little piece of consciousness she had left.

"Remus gave me the time he never got."

Remus didn't get multiple lives to break a curse put on him by a hateful sibling, but Vega did.

The world faded to black around her, and for the first time in days, Vega had a real smile on her lips as she repeated the words Marlena said to her fifty-five years ago.

"We're gods, sister."

41

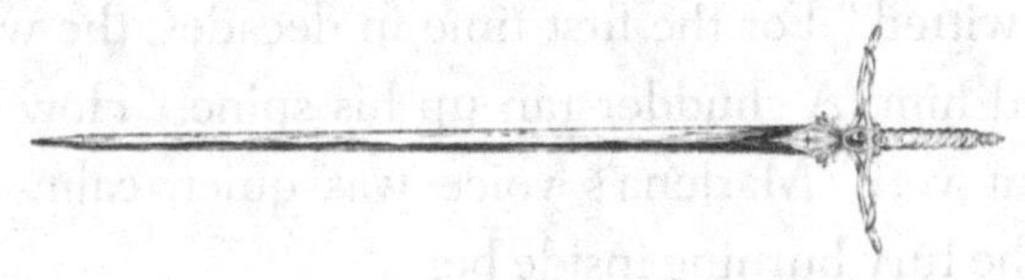

Bridger's horse reared as Marlena materialized under its nose—blood smeared her hands, splattered up her arms, and sprinkled the bridge of her nose in crimson. Bridger kept his saddle, pulling on the reins to gain control when the horse's hooves were back on the ground.

The sight of the blood sent his heart rate skyrocketing. *No, no, no.* "Marlena." Bridger dismounted the unsteady horse, charging towards her. He snatched Marlena's wrist in his hands, inspecting for a sign of struggle. "What have you done?"

Marlena tried to pull her arm back to her chest, her eyes wild with something unreadable. "Maybe you should ask what *she's* done." She escaped his grasp by traveling, smoke slipping through his fingers, and landed just outside his reach.

Bridger stood rooted to the dusty road beneath his feet. He'd never seen Marlena act this way. "Is she alive?" His words were a whisper.

"Of course she's alive," Marlena barked. "What does that matter? She'll be dead soon enough. As soon as she tells me how Remus did it."

"Did what?" Bridger couldn't keep up with her rambling.

"Cursed the gods to die!" Marlena's shriek pierced the night sky.

Bridger's skin prickled with invisible bugs crawling through him. He fought off the itch. "Why do you need to know that?" His mouth felt drier than the Ardor desert in summer.

Marlena didn't move, her eyes as big as a full moon. "You can't be that half-witted." For the first time in decades, the wild look she wore terrified him. A shudder ran up his spine. "How haven't you figured it out yet?" Marlena's voice was quiet, calm—completely opposite of the fury burning inside her.

Bridger asked again, "Marlena, what have you done?"

The shrillness in her tone was back as if it'd never left. "What have I done?! Ask yourself what you did, what my sister did to you! Why do you think you're stronger than you used to be? Why can you control the wind, help heal your wounded soldiers? How can you use your powers endlessly without getting fatigued anymore?"

He hadn't kept any of his new abilities a secret—hadn't been able to. All of them were changed. Bridger couldn't find the words to speak. Marlena had him in a metaphorical chokehold.

"What do you think happened to you four that night, Bridger?" Marlena's tone shifted and now sounded more melodic, like a siren luring a man to the deep sea, dragging him to his death.

"We were changed. Just like you."

Her smile was jagged and sharp. "Keep going. What am I, Bridger? What are we?" She kept saying his name to make this moment feel personal—as if she hadn't been keeping a secret for decades.

His mind swam with the facts he knew.

Marlena had summoned the twelve original gods, their souls and powers the only things left after Remus cursed himself and them to die thousands of years ago. *Check.* Marlena had all of their powers: electricity and wind from Jupiter, water control from Neptune, the ability to travel from Mercury, fire from Vulcan—the long list went on. *Check.* They'd taken what was left of the dead gods they'd summoned—Marlena, Vega, Arlet, Khort, himself.

Gods, no. The truth hit Bridger with the power of every god, and he staggered back in shock. "No."

"Yes," she said with a coolness only she could possess when altering someone's whole world. "Say it."

How did I not see this before? Marlena was known to keep secrets, but they should have figured this out sooner. Did the others know?

"We can't be." Bridger faltered, swallowing down his fear.

"Oh, but you are." Marlena took a confident step forward. Bridger took a step back. "Think about it. How else do you explain everything besides the simple truth: we are the new gods."

"How long have you known?"

"I've always known, and guess what?" Marlena's power of invisibility cloaked her, and when she allowed herself to be seen again, her mouth was to Bridger's ear. "Vega has too."

A sharp inhale filled Bridger's lungs with frigid air. "Impossible." He didn't back away from her this time, finding some composure to stand his ground.

Marlena reached out and caressed his cheek, her hand warm from the simmering anger underneath. "I told her."

The memory of Vega's eyes widening, Marlena's lips to her ear like they were on Bridger's now, before she struck that first killing blow made Bridger's knees wobble. "From her first life," he murmured.

"Yes." Marlena hissed the word like a serpent.

"She's been hiding it from all of us. Why?"

She cocked her head. "Maybe you should ask her that on the way to Fortis, where you'll be moving her tonight. I need a bigger torture chamber than what I have in my home."

I have a rising rebellion to worry about. I don't have time to babysit your sister. This defunct curse is your mess. You clean it up.

He should have said that, but the words never left his mind. Instead, he said, "Okay."

"She's being loaded up now. They're taking the pass through Pax." Marlena vanished after she spoke.

Bridger stood in the middle of the clearing, his horse yards away, still on high alert. His heart hadn't stopped the heavy beat rattling in his chest.

"I'm a god."

42

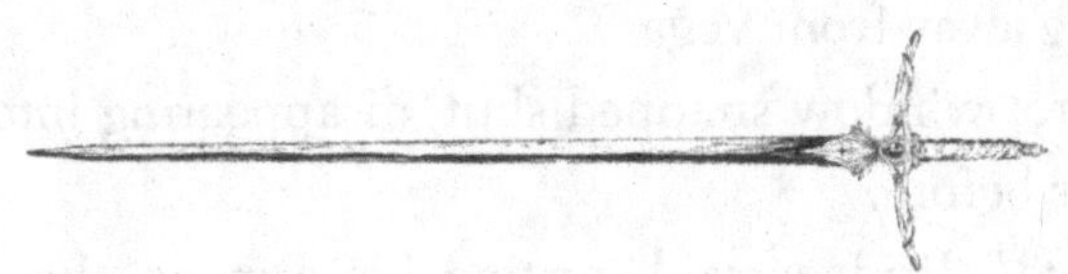

"Which vehicle is she in?" Bridger asked. Rain fell from the thick clouds above, wisps of his slicked back hair falling out of place. He was soaked through, running into rain after his world-shattering encounter with Marlena. Bridger pushed his horse to the brink of exhaustion, racing to get to Vega... He had to know if it was true—if she'd really kept a secret from everyone for fifty-five years.

The soldiers on horseback looked at each other. Two guards rode in the front on horses with two matching military vehicles sandwiched in between, and two more on horseback brought up the rear.

"Did I stutter? Which vehicle is the prisoner in?" Bridger hopped from his horse, water splashing from the puddle beneath his feet.

"The first one, sir," the other soldier answered.

Bridger handed off the reins to him and signaled the woman driving to open the door. The lock slid from its hold, and without hesitation, without thinking about anything other than *Vega*, he opened the door and slipped inside.

Vega's hands were cuffed behind her back, but she was alert, her eyes meeting his as he settled into the seat across from her. Bridger's stomach fell, and he had to forcefully snap his jaw shut at the new scar decorating Vega's left eye.

She glowered with distaste as he slapped the wall behind him and a hidden window opened. "Drive," he ordered in a neutral tone, never looking away from Vega.

The secret window snapped shut, disappearing into the cabin's wall as it was before.

"Your eye," Bridger said, resting his arm on the back of the cushioned bench.

Vega set her jaw and wiggled her shoulders like she was uncomfortable—and she should be. She'd been riding for hours with her arms trapped behind her.

"Marlena" was all she said as the engine roared to life again, and they lurched forward, down the dirt road with potholes around every corner. "Why are you here, Bridger? Did she send you as more torture? Because if she did, it's working. I can't think of a single reason why I'd want to spend more time with you than I have to."

Bridger masked his unease and the churning of his stomach as the vehicle dipped with the uneven path. "No torture at all. I just really wanted to spend some time with you, pick your brain about a few things."

Vega broke their staring contest, rolling her eyes before attempting to get comfortable. "Wake me when we get to my new prison. I should probably sleep before for my next round of torture." She rested her head against the interior wall.

Letting her sleep wouldn't get him the answers he needed. Before he lost his nerve, Bridger word-vomited. "Why didn't you tell me what happened to us when we summoned Remus? What we became?"

Vega's eyes flew open. "What?"

"Don't play stupid, Vega. Tell me why you kept it a secret—why you didn't tell me we're gods." His body had an unnatural stiffness, and he pressed his lips together in a tight line, fighting away the anger simmering underneath the surface.

"How do you..." Vega couldn't form the whole thought, her breath catching at the end.

"Marlena," Bridger answered. "You kept it from me... even before." He motioned between them with the arm resting on the bench. "Before we turned into this."

Shock turned to panic, her chest heaving and eyes growing wide as she fought for air. Her nerves lit the small cab up, searing into Bridger's chest.

Bridger removed his arm from the back of his seat and leaned forward. The vehicle was big enough he couldn't reach her without removing himself from the bench. "Hey," he drawled as she closed her eyes. "Breathe." Bridger's voice was deep and heavy like the thrum of a heartbeat. He got on his knees in front of her, hands gently grasping the backs of her calves. He hadn't remembered moving from his spot across from her...

Her piercing gaze met his, and suddenly they were in their twenties again, locked in a cottage in the woods. *"Do not break down now."* He heard his words inside his head like an echo.

She gulped air like a fish out of water—long inhales and shallow exhales. The speed of her breathing slowed.

"Good," he cooed.

It didn't take her long to find her words, the scared look in her eyes changing between blinks. "Get your hands off of me."

"Vega," Bridger started.

"I said." She took a controlled breath between words. "Get your fucking hands off me."

Bridger pulled his hands away and held them up in surrender. "I just want to know why you didn't trust me."

The laugh bubbling low in Vega's stomach surprised him. It blew through her lips with a puff of air. "Because maybe I knew you wouldn't choose me at the end of this, not when your destiny was so *perfectly* planned out for you." Bridger stiffened as she continued. "Because maybe I knew you didn't love me as much as I loved you, and that would be my downfall. I did it to protect myself and the people who truly loved me. I did it because I couldn't trust you, not really."

Bridger sat frozen on his knees below Vega, his eyes locked with hers in what felt like the ultimate showdown. Who would look away first this time? Those eyes twinkled with memories, her attitude the same one he'd fallen in love with all those years ago.

Her words sank in like a knife to the gut. Bridger's jaw flexed once, twice. *She'd never trusted you.* Maybe Vega was more like Marlena than he'd realized.

No. Could Vega see his internal struggle? She'd always been able to see right through him.

All this time, all these lives, Vega questioned his alliance—even before he'd switched sides. Shame annihilated him, shredding what was left of his soul. For fifteen years, Bridger had fought against his instincts, the role he'd been raised for—and for what?

Even in the beginning, the people of the rebellion never trusted him. They watched him like he'd betrayed them long before he actually did. They questioned his actions, never truly giving him a chance to fully become one of them—worried Bridger would take them down from the inside as a perfectly placed spy by his father, by Marlena.

He'd never felt at home during those fifteen years, not even when Vega was home—slowly becoming someone new altogether.

Finding out she'd been one of the people to question his intentions as well? It broke him. The dreams had started the crack, and Vega's words were what crumbled the entire foundation.

Bridger lost their stare-off, the turmoil inside him begging him to flee from Vega's soul-scorching stare. He forced himself off the floorboard, but before he returned to his side, Bridger reached for the cuffs behind her back, and they responded to his touch. The metal clasp opened and fell from her wrists. When his ass hit the plush bench, Bridger opened the storage underneath the seat beside him and tossed a pouch of mixed nuts to her, followed by a canteen of water. "Eat, drink. You're gonna need it."

Vega devoured her food and curled herself onto the bench, where she fell asleep in the most comfortable spot she'd been offered since Bridger took her as Marlena's prisoner.

Bridger watched the steady rise and fall of her chest, his mental shields shattering no matter how hard he tried to forge them back together.

It took a while to wind their way down the mountain and into the valleys of Pax that would eventually turn into Fortis. Bridger had taken more trips than he could count down this road to Vega before their lives came crashing down around them. He knew where he was without looking, knowing each bump in the road like a little landmark.

They were only a few hours from the fort city—where the start of her newest torment would begin. *Fuck.* Bridger didn't want to see Vega beaten even in his darkest days, the ones where he'd buried the real him so deep, he might as well be dead.

The torture awaiting her in Fortis was more than a beating. The punishment there would break her.

A bump shook the vehicle, rattling Vega from her snooze. "I have to pee." Her voice jostled Bridger from his daze.

"We're almost there," he lied. "Go back to sleep."

"Would you rather I squat in the corner?" She deadpanned. "Let me hold onto this one last sliver of dignity. You think Marlena is going to let me slip away to the bathroom? No, she's going to make me piss myself. I already smell bad enough." She paused, uncrossing her legs. "Let me pee on the side of the road like a lady." Her tone dripped with sarcasm.

Bridger sighed and swiveled his body to quickly tap on the wall separating them from the driver.

The vehicle quivered to a slower speed, and a squawky voice rang over the speaker into the cab. "Yes, Commander?"

"The pris—" He stopped himself. "Vega needs to pee. Send the soldiers up front on horseback ahead of us to keep watch, and tell the others to hold back and do the same."

Vega rolled her eyes at his correction.

The vehicle trembled to a stop. Bridger waved her out when the door opened, refocusing his eyes away from what little fabric covered her ass. *Act like a commander, not a horny teenager.* The time she'd spent locked away had stolen the weight that usually filled her out in Bridger's favorite places. *We're killing her.*

Marlena had been trying to end Vega since the moment she'd cursed her, and Bridger was a player in her game—a puppet she controlled. He knew his redemption was long gone, but that didn't mean he couldn't twist the narrative, didn't mean he couldn't try to say sorry in the only way that mattered.

She's getting to you, the darkness on his shoulder said. *Don't forget why you're in this position, why you chose to betray her.* And there was the light who'd recently reappeared. Bridger had only ever wanted to keep her safe.

Bridger honed in on her voice outside the vehicle through the small crack in the unclosed door.

"Can you turn around?" Vega asked, annoyed.

"No way. I don't trust you won't run," the soldier quipped.

"Please tell me how you expect me to run in this state." Bridger winced at the sadness in her tone. "Thanks to your serial killer ruler, I'm skin and bones."

There was a whoosh of air with a gurgling sound to follow. Bridger's senses swelled with danger. As silent as a leopard after its prey, he exited the vehicle.

His soldier held Vega by the throat, suspended in the air, while her feet kicked underneath for purchase. "You will not speak ill of Marlena." Vega's eyes bulged, her hands clawing at the man's arms. The soldier's gaze dropped to the ground, where liquid dripped from Vega's leg. "Gross. Are you pissing yourself?" He spat a laugh.

Bridger had been building an army to follow him, not Marlena. But there would always be outliers. The army was his, and he'd be damned if Marlena snaked her way in. She had enough control.

Crack.

The soldier's body folded to the ground after Bridger snapped his neck.

Vega barely caught herself on her feet, gasping for air as her fingers danced over the dark bruise already starting to form around her neck.

Bridger didn't reach for her, didn't help steady her. He looked behind him, waiting to see the next vehicle in their convoy. He could hear it in the distance, the engine stalled like he'd requested.

"Run."

Vega blinked rapidly. Her lips formed the question her voice couldn't find. *What?*

"Vega, *go*," he growled, detaching the cape of his uniform from the clasps.

She didn't question him this time, only hesitating for a second to grab the dagger off the dead soldier's leg. She kicked dirt up as she darted for the forest in the distance.

Bridger waited until she was inside the tree line to drive his dagger into his side, releasing a bellow of pain.

The second soldier from inside the vehicle jumped out, scurrying to Bridger's side as he ripped the blade from his flesh."Sir! What happened?"

A familiar soldier came barreling towards him on horseback. There was an X on the sleeve of his uniform, the numeral signifying he was a level ten warrior. The other from up ahead was close behind, the horse he handed over from earlier no longer with him.

The other soldiers of varying high ranks were on alert, searching the other side of the vehicle, awaiting their orders while calling the other piece of their convoy forward.

Bridger hastily reached inside the cab for his bonded sword with one hand pressed to his side. He ignored the nagging feel of his blood healing his self-induced stab wound. "I let her out to use the bathroom so she didn't pee inside my fucking vehicle, and she snapped Paulus's neck. When I got out to check on what was happening, she'd stolen his dagger and stabbed me." He slipped the scabbard over his back. "Three stay here in case she gets turned around and circles back. The rest of you spread out and keep eyes on the road."

"You shouldn't go alone. I'll come with you," the soldier with the X on his arm said.

"No," he barked quickly. "I can handle her on my own." Bridger stepped over his cape, glancing over his shoulder. "Do not sound the alarm yet. I don't need the rebels knowing she's trying to escape."

Bridger broke into a sprint, and with no one around to hear, he spoke to himself. "C'mon, Vega, I know you didn't get far."

43

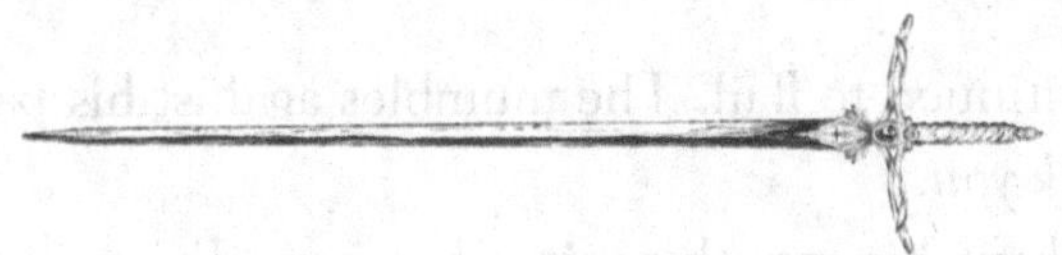

WHAT THE FUCK ARE YOU DOING, BRIDGER? HE ASKED HIMSELF as he pivoted toward a snapping twig. "Please come out." He spoke softly, knowing she was close. "I can feel you."

Their connection had always been strong, but since his shields came down, the tingle he felt had intensified like never before.

Another snap made Bridger spin in the opposite direction. "For such a tiny thing, you sure are making a lot of fucking noise," he grumbled. Standing in the same spot, Bridger took a deep breath and focused on the pull he could feel on the inside. It'd been so long since he followed the thread linking him to Vega.

His dark eyes shot open, and he moved on quiet feet.

Backed up against a large willow tree, Vega hid with the dagger she'd stolen clutched in her hand. Bridger stalked around in the shadows cast by the full moon.

Vega's head cocked, but with no powers, she wouldn't be able to feel him through the bond in their souls. She moved between trees, rustling leaves under her feet like a toddler without any balance.

Bridger rolled his eyes. *She's rusty.*

He made it behind the second tree she used for shelter and

343

didn't hesitate. Bridger sprung from behind, gripping her by the waist, and pulled her hard against his core. His free hand cupped over her mouth, muffling her screams after disarming her of the stolen dagger. The other Fortis-born warriors would know if he used his sound shields, so he was forced to do this the old-fashioned way.

Bridger's lips fluttered over Vega's ear. "Bite me, and I'll bite back."

Vega continued to flail. The mumbles against his palm sounded a lot like, *fuck you.*

Bridger kept his mouth against her ear. "I'm going to uncover your mouth. Don't you dare scream."

She screamed as soon as his hand pulled away. "Let me go!" Her voice pulsated through the woods. Birds scattered, squawking as they fled.

Bridger slapped his hand over her mouth again and sighed, his breath rustling her matted hair. She continued to thrash, but Bridger's hold was strong. "Why can't you do as you're asked?" He slid his hand down his leg and gripped a dagger at his side. "I let you go. Again. The least you could do is fucking *listen to me,*" he growled.

She did the exact opposite. His words made her fight harder, but with no powers and as awfully malnourished as she'd become, she was no match to Bridger. "Okay, fine. We'll do this the hard way then." He pulled the dagger up for her to see, dangling it in front of her face.

Vega's eyes grew wide with recognition, and her body went slack.

"Ah, that got your attention. Your dagger. Have you missed your bonded blade?" Vega shouldn't have been able to bond a weapon, but thanks to Remus and the gods he'd turned them into, the laws of their world didn't seem to apply to the four of them. "I don't know if this is going to work, but it's the only choice I have, and I'll apologize for it in advance because it's going to hurt. A lot."

Bridger let go of her waist and switched his hold to her forearm. Vega didn't have time to move before he drove the dagger through her flesh—through the brand that kept her powers locked away, shattering the bone as it came through the other side of her arm.

Vega's scream was blood-curdling, even muffled by Bridger's hand.

Bridger removed the dagger, and blood pumped from a major artery without slowing like it should have if his plan worked—if her powers had been restored.

"Fuck," he muttered. Bonded weapons held special ties to the person attached to them, and Bridger thought maybe, *just maybe*, it could break the block since it was her own.

He hadn't been certain it would work, but that didn't mean she was totally fucked. Vega could still get to Demuto—she could still get out of this and have her powers returned to her by one of the allies the rebellion had in their arsenal.

Blood continued to pour out, but Vega quieted. Bridger spun her around, dropping his hand from her mouth seconds before she chomped down with a bite that surely would've taken his finger off.

The look on Vega's face was lethal, the snarl on her lips pulling at a smile. She looked so much like Marlena, Bridger found himself stuck in place, blinking to clear his eyes of the image his brain was tricking him with.

No, it wasn't the shock. It was electricity. His hand was still on Vega's arm, and she was frying him from the inside. *It worked*, he thought, before realizing he needed to save himself. Bridger roared in pain, throwing a physical shield up that freed him of Vega's hold.

Light blue lightning sparked in Vega's palms, and wind whispered through the trees. She didn't say a word as she lunged forward, throwing a lightning bolt directly at Bridger's shield. It wasn't as strong as it could be, as it would be when she was fully healed, but it was enough to break his hold. His shield fell.

Is she really trying to kill me right now when I'm saving her life?

Her lightning cracked across the sky as the sprinkling rain from earlier turned into a torrential downpour.

"What the fuck are you doing?!" Bridger wailed, still slightly stunned by the shock she'd sent through him.

"Protecting myself! You stabbed me!" Another bolt of lightning flew towards him, narrowly missing his head.

"I stabbed you to try to give you your powers back, you lunatic!" Bridger didn't pull his weapon, only dodged her blows whenever they came hurtling towards him. "And look, it worked! You can thank me now."

Vega was weak, but she knew how to use those terrifying powers he knew too much about. This wasn't the same Vega he'd captured in the witch's cottage weeks ago.

She had her memories... And that made her dangerous.

"Vega, listen to me!" Bridger thundered. "You have to trust me!" He dodged another strike.

"Trust you?" Vega cackled. "Why would I ever trust you?" She crouched to grab the dagger Bridger stripped from her.

"Vega, please. I killed one of my own men to free you," he pleaded, looking over his shoulder at the sound of his other soldiers clamoring in the distance.

The footsteps from behind were getting louder, and Bridger watched as Vega's attention shot to the men coming from behind him.

"This way!" The voice of the leading soldier traveled through the wind.

"Why do you want to help me?" Her voice quieted, and the blood coming from her forearm finally ceased. Her powers were healing her.

"Because Marlena has been lying to all of us. Why would she need to know how Remus cursed the gods to die if your curse is just going to run out eventually?" He cocked his head, asking a question he was sure she already knew the answer to.

"My curse isn't going to run out. She cursed me as a demi, not a god. She doesn't know how to curse immortal gods. Remus is the only one to have ever done it, and he took the knowledge with him to his grave." Vega exhaled. "My curse is nothing more than an inconvenience. Marlena meant for it to be a drawn-out execution, a death sentence, but Remus gave me the time he wished he'd had when his own brother cursed him."

Bridger nodded. "He gave you more than time, Vega. He gave you the opportunity to save yourself, to save our realm like you asked. He wasn't talking to us that day. He was talking to you. We were merely caught in your orbit."

He could see the wheels in her head turning. "So what, you're looking for redemption? For forgiveness?"

Vega's storm rustled the trees, rain cleaning her of the dirt and grime from her cell.

Bridger swallowed with a click. "I'm not on your side. I belong here. That hasn't changed. *I* haven't changed." He said the words to convince himself, even though he didn't believe them. Bridger was changing... his shields faltering, failing, breaking down the walls he'd built up around his heart. "You deserve a chance to fight. I can't promise you'll win, but you can't try if you're locked away until Marlena figures out how Remus did it... and let's be honest with ourselves here, she will figure it out."

Lightning sputtered from her palms at his words. "What happens when we run into each other again? Because it'll happen. This isn't over."

"We pretend none of this ever happened. You escaped, killed my soldier, stabbed me, and learned how to regain your powers. No one's ever called you stupid, just unlucky." Bridger pulled his sword from the sheath on his back, rotating his wrist like he always did before striking. "We can fight it out, I'll win, and you'll end up in Fortis, where you'll never get the chance to figure out how to break your curse. Or you can save your energy for what's to come on your journey back to wherever it is you and the rebels have been hiding. What's it gonna be, Kitten?"

"What makes you so sure you'd win?" Bridger watched her move back and forth on the balls of her feet, contemplating her next move.

"You're weak, despite your memories and powers being back. You can't beat me in this state. You know it. I know it. There's no need to lie to each other." A cocky smile pricked at the corner of his mouth.

"Commander!" The voice of the level ten called out.

"Over here!" Bridger replied, continuing to play the part. "What's it gonna be?" he asked again.

A bolt of lightning whipped past Bridger's head, his ear ringing from the crack it made when it struck its target behind him.

She made her choice. And it wasn't to fight Bridger—not right now, at least.

Bridger swiveled on his heels to see two of his soldiers, one convulsing on the ground. His body twitched until his muscles tensed one last time, and he finally drifted off. *That's too bad. I really liked him.*

Vega didn't wait for the other soldier to act before she ran.

Bridger pointed back toward the vehicles, taking his eyes off the dead man at his feet. "Call for backup."

"We already did when we heard her screaming. General Ignis will be here in five minutes. Halo was called to transport him."

Fuck.

Bridger didn't have time to waste. "Go back and lead him this way," he called as he took off after Vega again.

When he caught up to her, she was bent over with her hands on her knees behind a tree, panting for air. Her powers were back, but her body would take a while to rebuild itself. Their blood helped them heal, but it didn't build muscle or aid endurance that wasn't already there.

Bridger reached out to touch her back, then quickly decided against it after the shock he'd received earlier. "Get up."

"I need a second." Vega didn't look up, her eyes fixated on the forest floor.

"We don't have a second." Bridger looked behind them, focusing on the sounds in the far-off distance. His heightened hearing picked up the sound of Meyer's booming voice. "Meyer is here, and if we don't move now, it'll be too late." Bridger didn't hesitate this time. His hand found what was left of the back of her training suit and hauled her up.

Vega batted him off, straightening herself and taking one last big gulp of air.

Meyer was fast—*too fast*.

The smell of smoke wafted in their direction. Bridger and Vega locked eyes. "He's trying to smoke us out," Vega gasped as the wind picked up in their direction, pushing against the storm she tried to keep alive.

Meyer knew Bridger could hide from the smoke and fire with his shields—shields he couldn't use to save Vega with other warriors around. They'd spent every moment together as young men training, playing off each other's abilities to excel further than anyone else could. It didn't matter the forest floor was damp from rain or even that Vega could conjure a storm—she couldn't control anything big enough to stop his fire right now.

"Go!" Bridger yelled.

Flames licked at the trees, rapidly encroaching on the space they'd briefly occupied. The storm of flames licked at their heels, the wind feeding oxygen for the fire to grow. Vega was slow, her body malnourished far more than Bridger realized. She tripped up, going down for a tumble. Bridger snatched her up before she had a chance to hit.

"Find your fucking footing!" he shouted over the howling wind.

Vega scowled, snarling. The heat from Meyer's fire scorched from behind by only a hundred yards.

We have to move faster.

Answering his thoughts, Vega pulled wind from in front of them and shot it back, gaining fifty yards between them and Meyer's fury.

Vega couldn't keep up much longer—she was gassed from the expelling of her freshly returned powers, and her body wasn't conditioned to fight for her life.

"Bridger." Her voice cracked, and he knew she couldn't go any further.

He reached for her hand and skidded to a stop. The fire began to catch up again. *Fuck, Meyer, fuck, fuck, fuck.* Vega pulled her hand away and crouched to the ground, steadying the sway of her body.

"Stay with me, Vega. Stay with me." Bridger ran a hand through his saturated hair, unsure of where they could go—of how he could give Vega a chance.

"The cliff," she croaked.

The cliff! Of course! Bridger could reach out and kiss her dirty, blood-smeared face. The cliff overlooking Lake Vehemens, the only lake big enough to hold some of the nastiest and most ruthless aquatic shifters known to Tolevarre.

It was their only choice.

The flames nipped behind them, growing closer by the second. "Get up," Bridger ordered.

Vega's face was pale, her skin glowing with a dew of sweat. "I can—"

He cut her off. "Yes, you can. Get. Up." Bridger hadn't done this for nothing. "Vega, get the fuck up!"

She struggled to her feet, and this time, Bridger didn't help her. He knew her—inside and out, in this life and in every other. Vega needed to do things for herself. She didn't need nor want people to always do things for her.

Vega was strong, even when broken, and she proved that by digging deep and shoving herself off the ground again.

Flames charred the tree behind them, blazing the side of Bridger's arm when the wind picked up from another gust. He yelped in pain, cradling his arm against his chest. The suits helped to an extent, but Meyer's fire roared with anger. Bridger's skin bubbled with third-degree burns.

She's going to live. She's going to make it. That was the echo in Bridger's mind, repeating over and over until the trees opened into a small clearing.

Vega stood on the edge of the cliff, peering into the lake. She turned from pale white to a shade of green, like she might hurl. "The water's too rough."

Bridger joined her on the edge. The water splashed against the cliff like an angry god, ready to seek its revenge. He shot a look behind him. The fire wasn't stopping at the tree line like it should.

Meyer was coming, pushing the fire forward so he could travel through unscathed. He'd recently told Bridger he deserved to make his own decision—to choose his own path.

Bridger's path had always been clear, and Vega Caelum got hung up in the wreckage. His love for her had burned like a thousand suns—suns since smothered by years of carnage. Slowly, they were igniting again, roaring to life with a vengeance.

But Bridger *had* made a choice—Meyer was wrong about him not getting the choice. He'd chosen to follow the path of darkness to keep the people he loved safe.

And somewhere, over the course of his lifetime, he'd lost sight of that—harming someone deserving of more than he'd ever be able to give her.

"We have to find another way around," she said, turning her back to the cliff.

Meyer's flames parted down the middle like a sea of madness. Bridger only had seconds to decide.

There was no other way.

Bridger whispered a hushed apology and shoved Vega off the cliff.

He watched Vega fall, fall, fall. Her frail body hit the roaring waters, and Bridger knew she had less than a minute.

A minute before she was gone again, before the brand around his wrist throbbed with the loss of a bond so strong it took a little piece of him with it every time. The shields could protect him from the memories but not their fated connection.

Meyer strode through the fire, worry lining his brows. "Gods be damned, I thought you were dead." He reached for Bridger, but he stepped back, his heel dangling off the edge. "Where is she?" Meyer looked around, stepping forward to gaze over the cliff.

"She jumped."

The general's jaw dropped. "She what?"

"She jumped... and I..." he lied. *Fifteen, sixteen, seventeen.* The clock on her life tick, tick, ticked. "I can't let her get away."

"If she jumped into the water, she's already dead. We'll try again next time, or maybe the curse will run out and we won't have to worry about a next time." He gripped Bridger's shoulder, yanking him away from the ledge.

Bridger thrust his hands into Meyer's chest, pushing him off. "You don't understand! The curse isn't going to run out!" he screamed. "We are bonded. I'm—fuck." Bridger yanked at his hair, the smell of smoke clinging to his body. "Meyer, we're..." Bridger inhaled, unable to keep this truth from him. "Remus bonded the four of us that night in a way I never—*no one* ever thought possible. We weren't supposed to live. Marlena shouldn't have lived. No one had ever lived when trying to summon any of the dead gods. But we did..." Bridger rambled, trying to process all he'd learned tonight out loud for the first time.

"Remus didn't just bond us." Bridger glanced over his shoulder quickly before finding Meyer's eyes again. "He turned us into gods.

I'm a god. Vega is a god. Arlet, Khort. *Marlena.*" Bridger swallowed the knot in his throat. "Her curse can't kill her, but Marlena can if she finds out how Remus cursed the gods."

Meyer's fire still raged on behind them, but he didn't dare make a move, stunned by Bridger's words. "That's what we want, what you want. For her to die forever."

Thirty-nine, forty, forty-one.

"I asked you what you thought would happen if one bonded soul died. I think I know now. Remus did to us what he did to the original gods. He joined our souls, but not to kill us. To make us stronger." Bridger retreated a step, both heels dangling from the ledge. "There's so much you don't know, Meyer. I wish I had time to explain it, but I can't let Marlena find a way to kill her. If she dies, I die. We all die. Everyone but Marlena."

Meyer exhaled. "You don't know that."

"It's not a risk I'm willing to take."

Meyer nodded behind him to the crashing waves of Lake Vehemens. "You've made your choice?"

"No, but I'll save her to save me."

Sixty. Bridger took one large step back and plummeted into the water below.

44

I'M FREE-FALLING TO MY DEATH. THE ICY COLD WATER IS GOING to lap me up and spit me out as a lifeless corpse before my body disappears altogether. And all of this, every revelation I've had in this life, will have been for nothing.

Vega sank, sank, sank, kept sinking until her feet touched the bottom. Stones rattled around her water-logged boots, and the current slammed Vega's already ravaged body against the rough rocks of the cliff. Maybe if she weren't already so weak, she'd have the strength to swim, to continue to fight for her life.

I'm going to die. This is what I deserve for putting my faith in Bridger.

Never again.

Vega wasn't worried about the shifters-turned-monsters—she was worried about the person she'd become in her next life. What kind of person would follow this one? Would she have it in her to keep fighting?

Her lungs burned, filling with water when the current slammed her against the rock again.

Vega saw Arlet's face, the smile that spread across her lips when they sang their favorite song. She saw Khort soaring in the night, fire ripping through the sky. *I'll never be able to apologize for always letting them down.*

At least she got to see her friends one last time...

When her vision started to blacken around the edges, Vega accepted her fate. *I'll try again next time. I'll get it right next time.*

Before she faded completely, arms wrapped around her waist, hoisting her out of the darkness.

Her head popped out of the water, and she devoured that first breath of air before hacking water out of her lungs.

"Kick your legs!" Bridger screamed over the rushing waves.

She didn't argue, couldn't argue, so Vega did as she was told and used whatever strength she could find in her to kick. Bridger turned their backs to the brunt of the waves, blanketing them with a shield.

Vega was beaten and exhausted, but she wasn't dead. She would heal, and she would live.

All she had to do was keep swimming and try not to think of the beasts lurking in the waters below.

She summoned her wind, battling against the rough waters. Vega pushed when the water pulled. After what felt like hours of swimming, Bridger's feet touched the shore, and he pulled Vega until hers did too.

Vega collapsed to her knees on the shore and hacked up whatever water remained in her lungs.

Even Bridger panted with his lean and muscular body, lungs stronger than steel, and powers to assist in grueling fights.

Bridger saved her, but she didn't forgive him—she would never forgive him, not fully.

She stood when she finally felt like her legs weren't made of jelly and locked a violent gaze on him. His eyes twinkled with something she couldn't pinpoint, but she didn't care—he'd pushed her off a fucking cliff! Vega trudged over to Bridger, and before she could stop herself, she slammed her fist into his mouth.

Bridger cupped his jaw, blood dripping down his palm. "What was that for?" he groaned, wiping blood from his busted lip.

"For pushing me off a cliff into waters infested with creatures that could have eaten me!"

Bridger walked over to the water and rinsed the blood from his face and hands. "What else did you want me to do?"

"A heads-up would've been nice!"

"That's what the apology was for," he scoffed.

Vega rolled her eyes and looked into the tree line. *Demuto*. It had been years since she'd stepped foot into this territory, and for good reason. The shifters left here had gone mad and didn't like strangers —more specifically, they didn't like Caelums, no matter which sister it was.

His bleeding lip stopped, and Bridger moved to stand beside her. "This is where I leave you."

Vega looked up at him, nodding. "And if I die in there?" she asked before returning her gaze to the dark forest illuminated by nothing but the moon.

"Then I guess you won't remember any of this happened and my little secret will be safe for now."

Vega cracked a smile, peeking at him with a sideways glance. *Why does he have to be so gods-damned beautiful?*

He returned her smile, looking like the fallen god he was. "I'm sure Khort already knows you're in his lands, and I know he won't waste a minute coming to your aid."

Vega's hand went to her side where she'd stuck the stolen dagger while they ran. A panic settled in her stomach when she realized it wasn't there. "Fuck." She searched around in the sand, hoping it fell out when they waddled out of the water but accepting that it'd probably sank to the bottom of the lake.

She had her powers back, but using her lightning and storms put a direct target on her back, like a big neon sign that screamed, *Here I am! Come get me!*

Bridger outstretched his hand, and in the center of his palm was her dagger, the one she'd lost several lives ago. Her eyes lit up excitedly as she took it from him, spinning it between her fingers.

She'd made this in her second life—her bonded blade. As an Aeris-born, she shouldn't be able to bond a weapon... but the four of them weren't Aeris-born, Fortis-born, Vates-born, or Demuto-born anymore—they were gods-born. Unlike anyone else in their realm.

It was all black, from the hilt to the blade's tip, except for the light blue gem at the pommel. Made with the same material as Bridger's sword, the same material the gem in her ring was made from, and it was just as beautiful as she remembered.

"Thank you," she said with a breath.

"Don't thank me yet." He glanced towards the eerie darkness ahead. "You still need to make it through the night, and Demuto might have what it takes to kill you."

Vega slid her blade into the holster on her suit, somehow still intact, and turned to face Bridger. Arlet's voice rang in her ears. *"We need Bridger to win this thing."* But could Vega's heart take letting him get close?

She took a step forward, testing the waters between them. Bridger stood as still as stone. "Why?" she asked, her voice lighter than the breeze threading through her fingers.

"Why what?" he responded.

"Why now?"

Bridger didn't break eye contact. "Because I've made a lot of mistakes in my life." He licked his lips, and Vega could hear the words before he spoke them out loud. "But none of those mistakes were you."

Her heart fluttered in her chest, and she would damn herself for this, but she had to do it. *They needed Bridger.*

Vega's body crashed against his. She lifted herself to her tippy-toes and pressed her lips against Bridger's. His body went rigid for no more than a second before his hands reached to cup one side of her face, the other tangling in her wet and knotted hair.

Vega melted at his touch, just like she always had. She'd planned to take the lead, to rattle Bridger to his core, but it was she who was rattled. Flustered by the sheer need in their kiss.

It had been forty years—forty years since she'd kissed the man whose soul was bonded to hers.

Bridger licked at her bottom lip, begging for entrance, and as big a mistake as Vega knew it was, she let him in. Their tongues slid together like they were revealing a secret. Slow and cautious at first, and then ravenous with the need to know more—to know what they'd missed while being apart.

The little voice in the back of her mind quieted, turning into a soft undertone, but Vega knew she had to escape. She would do anything to escape.

Her hand slid from Bridger's hip, moving down the curve of his body—gods, how she missed the feel of him.

With a control she didn't know she possessed, Vega pulled her lips away from Bridger and kissed a line down his jaw. Bridger groaned, fighting his own internal battle. "Do you want to know the real reason I never told you what Marlena said to me before she killed me?" Vega pulled back, meeting his gaze.

The hunger behind his eyes made her almost give in to the temptation she felt—just one last time.

Bridger's voice was pure gravel, his hand gliding to the spot on her chin he always loved to hold. "Yes."

Vega swallowed, steadied her breath, and leaned into his ear. With one hand on his hip and the other hovering over the hilt of his dagger, Vega spoke the truth. "Because I never had anyone I was willing to test the theory on." She nibbled his earlobe gently, drawing him in. Bridger's breath hitched. "After everything you've done to me, I finally don't care whether you live or die."

Vega leaned back to look him in the eyes as she slid his dagger from its sheath and struck him right through the heart. Her eyes didn't leave Bridger's, watching his emotions jump from lust to shock to betrayal, and back to cold and unreadable—the Bridger she was accustomed to seeing over the last forty years. But then the pain set in, and it was so strong she too could feel it.

There was pain, but life didn't drain from his eyes. Vega twisted the knife in his chest. "I guess Marlena's right. We are gods, Bridger."

When he dropped to his knees, Vega crouched at eye level and pulled the dagger out. She could still taste him on her lips, could feel his heartbeat pounding in time with hers.

She met his cold but very alive gaze. "Now you know how it feels to love someone even after they've killed you, after they chose a sister over you. You know what it feels like to hold on to hope that they'd come back, that they'd change their mind—like a knife to the heart." Vega stood. "I would've loved you until my very last breath. I would've kept the promises you couldn't keep."

And then she disappeared into the Demuto forest with his bonded dagger still in her hand.

45

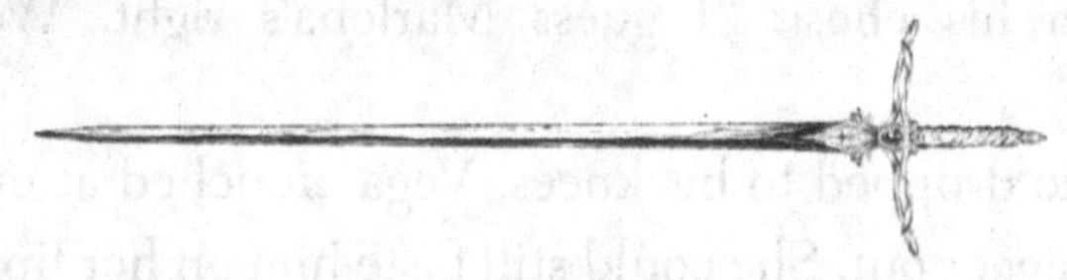

BRIDGER AND KHORT HAD BEEN BY THE PORTAL IN SILENCE FOR hours. Khort started to pace, driving Bridger mad as the seconds bore on. "Will you sit fucking still?" he barked, whipping his head to face him.

"Can't. Have to keep moving."

They'd felt Vega stir about a week ago, meaning Arlet found her on Earth. The tingling got more aggravating as the week came to an end, and this morning, the tingle turned into a burn that could only mean one thing: Arlet and Vega were close to home.

Bridger wanted to step through the portal and find Vega himself, but neither he nor Khort were right for the job—they could feel Vega here, once she was back in Tolevarre, but they couldn't sense her on Earth until Arlet made contact. The sisterhood they had before the summoning made their bond work differently—each of them had something the other didn't.

They'd tried to convince her to let them go with her, to help find her faster, but whether they wanted to admit it or not, Bridger and Khort knew they had to stay here and keep their people safe. The small but growing rebellion was at risk if they weren't there to fight if needed.

This was Vega's fourth life, and they were no closer to figuring out how to break the curse than they were during her last. There just wasn't enough information about the type of curse Marlena created.

"You're driving me mental. Please sit down," Bridger begged, running a hand through his hair. It had been months since he'd had a proper haircut or even a shower that wasn't cold as ice.

"I can't help it. I need to move or the burning will drive *me* mental." Khort kicked at a small rock while he paced, sending it back and forth with a pitter-patter sound.

Bridger used the wind he'd gained control of over the last year and sent the rock hurling far away from Khort.

"Hey!" Khort whined, stopping himself finally.

"Oh look, it worked," Bridger said with a hollow breath.

"Dude, you're about to get your girl back. Why are you so grumpy?" Khort had let go of the outward animosity towards him over the last few years, but Bridger could still hear the sneer in his voice when he said "your girl."

"Because what if she's not Vega again?" Bridger asked, opening a dark door he didn't need to fall into. "What if she's even farther from the person we love?"

Khort's back tensed. "She's always Vega, Bridger."

Bridger wanted so badly to disagree, but they'd had this fight before, and it got them nowhere. The two were finally at a place where they could consider themselves friends and partners in this rebellion, despite what the others might think of him—Bridger didn't have the energy to push right now. "Who knows what this last life has done to her."

"It's only been two years. Maybe Arlet got to her in time," Khort said with optimism Bridger didn't feel. It seemed the shorter timespans fucked Vega up more than the long ones did.

They'd been at this for ten years... How much longer could they keep it up before Vega wasn't herself at all anymore?

"Yeah, maybe," Bridger said as the portal flickered with movement. Bridger jumped to his feet, brushing off the grass stuck to his pants.

Arlet stepped through, and the first thing Bridger recognized was how tired she looked. The bags under her eyes were puffy, her black shirt wrinkled, and those definitely weren't the same boots she'd left with.

Vega appeared behind her seconds later, rubbing her eyes in bewilderment at the world around her. She was so tiny, skin and bones, with bruises up and down her arms.

Are those fingerprints? Bridger's anger could be felt in the rise of the temperature around them.

"I'd rather not talk about them," Vega said in a mousy tone that wasn't hers.

Bridger must be more sleep-deprived than he thought because he meant to say those words to himself, not out loud. Or maybe he had, and she'd just followed his gaze...

"It was tough getting her out this time," Arlet admitted.

Bridger forced himself forward, moving to reach out for Vega, but she flinched away, stopping him in his tracks.

"Vega, that's Bridger. He won't hurt you." Arlet reached out to tug her away from the portal, nodding in Khort's direction. "And that's Khort."

He smiled at her wide. "It's good to see you."

No, it's not. Not like this. Vega stared at Bridger, taking him in with wary eyes.

"Do I look different?" she asked, seeming to read his thoughts again.

Bridger bit his lip. "Just a little more banged up than I'd like you to be."

"But it's okay, we'll get you back to you," Khort promised as he pulled Arlet into a big hug.

Arlet wrapped her arms around Khort, and that was when Bridger saw the bruises on her too. The rumble of his anger shook the ground under them. "Who?" he growled, grabbing Arlet gently despite his growing rage.

"Bridger, it's fine." She tried to reassure him. "He's back on Earth. He can't hurt her anymore."

These lives Vega was living were quite literally beating her down until she crumbled.

"My ex," Vega squeaked. "I left him when I met Arlet, but he followed us when we went to leave."

Her ex. Bridger would never get used to the fact she was living a completely separate life on Earth, including being involved with other men. It wasn't her fault, but Bridger's heart broke with the knowledge that his Vega wasn't just his anymore—she became someone else's every time she left this life.

A wisp of cold air blew, raising the hairs on Bridger's arms, and Arlet jumped to hide Vega behind her. He knew before he turned around who he would see.

Marlena's grin was huge, spreading ear to ear. "That must suck, knowing someone else has been worshiping..." She paused, peeking her head around Bridger to get a view of her sister hiding behind Arlet. "Maybe that's not the right word. Let me rephrase—knowing that someone else has been beating the shit out of your girlfriend and there's nothing you can do about it. I'm sure that's worse than picturing her moaning someone else's name, right?"

Khort puffed smoke, his eyes turning to slits.

Marlena chuckled. "Calm down, big boy. I'm not here for her. Not this time, at least."

"Then what are you here for?" Bridger snapped.

"I'm here for you. Haven't you heard?" Marlena asked, her eyes darting between everyone. She gasped, the sound of practiced innocence. "Oh no, I'm sorry to be the one to tell you, Bridgey..." A fake frown pulled too deeply at her lips. "Your father is dead."

Arlet inhaled sharply, Khort unsteady on his legs. But they kept themselves in front of Vega, not allowing Marlena to get too close.

"What?" Bridger asked, dumbfounded. Tolevarre was without a commander for the first time in history.

"I killed him." Her words were melodic, *happy*. "And you're next in line for commander of Tolevarre."

Marlena stepped closer to Bridger, and while every nerve ending in his body told him to move, he wouldn't show Marlena fear—it was what she wanted.

That was a mistake, one he would think about for the rest of his life.

Marlena reached out with a swiftness she shouldn't possess, and the brand of a power block burned into his forearm where her hand had been. Bridger hissed against the pain.

"I know you won't agree to it without a little coaxing. So you're coming with me, where I can persuade you in different ways."

Khort shifted with a roar, steam billowing from his nose as his fire primed up.

Arlet and Vega ran, but a traveler, one they'd thought was on their side, appeared, blocking their escape. She *tsk*ed at Arlet's surprise. "You should know better than to let a fox in your hen house."

"Traitor!" Arlet spat, reaching into her pocket for a dagger. She flung it at the woman's chest with the precision Bridger taught her, but she disappeared, reappearing with Vega's head between her hands.

"I like to call it being an opportunist," the traveler replied, snapping Vega's neck.

Her body hit the ground with a thud, and the air left Bridger's lungs as Khort spit fire, charring the Fraus-born to ash where she'd stood.

Bridger felt himself inhale, but the air never returned to his lungs. The feeling of suffocating jarred him out of his restless slumber and threw him back into reality—the one where he'd fallen asleep on his trip back to Vincere after surviving a direct stab to the heart.

Marlena hunched over Bridger, her hands wrapped around his throat with anger unlike any he'd ever seen.

Bridger pulled his legs to his chest and kicked her across the cab. She landed with a bang but sprang back with cat-like reflexes.

"You let her get away! Twice! Twice in one life!" Marlena blustered, clawing at his outstretched legs. The space was tiny, too small for large powers.

He burned where she touched him, fire blistering his skin. Bridger hissed and threw a shield around the outside of his skin to keep her from searing any more of his body.

The soldier driving had no idea anything was happening back here, going about his drive like all was well. Bridger could feel the sound block Marlena put up.

"What did you think was going to happen when you gave her her memories back, huh?" Bridger grabbed Marlena's wrist while it was outstretched, aiming for a blow to his face. "She's not the meek Vega you hoped she'd be in every life! She's Vega, the Vega you've been in fear of your whole life."

Marlena screamed, her wrath rattling the windows. "You're fucking with me! What kind of game are you playing, Bridger?"

He kept his leg extended, holding Marlena back. She fought like a wild animal, clawing at anything she could. "I'm not playing any games. You're just making bad moves, setting yourself up for failure. You told me once I'm just a chess piece and you're the game master."

His words made her barbaric. Green lightning surged, flying from her palm. Bridger's shield sent it through the glass barricade between them and his soldier. It shattered around the cabin, glass raining down.

The bolt struck the driver in the back of the head, and the man slumped to the side, the vehicle sputtering to a stop without his foot on the pedal. He was dead, killed without warning.

Marlena lunged for Bridger, but her anger distracted her, slowing her reaction time. He landed on top, pinning her to the floor. Bridger held his sword to Marlena's throat, pressing hard enough to draw blood.

She was strong, bucking her hips to get out from underneath him, but Bridger was stronger as the wildness of his rage thundered around them. "You're losing it," he snarled.

Marlena ignored his words, still fighting to get herself free. Bridger wasn't going to budge, his strength growing the harder she fought.

"You can't kill me." She laughed, the pressure Bridger had on her throat muffling her voice. "I can't be killed."

"Oh, but I can make it hurt." Bridger pushed the blade harder, blood flowing faster from her growing wound.

Marlena's laugh gargled in her throat, madness consuming her the longer Bridger held her down. She tried every power she possessed to get her commander off, but his bodily shield protected him.

All she could do at this point was travel away, but Bridger knew better than that. She was here to fight, to show Bridger she was stronger than him... but the warrior had had enough.

Enough of being her pawn.

Enough of letting her think she always had the upper hand.

Enough of her.

"I might not be able to kill you, Marlena, but now I know you can't kill me either."

"Don't be so sure about that," she said with a grating laugh.

"Keep lying to me. See where it gets you." Bridger didn't let her up. "You might be strong, but don't forget I was made to be the strongest warrior this world has ever seen," he boomed. "And I've been going easy on you."

Marlena bared her teeth, her smile fading. "Don't get too comfortable, Commander."

"Or what?" he asked. "You know you can't lose me. We both know it. So here's what's going to happen." Marlena hissed when he pressed down harder on her throat. "The next time you think about putting your hands on me, remember that without me, you have no army and no one to defend you when the rebellion attacks."

"If you don't find her—"

Bridger chuckled. "Vega is your problem, not mine." He took his knee off her rib cage, the blade following soon after. Bridger exited the vehicle, and Marlena followed.

"I own you! You work for me!" Her raucous screams scared birds from the surrounding trees.

Bridger opened the driver's side door and pulled his soldier's limp body from the seat. He placed him over his shoulder and sat his body down in the back. Bridger would transport him back to Ardor, where his family would be alerted of his passing and thanked for his service. They would be allowed to take his body for proper burial or cremation.

"No, Marlena. Without me, without the army I saved and rebuilt from nothing after you let my father run it into the ground, after you murdered him as bait to lure me to your side because you knew I'd want to protect my people... you'd have nothing to rule over." He got into the driver's seat. "I am not your toy to torture Vega with. I am the commander of the strongest army our world has ever known, and it's about time you recognize that."

The engine whirred to life, but it didn't drown out Marlena's response. "I hold your life in the palm of my hand! Your life is tied to hers, to theirs! I am the key to your survival when I kill the rest of them, Bridger!"

He slammed the door, driving away from Marlena—but her voice reached him inside the vehicle.

"Don't make me kill you too!"

46

The smell of bacon pulled Vega from a death-like slumber. When her eyes peeled open, Khort was in the corner of her room, arranging a fresh bouquet of hydrangeas and pouring water into a glass on her desk.

She cleared her throat, and he jumped, knocking over the glass of water. "Shit!" He laughed, grabbing a towel from the tiny bathroom connected to her room.

Vega sat up against her headboard, stretching her sore muscles and limbs. "Morning." She yawned.

Khort smiled, tossing the sodden towel into the bathroom sink. "Welcome back to the land of the living." He sat at the end of her bed, handing her the plate he'd brought into her room. "I didn't mean to wake you. I figured you'd be hungry when you finally woke."

Bridger had been right. Khort was alerted when Vega crossed into Demuto—once his home, now a place he couldn't cross into without the possibility of being trapped forever. He met her at the border of Vates as the sun rose. Somehow, Vega survived a night in

Demuto with only one near-death experience. She shuddered at the memory of the bird-beast she'd had to fight off.

"Thanks." Vega smiled and reached for a piece of crunchy bacon, chomping down with a content hum. "How many days did I sleep this time?" she asked before tearing into a piece of toasted bread.

"Only two." Khort stared at the scar over Vega's eye.

Upon returning to Castra, Vega only had time to shower and look herself over in a mirror before she passed out. The version of herself that stared back at her was one she never wanted to see again... but the scar, the claw marks of her sister, became a reminder of what she'd survived, of *who* she'd survived.

It split her eyebrow in two, the first mark slicing through her brow and onto her cheek while the other two trailed off the corner of her eye.

Khort's lips were in a tight line. "Will you please let me see if a healer can mend that for you?"

Vega shook her head. "They have bigger things to worry about."

Khort reached across the small room, able to grab a new glass of water without leaving his spot on the edge of the bed.

Her eyes wandered to the flowers Khort brought in with breakfast, and her heart dropped to her stomach. *I can't avoid this conversation.*

Vega chugged the water in one go and sat the empty glass down. She took a breath and let it out in a sigh. "I think it's time we talk about something."

Khort met her gaze, nodding slowly. "I guess so."

Vega laced her fingers together, rubbing her thumbs together as a way to focus. "Khort, I love you, you know that. You're my best friend, my first friend." She bit her lip, working through the mess in her brain. "Our kiss was—you're a great kisser." She paused, trying to find the right words and not make this about the physical act.

"First, I want to thank you for stopping us. You're a better person than I am for not taking advantage of that situation."

His eyebrows drew together. "I would never."

"I know, I know." Vega reached out across the bed and squeezed the back of his hand resting on her blanket. "I mean, I know it's probably something you've wanted from me most of our lives, and I can only imagine how hard it was on you to experience it from me when I had no idea who you were."

He nodded, glancing at the door. Vega knew he was remembering the last time they entered this room together too.

"I've been through a lot, obviously... We all have." She huffed a small laugh. "But the last thing I need to think about right now is any kind of love life. You understand that, right?"

He turned his head to refocus his attention on her. "Yeah, I do."

"I'm not saying never. You've always been the best choice for me, the smart choice." She gave him a tiny, pursed lip smile. "But I can't make that choice right now. For the first time in my life, in my lives, I'm ready to focus on the one thing that matters. Me. Breaking my curse. Staying here with you, with Arlet, forever."

Khort returned her smile, but his seemed sadder than hers. "Of course."

Vega crawled out from under the covers, avoiding the plate of food on the bed, and sat beside Khort. Her legs dangled where his met the floor. Their thighs touched, and she rested her head on his shoulder. "I don't regret it. I want you to know that. That's not what this is about."

Khort leaned his head over and rested it on hers, then reached out to rub his hand on her exposed thigh—the touch was friendly. "I know, and I understand. I'll wait until you tell me not to."

They sat like that for a while in complete silence until Khort tapped her leg and stood. He grabbed the plate and handed it to her. "I have to meet Arlet for training. Come visit when you're done eating. She's been dying to see you."

I've been dying to see her. Arlet hadn't been here when she'd returned, and Vega hadn't had the energy to stay up to see her. "Okay."

Vega smiled big, waving Khort out before scarfing the food down and jumping into a warm shower.

She rushed through the motions, keeping her mind on one thing and one thing only: breaking the fucking curse that consumed her.

Vega stood at her armoire, and her eyes landed on a clean training suit. Her fingers skimmed over the new fabric, and she smiled as she removed it from the rack. *It's time to get me back.*

Her brain was there, but the body needed some more work. With a full stomach and a heart ready to save herself and the people caught in her sister's storm, Vega dressed and marched her way to the training room with her head held high the entire way.

Arlet and Khort were locked in a heated sparring match when Vega pushed through the doors... and from the looks of it, Arlet might be coming out on top.

No longer was she the scared girl she'd been at the start. Arlet could win this brewing war with nothing but her wits, but it definitely helped she was a complete badass too.

Staying in the shadows, Vega watched as her friends fought like they were choreographing a dance—so in sync with one another. She'd only felt that way with one other person in all her lives. Arlet whirled an axe, her skin glistening with sweat. Khort blocked her with a shield made of impenetrable steel. Vega watched his muscles constrict as he blocked Arlet blow for blow.

Arlet pinned Khort, his back whacking against the mat with a whoosh of the breath from his lungs. Vega clapped, and they both snapped their attention to her.

"Vega." Arlet let out a breath, dropping her weapon. She slipped through the ring's edge and dove into Vega for a big squeeze.

She inhaled the sweet scent of honey in Arlet's hair. "Gods, I've missed you." Vega didn't let her go. The pair stood in an embrace until Arlet pulled away.

"It's you. It's really you. You're in there?" Arlet asked with a single tear rolling down her cheek.

Vega wiped it away with her thumb, smiling. "It's me. I'm back."

Arlet choked on a sob and brought her into another hug. "I thought we'd lost you again."

"I did, too, but Marlena has made a few mistakes." Vega bit her lip, pulling away from Arlet to meet Khort's gaze as he sauntered across the room to join the girls.

"What do you mean?" Arlet asked.

"There's something I need to tell you two." Vega flexed her hand, her nerves rising inside with the beat of her heart. She nodded towards a table in the corner. "Do you have a minute to spare?"

"We have all the time in the world for you," Khort answered.

Vega sat, Arlet and Khort taking the chairs across from her. It was time to tell them what she'd been hiding—they might have time now, but the minutes were ticking by. Vega inhaled sharply before either could speak and spilled the secret that had been eating away at her for fifty-five years. "When we summoned Remus, we all knew something happened to us—that we were changed. Have either of you ever found out what it was?"

Khort shook his head. Arlet leaned forward in her chair and spoke. "We've always wondered, but we're the first of our people to make it out alive after summoning a dead god. There's no text, no rumors, nothing to give us the answers we wanted. We gave up eventually. Our priority has always been getting you back."

A piece of Vega's heart broke at her confession. "Marlena knew. She always knew what would happen if someone lived after successfully summoning a god. It's why she summoned them all. It was worth the risk to her, but she didn't expect Remus to answer us once she'd taken all the others." Vega wondered where Romulus was or if his brother's curse had sent him straight to the underworld.

"And my curse, it's not going to run out. The only thing at the end of its rope is Marlena's patience because she can't break the curse she put on me. Our summoning messed up her perfectly planned ploy."

Khort rolled his eyes. "We can't trust Marlena. We know that."

And you can't trust me, Vega thought before metaphorically pulling her knife out and jabbing both her best friends in the back. "She told me in my first life," she murmured, forcing her eyes up from the spot she'd been boring a hole through with her stare. "When she leaned in before killing me."

Vega knew she didn't have to ask if they remembered that detail—she knew they did. "She told me what we are, what happened to us, and I kept it from everyone because I didn't know how to test if what she'd told me was true." She wasn't ready to strike the final blow, but it had to be done—she'd put it off for too long. "It's true. I tested it with Bridger to get away, to stun him. When we survived the summoning and Remus bonded us, he strengthened us with whatever power he had left. He was a demi, and we were demis."

"What's true?" Arlet mused.

"Were?" Khort asked, and Vega watched as the wheels began to turn, the answer clicking before she said it.

"We're gods now. We have been all this time."

Arlet didn't move, looking at Vega like she had three heads. Khort began to laugh, light at first and then hard, like what Vega said was the funniest thing he'd ever heard. He slapped his knee and pushed himself away from the table.

"Oh gods, that's a good one." Khort straightened, his laugh tapering off.

Arlet's head swiveled between the two. She let out a forced laugh, but Vega didn't join in, and the laugh immediately caught in her throat. "You're not kidding."

As Vega shook her head, Khort went pale as a winter's night in Amora. "No, I'm not."

Khort grabbed the side of the desk to keep himself upright. "Wh-why didn't you tell us?"

"I didn't know if it was true or not. If she was trying to get in my head," Vega admitted.

"But now you say you know it's true because you tested it on Bridger?" Arlet was spearheading the questions while Khort broke out in a nervous sweat.

"I stabbed him in the heart."

Khort caught himself before his knees hit the ground. "You killed him?"

Vega shook her head. "He can't die. He's a god. He's alive. I can feel him. Can't you?"

Arlet froze completely, staring Vega down with eyes as wide as they could go.

"There's no way." Khort shook his head, pacing the room like he did when he needed to think. "Why would you keep this from us? We deserved to know this even if you didn't know if it were true."

Vega crossed her arms and held on to her shoulders, trying to comfort herself through the sadness she felt in her betrayal. "I know. I'm sorry. In some lives, I didn't think about it. Marlena never brought it up again after the first time. I think she was going to try to use it against me to make me look like the bad guy. And ya know, I'm not saying I'm not the bad guy here—"

"You're not," Arlet interrupted, turning to give Khort a look. "You're not the villain in this story, whether you kept this from us or not." She turned her attention back to Vega. "I'm upset you didn't tell us sooner, but you've been put through so much, and I can't imagine what it's like inside your head."

Khort crossed his arms, clamming up. He was mad, and Vega didn't blame him. Not everyone was Arlet—forgiveness came easier to her.

"I always thought it was a possibility." Arlet tapped her nails on the table, lost in her head.

"You knew?" Khort choked out.

"No, I just had a feeling that we could be. I mean, come on. We don't get tired anymore, we can fight for *hours* without burnout, and I have powers that no one has ever heard of. Vega and I can find each other anywhere, we can all feel each other's pull, and you have powers only warriors should have. And let's be real, Vega and Bridger are bonded in ways you and I will never understand." Arlet pointed between herself and Khort.

Vega physically hurt when Arlet spoke about her and Bridger. How could he have left her, knowing they were forever linked in such a unique way? *No, you're not going to feel anything for that bastard.* A feather fluttered inside her mind, like a tickle of a touch, but Vega forced the feeling away.

Khort's eyes clouded with the glaze he got before he shifted or when his anger rose, but it was gone before Vega could say anything about it.

"You said you stabbed Bridger, which obviously had to come after he let you go." Arlet leaned back in her chair. She needed the facts—it was how she had always been.

Vega nodded, deciding to keep the kiss to herself. If only to keep Khort from shifting into a fire-breathing death machine in a space not meant for his dragon size... and probably because she didn't want to think about how much she'd *liked* it.

"I thought about what you'd said, about his reaction to seeing me wearing the ring." The one Vega was wearing now—the one she wore the entire time she was locked away under her sister's estate. "How we need Bridger to win in any capacity."

Khort puffed steam. "You can't be serious."

Vega stood, the chair scraping against the floor in a shrill shriek. "Yes, I am serious. We don't win this thing without him, Khort."

"So you're just going to run back into the arms of the man who has stabbed you in the back, killed you, and brutalized you any chance he's gotten?" Khort clenched his fists, the conversation they'd had this morning apparently going up in smoke like it'd never happened.

Arlet spoke before Vega could. "Oh my gods! This isn't what this is about."

Vega felt the brush of his lips, the way Bridger's hands gripped her hips and pulled her against his body. "For fuck's sake!" She threw her hands up in the air, her voice rising an octave. "For once, can you push aside the knowledge that I chose him and focus on the facts?"

Arlet cringed at Vega's retort, air escaping her mouth on an exhale.

Khort completely froze, his green eyes turning to slits again. "I'm done worrying about your doltish choice, Vega. I'm now concerned with how it's affecting the people in our world, and how allowing Bridger a free pass because he's a *tortured soul*, as if your sister hasn't maimed us all, will get more people killed in the process."

"People die in war, and there's no sense in pretending this isn't going to end in a war. The citizens of Tolevarre are going to die. It's inevitable. Imagine what Bridger and the soldiers who would follow him could do for us, for this rebellion," Arlet offered and moved herself in front of Vega, blocking her path to Khort. "This isn't how we settle things, and I'll be damned if we start now."

Vega's jaw clenched. "Your jealousy is getting to you. Think about what I'm saying, Khort. Bridger is one of us. I'm not forgiving him for anything, but Marlena will win if we don't figure this out. Together. All of us."

Khort stormed to the door, looking back for a split second. "Find another way. I refuse to let that back-stabbing son of a bitch back in." He slammed the door so hard the weapons hanging on the wall fell off their hooks.

"Give him some time. He'll come around." Arlet rested her hand on Vega's shoulder, giving her that squeeze she loved so much.

"We don't even have a plan." Vega's eyes were planted on the door Khort had stormed through, hoping he would return if she stared long enough.

"We can come up with one later." Arlet let go of Vega's shoulder. "Did you eat?"

Vega nodded.

"Good. Let's train." Arlet handed her a sword. The weight pulled Vega's arms down, the tip hitting the floor. "We have a lot of work to do."

47

Castra's hall lights hadn't turned on yet. Keeping some semblance of normalcy under here while also managing electricity use was essential. Controlling the lighting in the underwater compound was the least that could be done to ensure the people who lived here had somewhat of an ordinary internal clock.

That didn't mean there weren't early birds who got up and started their day before the lights kicked on at five in the morning. The early risers usually stuck inside their rooms, spending their mornings with whatever routines they had built.

Two small lanterns sat by the sparring mats, flickering with her blue lightning to give her a beam to work by. Every day, Vega was returning to the strong fighter she used to be, tapping into the skills she'd lost while trapped on Earth.

Vega was already pouring sweat when the generators came to life and the lights came on. She fell to the mat with a huff, watching the punching bag swing above her from a chain.

Her muscles screamed, on fire from another hour of training. It had been two weeks since she'd escaped, and her nights were haunted by nightmares of her sister, of failing the people she loved.

Most mornings, she woke up screaming, worried about waking her neighbors.

Arlet came in the first couple times, racked with panic.

Khort never did.

They hadn't talked since she'd admitted they needed Bridger's help.

Vega took a sizable inhale through her nose and released the breath through her mouth. She wiped her forehead with the back of her hand, groaning as she pushed herself off the floor to get some water.

The door to the training room swung open as Vega downed her second cup of water, and in walked Khort and a few of the other rebel warriors.

"Do you ever sleep?" Leo asked, migrating over to her. His hair was the color of wet bark, his eyes glittering with specks of crimson over almost-black irises. He'd come from Ardor a few years ago, escaping the mining camps he'd been imprisoned in when he refused to join Marlena's army before Bridger took over.

Khort ignored her.

"Mmm, not much," she admitted.

"Well, if you'd ever like anyone to train with, I'm happy to assist in the early mornings. I haven't slept well since leaving the mines." The Ardor-born was handsome, devilishly so, and rumor had it he was strong, if not stronger than the original family of his land.

Vega smiled at the thought of Meyer Ignis being outfired.

"I appreciate that. You're welcome to join me any time. I'm here around four, four-thirty every morning." Vega took another sip of water as her eyes trailed to Khort, who'd approached while the two were lost in conversation.

"If you're done flirting, Acer, we have work to do." Khort's tone was rigid as he addressed Leo by his surname.

The fire-wielder chuckled, patting Khort on the shoulder. "Point taken. I'll see you around, Vega." He winked, poking the dragon further.

Vega turned her attention to Khort after waving goodbye to Leo. "Jealousy is unbecoming of you."

"Pfft." Khort crossed his arms over his chest.

"So what, we're talking again?" Vega quipped, cocking her head as she put her cup on the table.

"Maybe," Khort replied.

"Gods, Khort. We're not teenagers anymore. If you need to scream at me, scream at me. You wanna fight it out? Let's step in the ring, but I can't do this with you. We have too much to worry about, too much to plan for to act like we're feuding children again, especially over Bridger. We've done this before. I'm not doing it again."

Vega watched as Khort's features gave away every emotion crossing his face. Anger, jealousy, regret. "You're right, and I'm sorry. My feelings about the matter still stand, though. I don't trust him, and I don't think there's a place for him here." He shrugged his shoulders as if to say, *Do with that what you will.*

A sigh escaped Vega's lips. "I don't disagree with you, but we need to keep it as an option. He's not the same Bridger he's been. Something's happening behind the scenes that we don't know about."

"Sounds like he needs to figure it out then. I'm not here to help Bridger. I'm here to help you, our people. He's not welcome in my army."

Vega nodded once. "Okay. For now, Bridger is the last thing on my mind. I'm focused on finding out how to end this curse." She bent the truth slightly because Bridger, in fact, hadn't been the last thing on her mind. Some of the nightmares keeping her up were of his death—the dagger she'd stabbed through his heart being the kill shot.

"We have some books in the offices," Khort offered up as Leo and the other men stepped into the ring to start their warm-ups.

"Yeah, books I've read from cover to cover hundreds of times. They don't have what I'm looking for. I need to get to Littera."

"No," Khort said with finality, stepping away from Vega.

She followed him, not giving him the space he was trying to put in between her and this conversation. "I have to get to Littera. It's not an option anymore."

Khort spun on his heels, and Vega collided with his chest. "We don't have allies there. It's too dangerous."

"*You* don't have allies, but *I* used to," she objected.

"Used to. It's been fifteen years, and too much has changed."

"I am never going to figure out how to break this curse if you guys don't stop keeping me locked away like some helpless princess," Vega snapped.

Khort opened his mouth, but his words were silenced by the sound of an alarm ringing through the building. Red lights flashed in the hall, shooting red beams under the door.

Vega grabbed her daggers off the table by the mat and sheathed them at her sides. Bridger's dagger tingled in her palm, his bond to the blade calling to her own bond with its owner.

The alarms ringing meant there was trouble—an intruder.

Leo and the other soldiers scrambled to life, grabbing their weapons. They might have powers inside them more dangerous than anything they could arm themselves with, but getting caught in close-distance combat without something other than gods-given abilities could be a death wish, depending on who their opponent was.

Vega didn't wait for anyone. She burst through the training room's door, her electricity buzzing through her body, ready to strike at any second.

Vega focused on the pull in her chest, guiding herself through the maze of hallways and the people flooding through them. She had to find Arlet.

Khort was on her heels. "Vega, go to your room and wait until I come find you!" He gripped her arm, slowing them to a jog.

"Over my dead body! I'm going to Arlet!" she called over the sound of the alarm's wail.

"I can't keep you safe if you don't listen!"

"It's not your job to keep me safe!" Vega stopped, exhausted by his constant need to shelter her. "I'm in this fight! Fuck, Khort!" Her eyes shot side to side for anyone within earshot. "I'm a god. I'm not going to hide like a coward just because I'm a cursed one."

The tug in her chest was unbearable, prying her away from the spot she'd planted herself. Vega backed away from Khort. "I'm not going to hide anymore. I'm more me than I've ever been. It's time you and everyone else saw that." She turned and sprinted towards the direction her heart pulled her in.

Vega climbed the stairs, one, two, three levels. The people of Castra flooded the stairs, some fleeing to their rooms, others to the posts they were assigned during an attack.

What if she had been wrong? What if Bridger was angrier than she'd anticipated him to be after she plunged his dagger through his heart? *What if he tracked me here because I stole his stupid fucking bonded dagger?*

Was that possible?

Vega picked up speed, heart ticking faster the closer she got to the office where the rebellion leaders met. The entrance was hidden by Arlet at all times, but Vega knew where the door was through the illusion masking it as a blank wall.

She flung the door open, eyes landing on Arlet. *She's okay.* Vega scanned the room, her eyes finding a face she hadn't seen in at least twenty-five years: the now praefectus of Solum. "Urban," she gawked.

The redhead wasn't the young boy she remembered from the

start of her sister's rule—he had grown into himself, though he was still lanky and sported a patchy ginger beard. His hands were cuffed together in front of him. The rest of his body was roped to a chair, and who Vega assumed was his guard was slumped in the corner on the floor, unconscious.

He'd been on Marlena's side since the beginning.

"Hi, stranger. It's good to see you." His voice was more profound than she remembered.

Khort came up behind her, and Leo barged in with scarlet fire licking up his arms.

Arlet's hands rested on her hips, foot tapping against the flooring below with a *tink, tink, tink*. "I'm hoping this is a false alarm," she grumbled.

"How did you find this place?" Khort interrogated, zipping around Vega to stand between her and Urban.

"A rebel from my territory. He said I could find you on the south peak of Imber. I didn't actually know *where* you were until your guards snatched us up," Urban answered. "How is this place possible? How are you hiding it?"

Khort snatched a dagger out of its sheath so quickly Vega almost missed it. He pressed the tip to the bottom of Urban's chin, and a bead of blood instantly dripped down the blade. "Who told you that?"

"Khort," Arlet warned. If they killed Urban too early, they wouldn't be able to get any information out of him.

Urban went completely still. "Please don't kill me. I'm of no threat to you. I swear." His voice quivered with nerves.

The bacon.

It came from Solum. Vega knew there had been rebel uprisings there but hadn't expected help from Urban—not with his timid nature.

"I came here to talk, to offer an alliance," he blubbered. "If I were here to attack, would I have only brought one guard?"

Good point.

Vega stepped forward. "Put the dagger down, Khort." She reached out and lowered his arm away from Urban's jugular, giving the man at least another minute to live.

"Thank you. Oh my gods, thank you," Urban chattered.

"I only bought you enough time to explain yourself. He can still kill you if he doesn't like your answer." Vega wanted to save the people of Tolevarre, but she wasn't opposed to killing those who deserved to die.

Bridger had taught her not everyone was worth saving. What a shame he'd become exactly who he'd told Vega to give up on.

Arlet gave orders to Leo, sending him to do a perimeter check around the grounds of Imber. He left without a word. Arlet hit a button on the control board in the corner, and the blaring alarms finally came to a stop, followed by three staccato beeps alerting the people of Castra to stay in their rooms until the all-clear was given.

"Better start talking. I'm running out of patience." Khort stood straight, stepping back to line himself up with Vega.

"Marlena is killing my people. Innocent people who don't deserve to die. General Ignis has set up camp near the border of Littera to keep the rebels at bay. These rebels, most of them are my people standing up for themselves, refusing to work under the conditions Marlena has imposed. They don't want a war, but they'd rather fight than continue to live this way. They just want their lives back. Their happiness," he started.

"Innocent people are dying every day because of her. What makes your people special?" Arlet asked, crossing her arms over her chest like Khort.

Vega elbowed her. Arlet shrugged.

"My people are the reason this world eats, the reason you got fresh bacon for breakfast this week." Urban raised an eyebrow. "Where do you think that came from? I gave them to your rebels, who it seems are fighting a battle alone in my lands, and they gave them to you. I sent those pigs on their behalf."

Khort reached for his dagger again, but Vega stopped him, gripping his branded wrist tightly. "What do you mean by it seems they're fighting a battle alone in your lands?"

Urban's eyes bounced to Vega, a sad smile on his lips. "You've been gone a long time. There's a lot I'm sure your friends haven't been able to fill you in on." He nodded to Khort and Arlet.

Khort's jaw tensed so hard Vega could hear his teeth grind together. He spoke through gritted teeth. "I can't be everywhere at once."

"I know that." Urban nodded. "Which is why I've come to offer my help. I may not be a war hero, but I have resources that can help a rebellion rise and can easily cripple the other side."

"She'll just kill you all. Make you suffer for it," Vega added, dropping down on one knee to make herself eye level with Urban. "More of your people will die. Why would you subject them to exactly what you're trying to avoid?"

"I've been suffering since the day my parents died for her. Do you know what it feels like to be seen as weak your entire life because of where you were born? Because your gods-given powers aren't ones that can crumble an entire city or kill a dozen men in a single blow?" Urban had tears welling in his green eyes. "I have been scared to step out of line, to speak out against her. All because I thought it would save my people if I followed along and did what I was told." He didn't break his stare and neither did Vega. "She thinks I'm weak, that I couldn't destroy the entire foundation her malevolent council sits on with nothing but the root of a single tree. That I couldn't starve out Bridger's army in under a month."

Vega didn't dare react to Bridger's name, wrestling the muscles in her face not to move.

"You ask me why I would be willing to lose more of my people?" Urban shifted his gaze to Khort, then to Arlet and back to Vega.

"Because at least then I'll know they fought for the life they deserve, that they stood against tyranny. And if I die trying to give them their freedom back, then I'll be remembered as the last Silva to give a damn."

It took Vega hours for her and Arlet to convince Khort to accept Urban's proposal. He was right to be cautious, but Vega believed Urban—she could see it in his eyes, feel it in his soul. He was sick and tired of being played for a fool.

"Here's some water." Vega handed him and his guard each a glass.

"Thank you, Vega," Urban said while holding the cup between his still-cuffed hands. "I meant what I said before. It is really great to see you."

She gave him a warm smile. "You too. I'm sorry for what's happening to your people. I never wanted any of this to happen."

Urban handed the empty glass to his guard and then reached for her hand. Vega took it, his hands cold from being unadjusted to the temperature of Castra. "I know that. You were always so kind to my people. To everyone's people. You would have been a wonderful Curia member."

Vega squeezed his hand. "That's kind of you, but I never wanted to rule. I just wanted to live..." *My happily ever after with the man I loved.*

"We don't always get what we want, huh?" Urban asked, not expecting a reply.

"Has..." Vega stopped, looking over her shoulder. "Bridger—has he been in Solum with Meyer?"

Urban's smile slinked across his face. "Why do you ask?"

Vega huffed, blowing a piece of loose hair out of her face. "I like to know where my enemies are at all times," she lied. "Keep your friends close and your enemies closer."

"He doesn't come around often. I've only seen him there once since you returned."

Maybe because he was too busy dealing with me.

Khort popped up behind her, reaching over to unlock the cuffs around Urban's and his guard's wrists. "I'll have someone escort you out, and we'll be in touch soon about what the next step needs to be."

Vega helped untie Urban from the wooden chair. He stood and stretched his legs, rubbing his wrists where the manacles had been. "I look forward to it."

Khort nodded, stepping away to gather a few men to walk Urban back up to the hatch that would spit them back onto Imber's solid ground. Arlet left to fill in the other leaders of Castra after they'd come to an agreement on whether or not to accept Solum as a much-needed ally.

"I hope you'll be fighting beside us when this blows up," Urban said with a slightly nervous chuckle.

"As long as I'm here and breathing, I'll be fighting," Vega promised.

"Then I'll see you soon," Urban said as the Castra guards came to usher him out.

Vega nodded, giving him a genuine smile. Urban walked through the door, and it shut behind him as a thought struck her.

Khort was approaching, but Vega had no time to waste. She faked a yawn, rubbing her eyes. "Gods, I could use a nap." She looked down at her suit, which had finally dried from this morning's workout. Vega scrunched her nose. "And definitely a shower."

Khort laughed. "Yeah, I was gonna say something about that," he joked.

"Ha-ha." Vega rolled her eyes. "I'll catch you for dinner?" she asked, already heading out the door. She barely heard him agree as she broke out into a sprint to catch Urban.

"Urban!" she called when she saw his bouncy gait and red hair turn a corner.

He popped his head back around, his body following as he stepped back to meet her. "Is everything alright?" he asked, his eyebrows creased with worry.

"Yes, sorry. I almost forgot to ask you, and I don't know when I'll see you again." Vega made her smile relaxed, like the question she was about to ask was no big deal.

"I'm hoping very soon," Urban said with a snorted laugh. "I don't want to wait too long to get this started or I might lose my nerve."

Vega cocked her head.

"Kidding, kidding. Really, I've made up my mind." Urban didn't have a funny bone in his body. "What did you want to ask?"

Vega took a quick breath, pushing away the nerves settling in the pit of her stomach. If he said no... She didn't want to think about that. "Do you have any allies in Littera?"

Urban's eyes gleamed with excitement. "Ah, it's been so long since I've talked to her, but yes. I suppose you could call us that."

Vega's heart thrummed with excitement. "Do you think you could get in touch with her? I really need to make a visit. A secret visit." She whispered the last part through pursed lips, hoping the guard around the corner was far enough away not to hear her.

Urban turned his eyebrow up. "I think I can have that arranged."

Vega released a happy sigh. "That's fantastic. How soon?"

"Vega, for you, I'll make the call as soon as I get back to Solum. I'll be in touch." He winked and dipped back around the corner, disappearing from her sight.

Vega's chest warmed, and a smile so wide her cheeks hurt spread across her face. There it was, that feeling she'd gotten in the car driving to the portal with Arlet.

Hope.

Hope that she could break this fucking curse.

48

"Stop going so easy on me!" Vega ranted, lightning dancing from her wrist to the tip of her fingers and then back.

"I'm not!" Khort responded quickly.

Vega glared at him, shooting a bolt of lightning at his head. He dodged, blocking the blow with a roll across the mat. "You are, and you know it."

"Gods, maybe I'm going a little easy on you, but do you have to try and decapitate me for it?" Khort shot up to his feet, eyes slitted.

"At least then I'll get to use my full power," Vega sneered, and sweat rolled down her brow as the timer for their match went off.

Khort let loose a breath, obviously happy about the end of their training session. "Vega, you're training multiple times a day. Don't think I don't know you and Leo are meeting for early morning sparring. You're going to wear yourself out."

Vega rolled her eyes, grabbing her water and taking a long chug. "I'm fine." She couldn't help the thoughts that slinked into her mind, the voice that sounded so unlike her own. *Bridger never made you feel weak, never made you become less than yourself.* Vega couldn't rid herself of thoughts of him—that kiss had done her in, and she was working on clawing herself out of the depths of her heart every day because of it.

Khort leaned against the ring. "I don't mean physically. I mean mentally. You're not sleeping, you're overtraining, and any free time you have, you're buried in a book you've read a million times."

"What else do you expect me to do? Knit sweaters and tell ghost stories around a fire?" Her brows furrowed.

"I expect you to take a break every once in a while. That's all." Khort sipped his water, eyeing Vega as she exited the ring.

She slung her bag over her shoulder. "I just got back from a fifteen-year vacation. I'm still making up for it." Vega nodded in his direction as she turned. "I'll see you later."

Khort meant well, Vega knew that, but his constant need to protect was starting to wear on her nerves. Despite what some might think, Vega wasn't some stupid kid who needed to be put in a bubble forever.

If she wanted this curse to come to an end, she had to do it herself—and Littera was the first place she needed to begin her search. It had been a long time since she'd nosed around the endless books in their private collection.

Vega opened the door to her room, and the lamp in the corner by her bed caught her attention immediately. She knew she hadn't left it on...

She scanned the room, plopping her bag on the corner chair by her bookshelf. A note sat on her pillow, facing up.

Tomorrow. Sunrise at the docks. Don't be late. -U.S.

Vega sat silently at dinner, pushing her fish around the plate instead of scarfing it down to avoid the taste as she usually did.

The people around her, her friends turned family, didn't notice her stillness. No one but Arlet, who'd moved her seat and brought her tray of food over to snuggle in next to her. "What's on your mind?"

Vega dropped her fork with a clang that couldn't be heard over the noise in the mess hall. "Where should I start?"

Arlet bumped her with her shoulder, taking a sip of water. "Wherever you'd like. I'm all ears."

Secrets were hard to keep from Arlet. Vega lowered her voice enough for only her to hear. "It's just that..." She stopped, taking a breath and releasing it. "I kissed Bridger."

Arlet's jaw dropped, a gasp causing heads to turn toward their table.

Vega shot them all a look that said, *Mind your business.*

"You what?" Arlet whisper-shouted.

Vega's sheepish smile was the only apology she would give. "It was for a distraction so I could, ya know, stab him through the heart and see if he died."

Arlet shoveled the last bite of her food into her mouth, jumped off the bench, and nearly dragged Vega out the door. When they were out of earshot, the scolding began. "Vega Caelum, why did you keep this from me? What is it about you and kissing men you're not supposed to kiss?"

"Because I've secretly been hating myself for keeping it from you while also hating myself because I *liked* it!" Vega groaned, running a hand through her free hair. "It was so good. The feeling I got from it hasn't left me, and I'm crazy for that, right?" Vega panted out a laugh, choking on it. "There's something wrong with me for liking anything about him... right?" Her laughs stopped, the realization of her questions sinking in.

Arlet's face drooped, and she didn't hesitate to pull Vega into a hug. "There is nothing wrong with you, nothing. It's okay to love him still, Vega. He hurt you, but you've never had the chance to let him go properly. Not with the curse constantly sending you away, with the memories of the life you once had together so fresh in your mind. Not when he's showing you bits of who he used to be."

Vega buried her head into Arlet's shoulder, inhaling her sweet scent.

Tears forced their way through the emotional barrier Vega had built around herself. "I hate him. I hate what he's done to me, what he chose over me. But I hate that I'm why she came after him more. If it weren't for me, Marlena wouldn't have targeted him, tortured him. Gods, Arlet." It had been so long since she'd broken down because of Bridger—since she'd let herself *feel* what he'd done to her. "Being the object of her torment is something I'd never wish on anyone."

Vega wasn't over it, but she wanted to be.

"I want to break this curse." Vega pulled herself out of the hug, wiping the tears from her red-rimmed eyes. "I want it to be over, and I want to find a way to be over him too." She swallowed down the sob she felt. "If I have to use him to win this war between us and Marlena, I can't have these unresolved feelings for him."

Arlet nodded. "How can I help?"

Vega didn't deserve her—Arlet was the light in the darkest days of her life.

"I need to get to Littera," Vega admitted. "I need to find out how to break this curse finally. Breaking this curse means I can start to focus on how to beat Marlena to the next part... learning how Remus cursed the original gods. Now that she knows I know, she's going to try and kill me again to give herself more time."

Khort would have—*had*—shut her down, refusing to put Vega in harm's way. Arlet hesitated briefly before saying, "Okay."

"Tomorrow," Vega said flatly.

"Tomorrow?" Arlet echoed.

"Yes, tomorrow. We need to meet Urban at the docks in Solum at sunrise."

Arlet raised her eyebrow. "So you had this planned already?"

"Yes." There was no regret in Vega's voice. Arlet didn't need to know the details, only that Vega would have done it without her if she hadn't agreed to come with.

"Then I guess we're hitching a ride with Khort and his band of misfits in the morning since he's meeting with Urban." They only had one motorized boat.

Fuck.

Vega threw her hands in the air. "He already shut the idea down."

Arlet's smile was slow, troublesome. "Since when have you ever listened to Khort 'I'm the Boss' Fera?"

49

Getting on the boat with Khort went about as smoothly as Vega and Arlet had anticipated. He argued for nearly half an hour, causing them to approach the docks after sunrise.

"I swear to the gods—" Vega started.

"We are the gods. You can't swear on us anymore," Khort fired back.

Vega whacked him on the shoulder, coaxing a genuine smile from him for the first time since she boarded the boat. "Okay, I swear to the dead ones if I can't get to Littera because we're late, I'll fry you."

Arlet strode up beside them. "And I'll help."

"Wow, I need new best friends," he jeered.

Vega eyed the land in the distance, hoping to make out Urban's figure on the horizon.

Arlet scoffed, "Good luck with that. No one likes grumpy dragons."

Anxiously, Vega tapped her foot against the boat's deck.

"Don't worry, Vega. He's gonna be there." Arlet wrapped her arm around her shoulders, pulling her close.

The journey from Imber to Solum was half the distance of the one to Fraus, but this time Vega found herself counting every second sneaking by.

The docks came into view, and Vega scanned everyone bustling around the ships and market square. Urban's red hair stood out, rustling in the breeze.

Vega let out a sigh of relief.

He lifted his arm, fingers fluttering in a hello. Vega smiled big as Arlet squeezed her shoulder helping throw ropes to the merchants on the dock.

Khort stood at attention, eyes scrutinizing the people buzzing around Urban. He had no guards near him, only a small blonde with a white cloak wrapped around her shoulders for warmth.

Urban spoke loudly. "I almost thought you weren't coming."

Vega disembarked, her footsteps echoing across the wooden planks. She pulled Urban into a hug, and despite his shock, he wrapped his arms around her too. "Thank you."

She could hear the smile in his voice when he answered. "No need for thanks. I told you I'm in this. Reaching out to Colette is the least I could do to prove it."

Vega extended her hand to Colette. The blonde grabbed it and shook lightly. "It's nice to meet you," Vega said.

The young woman nodded her head. "I have been dying to meet the infamous Vega who has our world up in arms."

"You have no guards," Khort noted as he came up behind Vega, interrupting their conversation.

"There is no need for guards when the people in my territory are all on the same page," Urban replied with certainty. "The people in Solum are ready to fight." As he said it, the men and women working the docks put down their crates and shifted their attention to their praefectus, placing a balled fist over their hearts in unison.

Urban threw his hands up in a sweeping motion. "My people are with this rebellion. My people are with you, Khort. I understand your unease, but it is misplaced here. My people are your people."

Solum-born controlled plant life—some at a slow pace, great for farming year-round, while others could make a tree root system their weapon of choice—bonded with animals, and were the reason everyone in Tolevarre ate. No one would be alive if it weren't for the food they brought to everyone's tables—especially those in power.

Vega watched as more Solum workers surrounded the docks with their fists over their hearts—it was a sign from a long time ago that meant, *We are with you.* Arlet was the first to move, her hand mimicking Solum's people.

Vega joined her.

"See, I didn't come to you prematurely. Solum's people knew of the arrangement before I met with you. I wouldn't offer up their lives without first asking if they were willing to give them." Urban, who was once so feeble and shy, was now a man willing to die for a cause not many would.

Khort finally placed his fist over his heart.

Urban spoke again. "This is why I asked you to come here, so you could see for yourself that Solum is ready to fight. Fifty-five years of slavery is enough for one lifetime. And the letter I sent to Vega, well, it seems it's no longer a secret why you're here. You told me to keep quiet, so I planned to have you scurry off with Colette before Khort arrived today." His eyes met Vega's. "I guess silence on the matter is no longer needed."

Vega shook her head, letting her hand fall from her chest. "No." The people of Solum one by one dropped their hands and got back to work, loading crates and boxes to far-off territories. The seas were easier to navigate these days than the roadways littered with Tolevarre's army. "I can't leave the only people who have ever fought for me in the dark anymore." She'd done that too many times before. "And we only have one boat right now, so..."

Urban chuckled softly. "We have plenty of boats, which means you now have plenty as well." His eyes wandered over the three of them. "Your friendship always made me a little jealous. The way you had each other to lean on. You should consider yourselves lucky to have one another still. A lot of us have been left alone."

"You're not alone anymore," Arlet told him, touching his arm gently.

"Thank you. Now, Vega, you better get going. Colette doesn't have a huge window to sneak you in and out of the archives, and you're already behind schedule." Urban hurried them along.

Khort stepped forward, blocking Vega's path. "I'm going with you."

She shook her head. "No, Arlet is. You need to stay here and load the boat with food for Castra. Take some time to spend with the people we'll be fighting beside, who will be fighting under you. We aren't deviating from our plans today. We'll be quick."

"What if this is a trap?" he said to Arlet and Vega, his voice low.

"I know this is supposed to be a private conversation, but I will be honest about the risks." Colette butted in. "I can promise I won't tell a soul." Her voice was buttery sweet. "But I can't make that promise for the others of Littera."

The small woman was much younger than the rest of them—Vega could see it in the way her eyes sparkled with youth, and the bounce in her step still looked full of hopeful wonder.

The world hadn't broken her yet.

"We'll deal with that when it comes. For now, I need tomes, journals, everything and anything you can get me on curses."

Colette smiled. "You're in luck. That's my department."

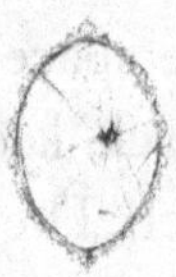

Vega couldn't remember the last time she rode horseback for over an hour. Her legs felt stuck in a bowed position when she dismounted her black mare. She griped, stretching her legs while Arlet did the same.

It was hard to tell they'd grown up with the best horses and stables in all of Aeris with how they hobbled behind Colette.

Vega leaned into Arlet, whispering close to her ear. "Hopefully we won't be fighting this war from the backs of horses."

Colette held her finger over her lips, turning only long enough to shush the girls as they walked into the main room of the oldest library in Tolevarre—the Minerva Archives. The building was spelled long ago to block the use of powers inside, a way to protect the history of their world and the one that came before it.

As they crossed through the door, Vega couldn't rely on anything other than her wits and physical skills to keep her safe. The buzz of her power simmered to nothing, bringing back memories of the nights she spent underground in her sister's dungeons.

As if Arlet knew where Vega's thoughts went, she slipped her hand into hers as they entered the main room and pulled their hoods over their heads for an added layer of camouflage.

The back entrance opened to a high ceiling with painted pictures of the dead gods. It rounded in the center, small windows illuminating the paintings on every ebony wooden wall. Any free inch of space was lined with floor-to-ceiling shelves. Vega took a deep breath, inhaling the glorious scent of old and loved books.

She used to love coming here for visits with her parents as a kid.

Colette shuffled them quickly through the main room and dipped off into a hallway that made Vega feel claustrophobic after the room they'd just left. The space was too small for the girls to walk side by side. Arlet fell back, keeping watch behind Vega, and Vega's head stayed on a swivel. They'd be ready for a fight if one came.

They walked down more halls, descending into the belly of the archives where not many got to go. It was darker down here too, the chemical breakdown of the ancient bindings creating a musty book smell that wasn't present up above.

Colette smiled as they passed another Littera-born, his eyes sweeping over Vega and Arlet with unease.

Arlet took a few large strides to get beside Vega when the hall widened a bit. "We get what we need, and we get out. We might not see them, but they see us."

Vega knew she was right—she could feel people watching at every corner.

Colette came to a stop at a door, and after entering a code on a beeping keypad, slipped them inside unnoticed. "This row"—she pointed—"the third one over, and a small section over there will have anything to do with curses. If it's not here, it doesn't exist."

Vega inhaled sharply at her words. *The answer has to be here. It has to be.*

"Is there anything in particular you're looking for?" the young girl asked. "I have a photographic memory, so I might be able to tell you exactly where something is."

Vega looked to Arlet, her best friend's eyebrow raised as if to say, *Your call.*

"Anything on breaking curses?" Vega didn't know if they could trust Colette fully, but she'd already damned herself by helping them.

A glimmer of excitement lit up her youthful features. "Ah, I wondered if that's what you were here for." She rubbed her hands together. "I have a few small tomes from before our people's time. They're not kept here, and I'm leery to let them leave, but..." Colette looked around, lowering her voice. "I'll lend them to you if you promise to let me know if whatever is in them helped."

Vega nodded vigorously, her ponytail bobbing up and down. "Yes, of course."

Colette grinned widely. "Great. I will be back soon. Find what you can quickly. The class rotating in will be here soon, and Nero is with them today."

That was the only warning they were going to get. Colette deserted the room, leaving Arlet and Vega alone. Turning to her best friend, Vega quickly clarified what she was looking for. "The few books I have talk about small curses, things that most Fraus-born can do. Cursing small animals with blood, using potions to sicken your enemies. Look for things that talk of larger curses, curses on people, curses that can't be broken. Things like that." Vega pulled a small bag from her jacket and handed it to Arlet. "And if you see anything, *anything*," she reiterated, "about Remus, Romulus, or the dead gods, you take it. I don't care if it's folklore from a children's book."

Arlet nodded, getting to work quickly in the far corner opposite Vega.

Vega gently thumbed through a few books before finding something worth sliding into her bag. The next ten books weren't of interest, talking of topics she already knew. At the end of the row, she found a book with a picture of the Colosseum on it that read *Roman Curses*.

She moved around the room, riffling through pages until she heard the door reopen. Vega popped her head out of the row, expecting to see Colette. Her stomach sank to her feet when her eyes landed on an old man, followed by a small group of students.

Nero.

Arlet scuttled down the aisle with a happy grin on her face. "I—"

Vega reared back into the aisle of books and pressed herself into the shelf. Her pointer finger rested against her lips, head shaking to keep Arlet quiet.

Arlet followed her move, stepping silently until she was hidden in the shadows of the bookcases.

"Alright, students." His voice was as shaky as Vega remembered it to be. "You will have ten minutes to find the book you'll use to write your final paper. Once we leave here, I will allow you three days' time to complete your research. As your final year of training comes to an end, you will spend your last six weeks working alongside the smartest Littera-born our world has to offer."

Vega didn't let out a breath, scared to make a single move.

"Your time here at the Minerva Archives will be nothing short of spectacular, but there are many sleepless nights ahead of you. I will be here every step of the way. Marlena has—" The beeping of the door's keypad interrupted him.

Vega cursed under her breath, dying to know why he'd brought Marlena up.

"Colette, what a nice surprise!" Nero cooed.

"Oh, Praefectus Nero, hello!" Her voice wavered. "You're early." She laughed nervously.

"Why, yes, these young minds are very eager to get their studies in curses started. Marlena has been very adamant about pushing them along faster if possible."

Vega and Arlet locked eyes, dread filling Vega's chest.

"Delightful," Colette blubbered.

"I heard you were off today. I was disappointed by the news. Students, this is Colette Sophia. My granddaughter."

Arlet inhaled in shock. Vega's hand shot to cover her own mouth. They had to get out of here, *now!*

"Oh, I am off. I was just going to swing by and grab some leisure reading." Colette tried to cover her tracks—hopefully Grandpa Sophia would fall for her lie.

"Colette was the top student in her class, and she got to pick the department she wanted to lead after graduation. If you all make it out of curse studies, you might be lucky enough to work under her." Nero sounded proud, like any grandfather of a star pupil would be.

Nero had held a Curia seat for over 300 years and was one of the oldest people in Tolevarre at somewhere around 450 years old.

He'd been one of the first territories to side with Marlena, but it was only because it was the easy way out—Littera-born weren't fighters. They used their brains, not brawn. Nero knew his best chance at survival was to get as close to Marlena as possible.

"You stick to the outsides of the room, you might find the best books in the shortest amount of time." Colette's voice rose, giving Vega and Arlet an escape.

Stick to the middle. Vega and Arlet locked eyes, nodding at one another as they slid their backs down the shelves.

"Thank you, Colette. Your time starts now, students," Nero told them, a beep going off as a timer started.

Vega snooped around the corner, finding the doorway empty. She nodded to Arlet, who followed close behind. They stepped out into the open, working quickly to line themselves up in a new row. The pair worked quietly, row by row, until they were at the door.

Arlet reached for the handle, but Colette stopped her with her hand around the knob. "Get out of here. Do not look back. Head straight to Solum. Get on your boat and leave." The blonde sank into the row of books, disappearing from their sight.

The door creaked open, and Vega was so close to freedom she could taste it...

"Colette?" Nero rounded the corner with a book in his hand.

Vega locked eyes with the ancient man and watched his grow wide with recognition. "Arlet, go," she squawked, shoving her through the door.

"Colette!" Nero screamed as the door clanged shut.

Vega and Arlet tucked their bags under their arms, sprinting through the maze of halls.

"I saw her! Stop her! Stop them!"

Arlet took a right, but Vega snatched her by the arm, pulling her to the left. It was easy to get lost in the archive's cavern-like underbelly. "Through those double doors," Vega pushed, pointing ahead.

The two burst through them at the same time, the doors cracking against the wall.

Arlet's long legs took her farther faster, but Vega was on her heels, pumping her arms to keep her accelerating forward.

The side door they'd come in through was only a few paces away—they were so close to Arlet being able to make them vanish.

Vega could feel her own powers tingling the closer they got to freedom.

Nero was old, slowly working himself to his own grave, but he made it to the main room before they could exit. His shaky voice roared through the quiet building. "Why isn't anyone stopping her?"

Heads popped out from the rows of books, shaken by the sudden screams in the perpetually quiet building.

They didn't slow down. *I will not become a prisoner again. I will not!*

Arlet pushed through the door, freeing them into the afternoon chill. Vega's body buzzed with the full force of her power.

Arlet snatched her this time, yanking her against the wall. The girls caught their breath, chests rising and falling in quiet gasps. "We're covered. Stay still."

Nero stumbled through the door, hopping down the steps with Colette right behind him.

"Where is she? I know I saw her!" His breaths were shallow, fit for a man who wasn't used to exerting himself.

"Grandfather." Colette spoke, reaching out to grab his arm. "Are you okay?"

Vega and Arlet watched from feet away as Nero turned in circles, looking for two women who were no longer there.

"I saw them!" He continued to search, looking behind pillars and under the steps.

"Who? What are you talking about?" Colette showed her true colors as she played her own blood for a fool.

"Vega and her useless friend!" He was getting angrier as time passed, unable to find them.

"Grandfather," Colette repeated, stepping into his line of sight. "Are you feeling unwell? There was no one... Vega wasn't here."

He stuttered over his words. "No, I know she was here. I saw her! I saw them!" he rambled.

"No, no one was here. You must be seeing things."

Nero was as red as a tomato. "I know what I saw!"

Colette sighed, her shoulders heaving. "Let's get you inside. I think you might be coming down with something."

The old man jabbered on as Colette walked him back through the doors. She looked over her shoulder, scanning the tree line before ducking back into the archives.

They never slowed or gave their horses a break until they were back at the docks.

Khort and his soldiers ate lamb stew near a fire at a rebel camp, laughing it up like a bunch of old chums. Their merriment ended when Vega and Arlet returned.

No one spoke a word until after they were loaded on the boat and on their way back to Imber.

"I'm sorry it ended like that," Khort said, patting her on the shoulder as they descended into the hull of the boat.

"It's not your fault. Thank you again for the help," Vega said, wrapping herself in a larger fleece-lined jacket Urban gifted her. Since the trek back, she hadn't been able to escape the cold.

Vega was too tired to ask or answer any questions. She found herself a comfortable place to curl up and rest, but the disappointment of not getting the old tomes kept her from dozing off.

Vega opened the bag Arlet stuffed full of books, sorting through what she'd taken. She did the same with her own, wondering if the answer would be inside any of these or if the answer lay in what she hadn't gotten her hands on.

Her eyebrows met in the center when she pulled out a book she didn't remember grabbing. *Where did these come from?* Vega pulled out another as a smile spread across her face.

"Oh my gods," Vega gasped.

Roman Blood Curses: Vol. 1.

"Colette, you sneaky girl." Somehow, the young girl had deposited the two tomes she'd gone to fetch inside her bag without Vega knowing.

Alone in her corner with no one paying attention to her, Vega started to giggle, kicking her feet in excitement. "I'm going to break this fucking curse."

Vega ran until her lungs begged for a break. She'd spent another sleepless night tossing and turning, fighting away nightmares and an insistent itch on her wrist.

When she wasn't training, she was reading through the books and tomes she and Arlet brought back. She'd learned more than she had in any other life on ways to trick curses, to bind them to someone else, but nothing about how to break them, nothing about how Remus cursed the original gods.

Vega finally got her way after weeks of arguing with Khort about being cooped up like a prisoner, and he allowed an hour of air time... but only if she agreed to a guard. Vega chose Leo, knowing at least he would make it seem like training time and not babysitting.

He turned backwards, continuing his jogging pace. "Oh, come on, Princess. You're not giving up so soon, are you?"

Vega's eyes shot daggers at Leo and the nickname he'd chosen. "Leo, I'm going to drown you in that puddle." She pointed at the stagnant, muddy water behind him.

He laughed. "Okay, but it makes sense. You were the daughter of the head Curia seat, kind of making you a princess to lowly families like mine."

"And now, I'm just like you, but cursed," Vega said while she shoved his shoulder, picking back up on her run. "Let's go, lowlife." She winked playfully.

Vega wasn't interested in Leo—sure, he was *gorgeous*. But her life was already too complicated without adding him into the mix. Vega's focus was on herself and the curse consuming her every single thought, and only that.

Leo's laugh followed her as she sprinted the last half mile. When they got back to the crumbled pile of buildings the hatch was hidden in, Vega sat down against a rock to catch her breath.

He checked the watch on his wrist, standing tall as he took in deep breaths. "You broke five minutes a mile until that last one." The abilities in Tolevarre made everything easier, faster.

When Vega returned, she couldn't run a mile in under ten. She was officially back at her old running speed. "Good, so I have a little time to read in the sun." She smiled, pulling her bag out of its hiding place.

Leo had learned not to argue with her anymore—Vega would do whatever she wanted and take whatever Khort wanted to throw at her later for being "late."

She didn't answer to Khort.

Vega guzzled water as Leo took up a spot to stretch in the shade. Her skin had begun to glow again, her porcelain complexion taking on a golden tan from her time above Castra.

She couldn't wait for the day she and her people didn't have to hide thousands of feet underwater, when they could all bask under the sunshine freely.

Winter was creeping in, and Imber was usually cold this time of the year, but it was unseasonably warm this week, and Vega wasn't complaining.

Unzipping her skintight black jacket, Vega slipped it off her shoulders, exposing a training suit with no sleeves underneath.

Her heart rate slowed by the time she opened the old tome she'd been reading through for the last five nights. Of course it had to be in Latin, a language rarely used here by anyone other than those in Littera. Vega had never been great at reading it... That was a skill her sister had mastered before Vega even learned to read a single book.

She translated words slowly.

> Curses are fickle things, varying depending on the
> creator. All curses need a living thing to
> attach to.

Marlena mentioned she was the first of her kind to be able to curse non-living items, which was where the mirrors in her home came from. Could that mean her curse wasn't just linked to her? The mirrors weren't directly attached, she knew that much—Marlena said they were only pieces of it. Vega knew she'd be long dead if the mirrors were connected to her life. Marlena would have smashed them with her bare hands.

> In some very rare occasions, a curse can hold
> someone to a specific location if the curse is
> created by blood.

Vega read that line again and again, her jaw dropping as she gasped, making Leo jump to his feet. She reread the line five more times before he made it to her.

"Leo, do you read Latin?" she asked, looking up at him, wide-eyed.

"Barely, but I can try," he said with an outstretched hand.

Vega passed the tome to him. "Careful. It's old." Leo cracked a smile, and Vega pointed out the line she needed him to read.

"Uh, so it's saying something about a curse being..." He pointed to a word he didn't know.

"*Locus.* Location," Vega translated.

"Tied to a location by blood?"

Speaking of blood, all of it seemed to rush to Vega's head.

"Oh my gods." She exhaled, snatching her bag and jacket off the ground. Vega gently grabbed the tome from his hands and put it back in her bag. "Let's go back down. Right now." Vega didn't wait for him, marching to the hidden hatch.

Leo's eyebrows creased in the middle of his forehead. "Is everything okay?"

Vega pulled the latch open. "I think I figured out how to break my curse."

51

"No fucking way."

It was Arlet who spoke up, vetoing her idea immediately.

Khort chimed in with a furious look, his eyes shifting between slits and normal pupils.

"You guys—" Vega began.

"Absolutely not, Vega. I haven't worked tirelessly for fifty-five years, traveling back and forth from Earth twenty times for you to purposely send yourself back there." It'd been a long time since Vega had seen Arlet this pissed.

"Khort!" Vega stomped her foot like a child who'd been told she wasn't allowed ice cream after dinner.

"Don't look at me. I'm with her. We've worked too hard to get you back." Khort leaned against the wall of the meeting room, an angry frown sagging his face.

In the same tome pages earlier, Vega had already learned that sometimes there was a way to trick curses. Granted, there was no information about how her specific curse worked, but it was closer than they'd ever gotten to an idea. She understood more about her curse in this life than she had in any other.

"My curse is obviously tied to Earth. Why else would I continuously get sent back there after every death?" Vega flailed her arms as she continued to explain. "All we have to do is trick the curse into thinking I've died, to stop my heart for less than a minute, right? That's how long you two said it takes my body to disappear after I've died." They didn't answer her, and Vega didn't give them enough time to interrupt. "I get back to Earth, have my memories, and then I can find out what it is that keeps pulling me back there. And if you're so worried about me, you'll know how to find me! Just come to me, and we can do it together, but this time, it's *me*. Me, with memories and hopefully the knowledge of how to end this thing."

Arlet shook her head, curls bouncing freely. "We're starting a war, Vega. After the new year, Urban is shutting off the food supply to Tolevarre. I don't have time to come chase you down again. I have to be here. *We* have to be here."

Vega felt a pang of sadness tug at her heart. Her hand shot up to knead at the spot on her chest like she could get it to go away if she applied enough pressure. "*You* need to be here. *I* need to break this curse."

Khort pushed himself off the wall. "It's too dangerous. We don't even know if it would work."

Vega slid the tome across the table again. "Read it. It's there. All the signs are there. All the *facts* are there. Marlena made this curse with her blood. Blood that she and I share. Blood from gods who used to call Earth their home." She jabbed her finger at the page. "Earth holds the key to ending this, to keeping me here forever with no chance of having to do it all over again."

Vega saw a flicker of hope in Arlet's eyes, but it was gone too quickly.

"Keep reading. There has to be another way." Arlet wasn't budging.

"There isn't another way!" Vega yelled, slamming her hand against the table as her anger crashed to the surface. Sparks flew from her palm, landing on the floor with no intended target. "I have spent nearly all of my lives trying to figure out how to end this curse, to end this plague on my body, my mind. Now we know we're gods, and there's a way for me to stop dying, to feel like I don't have to worry about someone snapping my neck in the middle of the night and waking to a life that doesn't want me! Spending another five, ten, fifteen years away from here while everyone I love, our people, get slaughtered." Vega drew in a shaky breath. "If I don't figure this out, if I don't end this, Marlena will. And if Marlena figures out how Remus cursed the gods to die before we can, this is all over. You can kiss me goodbye forever."

A lone tear rolled down her cheek.

"Vega." Khort reached out across the table, grasping at her hand.

"No!" She jerked away, taking a couple steps back. "You heard what Nero said, Arlet." Her attention dragged to her best friend. "Marlena wants more people researching curses. Why do you think that is? Because if she can curse us like Remus cursed Jupiter, Apollo, Diana"—she used the names of the gods they'd gotten powers from—"we're dead, and she's the only god left."

Khort sighed. "It sounds like we need to research how Remus cursed the original gods instead of worrying about how to break your curse."

It wasn't Vega's curse that had a ticking clock attached to it like they originally believed. It was a race to the finish line with her sister on who could kill who first... and Marlena rarely lost.

"Marlena knows I don't know how to break it now. She spent weeks trying to torture it out of me. She will kill me again—she will send me back to Earth to buy herself more time. And what happens when I'm gone for another fifteen years? Hmm? And she figures out how to kill us?" Vega scoffed, shaking her head frantically. "I'm no good to this revolution if I'm lost on Earth and certainly no good if I'm locked away because a curse weakens me. I'm useless, and so are the both of you if during every battle, you're worried I'll be killed and reset again." Vega snatched the tome up, marching towards the exit. "Remus foiled Marlena's original plan, but it's working in her favor. Keeping me alive but without my memories, without my powers, a realm away where I can't figure it out before her."

She turned one last time, glancing over her shoulder. Khort crossed his arms, closed off from the conversation already. Arlet held her gaze, sadness deflating her face. Vega opened the door, and before she shut it, she took a breath. "I realized how flawed my plan was after I stabbed Bridger. I didn't just put him in danger. I put the rest of us in danger too. Why do you think Marlena hasn't tried to kill you two to break me? Because she can't. You can't die until I do." The door slammed on a gust of Vega's wind.

52

THE WEATHER FLIPPED, AND THE BITE IN THE AIR WASN'T going away anytime soon. Winter had arrived in Tolevarre, officially bringing cold weather to most of the eastern territories.

A winter storm brought a blizzard to Imber and the mountain ranges throughout the realm. The people of Solum were working overtime to prevent the crops from being damaged by the frost drifting into the rolling hills.

Amora, the coldest territory in the realm, was used to year-round winter weather, but even it was getting buried by the storm.

Vega wrapped her coat tighter, burrowing into the warmth of the collar from the blowing wind, wishing she could find the heat of a summer storm right now. Vega could still summon storms in the cold, but they would only increase the windchill to a level no one would be happy with.

The Solum rebels called for backup at midnight, reporting an unruly group of soldiers wreaking havoc on the locals of a small village called Schoenus that bordered the main city.

Arlet and Vega had been looking through books from Littera,

attempting to find an alternative solution Vega knew they wouldn't find when the call came in. They had both jumped up simultaneously, never once second-guessing where they should be during a fight.

At least Arlet and Khort stopped fighting Vega on that front. It'd been nearly a week since she'd realized what it was going to take to break her curse and only an hour less than that for Vega to realize her friends wouldn't budge on their decision not to help her try.

She'd already decided she would try herself if they didn't find a backup by the turn of the new year. But at least their impromptu trip to Solum brought another option to the table.

For too long, Vega had spent her time hiding, allowing herself to be locked away like a porcelain doll—no longer would she hide, cursed or not.

What was the point of being found if she wasn't allowed to live?

Vega left a trail of bodies across the back roads of Schoenus. She didn't leave a single soldier alive if she came across them. Killing didn't hurt anymore, dulling over time to a small ache in her chest. She'd never been keen on taking someone's life, but it had been thrust upon her, and she was sick of being on the other end.

Vega helped the locals move the bodies to a mass burn pit. People died in war, she reminded herself. And war was here…

Vega took a deep breath as she approached Khort and Quinley. Thanks to her and her spying, they knew their rebuttal hadn't sounded an alarm in Stella. Meyer was too busy wrangling up what soldiers he had left in Solum, and Bridger hadn't been seen in weeks.

For whatever sick and twisted reason, Vega had hoped at least the latter showed up.

"I've never seen you in action like that," Quinley.

Vega had only known her for a brief moment in her last life—a life in which she was so far from who she was now. "I've never been this version of myself," she replied honestly, pulling her wild battle hair back in a high pony, her usual braids pinning her flyaways down to her scalp.

"I think I like this version." The girl bowed her head, reaching her hand out to brush Khort's arm.

He stiffened at Quinley's touch in Vega's presence. She pretended not to notice, staring as a flame took over the dead bodies, sending their souls to whatever afterlife they deserved.

"I'm going to head back to my post. Let me know if there is anything else I can help with." Quinley waved goodbye to Vega, disappearing before their eyes.

Her invisibility reminded Vega too much of Marlena.

She pulled herself farther into her coat despite the warmth coming from the flame. The fire sizzled, the smell of flesh burning too overwhelming to ignore. Vega swallowed down the bile forcing its way up.

"You okay?" Khort asked, turning from the flame.

His voice distracted her from the smell she'd been fixated on. "Fine," she said, offering a small smile as they walked through the now-empty streets.

The sun peeked over the horizon, bringing forth a new day.

"Meaning you don't want to talk about it?" Khort raised an eyebrow.

"No, you don't want to talk about what's on my mind, so why bother?" Vega watched as the sun rose slowly from behind the hills and sank behind the winter storm clouds looming in the distance.

"You're still thinking about Earth," he stated.

"I'll never stop thinking about it." Vega shook her head. "Not when it's the only viable option we've got."

Khort sighed. "Vega."

"Please, I can't talk about it anymore." Not with someone who couldn't see what was so clear.

Vega loved her friends, she did... but they'd begun to baby her in ways she wasn't used to, in ways that made her feel inferior because of a curse she couldn't control.

She tried to understand, putting herself in their shoes, trying to fathom what it would feel like if it were Arlet with the curse and not herself.

But all she could think about was how Bridger never once made her feel like she couldn't do something—with or without a curse.

And that was a problem because Vega shouldn't be thinking positively about Bridger in any sort of way—not after everything.

Certainly not after the way their kiss made her feel.

"I hope you know Arlet and I are doing what we can to keep you safe."

Vega bit back a scoff, her teeth cutting into the inside of her lip. "Yeah" was all she said.

They reached the hut where Arlet was helping fix up some wounded rebels. She smiled at them both as they approached, but it didn't reach her eyes. There was nothing happy about burning bodies, no matter what side of the line they came from.

"What did Quinley say?" Arlet asked, passing the supplies in her hands to a healer.

"No movement in Aeris, Fortis, or Ardor. It seems they're going to let us have this battle," Khort answered.

And really, that was what this was—*a* little *battle*.

Seventy dead soldiers with rankings under level three, who were looking for trouble, was nothing more than a bothersome morning to those in power.

"Hmm," Arlet hummed. She nibbled the inside of her lip.

"What?" Vega asked.

"It's just curious. Why wouldn't they show up when they've been jumping at every opportunity to squander this rebellion since the beginning?"

"Because she's planning something bigger," Vega answered, her brow raised as if it were obvious.

She left Khort and Arlet to banter back and forth, something more important weighing on her mind. Vega wandered off towards a small group of Schoenus locals tending to their horses. A petite elderly woman with a curved back and kind eyes smiled at her, chattering to her horse. It whinnied, attention flickering to Vega as she approached.

"What did she say?" Vega asked, reaching out to stroke the horse's soft muzzle. The mare pressed her nose into Vega's hand in a sweet hello.

The woman brushed the horse, its white hair full with a winter coat. "She asked if you were the one with the lightning." Her voice quivered with old age.

Some of Solum's people bonded with animals, allowing them to speak to the creature who chose them—and it was the animal who chose the bond, not the other way around.

Vega nodded with a smile as the horse nickered. "Yes, that's me. Sorry if I startled you."

The little old woman laughed a happy sound, patting the mare on the back after she put the brush away in her basket. "She's okay. Pip has been through worse."

Vega's heart ached. Bonded animals lived as long as their person did, which meant Pip had to be hundreds of years old.

"She and I want to thank you for coming to our aid. It's been ugly around here with the soldiers using our town as a base. They take what they want without respect to those who live here." The woman shuffled her feet, slowly standing beside Vega, where she continued stroking Pip's head. "I'm Belva."

"Belva, it's nice to meet you. Vega." She held out her hand. The woman's grip was surprisingly strong for how fragile she seemed.

Belva's smile revealed she knew who Vega was, but she didn't say it... and for that, she was grateful.

Vega peered over her shoulder, not seeing Khort and Arlet where she'd left them.

Perfect.

"Is there a horse I might be able to borrow for an hour or so? It's been too long since I've gotten any alone time, and after this morning, I could really use some quiet to read." Vega let her hand drop away from Pip and fall to her side.

Belva eyed Vega, nodding to a stable at the end of the road. "Come with us. We'll get you set up with someone."

Much to Vega's surprise, a horse was already saddled and ready to ride. She'd snuck out the back stables without notice from Khort and Arlet, a small satchel of books strung along the saddle.

Schoenus was only twenty minutes from Littera and the Minerva Archives, where she was hoping she could find Colette.

She was Vega's last hope—the last option she might have to convince someone to give her absurd idea a chance.

Vega pulled the cloak's hood up as she approached the city's main road to hide from prying eyes. She suddenly felt thankful for the snow falling in fat flakes around her now at a higher altitude. Everyone who passed was bundled up, their heads down as they shuffled to wherever they were headed.

She tied the stallion to a tree, giving herself an exit into the forest if needed. Vega felt the prickle of eyes on her, the hairs on the back of her neck standing up. She pivoted in the fresh snow, scanning the area around her.

No one paid her any mind, but the tingle remained.

Vega reached into her jacket pocket. She gave the horse a sugar cube and a pat on his muscular neck before she snuck into the library's side entrance.

Vega felt the strain on her powers as the door closed behind her, unsettling her. She had spent too much time without the steady thrum of electricity and the whirl of her storms. Vega didn't want to be powerless for even a second. Her hands slid to her sides, confirming her daggers were in their places.

The feeling of being watched had yet to leave her.

She would know if it were one of the bonded.

Vega trailed her eyes across the main room, the light from the glass ceiling above dimmed by a layer of snow. There was no one behind her and no one but the students bustling through the aisles in their white robes.

Vega turned a corner, hurrying down the hall towards Colette's wing.

What if she wasn't here? What was her plan then?

Vega pushed those thoughts from her mind, focusing on what she could guarantee—not getting caught in the main library of Littera by the enemy.

She looked behind once more, and with her eyes focused in the wrong direction, Vega came crashing into someone. A startled peep escaped the woman now on her ass from the collision.

Vega whipped her head around, eyes landing on Colette. A smile pulled at her lips, still hidden behind the hood cloaking her. "Oh my gods. I'm so sorry," she cooed, reaching out to help her up.

Colette's soft voice murmured her own apology, accepting the helping hand. "You're fi—"

Vega let her hood down, releasing Colette's hand.

"Vega," she hissed, pulling her behind an open door. "What are you doing here?"

Vega found her words before speaking. "I have a couple books I wanted to return." It was partially true. She dug around in her bag and pressed two against Colette's chest.

The blonde's eyebrows met in a V shape. "You shouldn't be here. There are too many eyes. The books could have waited." Her voice was a hushed murmur.

"Well," Vega paused, biting her lip. *It's now or never.* "That's not the only reason I'm here." She looked around the room, catching a student ogling at her from the corner.

Colette followed her gaze, snapping her fingers at the young boy. His eyes diverted from them, and he tottered away.

It wouldn't be long before people learned Vega was here.

"Colette, I need your help with something. You told me to tell you if something in one of the tomes worked." Vega pulled the last book out of her bag.

Colette shook her head, placing a finger over Vega's lip. "Not here." She grabbed her wrist and led her to a small office. The lights winked to life as they walked in, and the door squeaked shut. "You don't have much time. Start talking."

Vega swallowed her fear and delved into the gritty details. As she spoke, she flipped to the page numbers she'd memorized. Vega pointed out the most important details, not missing a beat.

"I keep getting returned back to Earth. That has to mean my curse is there, tied to that world somehow. Maybe the key is just being able to outsmart it... but regardless of what it is, I need to get back to Earth, and I need to trick this curse into thinking I'm dead so I keep my memories this time." Vega felt breathless after spilling her guts to an ally who might be too new to trust—an ally who was the granddaughter of one of Marlena's most loyal praefecti.

Colette shook her head, the ends of her blonde hair rustling over the shoulder of her robe. "I can't help you with this." She walked to the door and peeked outside, searching the corners for watchful eyes.

Vega stepped forward, reaching for her hand, but Colette pulled back. "Colette, please. You're my last hope."

"No. It puts me in too much danger, and I refuse to be put in the middle of a war I can't fight myself out of." Colette's bronze skin had gone pale, fear prickling her skin.

Vega's expression was tight, lips pursed. "You've already put yourself in the middle by helping me."

"I owed Urban a favor. I do not owe you anything. I got you out of here safe, and now I must protect myself. My grandfather has been babbling about seeing you here for days. It's only a matter of time before Marlena shows up here, questioning all of us. Or that Bridger shows up with his army ready to burn this place to the ground for harboring secrets we've been keeping for centuries." Colette ushered Vega out the door and back down the hall. "I'm sorry I'm not the fearless ally you were hoping for, but I want to live just like the others here in Littera. I will do what I can, when I can to help, but this is not something I will help with."

Colette pulled Vega's hood up for her, moving them quickly through the halls.

Vega wanted to argue, to fight and claw to get her way—but she wouldn't. That was what Marlena did, not her. Vega would find another way. She always found another way.

When they got back to the door Vega entered through, Colette stood outside on the stoop and bowed her head as Vega descended the stone stairs. "I am sorry, Vega. Truly. I'm rooting for you, but I'm not equipped to fight off Marlena if this goes badly. And I'm certainly not sure I'd want to have an angry Arlet or Khort on my ass, either."

Snowflakes were coming down thicker, a white coat layering the ground she stood on. "I hope you know this will end in war, Colette. It's already started. My sister has gotten away with far too much. I will not rest until she's dead, but first, I have to get the upper hand and break the curse she's been using to keep me prisoner inside my own body." Vega turned, heading back to her horse. "If you're not with us when it's time to choose a side, you'll be dead too," she called back to the young girl standing on the steps of a building Vega would watch crumble if she had to, taking all of Tolevarre's history with it.

Vega was sick of people playing whatever side benefited them. Colette would have to choose, one way or another.

Her borrowed horse whinnied when she walked up, his head falling to Vega's pocket where more sugar cubes hid. She reached in and nabbed another for him to crunch on while she readied herself to get back and start formulating a new plan.

Vega began to untie the horse's reins from the tree when a voice froze her in place.

"How far are you willing to go to set your scheme into motion?"

Quicker than she'd ever moved, Vega twisted away from the horse, and lightning licked at her fingertips with power so strong it raised the heat inside her body.

Meyer's golden eyes gleamed as he raked them up her body, sizing up his opponent. "Hello, Sparks."

53

She'd felt eyes on her, knew she was being watched, and now Vega was kicking herself in the ass for not trusting that gut feeling.

She didn't let her lightning free, but she did let the cold wind pick up—warning Meyer she would strike if needed.

His lips twitched in a devious smile. "Oh, c'mon. Aren't you happy to see me?"

"No," Vega spat, the horse behind her braying with nerves, his ears shooting back.

Meyer poked his lip out, fake pouting. "You wound me."

Vega slid her hand down her leg, gripping Bridger's dagger.

"Ah-ah. There's no reason to start reaching for your weapons," he cooed, eyes fluttering to her fingers curled around the blade. "I came here looking for you, hoping we could chat, and somehow I got oh so lucky to follow you—I can't believe you didn't see me, by the way. I've been trailing you since you left Schoenus." He pointed towards the path she'd taken through the woods. "And came upon the stunning realization that you might know how to break your curse."

If Marlena finds out...

Vega kept her reactions under control—she wouldn't let him get under her skin.

"You have no idea what you're talking about," Vega lied, resting a hand on the horse to keep him calm.

Meyer rolled his eyes, taking a step closer. "Don't play dumb, Sparks. I heard it all. One quick bolt of internal lightning, strong enough to stop the heart for a minute but not strong enough to kill you. A dagger just beside the heart, but make it look like it's been pierced. It is a brilliant plan. Simple and effective."

The use of the nickname again made her lip curl in disgust—it had been a way for him to get under her skin years ago, and it still worked. When Meyer stepped closer, Vega let her lightning crackle to life in her hand.

"And I want to help you with your problem if you don't sizzle me to a crisp."

Vega's look of disgust turned into one of confusion, her eyebrows pinching in the middle. "You what?"

"I didn't stutter. Gods, has the dying fried your brain?" Meyer retorted.

Meyer, in no life, was ever a fan of Vega. She'd always known he felt Vega was the reason Bridger had fallen off his life's path, and maybe she was, but he had chosen to follow her all on his own—just like when he'd chosen to stab her in the back. He'd done that all on his own too.

"Watch your tone, or maybe I'll fry you instead." Vega let her lightning scurry up and down her arm as a reminder of what she could do.

Meyer laughed, and there was a lightness to it Vega had never heard before. "If you did that, then you'd really have no one willing to help you. As you said, Colette was your last hope... and here I am, giving you one last solution, and you're about to blow it."

Vega chose not to let the lightning or the wind die down, keeping her power flowing through her. She'd never once trusted Meyer, and she wouldn't start today, no matter what he said.

"And you would want to help me why?" she asked, cocking her head to the right.

Meyer looked around their secluded surroundings. "For Bridger."

Vega felt her stomach drop, a flutter of something deep inside her coming to life. A laugh bubbled from somewhere deep. "You've lost it." She turned to grab the reins.

Meyer snatched her by the wrist before she could and spun her around. The horse let out a frightened screech.

His hand was warm around her wrist, sending Vega into fight or flight mode... and she was sick of running. Her electricity seared through her, prickling into Meyer's hand. Not enough to kill, only to forewarn him what she would do if he laid a hand on her again.

He jumped back, shaking his palm out. "You bitch," he sneered.

"Keep your hands to yourself, and we won't have a problem," she said with a promising smile.

"Then listen to what I have to say." His voice was menacing, but Vega had seen scarier things and lived through them.

The snow fell harder, hiding them from prying eyes.

"You have two minutes," she warned.

Meyer's jaw flexed, annoyance written in his face's hard lines. "Do you know Bridger has been dreaming of you, of his past, for months? Since Arlet found you on Earth?"

He's dreaming of me too.

Vega raised an eyebrow, her arms crossed over her chest. "How would I know that?" She forced herself to keep her edge, to maintain the air of distaste she needed.

He didn't answer Vega's question. "You're haunting his every dream and then every waking minute because he can't wash you away with booze, training, war. Nothing. He's not sleeping, petrified of seeing memories he buried away for decades come to the surface. And then this time, you're so you. Witty, strong, brave."

Vega wasn't used to hearing compliments coming from Meyer.

"He sees the girl you once were. The one he fell in love with. The one he waited for, fought fifteen years for. The one he's let go twice in a single life."

Vega took a deep breath in, steadying the thrum of her heart. "You're delusional."

"Delusional?" he asked. "This curse wasn't made to torture only you, Vega. Marlena designed it to fuck with everyone who loves you too. How do you think it made Bridger feel when you came back from a life and couldn't remember him, but had the memories of another man, another life? Or how Arlet feels having to leave her own world behind to go chase your lost ass down all the time? And don't even get me started on lovesick Fera. May I remind you that while you have been tortured on and off by your sister, Bridger endured two full years of it with her only intent being to break him."

Vega didn't need the reminder. "So what are you saying? That I owe him because my sister's a psychopath?"

Meyer sighed, his shoulders sagging. "I'm saying if it weren't for your sister, Bridger would have chosen you in every lifetime without any hesitation. Marlena made certain Bridger had no other choice... and I'm trying to make the decision he would have made for himself if she hadn't fucked him up so badly—the decision he would have made had his parents not sold his soul long before he got the chance to save himself."

Vega could see her breaths coming out in short bursts. "I will never forgive him, Meyer. If that's what you came here to do—"

He cut her off. "That's absolutely not what I'm here to do. I'm here to save my best friend, and unfortunately, I think you're the only person who can do that."

"Why would breaking this curse set him free?" she asked.

"Because your curse is his curse, right? Since you're bonded gods and all." Meyer's smirk started on one side of his face and twisted to the other.

Vega went white, her mouth opening to ask, *How?*

"It doesn't matter *how* I know. It only matters that I *do* know." He waved his hand, moving the conversation along. "And if this doesn't work, then no harm, no foul. It wouldn't be the first time you had to start all over. You should be good at it by now."

Vega clenched her jaw. She wanted to reach out and slap him, but she didn't... Meyer was offering her the help she needed.

And if it worked, well, then she'd be one step ahead.

"I'll think about it, and if I decide I'm desperate enough to work with you, then I'll come find you." Vega pulled the reins down and hoisted herself up onto the horse. He took a few steps back, the sound of snapping twigs under his hooves insulated by the snow.

This time Meyer didn't try to stop her. He stood stuck in his place, rooted to the ground below. "Hey, Vega!" he called.

She twisted her body as the horse continued in the opposite direction.

"Marlena knows Solum's joining the rebellion, and after today's retaliation, she and Bridger are planning on wiping it clean after the new year."

Vega had a choice to make... and she didn't have much time to make it.

54

THE TOME IN HER HANDS HAD PAPER SO BRITTLE, VEGA worried it might disintegrate if she pinched too hard. Every bit of information she'd come across pointed towards one thing: she had to die.

Or at least trick the curse into thinking that was what was happening.

Thankfully, upon Vega's return to Schoenus, Quinley had warned Arlet and Khort about the planned attack on Solum after the turn of the new year, and Vega didn't have to come up with a lie about how she knew before they did.

Once back in Castra, Vega inserted herself into everything she could. There was a lot she'd missed out on in fifteen years. She reread every book she and Arlet borrowed from the archives a couple times through, looking for another way that might free her from her curse.

There was nothing, not a sliver of hope she could break this thing here in Tolevarre. Something on Earth kept pulling her back for a reason.

Every time Vega got close to convincing herself there was another way, she came to the same conclusion... she needed to move forward with her plan, regardless of how mad Arlet and Khort would be. Vega couldn't wait—there was no time to wait.

As badly as she wanted to leave right now, she couldn't sneak out on a night like tonight. *But maybe when everyone is drunk and not paying attention.* Vega's mind was made up.

Books, tomes, and letters scattered across the floor of her tiny room, and Vega was sitting in the middle. She took inventory of everything, jetting air through pursed lips. A knock at the door yanked her out of scholar-mode. "Come in," she called, turning her head to see Arlet stepping through the door.

"What are you doing?" she rasped.

Arlet was dressed in an off the shoulder gown with a sweetheart neckline, the color gold with jewels that shimmered with her every move. Fringe started at her hip, cascading down her long legs in a flowing fit. Arlet's bouncy curls were pulled out of her face in an updo.

Arlet looked like every god they had learned to pray to growing up—like the god she had become.

Lifting herself off the floor, Vega gave Arlet an apologetic smile. "Sorry, I got distracted, but look, I'm dressed and ready!" She gestured towards the mess on the floor and then to herself. Vega stored all the information she'd been thrumming through in a safe spot inside her dresser. "You look beautiful." Vega reached out to run a hand over the straps hanging off her arm.

Arlet's annoyance fizzled out when their eyes met. "It's been so long since we've celebrated Saturnalia together." Her eyes raked up Vega's body, and she reached out to straighten her dress where it was bunched from sitting on the floor.

It was made just for her. The straps thin, neckline plunging below her sternum, with the same V-shape diving down her back. The sheer black fabric allowed for her black undergarments to be seen, a fact that would have made her flustered in any life on Earth—but here in Tolevarre, it made her feel fierce and every bit of the lethal woman she was learning to become again. Similar to Arlet's dress, Vega had jewels of her own littering the gossamer material, but they were as black as her dress and only sparkled under the right lighting.

She kept her dark hair down, no braids to hold her hair out of her face tonight.

"Since Bridger's last year with us," Vega said, exhaling. The celebration had been nothing like the one Castra was throwing tonight.

"Don't," Arlet said, reaching out to brush Vega's cheek. "Don't let him ruin this night for you."

He already has.

"I won't," Vega said instead. But her brain couldn't stop thinking about him, about how he'd let her go or about the look in his eyes after she'd kissed him and drove his own dagger through his heart—how she'd used him as an experiment. She reached out and grabbed Arlet's hand. "Let's go. We're already late."

They were the only two left in the halls. Vega could hear the thrum of the music as they approached the room she still thought felt like a fishbowl. The residents of Castra had decorated the inside with sparkling string lights and wreaths made of natural growth from the land over a mile above them, and whoever was musically talented spent their night entertaining their neighbors.

Happy laughter floated through the air, smiles on faces around them as people said their hellos. Vega grabbed them two flutes of bubbly wine from a table and tapped her glass against Arlet's before taking her first sip.

It tasted like Saturnalia.

She hadn't been drinking since the return of her memories—she hadn't had time, and really, she hadn't felt the need. When her life was falling apart on Earth, it was the way she coped with having nothing to live for. This Vega not only had something to live and fight for—but something to die for too.

Arlet pulled her onto the dance floor after another glass of bubbles, just in time for the band to start a song with an all too familiar tempo. Couples shuffled to the floor, but Vega's eyes blurred over with tears, unable to focus on anyone but her best friend.

"What did you do?" Vega bubbled with laughter as the crescendo of the music picked up.

Amusement rippled from Arlet. "I might have taught them a new song."

"Over My Head (Cable Car)" was being played by the band, and Vega couldn't contain the tears spilling over.

"No! No crying, only dancing!"

The girls danced, screaming the lyrics only they knew at the top of their lungs. They didn't pay attention to the eyes on them, didn't care what people thought. For a moment in time, there was nothing for them to worry about—they were just two best friends, singing their favorite song, lost in a moment neither ever thought they'd have.

Khort joined them at some point, spinning each other around, their smiles so big it was hard to remember a time when they weren't all happy and safe. Hours passed, and Vega hadn't thought about what she was about to do tonight—about the deception hiding just below the surface.

Eventually, Arlet sauntered off somewhere, leaving Vega and Khort alone. "Do you remember the Saturnalia we spent in Vates with Arlet and her family? The one right before they left?" Vega questioned.

Khort placed his hand on the small of Vega's back, pulling her in while they danced to a slow song. "Yeah, what about it?" he asked, dipping his head to meet her eyes.

Vega contemplated if she should mention this tidbit of information or not. The little voice in her head told her not to, but the beating in her chest reminded her she might not have this memory much longer. "That night your mom came to me and told me how happy it would make her to see us together." Vega's voice was low enough only Khort could hear her.

"Why are you telling me this?" he asked.

"Because sometimes I wonder, if I listened to what she was telling me, if we'd be in the same situation now. If maybe Marlena would have left us alone because I wasn't after someone who was supposed to be hers." Vega's hands looped behind Khort's neck, her forearms resting on his shoulders.

Could I have been happy with Khort? It was a question she'd asked herself a million times. Could *I be happy with Khort now?* The second question was new to this life.

Khort exhaled. "You can't blame yourself. This isn't your fault."

"But it is, isn't it? I'm the reason she's dragged you all into this." The two of them stopped dancing and stood in the middle of the floor with their arms still around each other. "If you weren't my friend, then you'd be safe. Your parents." Vega choked on the words, forcing tears back. "They would still be alive. Your sister wouldn't have—you'd be—"

Khort's hands shot up to the sides of her face, his calloused palms cupping her cheeks. "No. Stop." His forest-green eyes bore into hers, like he was searching for something.

Vega clenched her jaw and averted her gaze. "Khort, this is all because of me. I have to be the one to fix it."

She wrapped her hands around his wrists, pulling his palms away from her face—not because she didn't like his touch, but because she didn't want him to see her break down, to catch on to the secret that was threatening to spill out.

She was leaving tonight, and Vega couldn't stray from that.

"Stop pulling away from me. Please." His voice was soft, pleading.

Vega stopped trying to retreat, her focus returning to him.

"There's only one way to end this." Her throat bobbled when she swallowed. Why was she trying to convince him again? He'd taken his final stance on this topic. *One last time. Give him one last chance.*

"No." Khort shook his head, letting his hands fall to his sides. Vega took a step away from him when he began to speak again. "Arlet and I both agree it's too dangerous. We will try other ways."

Vega's hair fell into her face as she shook her head. "There are no other ways, Khort. We've tried them, hundreds of times."

Khort reached out to brush the strand out of her eyes, but Vega took another step back and did it herself, sighing heavily at the look in his eyes.

"We're just not willing to lose you," Khort said with a sigh.

"You're going to lose me if you don't let me try." Vega's voice shook, using the same words she'd been using incessantly to convince both Khort and Arlet to give in. "We'll all lose."

"Vega, please. We've talked about this. Let us keep you safe."

This. This is why I didn't choose him.

Khort always spent all his time worrying about how he could make sure Vega was safe from harm, protecting her like she was a small child no matter how strong she'd become. Bridger had let her fight, let her figure things out on her own—he'd believed in her once... even if that felt like eons ago.

"Sure," Vega finally agreed. "Keep me safe." She needed to not raise suspicions, and their little tiff was enough to have Khort questioning her.

"Can I please touch you again?" he whispered, reaching for her delicately.

She shook her head, eyes falling to the floor. "I'm going to go to bed," Vega said lightly. "I'm tired."

"Let me walk you to your room."

"You should stay here." She nodded towards the new set of eyes on them. "Give Quinley her turn to dance with you." Vega smiled softly. "Goodnight, Khort."

Vega left him in the middle of the dance floor, wiping a tear from her scarred cheek.

Arlet and Khort had never let her feel alone before—not until now.

No backing down. You're on your own this time.

55

My dearest Arlet & Khort,

By the time you read this letter, I'll be a world away. I'm sure you know that. I'm sure you'll feel it before even finding this.

I love you both more than you'll ever know. Your friendship has been the anchor that holds me here, in this life and all the others before it. Unfortunately, there is also something holding me to a world that doesn't want me. I cannot be fully here, fighting for us and the people who need it, if Death lurks at every corner.

I hope you understand why I've made this decision without you. Be here, protect our people.

I'll be back soon.

Dum vita est, spes est—while there is life, there is hope.

All my love & until the very end,

Vega

THE SUNRISE OVER THE WATER ILLUMINATED THE SKY IN PINK and purple pastels, birds flying over with happy morning tweets.

Vega's eyes never left the horizon, taking in what very well could end up being her last Tolevarre sunrise. *Gods, I hope not.*

There were so many unknown variables. What if it didn't work and she did end up back on Earth with no memories? How long would Arlet wait before coming to look for her this time? Would she even come to find her?

It wasn't a matter of if the war broke out. Now it was a matter of when—when was only a week away. And Arlet was needed here, not out gallivanting to find Vega.

She shook the doubts away, focusing on the coastline ahead. *This will work. I will make it out alive, and I'll show my sister who she's been messing with.*

By the time she'd made it to the secluded docks, Vega's boots were under at least an inch of water. The tiny boat had somehow made the hour-long journey, keeping Vega afloat and safe from a cold plunge into the Sea of Ros.

It was the morning of Saturnalia, and families were huddled in their homes, opening gifts and enjoying their time together. It was the one day a year most people took off from their daily lives to simply enjoy what peace they could find in the world today.

Vega passed very few people moving through the quiet streets. They waved as she walked by, giving her pleasant smiles and blessings of happiness for the holiday.

She decided against covering her face or hiding behind a cloak. Vega was dressed in her training suit, letting her lightning hum through her body to keep warm.

By the time word got back to Marlena, Vega would be gone.

After the attack Vega assisted with in Schoenus, the army increased the number of soldiers in and around Solum, but they'd been rather well behaved according to Urban.

They knew it was because they were lying in wait to attack, but their people didn't. It was important to Urban to let them have one last holiday—they'd agreed to slowly start moving as many people as they could to Castra and deep into the forest of Vates.

Anyone who didn't want to fight didn't have to.

Vega knew she was getting close when she passed a few soldiers flirting with young locals, the insignias on their uniforms proudly displayed.

They didn't pay Vega any mind while the girls twirled their pretty hair and laughed at whatever the boys were saying.

She felt a pang of jealousy for the lightness in their hearts, the free way they laughed with no worries. One day—one day she would be able to feel that way again.

When her sister was dead and they were free from her fatal clutch.

Vega walked for a few more minutes, moving herself to the shadows and alleyways when the groups of soldiers started to thicken. There were a few moving large bins into old cabins, families standing outside with their hands up, their kids crying with fear and confusion.

"Today? But it's Saturnalia," a mother holding her wailing baby asked a level eight soldier.

"I don't make the rules, lady. Boss said get out, so you've gotta go."

"Where am I supposed to go?" the woman asked, containing her own tears.

"That's not my problem," he responded, pushing by to continue moving things into the house.

The local wiped at her face, handing the baby in her arms to the oldest child in the group while she gathered the few things she'd been allowed to grab from her home off the front lawn.

Vega's heart broke for the misplaced family. "Pssst!" she hissed.

It took a couple tries before the woman found where Vega was hiding. Carefully she walked forward, cautious like a fawn ready to bolt.

"You and your kids have nowhere to go?" Vega asked, the woman finally laying eyes on her.

"Vega," she cooed, reaching out to grab her hands as if Vega would disappear if she didn't.

People acted like she was part of some prophecy—that by her being back, their land would be saved.

Vega wished she could promise that.

"No, it's only me and the kids." Her voice shook.

Vega squeezed her hand. "Okay, I need you to listen closely. There's a rowboat east of the main docks. I hid it underneath the middle row. It has some holes so it won't hold all of you, but if you get on alone and paddle to Imber, someone will come find you. And they will come back for the kids. They'll take you to a safe spot, but you need to go now." Her voice was hushed but firm.

The woman started to protest. "I can't leave here."

"You have to. There is going to be an attack. Soon. Marlena's calling for a kill-all in Solum, and if you don't get out of here, you and your children will die." Vega saw no sense in sugarcoating what would happen if they stayed.

The mother's eyes grew wide, panic setting in. "No."

Vega nodded, patting her hand and letting it go. "I wish I was lying, but I'm not. You need to get your kids out. They'll be safe where I'm sending you."

The woman finally nodded. "Okay. Okay, I will go." She looked over her shoulder at her four children, eyes filled with tears. "I lost my husband last month to the flu. I can't lose them too."

"Then get them to safety."

Vega was snatched into a quick hug, and the woman mumbled a goodbye before scurrying off to round her kids up.

The silence didn't last long.

"That was very nice of you, Kitten."

Vega hadn't felt him approach, but now that he was near, she couldn't ignore the tug in her chest or the featherlight whisper of his words inside her head.

Bridger wore his commander's uniform, no cape hanging from his shoulders, and he was strapped to the nines with weapons. The uniform wasn't the one for show—it was the one for battle.

No. Vega felt her face fall, and her body went ice cold with a rush of blood.

"It's Saturnalia, Bridger. You can't." Fear shook her voice, her powers inside begging to be set free.

"War waits for no one, and you and your friends slaughtered seventy of my soldiers. It's only fair we answer back." Bridger's eyes were hollow with dark circles underneath, his hair longer than he was known to keep it. He was disheveled, and it looked as if he hadn't slept in weeks.

"Your men were hurting innocent people," Vega bit back.

Bridger's throat bobbed when he laughed dryly. "So killing them is okay? I thought you were against people dying?" He cocked his head to the side, waiting for an answer.

"You once told me not everyone is worth saving." Vega locked her eyes on his. "And I don't believe anyone who would willingly follow my sister is worth saving."

Her dig hit home, right where it was supposed to.

The smile that took over his face was sinister, coated with ice, and dipped in darkness. "I was never meant to be saved."

Bridger took another step towards her, and Vega stood her ground, feeling not a drop of fear in his presence like she might have in previous lives.

"Is that how you feel about the dreams you're having of me? Of the feelings you're trying to suppress whenever you see me, get to touch me, kiss me? That you don't deserve to be saved?" Vega took a step forward too, closing the distance until her chest grazed against him. Their height difference was on display, Bridger towering over a foot above her with a menacing glare.

Bridger's jaw flexed with anger, bringing a smile to Vega's face.

"Do I see a crack in that impenetrable shell?" She licked her lips slowly, watching Bridger's eyes flick to them. "Has Vega Caelum ruined Tolevarre's greatest warrior? Have I finally become the undoing you told me I'd be?"

Speaking through a clenched jaw, Bridger replied with a growl, "Don't flatter yourself." His hand reached out, brushing against her cheek. "Where've you been hiding in Imber, baby?"

Vega wrapped her hand around his, their eyes locked in a battle of wills. "If you want to know so badly, you'll have to come find me."

"I can feel you, feel my blade. The pull led me to the middle of the Sea of Ros, just off the coast. Have you grown gills?" Bridger's hand slid down to Vega's neck, his fingers applying pressure where her pulse was.

"Don't make a rash decision, Dimico, or I'll make you wish you *could* die." Vega let a purr of electricity buzz over her skin—enough for Bridger to feel a slight tingle under his fingers.

The anger melted from his face, a look of amusement taking its place. "I like it when you threaten me with a good time." Bridger pulled her roughly by her neck, and a traitorous gasp slipped from Vega's parted lips. "Do me a favor and get the fuck out of here before you get yourself caught up in something you'll regret."

Bridger shoved her away with enough force she staggered back. "I'm not running from this fight," Vega declared.

Thunder rumbled overhead as a storm formed in the distance. It wasn't a natural occurrence this time of year. Vega sent a warning she was here. *Here and ready to fight.*

Bridger's lips parted, his gaze nowhere near as cold as it'd been in lives before. He looked like he was about to say something, but then his eyes shifted, a flicker of fear flashing across his face before it returned to impassive.

"Why must you always play the hero?" Her sister's question grated like nails on a chalkboard. Vega turned slowly, and Marlena was smiling as tendrils of smoke disappeared behind her. "Hello, sister."

Vega returned the smile, her senses on overdrive as she let her lightning finally roar to life in her hands.

Marlena stood in place, eyeing Vega like a bullseye. "I knew if I found Bridger, I'd find you. Still trying to get him back? How pathetic."

"Still trying to sneak into his bed and have your sister's sloppy seconds?" Vega rolled her eyes. They could stand there all day arguing, but it would only prolong the inevitable.

Marlena snaked forward as the wind picked up overhead and Vega's storm rolled in, sitting on top of them. Vega wouldn't wait for her sister to strike first.

The time for playing with emotions was over.

Vega lunged forward with her lightning, the bolt cracking a tree behind Marlena. Her sister laughed, beginning to point out that Vega had missed—but the diversion was just what she needed. Vega looked up at the sky, a funnel cloud breaking the surface.

In no life had she been strong enough, either mentally or physically, to conjure a tornado. But this life, *oh boy*, this life Vega was ready to fight.

"Your soldiers better run," Vega said over her shoulder to Bridger. Lightning flickered inside the descending storm, screams rattling from the people at the newly assigned war camp.

Vega saw the storm inside her head, pushing her powers to twirl and dance with the clouds above.

Marlena's mask fell for a sliver of a second—long enough for Vega to see the look of shock mangling her features.

The thin tornado touched down, and Vega spun her finger out in front of her, a gust of wind mimicking the rampant storm beyond the cover of trees.

Bridger unsheathed his sword, taking a step closer to Vega when she threw the wind at him, knocking him down.

"You both have made a grave mistake this time. You've underestimated the hatred that has grown for the both of you over the last half-century. I no longer feel sorry for the lives you've lived." Her voice grew louder. "I no longer care who either of you once were to me!" Vega unleashed, sending a lightning bolt through the air directly at her sister's pretty blonde head. "I'm going to make sure I find a way to send you both straight to the underworld where you belong!"

Another lightning bolt shot out from the palm facing backwards, nearly striking Bridger—but he was fast, and unfortunately, he knew her moves. Whether Vega wanted to admit it or not, he knew her better than anyone else.

Better than Arlet. Better than Khort. And even better than Marlena.

The tornado ravaged through the town, overturning caravans of army vehicles, sending their supplies flying and taking whoever got too close with it.

Marlena's emerald fire tore through the whipping wind beside Vega's face. The heat from the flame forced her to duck and roll. She popped up, reaching for a dagger at her side.

Spinning on her heels, Vega flung the dagger towards Marlena, who caught it midair.

None of them could die, but that didn't mean they couldn't become incapacitated long enough to find themselves imprisoned.

Bridger came from behind, knocking Vega off her feet. She flipped herself over, ready to claw his eyes out of his skull until she realized he'd sent her flying to the ground seconds before Marlena chucked the blade back at her. It would've landed its target.

Sinking through Vega's heart.

Except it didn't. It hit the tree behind her.

Bridger ripped the dagger from the tree and spun it in his hand. The blade shined, reunited with him, and a smile broke his face in two. *Menacingly beautiful.* And she'd just made Bridger stronger than he needed to be with the return of his bonded dagger. *Fuck.*

She was outnumbered. Stronger than she'd ever been but outnumbered by two others who were also stronger than they'd ever been—all now with the knowledge of what they were.

Gods.

Vega, you're a god, she reminded herself as a snap of lightning shook the ground, breaking the grassy floor under Marlena and Bridger's feet. Watching her sister stumble to her knees filled Vega with the best reminder she could have asked for: *you're one step ahead of her. You can stop this curse.*

The pitter patter of rain began to fall down in waves, drenching them.

Vega stood, the wind from her storm blowing her loose hair around her face. Her eyes simmered with rage, reflecting off the lightning bolts shattering the land around her, keeping her enemies locked in their places.

Marlena released a scream so feral it could be heard over the tornado desecrating the town. "When I get my hands on you, I'm going to rip your heart out for the fun of it! I'm happy to send you back to Earth while I kill every single rebel in these lands!"

A gust of Marlena's wind pushed at Vega's tornado, attempting to switch its path. She had no luck—Vega's storm was finally too powerful for her.

The townspeople of Solum ran in packs, avoiding the destruction Vega caused. Her storm jumped mid-air to avoid them, on a strict path to kill those aiding in the start of a war Vega had every plan of winning.

"You're going to have to try harder to kill me this time," Vega gloated, egging Marlena on.

Tree roots cracked around them, shooting from the ground like missiles shooting into the sky. Vega jumped back, digging her boots into the muddy ground.

Behind her, Bridger dodged the intruding branches by wielding his invisible shield around his body, breaking off pieces and sending sharp fragments of wood flying through the air.

A chunk pierced Vega in the side. She gasped from the pain, immediately ripping it from her body. She gave Bridger the middle finger before zapping him with a surprise bolt of lightning from the dark, angry sky.

His roar of pain was drowned out by the sound of trees cracking and bending to encase Marlena in a cage of branches. Her fire was useless in the pouring rain, stealing her favorite power.

Vega thought the manipulation of plant life was hers, but when the cage grew smaller, crushing against her, Vega knew exactly who it was stepping through the newly made clearing.

Urban's shoulder length hair was down, plastered around his face, and his hands were beside his body, fingers wiggling while plants continued to grow and move by his decree.

His power wouldn't keep Marlena held for long, but it gave Vega the upper hand for a breath longer than she needed. A dart of lightning cracked from her palm, striking Marlena's chest.

Her eyes rolled into the back of her head as she slumped against her wooden cage.

Vega smiled at Urban. "Perfect timing!" she called over her raging storm. Her attention bounced between the inside of her head to control the tornado taking out half the small town, to fighting what was happening right in front of her. "Sorry for the destruction!"

Urban's roots crushed Marlena, her skin turning purple from lack of oxygen. "We can rebuild! Try to keep our people out of harm's way!"

Rebel soldiers ran through the clearing, circling Bridger, whose sword was drawn. Vega turned to him, shrugging her shoulders to say, *Make a choice.*

She wasn't dense enough to think Bridger couldn't fight his way out of a circle twice the size that had formed around him. Vega only hoped he'd do the right thing: flee.

His sword sliced through the first rebel brave enough to come after him.

The tornado of Vega's wrath sucked back into the sky, looming over the town as a warning—it would be back.

Her bonded blade hummed at her side, warming her hand when it met skin.

Flocks of Bridger's soldiers who survived Vega's twisted storm rushed through the trees. As Bridger had said, war waited for no one.

The funnel cloud Vega held above the town split, turning into twin twisters. They dropped from the sky at the same time, plucking soldiers from their places and sending debris crashing into anyone too close.

Bridger sliced and diced, obliterating rebels into pieces. "Twins?!" He cackled, fighting on. His night-kissed sword stuck through the chest of a young rebel Vega had seen around Castra multiple times. Her body slumped to the sodden forest floor as Bridger pulled his sword from her. "You brilliant goddess!"

Vega wasn't sure she'd heard his words, not over the sound of a bellow she knew too well.

She tossed her dagger, sending it end over end to strike a Tolevarre soldier through the eye socket. The strength he ran with caused him to slide through the mud until he was underneath her feet. Using her wind, Vega's dagger flew from the now-dead soldier's eye and landed back in her palm.

Trees were gone, ripped from the ground by Vega's storm, crumbled by Urban's power, and the cover they'd been under earlier was now open to the sky.

Khort came into view, flying faster than Vega had ever seen him travel. In the blink of an eye, he'd gone from being a speck on the horizon to overhead with a blaze of fire spewing from his unlatched jaw.

Dropping from behind the clouds was a second dragon, causing Vega to stumble, her eyes growing wide in shock. Its golden gleam against brown scales made Vega's heart skip a beat.

No way.

Soldiers screamed painfully on the battleground, trying to find whatever cover they could to get away from the flying beasts above their head.

The brown one dropped down, flames shooting out of its mouth as the fire turned the water from the sky into steam. Jagged teeth snapped, sending anyone near it scattering like ants.

Khort dipped to the ground close enough to Vega she could see his once-over glance and the look behind it that said, *You're in so much trouble.*

From his back, a blur of curls and graceful footing dismounted without Khort having to stop. She caught Vega's gaze, winking before glancing over at the second dragon.

It was all an illusion, made up by Arlet to distract. But when soldiers got too close, the dragon reached out with its serpent-like neck and gobbled them up. The blood was too real to be an illusion. What had Arlet been hiding from her?

Arlet gripped a weapon Vega had seen her use for the last two decades in every battle she'd fought. The double-edged sword—her swallow—was forged from the same dark metal Bridger's blade was made from, the same bonded metal as Vega's dagger.

She twisted the shaft, the double blades making a *whoosh* sound above her head before she brought it down and met the blade of the man Vega came here for.

"Arlet Videri, hello again." His gravel-laced voice sounded like he was purring at her best friend, like he wanted to make her his midnight snack. Meyer's hands glowed against the handles of his short-bladed swords, but his fire was doused by the continuous rain.

Arlet clamored in reply, twisting her swallow to strike again.

The twin tornadoes danced around the sky, waiting to be called back down. Khort dodged them effortlessly, diving to scoop up a mouthful of enemy soldiers.

Vega scanned the battlefield, eyes finding all the people she knew. Bridger was out of sight, but she could hear the thunder of his blows. Urban commanded a tree root up, crushing the skull of a man attacking a rebel soldier.

Blood. Blood everywhere. It covered the ground, mixing with mud and guts. A red sheen painted the battlefield.

Vega lost herself in the decimation. *It has to stop.* Her eyes met Meyer's. A single nod in his direction was the agreement she'd come here to give him.

Meyer dodged a blow, rolling in the mess underneath him to pop back up and strike a return on Arlet's blade. Sparks flew as metal met metal. He kicked out, knocking her to the ground.

Meyer called for backup, a couple soldiers turning their attention to Arlet as he beelined for Vega, blades raised. Before he made contact, he stopped dead in his tracks, eyes floating behind her as the sound of Marlena's pain and anger pierced the sky.

Warmth radiated down Vega's spine, but she had no time to turn and face who she knew would be behind her before the cold blade of a dagger was against her neck.

"Don't move," Bridger warned.

Splinters from Marlena's cage exploded, stabbing through rebel soldiers at the same time smoke billowed between Meyer and Vega. Marlena came into view. Bruises lined the exposed parts of her ivory skin, disappearing slowly before their eyes.

Vega bucked, sending an electric shock through her body. Her intended target had been Bridger, but he shielded himself, protecting him from her voltaic touch.

"You've created a fucking mess, little sister." Marlena traveled, disappearing only to reappear beside Urban. A single hand wrapped around his throat and lifted him off the ground. The hand around his throat was no longer that of a woman, but of a beast—black claws tearing from the tips of her fingers like the ones that had lacerated Vega's face. They dug into Urban's neck, blood pouring from the puncture wounds. "And so have you, Urban. If only I would have killed you sooner, you useless waste of power."

Marlena's claws sliced through Urban's neck, muscles and tendons snapping, his body detaching from his head.

The noise of battle fell silent to Vega's screams.

56

Urban's head rolled to a stop at Vega's feet. Her eyes welled with tears, her tornadoes dropping from the sky in a fit of outrage.

"Put those away, or she's going to kill more people you care about." Bridger's lips fluttered over her ear, his breath warm and his heart pattering faster from battle—she could *feel* it inside her chest.

"No!" Vega screamed, her voice raspy.

"*Vega, please.*" The words tickled her brain like a light breeze.

His blade lifted slightly, giving Vega space to breathe. "She's going to kill them all, and then she's going to kill you again."

She turned her head, her lips grazing the side of his face as she spoke venomous words. "And if she does, what does that mean for you, huh? How many years of the dreams can you take before they eat you alive?" She continued fighting Bridger's hold—but it was no use. He wasn't going to let her go.

Her sister stomped her foot, a crack opening and dividing in two. Soldiers from both sides fell to their deaths, their screams heard until a splat echoed back up.

The fight began to lull to a stop, everyone's attention turning to Marlena. They were too afraid to move.

Meyer twisted, taking Arlet to the ground. Her breath huffed, catching in her throat, and before she could hop back to her feet, Marlena pinned her in place, shielding her to the ground with an outstretched hand.

She can't die. Marlena can't kill her. This knowledge kept Vega from screaming, begging.

Khort was no longer in sight, and the dragon that had been used as a distraction withered away when Marlena's power pinned Arlet down.

Her sister's eyes grew wide, fascination bubbling to life in her eyes. She laughed, high-pitched and otherworldly. "You sneaky girl." Marlena sauntered over to Arlet and toed her hand with a dirty boot. "You've been hiding something from me, Pet."

Vega could do nothing but watch from afar. She wanted to split Marlena in two, rain lightning down until she combusted, let her storm suck her up and spit her out into the sea. But she didn't move. She barely breathed.

"Are you the reason your underwater bunker has stayed hidden for so long?" Marlena's lips twitched with a smile.

"No." Vega trembled. "No!"

Fuck staying calm, and screw listening to Bridger. The people she cared about had been dying since this started—it wouldn't stop if she caved to the darkness around her.

Lightning popped in the sky, causing hairs to stand up on arms as it charged into a super bolt—ready to take down everything in its path.

Marlena turned to Vega, tapping her chin like she was pretending to think. "What did you call it? Castra?" Her eyes scanned Bridger's hold on Vega, eyeing them like a cat in a mouse hunt. "They all drowned at the bottom of the sea, and now the rest of your insurgents are going to join them."

The bolt came down hard, cracking against a shield before it splintered out around like raindrops.

Vega cried out in frustration. "I'm going to kill you!" Tears ran down her cheeks, mixing with the still falling rain. "It won't be today, tomorrow, but one day, Marlena, I will skin you until there's nothing left," Vega spat, her promise ringing in her ears.

Marlena stalked over, leaving Arlet trapped in the mud. "You sound a lot like me. And to think, people really believe you're the good one."

"I sound nothing like you. You promised to take everyone I love. I'm promising to take the *only* person you love." Vega cocked her head, not caring that it caused Bridger's dagger to sink in further, blood oozing down her neck. "Yourself."

Marlena snickered. "Your threats mean nothing to me. I will always be one step ahead of you."

One step ahead.

It was now or never.

When Marlena turned her back, Vega lifted a hand from her side and wrapped it around Bridger's wrist. His muscles tensed under her touch, heat searing her branded wrist.

Vega didn't try to jar away from the knife, only extended her pointer finger to tap beside her heart three times very slowly. Meyer's golden gaze was dulled by the cloud-covered sky, but he was staring straight at Vega.

He moved his head once to the right and once to the left so inconspicuously it would be missed by anyone except for Vega.

He wasn't going to help... not in front of everyone.

"Coward," Vega whispered, choking on the word.

Be your own god.

Marlena strolled around the gruesome battlefield, leaning down to look at the faces of the fallen. "It's a shame all of you have to die." Her chest fell in a sigh, like that was the last thing she wanted to do.

"But it's what has to be done. It's your punishment for picking the wrong side."

Arlet thrashed, trying to free herself from Marlena's power.

Vega had been there before, had seen the way this ended. Marlena would kill her just to prove a point. She would send Vega right back to her own personal hell like this was all a fun game she liked to play.

No one was going to help her break her curse.

She was going to die and have to start all over again.

No, she wouldn't let that happen. Vega wouldn't allow this to be just another life where she got it wrong, where she couldn't save herself or her family.

Never again.

The hand hanging by her side slowly moved over to the sheath on her leg. Vega's fingers wrapped around the hilt of her dagger.

Khort's wings fanned out above them, the shadow of his dragon form growing bigger before he landed, tottering to the ground.

Blood dripped from his teeth to the grass like rain. Vega's eyes trailed his massive front legs, focusing on the limp body in his jaws.

The body hit the ground, audible gasps ringing throughout the crowd. Khort huffed, but it sounded like a chortle.

Ivelle's body lay crushed underneath him, limbs facing all the wrong directions.

Havoc rained down as rebels and soldiers alike began to run, fearing for their lives. They knew what would come from Marlena's rage.

Marlena traveled to Ivelle's body in the blink of an eye, dropping to her knees, showing her first sign of weakness. With her attention elsewhere, her hold over Arlet faltered.

Ivelle was Marlena's weakness. A distant cousin with a taste for anarchy.

Khort shifted, standing over the blonde and her dead praefectus. "That's for Delori."

An eye for an eye.

Marlena took Delori. Khort took Ivelle.

It has to be now, Vega. You have to do it.

Before Marlena could blow the whole world up, Vega unsheathed her dagger and met Arlet's gaze. "I'm sorry." She shot her hand up to her chest and pressed the blade over her heart. "This is how the forgotten get their revenge."

Vega shoved the blade through her chest, and with a surge of electricity, she stopped her heart.

Before everything went black, Vega heard Bridger's voice inside her head, begging her to come back.

- MENTION OF DOMESTIC VIOLENCE & MENTAL ABUSE.
- DEATH BY CANCER (OFF PAGE).
- TORTURE, MAIMING, DEATH, GRAPHIC DESCRIPTIONS OF KILLING.
- CHEATING (NOT FROM THE MMC)
- SIBLING TRAUMA
- WAR
- MENTION OF HOMELESSNESS
- MENTION OF SUICIDE
- LOSS OF PARENTS
- LOSS OF SIBLING
- ABANDONMENT
- BEING HELD CAPTIVE

If there is a theme you are looking to avoid and it is not listed, or you think I should add one to this list, please reach out on my website and myself or someone from my team will respond as quickly as possible!

Acknowledgments

This book has been a labor of love. I have laughed, cried, and nearly given up 223 times. There are so many people to thank. When they say it takes a village, they really mean it.

Josh, your unwavering support helped me through the days when I wanted to give up and call this whole thing quits. Thank you for sticking through the late nights when I had to lock myself away in my dungeon and do the damn thing! I am endlessly proud to call you mine. I wouldn't have been able to do this without you. I love you more than I can ever put into words.

Mom, thanks for everything... and I don't mean just with what you've done to help get this book out into the world—I mean everything. You've always been my number one fan and I am forever grateful to have you.

Dad, you always told me I could be anything I put my mind to and I know you really thought the tiger trainer thing would stick, but how cool does "published author" sound?

Mollie, my sippin' sister and the friend I had no idea I was missing. Thank you for the laughs, the late nights, and knowing that whatever you tell me will need a reminder a few days later. Your friendship has been the best surprise I could've asked for. Thanks for sliding into my DMs.

Kristen, I wouldn't have made this deadline without you. Thank you for your endless hours of hard work, support, helping me build my brand, and being a surprise best friend in the process!

Julissa, guess what? I finally finished my book! Thank you for being my real life Arlet (I would travel realms for you any day too), and being there when I just needed a marg and a good cry. I thank my lucky stars every day that I found a friend like you. My brother for life.

Ferg, thanks for being the sister I missed out on. Marlena is the furthest thing from you.

Hailey, because of you, this book happened. Thank you for giving me the push I needed to chase a dream I never thought could become a reality. Without your guidance, I never would've made it this far.

Addey, this story wouldn't be half of what it is without you! Thank you for being the best first reader anyone could ever ask for, my best hype woman, and an even better friend.

Bobbi, Daddy Dimico is yours to keep. Thank you for not just reading my book once, but TWICE! You made me a better writer, never allowing me to get away with the little things. I can't promise it'll stick. but I promise to try. See you back in Tolevarre real soon!

My Sprint Baddies, thank you for keeping me accountable and for pushing me when all I wanted to do was cry. I forever cherish the late nights we've all spent together on the other side of a computer screen.

My beta readers, Bri R., A.M Wright., Haley C., Sarah G., Karley B., Bobbi M., and Kristen O. Thanks for the hours of reading you did when Revenge wasn't polished, and for all the feedback that made me tear my story apart, only to rebuild stronger.

Maria Spada, thank you for the cover of my dreams.

Katie Wolf, my editor, thank you for the countless hours, and for loving Revenge in the process.

And last, but certainly not least, thank you to my readers. Without you, I wouldn't have anyone to tell my story to. Thank you for taking a chance on a new indie author. Vega and Bridger's story isn't even close to done, so sit down, buckle up, and get ready for book two!

ABOUT THE AUTHOR

Dany is an adult romance author currently living in southwest Michigan with her husband and four fur babies. Revenge of the Forgotten was her debut, introducing the world to Tolevarre and the bonded. Whenever she's not stuck in a fictional world, she enjoys traveling, diving into books that make her cry, and belting songs anywhere she goes like it's her own concert. She's known for her mid-scene cliffhangers and emotional twists with a side of comedy to lighten the blow.

INSTAGRAM: @DANYCROOKSAUTHOR
WEBSITE: WWW.DANYCROOKS.COM

Also by Dany Crooks

Romantasy:

Heart of the Villain (Cursed Gods Series Book 1.5)

Vengeance of the Gods (Cursed Gods Series Book 2)

Rom-Com:

Make Me Laugh (The Headliners Duology Book 1)

Releases September 18, 2026

Join my newsletter to get the inside scoop about
what's going on in the Dany Crooks Multiverse.